STOLEN SOULS

DETECTIVE NIKKI GILL
BOOK 1

M.L. ROSE

D1176734

Storm
PUBLISHING

Ebook ISBN: 978-1-80508-002-2
Paperback ISBN: 978-1-80508-003-9

Cover design by: Lisa Horton
Cover images by: Trevillion, Shutterstock

Published by Storm Publishing.
For further information, visit:
www.stormpublishing.co

For Carol and Ounali Jaffer

ONE

Thirty years ago

The two little boys clutched each other's hands, shivering. It was several degrees below zero outside and not much better inside the care home where they lived. Wind whistled through the cracks in the window frames. Faint fragments of silvery moonlight shone like shards of illuminated glass on the dark floor. The boys could hear the sounds from outside. Loud voices, doors opening and slamming shut. They heard footsteps coming closer.

'Paul,' the smaller boy whimpered. 'I don't want to go. Don't let them take me.'

'Stop talking,' Paul said. 'They can hear you.' He clutched Tommy's hand and dragged him back to the lower bunk bed. They lay down on the thin mattress and the equally thin duvet, neither of which did much for the cold. The boys huddled closer together.

Lights came on outside, a sliver of yellow appearing under the door. Tommy grabbed Paul's arm harder.

'Please, Paul. Don't let them take me.' Tommy buried his face in Paul's shoulder.

'Shhh,' Paul said. 'Get back in bed. Pretend you're asleep. If they see you're awake that makes it worse.'

Tommy snuck in under the duvet, his thin shoulders shaking. Paul climbed to the upper bunk and lay down. Both squeezed their eyes shut, their hearts hammering in their chests.

Footsteps crunched loudly on the flimsy floorboards under the carpets and came to a stop outside the door. Keys rattled, then the door handle turned. A man entered, then a harsh light blinded Paul. The man's hateful eyes peered at the lower bunk, where Tommy lay. The man had fat cheeks that rolled down his face. His arms were large, and his protruding belly walked in front of him. As long as Paul lived, he wouldn't forget that face. He didn't move or stir. He could smell alcohol on the man's breath.

The man knelt and got closer to the lower bunk. 'Come on, then,' he said in a gruff voice, then burped loudly.

To his dismay, Paul heard Tommy move on the bed. He knew it was terrifying to lie still and play dead. Tommy had a lot to learn.

It was Friday night. The man and his friends had just been to the pub. Friday night and the weekend were like days of the week in this place.

'Come on.'

The man pulled Tommy towards him, and the boy cried out, then kicked and fought. He was seven years old and not hard to overpower. The man hit him, but Tommy continued to scream and fight. 'Leave him alone,' Paul cried. He sat up in his bed and dangled his feet over the side.

The man released Tommy, who scuttled back into his bed, sobbing.

The man glared at Paul for a few seconds. His colourless eyes were like the Devil's, roaming all over Paul's body, from his feet up to his head. Paul's skin tightened and his spine shook with revulsion.

'And what are you going to do if I don't?'

'I'll tell my school teacher.' Paul's heart was rattling against his ribs like machine-gun fire. His breath came in gasps and fear surged in his veins. But he had learned to stare down the bully.

The last time he told his teacher, an inspector had come. He was shown around the care home, with all the boys lined up for him to inspect. He had some cake and tea, then off he went. That useless inspector did nothing but earn Paul a good beating. He was thrashed, turned black and blue all over, and he was sore for days. But Paul was ready for it again. A complaint to the right teacher was the only thing that worked.

The man snarled, baring his yellow, nicotine-stained teeth. He grabbed Paul's legs and pulled him. Paul fell on top of the man, hitting him with his fists, but his little hands were no use against the man's huge arms. Paul was thrown on the floor and then kicked on the side. He cried out as pain mushroomed in his ribs, but he managed to move away and pull himself up against the wall, shaking.

The door opened again and another man came in. He was thin, with a moustache. The two of them ran this place. The thin man was called Bert, and the fat one Robert. An evil pair that had blighted their lives.

'What's all this noise about?' Bert sniffed. Paul hated the sight of him. He glowered at Paul till he looked away.

'These two, kicking up a fuss. And this one' – Robert hooked a thumb – 'tells me to leave Tommy alone.'

'Telling you, is he?' Bert advanced upon Paul, his mouth forming a sickening grin. He looked like a rabid dog.

Paul slapped Bert's hand away, but a stinging blow to the head, followed by another kick to his legs, sent him sprawling to the ground. Tommy started howling again as Robert grabbed him. Paul lay on the floor for a while, helpless. He was getting taller, and skinnier, while Tommy was still chubby and cute. The man seemed to prefer the more rotund boys, for reasons Paul didn't understand, nor did he care. It made him want to vomit.

Tears blurred his eyes as the men carried Tommy out and slammed the door shut. He lay on the floor, listening to Tommy's cries as they faded down the corridor. They haunted him, like a never-ending echo that took away his sleep and left a withering pain that was worse than the beatings he got.

Paul got into Tommy's bed and pulled the thin duvet around him. The lights went off outside, plunging the house into darkness. Through the shutters, a wan moonlight sent a stab of luminescence into the room, perforating the suffocating darkness. Paul dried his tears and tried to close his eyes. Sleep never came easy, and when it did, it was filled with demons.

TWO

Professor Brian Allerton knew it was his time to die.

Death came to those who had intimations of mortality. An acceptance of nature's inexorable ways. But Brian didn't have this morbid thought because he was getting older. For him, the intimation with mortality came in the form of a text message.

Though it was a cold night, and he found himself sweating. He dug into his pockets and took out a silk handkerchief, dabbing at his forehead with it. His heart thudded painfully in its bony cage as he looked around in the darkness. Only a faint breeze stirred the trees, the sound of the leaves rustling like voices above his head.

Brian knew it was stupid to come here so late. But the text he'd received had revealed his worst fears. He had to confront it, now, before it spiralled out of control. He did a three-sixty, looking all around him. The University Parks was large, and it was closed at this time, after 9 p.m. Brian had left the drinks party at the college, making some excuse about an early morning tomorrow. He had no choice.

Like many students and academics, Brian knew the few secret passages that allowed access into the Parks after dark. He wasn't far from the main road, the silent, tall trees watching him like menacing guards.

He heard the crunch of feet on the dry grass and whirled around. A shadow separated from a tree trunk. The man was broad and muscular. He stood there, silently, watching him. 'Who... who are you?' Brian stammered, his throat dry.

The man said nothing, but stepped forward. The moon was behind the trees, and its light did nothing to reveal the man's features.

'You know who I am,' the man said.

A very distant memory flamed to life at the back of Brian's mind. Memories he kept suppressed, hidden at all costs. Brian's mouth opened as his breathing quickened. A cold knot of fear gripped his spine, lashing it straight. It couldn't be... 'What do you want?'

The grass blades bending, crushing under the man's shoes was the only sound as he came further forward. He was now within striking distance, and Brian took another step back. He still couldn't see the man's face, but for some reason his shape looked familiar.

'What I have always wanted,' the man said. His voice was guttural, low.

Brian tried to stand his ground, but fear directed his feet backward. It had been a mistake to come here, he realised. He could still make a run for it, but the gates were some distance away.

'You're wasting your time,' he said, gulping. 'I've told others that I'm coming here. They know about you.'

The man laughed, a harsh, mocking sound. 'No you haven't. You're a liar. Always been a liar.'

'I haven't got time for this.'

Brian turned to leave, but the man leaped towards him. He was strong as an ox, his iron fingers gripping Brian's collar, crushing the soft, flabby skin on his throat. Brian gagged, then croaked as the pressure in his throat increased. He could smell the stench of cigarettes on the man's breath. He pulled Brian's face closer, and suddenly Brian recognised him. His eyes widened as a newfound fear unfurled in his guts like a vulture spreading its wings. 'You know me now, don't you?' the man spoke between clenched teeth. 'I've been watching you for months. I know all about you, Brian.'

The man spat into his face, then punched him, sending Brian sprawling on the ground. A red-hot ball of pain seared across Brian's nose, and his vision rocked as his back hit the grass. He grunted, then looked up to see the man advancing on him. He turned quickly on all fours, then managed to get up. Saliva and blood drooled from his lips, trickled down his chin. His knees hurt from the fall. Brian whimpered as he stumbled away. He didn't look behind, but felt the sudden slash of sharp pain in the middle of his back. Something sharp ripped into him and then again, in his neck. A crescendo of unbearable pain, cutting across him like a chainsaw.

He screamed but no sound came, his eyes closing to the blackness engulfing him.

THREE

Summer was the cruellest time in Oxford, Detective Inspector Nikki Gill reflected as she hunched her shoulders against the cold.

Summer meant lots of gawking, photo-clicking tourists who arrived by the busload, dodging the tired and hungover students eager to get home after finishing their exams.

Winter was far more agreeable, with the dreaming spires and cobblestone streets left to silence – as it was designed to be. Maybe the cold suited contemplation.

Nikki's boots crunched gravel as she walked into the quad of New College.

She had just listened to evensong in the chapel and, like always, it was a moving experience. Not that she was religious. But when she heard the high notes of the organ, and the voices of the choir singers echoing around the centuries-old chapel, she closed her eyes and let herself go. The music took her to a place of endless peace and comfort. Everyone needed a refuge from the storms of life, and for Nikki it was the chapel choir.

She thrust her hands deep into her pockets as the chilly air swirled around the large quad. Wonderful crenelations rose high in the air above the quadrangle buildings, where warm yellow lights glowed in the windows.

It was peculiar, Nikki thought, that New College, despite its name, was one of the oldest colleges in Oxford. Most guide books omitted this fact. The grounds were huge, but well hidden behind the original walls. It was far less accessible than other larger Oxford colleges, and Nikki liked that.

She didn't have an alumni card, but she did have a security pass.

Selected senior members of Thames Valley Police were allowed to work in security at the college's discretion. It was essentially gate duty, way below Nikki's normal abilities, but she loved the relative relaxation of dealing with nothing but drunk students. So far this week she had done two evenings, and enjoyed it immensely.

Her daughter, Rita, had been to see her for two days recently. The sixteen-year-old had loved Oxford, and especially their visits to Christ Church and New College. She would miss Rita. The teenager had her GCSEs coming up, and staying in London with her ex-husband made sense. Oxford wasn't far, and Rita could visit as often as she liked.

Could Rita study in Oxford one day? The thought made Nikki smile. Now that would be something. But the smile vanished from her face as she thought of the reality of her new life.

She hadn't started her new job in Kidlington. Following her divorce, she had transferred from the London Metropolitan Police Force last week. Kidlington was the base for the Criminal Investigations Directorate, or CID, of the Thames Valley Police.

Oxford wasn't new to her. She had grown up here what seemed like a lifetime ago. Apart from the colleges, which were eternal, a lot had changed. Oxford had become a buzzier, busier place over the past twenty years.

Her new temporary home was a boring small town but maybe sleepy was what she needed, she thought as her boot kicked at the gravel. That, and some rest. She never thought rest would help, but bloody hell it had. Just one week of doing nothing but walking around a new town, not having to attend 8 a.m. meetings, not dealing with an in-tray full of crap, had done wonders for her wellbeing. She had loved her old job, but the paperwork was getting worse by the day. She was a copper, not a paper pusher.

The gate duty at New College was a nice little introduction to her life here. Her cottage in Kidlington was less than twenty minutes' drive when traffic was OK, next to the canal. It was small, but perfect for her needs. A bedroom each for her and Rita, and a small garden.

Nikki checked her phone to see if Rita had sent her a text. She had finished her homework and was watching TV. Nikki replied with a smiley face emoji, then reminded her to stop watching after 9 p.m.

Then she walked swiftly, eager to get to the Holywell Street Lodge, where the general entrance was located.

A sudden blood-curdling scream stopped her in her tracks.

It came from the right, across the lawn. She whipped her head and found an open window on the second floor. The scream came again, and Nikki didn't wait. She ran across the carefully mown lawn, aware she was breaking the rules

A narrow archway allowed access into the stone-walled quad. She sprinted down to the wooden door with a sign in large letters that read PRIVATE. The door was open and she bounded up the staircase, finding herself in a darker corridor. This was the fellows' and professorial quarters. Only one door was open, light spilling out from it. It cast the arched hollows of the ceiling in strange shadows. Gasping sounds came from within the room.

Nikki stopped at the entrance when she saw the man lying

on the floor, blood congealing in a thick crimson pool around his head and neck. He had receding white hair, a pale face and glassy eyes that stared at the ceiling. His chest wasn't moving. The deep gashes on the man's neck and the rips on his white shirt could only be the result of a long, sharp blade. Nikki's trained eyes scanned the floor around the body to check for a weapon. They found none.

A woman sat on the floor beside the man. She was dressed in a black evening gown, bare at the shoulders. She held her head in her hands, and the dainty shoulders shuddered as she sobbed. Nikki didn't enter. The man was clearly dead, and there was enough contamination of the crime scene already. She crouched in the doorway and used her calm, authoritarian voice.

'Ma'am, I am Detective Inspector Nikki Gill of the Thames Valley Police.' She had to repeat herself in a louder voice before the woman lowered her hands and turned towards her. She was older than Nikki had imagined. Her blonde hair was turning to white. Age had left wrinkles around her eyes, and mascara smudged her cheeks.

'Could you please come out of the room?' Nikki asked.

The woman stared at her as if she was speaking another language. She glanced at the body before looking back.

'But... but... he's dead.'

Nikki lowered her voice. The poor woman was in shock.

'I know. But if you come out, I can have a look and decide on the best course of action.' Nikki knew she sounded absurdly formal, even to herself. Best course of action? There was a dead body in front of her!

The woman continued to stare at her. Nikki stepped inside, but didn't go too far into the room. She knelt on the floor, and stretched out her hand, gently touching the woman's arm.

'Come here,' she said to the woman. The woman moved, and clutched Nikki's hand. She was tall, only a few inches shorter than Nikki, who was five feet ten with small heels. Nikki touched the woman's arm.

'I'm sorry about this. I can help, OK?'

The woman blinked, then nodded.

Nikki said, 'Do you know who he is?'

She nodded. 'My husband. He's a professor at the college.'

'What's his name?'

'Brian. Brian Allerton.'

'I see. How did you happen to come here to find him?'

She nodded again, then sniffed. 'We were going to attend a wine and cheese party at the Senior Common Room tonight. Brian was lecturing at a seminar here, and I was meant to join him when the seminar finished.'

'I see. Thank you. And you came here to find him like this?' Nikki asked gently.

The woman sniffed again, wiping her nose on the back of her hand, and nodded, her eyes downcast.

There was a commotion in the corridor, followed by running footsteps. Winston appeared, sweat running down his face. He had tightly cropped curly hair and a protruding belly.

'What's going on?' the gate-keeper asked, trying to catch his breath and not succeeding very well. He put thick arms on his waist. 'A couple of the students said they heard someone screaming.'

He frowned. 'What're you doing here anyway?' He addressed Nikki, then eyed the woman who towered above him. His eyes softened. 'Sorry, ma'am.'

'There's a body in there,' Nikki pointed towards the room. 'A professor called Brian Allerton.'

The woman had retreated to the shadows, her black gown merging with the dark wall.

Winston stepped forward. 'Professor Brian Allerton?' He swore, then peeked inside the room. He staggered backwards, bumping his ponderous bulk into Nikki's angular frame.

'Easy, mate.' Nikki steadied the older man who was clearly in shock.

She grabbed Winston's slumped shoulders, then guided him gently to the wall.

Nikki turned to the woman. 'I'm sorry, I don't know your name.'

'Mrs Arabella Allerton. Please call me Arabella.'

'Please stay here. Thank you.' Nikki glanced at her, smiling briefly. She took a deep breath, and turned back towards the room, which needed her undivided attention.

FOUR

Nikki's instincts kicked in. She needed to preserve the crime scene and also establish a perimeter. The blood looked fresh. It wasn't turning black. The dead man's skin tone was turning white, but it had not yet acquired that stiff lemony texture of advanced rigor mortis.

But... should she even be doing this? She wasn't meant to start till tomorrow. At 8 a.m. she had to report at Kidlington's CID HQ.

Winston spoke from behind her. He'd been in the job for many years and was an ex-traffic cop to boot.

'I'm calling 999.'

'Good. Call St Aldate's and ask them for a rapid response team for a suspected homicide.'

There was a pause as Winston took out his phone. 'Do you want to speak to them?'

She eyed the body as she took the phone. The switchboard operator's voice crackled in her ear. Nikki outlined the situation, then gave her name and rank.

'DI Nikki Gill?' the female voice asked, her tone hesitant.

'Yes,' Nikki said shortly.

'OK, ma'am. On-call crime unit on their way. You said it was a suspected homicide?'

'Yes,' Nikki replied grimly, and then gave Winston his phone back.

The dead man was in his early sixties, she guessed. A well-trimmed beard covered his cheeks. The deep lacerations in his neck had probably sliced the carotid artery and veins, hence the blood spillage which had soaked the large rug that covered most of the floor. His white shirt was ripped at the chest by several strokes, and already some of the blood was darkening.

She turned her attention to the room. A mahogany desk took up almost a third of the space, a red leather-trimmed blotter in the centre. There was a smell of cigar smoke, and she saw an ashtray on the desk. A laptop and printer were on the desk, a stack of printout papers beside the printer. A pair of reading glasses lay next to the stack of papers. There was also a wine glass with dark-red liquid inside, and a bottle of port on the desk.

Cold air entered through an open window that looked out onto the lawn and quadrangle. The drop from here must be about twelve feet to the gravel path below, she guessed. The killer wouldn't have jumped, though, or would he? Assuming it was a he. She knew a strong woman could overpower an older man, especially with a weapon. That made her think again about Arabella, now sitting on the floor outside. She was an automatic suspect, but Nikki doubted she would attract attention to herself by screaming not just once, but twice.

But... stranger things had happened in the course of Nikki's career. Right now, she needed to keep an open mind more than anything else.

Through the window she could see the chapel on her right. Lights also glowed in the old dormitory directly in front, and she knew some of the floors were closed for renovation. A couple of the rooms had lights on, and she wondered if those students had alerted Winston.

Nikki knelt, casting her eyes under the desk, armchair and chaise longue in front of a bookshelf. Nothing met her eyes. Daylight would be a better time to carry out a detailed search for the weapon. Whoever had killed this man had made a swift escape, and they had taken the weapon, more than likely. It wasn't easy to get in and out of an Oxford college, though, unless one knew the layout well. New College was less accessible than most, with high walls on all sides.

Nikki pursed her lips in thought. There was a chance the killer was still in the grounds. She went out of the room, closing the door. Winston had turned on the corridor lights, and Arabella sat on the floor, back against the wall, in the same position.

Nikki knelt next to her. 'Arabella, please come with me to the security guard's office so we can take some details.'

The woman looked at her blankly. She was still in shock. Nikki squeezed her shoulder, then offered a hand. Arabella took it. They went down the old-fashioned, winding staircase, Arabella's heels clicking on the sandstone floor.

Winston was waiting for them downstairs. He was speaking to two men in suits, who Nikki suspected were detectives. A couple of uniformed officers also appeared, each from one end of the quad. Coming from a quick patrol, she guessed. One of the uniformed officers was unwinding a reel of blue and white tape to secure the area. Nikki was impressed how quickly they were protecting the crime scene.

One of the detectives cleared his throat. He was the taller of the two, and older. Late thirties to early forties, Nikki thought as he asked, 'Excuse me, who are you?'

Nikki gave him the once-over.

Abruptly, he looked away.

'Detective Inspector Nikki Gill,' she snapped, feeling cross with herself for getting flustered by a handsome face. She had her new warrant card from the Kidlington South HQ. Until now, she'd never had the occasion to use it. Well, she had shown it to Winston the first day she arrived, just a week ago.

The detectives leaned close to examine the card. 'Detective Inspector Monty Sen, and this is Detective Constable Nish Bhatt.' Both showed her their warrant cards.

Nikki nodded. DI Sen extended his hand and she shook it, feeling his warm grip. She gave Detective Constable Nish Bhatt a reassuring smile. Her smile vanished quickly, though. She could sense a conflict brewing already.

Despite his seemingly easy attitude, DI Monty Sen had a tight smile on his face.

'You're joining the Kidlington South office, aren't you?' he said to her.

She finished taking Arabella's details, then handed her over to Winston.

'Please stay in the security room. I need to arrange a time to take a formal statement from you.'

Nikki raised her eyebrows and turned back to Monty. 'Word travels fast.'

'Sure you'll find your feet quickly,' he said. 'By the way' – a steeliness now appeared in his dark eyes – 'I'll be SIO on this case.'

There it was, as Nikki had expected. She was damned if she was giving up that easily. 'You will find that I was first on the scene, DI Sen, and it was me who made the call.'

The smile remained on his face, even though it was forced. 'Monty, please.'

'OK, Monty. I start tomorrow, but I could easily have started a few days ago. And as I was the first senior officer on scene, it should be my responsibility.'

'But you haven't started yet, and I am the duty SIO for the week.'

He did have a point, Nikki agreed. 'But most duty SIO hand it over to the local team when they finish duty. Are you from the Kidlington South nick?'

The smile slipped further from Monty's lips. 'No, I'm Kidlington North.'

'I see. In that case, you'll be handing over to me first thing tomorrow morning anyway, correct?'

'I guess so.'

'How about you?' Nikki looked at Nish, who was still wide-eyed and gazing at her.

'I'm in the South HQ, guv. The major crime unit there doesn't have a DI.'

'That's why I'm here. Looks like you'll be in my team.' Nikki added a smile to her voice, to put him at ease. 'Nice to meet you.'

'Same here, guv.'

She touched the phone inside her jacket pocket. 'I will ring the super and clarify with him.'

'Of course,' Monty agreed, and Nikki walked a few paces away to make the call.

Detective Superintendent Dean Patmore's voice was gruff, roughened by decades of smoking twenty a day.

'Hello?'

'Sir, this is Nikki Gill, the new DI joining the South HQ.'

Patmore's voice softened. 'I see. How can I help, Nikki?'

'I'm in New College, sir. I was doing gate duty here, prior to starting, if you remember.' Patmore had interviewed her last month and agreed on her transfer from the Met.

He grunted, and Nikki continued. 'We have a situation here, sir. A professor's been stabbed to death, and I was first on scene. A DI Sen and DC Bhatt have turned up to respond. Permission to take over as SIO, sir?'

Patmore was silent for a few seconds. 'Bloody unusual, this. Happened inside the college?'

'Yes, sir.'

'Is the suspect's whereabouts known?'

'No, sir. He might well be in the college grounds. We need to secure the area. Permission to be SIO?'

Patmore sighed. 'It's your first case back. Are you sure you can handle it?'

Nikki bit down the tingle of irritation on her tongue. 'I have handled homicides all my career, sir, and I was lead investigator at my old nick.'

'That's not what I mean, Nikki, and you know it. After what you've just been through, are you sure this is wise? Your former commander was quite adamant that you take things easy.'

Nikki wanted to reply that this wasn't a gang warfare with bullets flying around. As for what she had been through, well, she needed to be active in order to put it out of her mind. She had rested for long enough.

'I'll hit the ground running, sir. Nothing like a new case to get my eye in. Trust me, I'm ready.'

Nikki could hear the hum of a TV in the background. Patmore was probably at home in Kingham, a picturesque Cotswolds village not far from Oxford.

Patmore sighed down the line. 'This is tricky, Nikki. I don't have to remind you what happened. The trial from that case is still ongoing. If anything happens on this investigation, I'm going to get roasted for putting you back on a case like this so soon.'

'I'm ready.' Nikki hardened her voice.

She didn't talk about the time she'd spent counting the hours. Or endless walks around the city, and in the dreamy Cotswolds landscape. Nights spent in a tent in the middle of a farm, just her, and she was better for it. She felt ready.

'Are you sure?'

'Yes, sir.'

Another pause, which seemed endless. Patmore cleared his throat. 'Very well. I will inform the chief constable and his deputy. You are the SIO on this case now. And Nikki?'

'Yes?'

Patmore hesitated. 'Just take it easy, all right? Don't go in—'

Nikki cut in quickly. 'I know, sir. Will that be all?'

Patmore breathed down the line. 'Yes, for now. I want to see you tomorrow in the office.'

'No problem, sir.'

FIVE

Nikki turned back to the two men standing by the entrance to the gates, chatting to each other in low voices. They straightened when she approached.

'I just spoke to DS Patmore. I'll be SIO on this case, starting now.'

Monty inclined his head to acknowledge, and she knew he was less than happy.

She glanced at the fresh-faced DC, who grinned.

'Nice one, guv.'

'Glad we got that sorted, gentlemen,' Nikki said.

She turned as one of the uniformed officers spoke to them. 'DI Nikki Gill, SIO.'

'Evening, guv,' the officer said. She had blonde hair and a mass of freckles on her nose. Her name badge said *Justina*. 'How far do you want the perimeter?'

Nikki looked around the quad. It was large, half the size of a football pitch. She couldn't shut down the whole area, useful as that would be for the scene of crime officers.

'This section,' she pointed. 'Also at the back, but I'm not sure what we have there.'

Winston would know, but he had disappeared.

'I'll have a look?' Monty offered.

Nikki considered for a few seconds, then nodded. 'Yes, good idea. How many officers do we have on duty tonight?'

'Er...' Justina looked perplexed.

'I want to set up patrol units around the perimeter of the gate, and also inside the grounds. Three uniformed units should be enough. Each unit has four members, unless I'm mistaken?'

Justina looked impressed. 'That's right, guv.'

'OK. I'll call three more units. Set the perimeter up here and also at the back. The murderer escaped from here recently, and we don't want him or her to be hiding in plain sight.'

'No, guv,' Justina agreed. She waved at her male colleague, who jogged over.

'While one unit searches the perimeter, please ask the other to do a stop and question patrol outside the perimeter walls. It's not that late, there should be pedestrians, one of them might have seen something.'

Monty had wandered through to the back, but Nish was still there.

Nikki said, 'Tomorrow morning we need a door to door over a two-mile radius, which pretty much covers the surrounding colleges. I want posters up everywhere, as well as police notices asking for any witnesses.'

'No problem, guv,' Nish said.

Nikki looked up at the open window of the professor's study. Ivy covered the windowsill and grew around it, all along the ancient limestone that characterised most of Oxford's buildings. The windows on either side were dark and closed. Now that she looked from the ground level, she realised it wouldn't be too difficult to dangle from the windowsill, then drop to the ground below. She strode forward and stood right under the window.

She heard footsteps behind her and raised a hand. She half turned. Nish had come to a halt, looking confused.

'Stay back. I want to have a look around here.'

Nikki craned her neck up. The thick knots of ivy dropped down to the arched walkway that wrapped around the quad. The regular openings of the walkway were covered in ivy, with white flowers that were visible in the light inside the archways.

She couldn't see any breaks in the ivy that might signify someone had hung from them, then dropped. She turned her attention to the stone floor. A few minutes of careful attention gave her the pay dirt she was looking for.

Boot prints. Right under the window. A couple of them, followed by some more down the side of the lawn. Had someone jumped from the window, then run away? She looked up, adrenaline coursing in her veins. This is why she wanted the whole quad blocked. She also knew come daybreak, when the students and staff discovered the blockade, there might be uproar. She didn't want to make a bad situation worse. Neither did she want to make enemies right off the bat.

She called Nish and Justina over and pointed at the boot prints. Then she pointed up. Monty came back and joined them.

'Less than a ten-foot drop, don't you think?'

'I'd say about right,' Monty murmured. He knelt on his haunches and looked at the boot prints then walked a few steps ahead, observing them. He stayed to the sides of the walkway, trying to preserve the crime scene as much as possible.

'I think they're the same prints, but I could be mistaken. They're very faint here,' he said.

Nikki turned to look beyond the arched entrance of the walkway. She couldn't see boot prints there. They were only under the window because someone had jumped from a height. If so, then someone in the halls opposite might have seen something.

She looked at the lights in the windows, rubbing her chin. 'Nish, come here, please.'

Nish walked over eagerly, Justina following. Monty stayed where he was, observing the scene, lips pressed together in thought.

'We might have a witness in the student halls there.' Nikki pointed to the building opposite. It was exactly the same structure that wrapped around the lawn of the quad. 'You two go up there and see if you can get a statement from someone. Specifically, if they saw a person jump from this window.' She added, 'Or heard the wife scream.'

'OK, guv.'

Nish and Justina walked off.

A group of three made their way over. Two of them, a man and a woman, wore bright-yellow visibility vests over the dark-green uniform of paramedics. Ahead of them walked a shorter woman with a no-nonsense attitude. She advanced briskly, her heels clicking on the centuries-old stone path. She had jet-black hair, cut short. Nikki imagined she was in her late fifties or early sixties. Her large, dark eyes lingered over Nikki. She came to a halt, glared at Monty, then gave Nikki the once-over.

Nikki introduced herself, 'DI Nikki Gill, SIO. And you are?'

'Dr Raman, the county pathologist. What did you say your name was?'

Nikki held up her warrant card, wondering if everyone in Oxford was rude. Dr Raman's face softened, and her voice dropped an octave.

'Not seen you around before.'

'That's because I don't start till tomorrow.'

'Ah, I see.' Dr Raman was silent for a while, observing Nikki.

Nikki knew she was trying to guess her background. Well, all would be revealed in due course.

'What happened here?' the pathologist asked.

'I was walking home after evensong at the chapel when I heard a scream.' Nikki pointed up. 'Came from there. I went up and found a dead body.'

'Definitely dead?' Dr Raman raised a shapely eyebrow, and the hint of a smile played on her lips.

'I will defer to your professional opinion, but eighteen years of investigating murders means I know a dead man when I see one.'

'Quite,' Dr Raman said. Her accent was polished, clipped. 'Shall we take a look?'

'Just one second.' Nikki raised a hand, then turned to Monty. 'Can you please ask one of the uniform units to search outside the wall overlooking Longwall Street?'

When he didn't immediately answer, Nikki lifted her chin. 'You have a problem with that, DI Sen?'

'Not Holywell Street?'

Nikki had walked around the colleges a lot since arriving in the city. New College had large grounds, and their medieval boundary walls butted up against pavements and roads that formed the perimeter.

'No, that's the main entrance. If the culprit tries to escape, he might as well use the road that leads to Magdalen College and its grounds. Winston's at Holywell,' Nikki added.

'He would've seen something.'

'OK,' she said before continuing. 'New College is close to other colleges, and only Magdalen has grounds big enough for someone to hide in. From the back of Magdalen, one could escape into the Water Meadows and Headington. Maybe also down the Thames in a boat.'

Monty said, 'If it was me, I'd do everything possible to get away from the cluster of colleges.' Nikki nodded. He was right. 'Unless he's an insider and is still on the premises. Unlikely but still worth a search.'

'Let's see what they find,' Monty agreed.

Dr Raman said, 'Shall we?'

'Certainly. After you,' Nikki murmured.

A familiar drumbeat was stirring in her blood. Her mind was alive, eager to hunt down the killer. It suddenly hit her how much she'd missed her job.

SIX

Nikki followed Dr Raman up the narrow, winding stairs.

Once inside the room, the pathologist put on her gloves, mask and apron, and took a long, thin instrument, which Nikki knew was a rectal probe thermometer. She then signalled for Nikki to come inside.

Nikki used a gloved hand to extricate a plastic apron from her bag and tied it around her waist and neck. Then she helped the pathologist to lower the trousers and turn the body on its side. Blood congealed on the carpet, disguising its real colour. When the doctor was done, she helped to pull the trousers back up.

The professor wasn't a small man. His shoulders were meaty, and he had a paunch. He wasn't short either, close to six feet, Nikki thought. Whoever had killed him had to be pretty strong.

Shoe marks had scuffed the desk legs. The two chairs opposite the desk had also been moved, and one was still on its back. Scene of crime would hopefully get some prints and DNA samples. Her eyes scanned the leather-bound tomes in the bookcases carved into the stone walls. All seemed to be in place.

A couple of framed photos showed the professor with his family. Five original pieces of art work hung on the wall. One of them was a landscape, and the other four were portraits of women. All five looked like they were drawn by an Old Master. Dutch perhaps, or Italian, turn of the sixteenth century. Nikki was far from an art enthusiast, but she remembered what she had read when she browsed the Old Masters' section at the Ashmolean Museum.

Dr Raman was on her knees, staring down at the body. 'Core body temperature is thirty-three point five degrees, which is almost normal. Death is recent. He's barely lost any of his core temp. When did you get the call?'

'I didn't. I heard someone scream, which turned out to be his wife. This was' – Nikki checked her watch – 'about fifty minutes ago.'

Dr Raman nodded. 'That makes sense. Was the window open when you came in?'

'Yes. That's how I heard the scream. What's the time of death?'

The pathologist frowned. 'Can't be any more than three to four hours. I know the window's open, but it's not that cold.'

'One degree an hour, right?' Nikki said, referring to a dead person's rate of body temperature loss.

Dr Raman gave her a smile. 'Under normal conditions, yes. Any sign of the weapon?'

'No. Has to be a knife or something sharp anyway. Nothing on the floor.' Nikki went over to the desk. With a gloved hand she opened the drawers. She found papers and boxes of cigars.

Nikki turned to face the pathologist.

'Pretty obvious what the cause of death is,' Dr Raman said, shrugging. 'Exhaustion due to exsanguination.'

'In plain English, he bled to death,' Nikki said. 'If it wasn't for the thick rug, there would be pooling of blood.'

'But there's another reason for the relative lack of blood here. I think he was killed somewhere else, and then brought here.'

Nikki frowned. That put a whole new twist on things. 'Why do you say that?'

'As I mentioned, not as much blood. If you look at the soles of his feet here' – Dr Raman pointed to the lower half of the body – 'Flecks of mud, and there's grass on the soles of his shoe. He could've been on the lawns outside, or somewhere else.'

Nikki pursed her lips together. 'Someone carried him in here tonight?'

'Has to be. The body's relatively fresh. I would look at CCTV around the college if I were you.'

Nikki stared at the dead professor, thoughts whirling in her mind. She spoke aloud. 'He wanted to make a statement by bringing him back in here. Perhaps to make it obvious who he is. Don't you think?'

Dr Raman smiled. 'You're the detective, I'll leave that to you. We'll put him in the morgue tonight, and I'll get to work first thing tomorrow.'

'Keep me posted,' Nikki murmured, her eyes drifting down to the body. 'Shall I call the paramedics to take the body away?'

'I'll do that, no problem,' Dr Raman said.

'Thank you, doc,' Nikki said.

'Sheila, please.'

'OK, Sheila, nice to meet you.'

'And you.'

They shook hands, and Nikki liked the doctor already. She didn't fuss and got down to work. That was also her style. She stifled a yawn.

She went down the stairs, followed by the doctor. At the base, she realised there was another entrance behind her that must lead to the back garden. She tried the solid wooden door, but it was locked. She knelt to take a closer look. There were no boot prints but the floor did have marks. Maybe a gait analyst could find something of interest here.

She walked out of the landing and into the arched passage. It was empty, but through the large windows that opened out to the green lawn in the quad, she could see the paramedics walking in with their stretchers. Monty, Nish and the uniformed PC Justina were chatting.

Nikki said goodbye to Sheila, who promised to call tomorrow with any further information, and walked towards the team.

'Guv.' Nish almost bowed, and Monty frowned. Nikki suppressed a smile. She knew her predecessor had been a man. Inspector James Rutland. She didn't know the exact reason he wasn't around any more. In any case, it was nice that Nish, at least, deferred to her.

'We knocked on doors upstairs and spoke to three students who were still awake. Neither of them saw anything, but then they were watching TV.'

'Apart from the girl, who was reading,' Justina reminded him.

'Yes.' Nish lowered his eyebrows. 'I was just getting to that. The girl heard the scream and the second time she heard it, she looked out the window. She saw a figure running inside the archway, who was...' Nish looked at her.

'Me,' Nikki said. 'OK, what else did she see?'

'Not much else, guv. She said nothing happened after that. The window remained open. She did say she didn't know why the window was open on a cold night.'

'Good. I think the professor smoked cigars, I saw an ashtray on the desk. He might have opened the window for that reason.'

Nikki thought for a while. 'It's not surprising the girl didn't see anyone jump out the window, or run away. By the time the wife arrived, the prof was dead. The killer had bolted.'

Monty cleared his throat. 'Did Dr Raman give a time of death?'

'Between 3 p.m. and 6:30 p.m., she said. Not that long ago. Hence I wanted the patrols in and around the college.' She blew out her cheeks. 'Where is the scene of crime?'

Monty looked away, and so did Nish. Nikki knew the answer to her question wouldn't be an agreeable one.

'Well?' she asked, when the silence lengthened.

'There's only one SOC team,' Monty said. 'They're based in Kidlington North HQ, and they have to cover a large area. They won't make it tonight.'

Nikki pursed her lips. It wasn't ideal, but she didn't want to come across as the impatient heavy-hitter from the London Met. Which, she imagined, some would inevitably see her as. Especially when she was surrounded by men, who she had always found to be more judgemental when it came to their female colleagues in the force. She had battled it in London and suspected it would be no different here.

'At least we got the place secure,' she said aloud. 'I want to check the CCTV. I think that will be in the porter's lodge.'

The two men followed her as she walked over to the gates. Winston opened the door for her and they stepped inside. Nikki pointed at the bank of TV screens, adjacent to the Perspex screen that allowed them to see outside.

'Can you bring up all the car movements in and out from the college today?'

Winston nodded and pulled out the keyboard from a sliding drawer under the desk. 'All day will be a lot of vehicles for food delivery etc. Do you have a more precise time?'

Nikki thought about the time of death and how the body could've been transported.

'How about this evening from five p.m.'

Winston scrolled and then pressed play. A few vehicles and the usual crowd of students walked in and out of the gates.

Then the screen went blank. Winston stopped the feed and rewound it. He shook his head. 'This has happened before. The cameras stop working sometimes. We're getting them changed.'

Nikki leaned over him. 'What time do the cameras stop working?'

'Around 9:30 p.m. They black out till 10 p.m.'

'So about a half hour ago.'

'But we were here.' Winston turned to look at Nikki. 'Jonty, my colleague too. Yo, Jonty,' Winston called, and Jonty appeared. He was a stocky man in his blue uniform.

'I haven't seen anyone come in through the gates in the last two hours. Have you?'

Jonty shook his head. 'Nope, me neither.'

'Camera was on the blink again.' Winston pointed to the TV. 'We lost half hour of footage.'

Nikki was still thinking. 'Can you get me all the CCTV over the last week, please? Send it to my team' – she pointed at Nish and Monty – 'and we'll have a look. By the way, could anyone have tampered with the cameras?'

Winston and Jonty exchanged a glance. 'It has happened before,' Winston said. 'A couple of drunk students did it, we think, but no one was caught. We reported it.' He looked pointedly at Nikki.

Nish cleared his throat.

'We can go back to the nick and look at the PCN you filed for this. See if there's any progress.'

Nikki turned back to Winston. 'Did you catch any students in the act?'

'No, but they have vandalised them in the past. Some of the drinking clubs make stupid dares, and sometimes we catch them.'

It would be one hell of a coincidence, Nikki thought, if the students messed with the cameras on the same night as the professor's murder. But it could happen.

'Keep an eye on them from now on. Do regular patrols. And we will keep a unit stationed here all night.'

'Thank you.'

SEVEN

Nikki waited till the others had left. Nish waved goodbye, and Monty gave a stiff nod from the driver's seat of his BMW.

Nikki watched the two men drive away, and her mind lingered on young Nish's face. He was so fresh and new. A brief spasm contorted in her heart, a sudden pain that stopped her breathing. Maybe it was being back in Oxford. Maybe she shouldn't have come back, after all.

If her brother Tommy were alive, he'd be like Nish. Young, vibrant, full of enthusiasm. Nikki had constructed her memories of Tommy from looking at old photos and hearing stories from Clarissa, her mother. She never saw much of her brother, and that left her with even more regrets. It was strange, thinking about Tommy now. Wisps of regret danced around her face like dust motes. She shook her head and turned away. Head bent, she walked to her car. Tommy and her mother were the real reason she had come back. To seek closure, but she knew she would rattle the demons of the past. Better that, she thought, better risk ruin, than live a life of silent torture.

She took Banbury Road to Kidlington. The roads here were never too busy, and right now they were deserted. It was the one thing she liked about the place. The relentless grind of London traffic was absent. It was nice.

The village's main street was ghostly with all the shop shutters down. A couple of drunks stumbled on the pavement. She passed the cute little post office and shop, and took the lane that went down to the canal. Her cottage was semi-detached and had two floors. It also had a thatched roof which, to her surprise, was quite common in the village. As a child, she had always wanted to live in a thatched house.

Some post had been delivered, and she went through it as she put her bag down. Letters for council tax and the census. She was in the process of changing everything from south London to Kidlington. Seemed strange to think that she was actually out of London. The city grew in her soul like ivy on the walls, and she had always been a city girl. How would she cope here?

Down in the kitchen, she poured herself a drink. The dining room next to the kitchen was small, and its glass-panelled door opened out into the garden. She sipped the white wine, and, keeping the light off, looked out at the dark garden. The canal was at the bottom of the slope, and she could see it from here. Lights from the canal path shone on the muddy water. A couple of houseboats were moored there, but they would move by morning.

Nikki went upstairs and checked Rita's room. Rita wanted to put posters up, and while Nikki wanted her to make the room her own, this was a rental property, and she didn't want to redecorate it before she had to leave.

She had separated from Rita's father when Rita was fourteen, two years ago. Rita had coped with it well, but Nikki regretted the fact that her job was often all-consuming and she wasn't always there for her daughter in the way she wanted to be. It had become a lot easier as Rita had grown older. They were more like friends now. The wine was helping to lighten her mood. She wanted to give Rita what she didn't have during her teenage years. Happiness and a sense of belonging. Her own childhood was scarred by her mother's sadness, and father's drinking. Over it all, like a huge, dark cloud, hung the memory of Tommy. Despite the divorce, which she delayed on purpose for Rita's sake, she strived to make life as easy for Rita as she could. Rita knew she could contact her mother anytime, and also come over. Once her school was over, she'd spend more time with Nikki in Oxford.

It was funny how every generation went through the same pressures, thought the same thoughts.

Nikki took a ready meal out of the fridge. She was going to prepare a salad but it would have to wait. She was knackered. She stuck the lamb hot pot into the microwave.

Tomorrow would be interesting. She cringed when she thought of meeting new people, having to establish new professional relationships. The brief introduction today with DI Monty Sen and DC Nish Bhatt was enlightening. She hoped the rest of them would be more like Nish. Maybe not. The microwave pinged and she took out the lamb hot pot. She poured herself another glass of wine. Her job might be starting tomorrow, but her real work had already begun. Her phone pinged with a text from her mentor, Detective Chief Inspector Arla Baker, of the Met. She had worked with Arla extensively, and Arla had taught her not just the ropes, but to trust her own instincts. Nikki called her back.

'How are you?' Arla's warm voice came down the line.

'Good. Settling in with a dead professor after just a week. My first case as SIO.'

'Trouble follows you everywhere,' Arla laughed.

Nikki told her about the case, and Arla listened attentively. 'Take your time. This will be a big case. You ready for it?'

'Yes.'

Nikki bit her lower lip. Arla sounded like Patmore, and with

good reason. Six months ago, Nikki had been the spearhead of
Operation Yardstick It was the result of a two-year surveillance
of an Albanian drug-smuggling gang in London's East End
dockyards. Nikki had gone in behind the armed response unit
into the warehouse to catch the gang red-handed. But it wasn't
just the gang who were there. Inside a room, there was also a
woman and her child, a five-year-old boy. A gunfight ensued,
and most of the men died, and the woman and the boy were
killed, too. Nikki would never forget opening the door and stepping inside that room...

'Nikki?'

'Hi, yes. I'm here. What did you say?'

'I asked if you're ready for a big case,' Arla's voice was low
and measured.

Nikki could hear the hesitancy.

'Yes, I'm fine. I'm doing all right, to be honest. Moving on
and all that.'

'Have you seen Rita recently?'

'Yes, she came once, that was good.'

'OK. Take care of yourself. Here to talk if you need me.'

'Thanks, Arla.'

EIGHT

Thirty years ago

Tepid, cold sunlight flickered in through the shutters. There was a crashing sound as a hand hammered against the door, and the sound reverberated through the corridor, as the same person went to all the doors, waking the boys up. It was school time, and in the absence of an alarm, either Robert or Bert did the honours.

Paul stirred. Sleep had come late, and he felt exhausted. He got up and peered down. To his relief, he saw Tommy on the bed. The seven-year-old was curled up tight. His feet moved, and Paul knew he was awake. He didn't disturb the younger boy.

Paul took his toothbrush and went to the bathroom, where there was a little pushing and shoving as all the boys lined up to use the loos. When Paul returned, Tommy was still curled up in the bed. Paul went to the single wardrobe they shared and got dressed in his school uniform.

Then he sat on the bed and gently squeezed Tommy's shoulder. The boy flinched, but Paul shushed him.

'It's me, it's OK. Don't worry.'

Tommy trembled under his touch, and Paul felt a heavy, oppressive weight settle on his heart. He knew what they'd done to Tommy. Those horrible men had done the same to him, a couple of years ago. The boys didn't know who to tell, or even how to say it. No one talked about it. Everyone was shamed into silence. As far as Paul knew, he was the only one who had told his teacher. She had been appalled, and hence the inspector was sent around.

Paul didn't understand why no one did anything about it. How could no one care? Despair had hardened his heart over time. One by one, every adult he had spoken to had turned away.

They took my clothes off. They touched me.

The words were horrible, terrifying and shameful to utter. But after two years, he had picked up the courage.

Fat lot of good it did. Paul shook away the weight in his soul. He wished he couldn't feel anything. Wished he was numb, like a block of ice that never melted.

'You'll feel better in school. We'll go together, come on. Better than being here, isn't it?'

He coaxed Tommy to sit up, and then get ready for school. He watched the bruises on Tommy's back and ribs slowly turning blue. He had fought them last night. Paul looked down at his clenched hands. Tommy put his clothes on slowly, because it hurt him.

'I'll carry your bag,' Paul offered, but Tommy declined.

They went downstairs, into the large dining hall. It was busy, with boys filling their porridge bowls at the counter, then sitting down at the long table. Robert and Bert stood at the corners, watching them with sharp eyes. Another man had joined them, helping to serve breakfast.

Paul couldn't look him in the face. His name was Stuart, and he had done unspeakable things to Paul when he was younger. Stuart's thin, sallow face and weird, widely spaced eyes lit up when he saw Paul. He bared his teeth in a smile that looked like a wolf licking his lips.

'Not seen you for a while,' he told Paul as the boy held out his bowl, looking away from him. He poured a ladle of porridge into his bowl, and Paul shuffled away.

'Well you're nice, aren't you?' Stuart said, and Paul looked over his shoulder. Stuart was staring at Tommy with an evil glint in his eyes. Tommy was staring down at his bowl.

'Come on,' Paul said, hurrying Tommy along.

They sat down next to each other and finished the bland porridge quickly. Every time Paul looked up, he caught either Robert's, Bert's, or Stuart's eyes.

Paul and Tommy filed out of the dining hall. Their route took them past an industrial estate that skirted the Cherwell River. The tall spikes of the factory fences gave way to open land and tall trees. The Cherwell's muddy waters rushed past.

'One day, we'll get out of here,' Paul said. 'I promise.' He put an arm around Tommy's shoulders. 'Then we can live in a house of our own.'

Tommy said nothing. He kicked a stone. He wanted to tell Paul about his mother, but wasn't sure if he should. Tommy had only seen his mother a few times. She came with a girl who she said was his sister. The girl was little, younger than him. She stared at Tommy as his mother did the talking. There was never much to say. Tommy barely knew her. He was told his mother couldn't have him at her house, but he didn't understand how she could have the girl who was meant to be his sister. A woman who came to the care home told him it was because when Tommy was younger, his mother couldn't cope looking after him.

Maybe that's why his mother cried so much when she came to see him. She simply held his hands and wept. Then either Robert, or Bert, put a hand on her shoulder and told her to leave. His mother said she would be back soon, but months went past, and she never came.

With time, Tommy had realised his mother either lied, or she didn't care. Perhaps she felt bad, and that's why she was so upset when she saw him. But like everything else in his bleak, colourless life, his so-called mother was also distant and hopeless, always fading into the grey background. He had learned not to expect anything from her.

'You all right, our kid?' Paul asked. He had gone ahead and now came back. Tommy nodded in silence. He thought of the wide-eyed girl who sat next to his mother when she came. She was cute, with her hair done up in two pigtails at the side. She stared at Tommy like she was trying to memorise his face. As his mother walked away, ushered along by Robert, the little girl always turned and looked at Tommy. He waved at her once, and she waved back.

Tommy felt no emotion when these memories surfaced. He felt like he was looking out the window at a wintry landscape. He couldn't change the snow, or the sky, or his life. He had accepted there would never be any change.

'Our own house,' Paul's words brought him back to reality. 'Can you imagine? I'd buy a pool table like you see in the pubs.'

They walked along in silence, the memories slowly falling away from Tommy's mind with each step.

'You've never been to a pub,' he said.

'Yes I have,' Paul said, a bit defensive. 'I popped in on the way back from school last week.'

'What for?'

Paul took his time to answer, and Tommy had to nudge him once. 'He told me not to tell anyone, so keep it schtum. He wants me to do a job for him. He wants me as I don't have a police record.'

Tommy had no idea what Paul was talking about. 'Who's he?'

'A school teacher.'

Tommy stopped, and his eyes widened. 'Really?'

Paul laughed. 'No, you idiot, I'm only joking.'

Paul skipped ahead and kicked an imaginary football, then celebrated a goal, running with his hands in the air. To Tommy he looked as if he felt free for a few seconds in his enclosed, tedious life. Paul closed his eyes and breathed deeply, and Tommy thought he'd be hearing the wind roar past his ears. Paul looked behind him and saw Tommy watching him.

'Listen, don't tell that to anyone, OK?' Paul grew serious. 'About the man in the pub, that is.'

'Pinky promise, I won't.' Tommy raised his little finger and the boys shook hands.

'Oh, look who it is,' a voice said behind them.

Tommy felt a hand pull at his shirt collar and yank him backwards. With a gasp, he fell on the ground, stones digging into his back. Jack, one of the older boys and a schoolyard bully, grinned at him, then slapped him across the face. His two accomplices, bigger than both Paul and Tommy, stood on either side, laughing.

'Let's see what you got,' Jack said, his hands diving into Tommy's pockets.

Paul lunged at them, but one of the other boys held him back with an arm, then pushed him to the side. Jack found some spare change in Tommy's trousers and took it.

'That's my lunch money,' Tommy said, tears coming to his eyes.

'Give it back!' Paul shouted and hurled himself at the boys again. This time he was shoved to the ground and got a kick to his belly. Paul screamed and curled up in the foetal position. Tommy got to his feet and scrambled away. Jack and his two friends stood there, laughing.

Tommy wiped his eyes. He caught Paul getting to his feet, behind the boys. Quick as lightning, Paul jumped on Jack, hitting his head with a heavy stone. Jack crumpled to his knees, holding his head. Paul pummelled his head with the stone, and Jack screamed, but couldn't stop him. Blood poured down Jack's head, and one side of the stone was tinged with crimson. The two boys scattered, shocked. Paul hit Jack one last time, then kicked him to the ground. Jack lay there, clutching his head, blood cascading down his face.

Paul raised the stone and advanced upon the other boys. 'Come near us again and I'll do it to you. Got it?' he screamed.

The two boys took off, their bags bouncing on their backs.

Paul knelt and went through Jack's pockets. He took all the money out and gave it to Tommy.

'Come on. We'll be late for school.'

NINE

The mist that clung to the river was diffusing slowly over the fields and road like a slow-moving cloud. Nikki's car sliced through it, racing down the road to Kidlington. Traffic was starting to build, but it was always less here than in Oxford.

She showed her warrant card at the gates, and the barriers lifted. The compound was as large as it was at Thames Valley Police's HQ. There was a central admin section, and then two sections on either side. All three of the buildings were modern and purpose-built – squat and ugly in Nikki's view. They had a sloping steel roof that bulged at either end. It was meant to be minimalistic and chic, but ended up looking like three giant sausage rolls with steel hats. The CID wing occupied the left section, on the top floor, with Uniform, Traffic and Cyber Security below it.

The lobby was empty when she entered. The desk where she expected a uniformed constable to be on duty only had two flower pots on either side, and a Perspex glass barrier over the desk. The blue carpet was soft under her shoes. She strode past the posters and the Crimestoppers notices on the walls. She took the lift to the top floor, wondering if it was always this quiet around here. So far, she hadn't seen anyone.

Nikki took a deep breath, readjusted her blazer and looked down at her newly polished black flats just as the lift doors pinged open. There was a landing, then a steel-and-glass barrier through which she could see the desks of the open-plan office. A corridor ran down the middle, with offices opening up on the right – all the doors were shut. There was a hubbub of voices coming from inside the area. She could see white-shirted uniformed officers and a few plain-clothes detectives at their desks.

Nikki went up to the double doors at the end of the landing. She took out her newly minted card, with a photo of her which was, thankfully, taken more than eight years ago, when she looked younger. She pressed the barcode against the machine on the side of the door, and there was a soft beep, then a click as the locks on the door released. She pushed it open and stepped through. The gentle murmur of collective voices became slightly louder.

She walked swiftly through. No one paid her any attention. Her eyes scanned the open-plan office, making eye contact with a few of the faces. A couple of the women smiled back at her and she acknowledged them.

She noted the names on the office doors on the right as she walked past them and stopped at the one that read 'Detective Superintendent Dean Patmore'. It was right at the end of the corridor. To her left, the glass-and-metal barrier had started up again, blocking off the open-plan office space. Nikki knocked on the door and waited. It was 7:50 a.m., she noted on her watch.

A gruff voice asked her to enter. Patmore was on his own. His hair was balding, and he had a heavy-jowled, swarthy face. His eyebrows were like caterpillars hanging over wrinkled eyes. His cheeks had lost the battle with gravity, giving him that hangdog, forlorn but angry look that most senior police officers got at an advanced stage of their careers. Decades of stress, form-filling, and pleasing the top brass.

A faint smell of cigarette smoke emanated from DS Patmore's seated figure as Nikki got closer. Smoking was definitely not allowed, but the window was open at the top, letting in frigid air. Nikki shivered, looking at the window, then at her new boss.

'Good morning, sir.'

'Morning, Nikki,' Patmore drawled, then succumbed to a bout of coughing. Behind him, there was a bookshelf with photos of him shaking hands with a bunch of faceless dignitaries. A couple of plaques that looked like award shields stood between the photos.

'So you hit the ground running,' Patmore said. He settled back into his leather armchair, and it creaked. He looked up at Nikki, who remained standing. She had met him only once, at the interview, when he'd been joined by another woman and a man, both assistant commissioners in the Thames Valley Police Force. She didn't like the way his beady blue eyes rested on her. He sensed her discomfort and sat up straighter in his chair.

'Have a seat.'

Nikki nodded and pushed a chair back, then sat down, her spine erect.

'I gather you met some of the team last night,' Patmore drawled.

'Yes, sir. DI Monty Sen and DC Nish Bhatt. Dr Raman was also there, but SOC didn't turn up.'

'You'll find getting hold of SOC can be difficult at times. They're thinly spread. We don't have the same resources you lot do in London.' A sarcastic smile played on his lips.

'I understand that, sir,' Nikki said plainly. 'I'm not in London any more.'

'The SOC lead will contact you today, I'm sure.' He pressed

his lips together. A draught came in through the window and Nikki shivered again. Patmore stood and slammed the window shut. He sat down on the armchair and put his elbows on the table.

'You are well regarded in the London Met, Nikki. But we both know what you've been through recently. This murder last night, it's likely to be a high-profile case. You might have to face the media. You know what that's like. Are you sure you're up for that?'

Nikki held his eyes. 'I can't tread softly around, sir. Besides, I was first on the scene. I hope you will agree that I have the right to be SIO.'

'I know,' Patmore sighed. 'I've already agreed. Just don't make me regret that decision.'

'You won't, sir, I promise.'

He narrowed his eyes, the tanned crow's feet at their corners crinkling. 'Are you talking to someone about what happened?'

Nikki sighed softly, then inspected her nails. 'I have, sir. It's all OK now.'

'But still,' Patmore said. 'These things play on our minds. I want you to continue seeing someone for the next four weeks. Once a week is fine.'

Nikki shook her head slowly. 'Is that necessary, sir?'

'Yes, it is,' Patmore said with an air of finality. He reached for a sheaf of papers on his desk. 'About the murder last night. I want a report on my desk by tomorrow morning.'

Nikki stood, glad the meeting was over. 'No problem, sir.'

She turned to leave but there was a brisk knock on the door, and DI Monty Sen stepped inside. Nikki stared at him, wondering why he was here.

Monty nodded at her, then at Patmore. 'Sir.'

'Ah yes, Monty. I know you two have met already.'

Nikki acknowledged Monty with a slight nod of her own.

Both of them faced Patmore. A sense of dread was curdling in Nikki's stomach.

'Nikki, Monty will be helping you settle in. Just to make matters easier for you.'

She frowned, tension sparking in her spine. '*Easier*, sir?'

'Yes. To give you a hand, if you need it.'

'I don't need a hand, sir. I can do my job perfectly well. You know my record, sir. I have one of the highest prosecution to arrest ratios in south London.'

Patmore exhaled and settled back in his chair. 'I know that. But after what happened—'

Nikki stepped forward, her mouth working, irritation flaring in her mind. 'I need to manage the team independently, sir. Having someone else stick their oar in will only make things difficult.' She hooked a thumb to her left. 'I don't need him to look over my shoulder. And if he does, I'll tell him where to shove it.' She stopped, aware she might have overstepped the mark. She looked down at her feet. 'Sorry, sir. But I feel strongly about this.'

Monty said. 'I have no intention of looking over your shoulder.'

Nikki glanced at him. 'Then what do you intend to do?'

Monty sighed. 'Look, I'm just following orders, OK?' He glanced pointedly at Patmore, and Nikki turned her attention back to the super.

Patmore bit down on his jaw. He gave Monty a murderous stare, and shook his head slightly.

'You think I give a damn?' He raised his gravelly voice. He was normally a soft-spoken man, but he could thunder when he wanted to. 'You can do what the hell you like. This comes from above, Nikki. Not my decision. Both of you are adults. I only care about getting the job done.' He pointed a meaty finger at Monty, but spoke to Nikki. "His job is to make sure you have the support necessary. You know how to do the job, but it's a new location, new office, and so on. We do things differently at Thames Valley Police. Someone like Monty who's been a DI here for a few years can help you settle in.'

'As long as I can do my job properly, sir, I don't really care,' Nikki said. She realised that this was an offer of help, one she should grudgingly accept. But she didn't want Monty acting like another SIO on the case. She decided to put things right from the start. She turned to Monty.

'For the current investigation, I'm in charge. I just wanted to make that clear.'

Monty shrugged wide shoulders. He was built like a craggy rock, all sinew and bone. Even his cheeks were sunken, but stubble filled out his face. His eyes were focused on her.

'We established that last night, didn't we? I don't have a problem with that.'

Nikki nodded, but there was something in Monty's manner that didn't quite reassure her. He had wanted to be the SIO last night. He was used to being a DI. She didn't want him to think he had to play second fiddle to her, but she genuinely felt this case was hers, as she was on scene first. She hoped Monty would see that.

'That's agreed, then,' Patmore said. 'Now clear out, both of you.'

TEN

Outside Patmore's door, she folded her hands across her chest and walked down the corridor with Monty.

She was trying to ignore that he looked ridiculously handsome in a well-fitted dark-blue suit. The suit was so nice, in fact, it seemed he was off to some dinner party instead of working in a police station. His cheekbones were high and sculpted, jawline firm and masculine.

Nikki said, 'I just want to get this out in the open, alright?' She stopped walking, and so did Monty. From experience, Nikki knew that personality clashes within teams tended to fester if they weren't dealt with at the outset. She didn't want to start a new job on the wrong foot.

'I know you're a DI. You probably don't want to work with me, but you have to. Are you happy to follow my lead?'

Monty stared at her for a while, his chestnut-brown eyes boring into hers. 'Just so you know,' he said, 'I didn't ask for this. I don't think I need to babysit you. But I need to let the super know if you're struggling.' He spread his large hands. 'I've never done this before, either. Keeping an eye on a colleague the same rank as me, I mean.'

'Guess it's new for both of us then.' Nikki smiled, and the corners of Monty's lips tugged in response. Then his smile faded.

'I should clear one thing with you, too,' he said. 'Like you mentioned, we're both the same rank. I don't want you to treat me as sergeant. I'm happy to go along with what you suggest, and your orders will remain orders. But if I offer ideas, they will be based on what I suspect.'

Nikki nodded. 'I will give your ideas the importance they deserve. As long as I have the last word on them. I know you won't say things that aren't important.'

Monty smiled wider, and his chestnut-brown eyes swirled. Nice lips, but she tried not to look at them.

'Glad that's sorted then,' he said.

He opened the brown door, and Nish Bhatt scrambled to his feet from a desk in the corner of the room as she entered the Murder Investigation team office. So did a woman Nikki had never seen before. She was young and petite. Her brown hair was tied up in a ponytail. She regarded Nikki with avid curiosity.

Nikki turned to the young woman and smiled. 'Are you one of the DCs?'

'Yes, ma'am. My name is Kristiana Young. Everyone calls me Kristy.'

'OK, Kristy.' Nikki shook hands with her. 'Don't call me ma'am. Guv or boss is fine.'

'OK, guv.'

'Right.' Nikki took a look around the office. It was a large room with filing cabinets, fax machines and printers stacked in one corner. A whiteboard hung on the wall, and a map of Oxfordshire and the Cotswolds hung on the wall opposite. Four desks were arranged around the room, and Nikki wondered who the fourth desk was for. She decided to ask them.

'No one, guv,' Nish said. 'DI Rutland wanted to keep a spare desk in case there was a new team member.'

'I see.' She eyed Nish, wondering whether to press him about James Rutland, her predecessor. She decided to leave it for now. Patmore had only told her that he had left, without giving a reason why. With time, she hoped the reason would reveal itself.

Nish walked over to the largest desk, in the right-hand corner. It had a red leather top, shiny edges, and a plush-looking armchair behind it.

'This one is yours, guv.' Nish smiled. 'Well, it belonged to DI Rutland. It's been cleaned and everything,' he added quickly.

'Thank you. Any news from last night?' Nikki asked as she took a seat and pulled her laptop out of her backpack.

Nish shook his head. 'SOC will be visiting this morning, guv. The autopsy should also happen today and I need to catch up with Dr Raman.'

'OK, right. I need to tell you guys something. I like playing by the book. Which means gather evidence, develop a timeline, and dig deep into the victim's and suspects' backgrounds. Got that?'

Both of them nodded. There was a knock on the door and Monty entered. He raised his eyebrows at Nikki.

'Started without me?' He grinned, then sat down at his desk. Nikki kept his attention. 'I was just telling the others how I operate.'

Monty grinned. 'Sure. I liked what I saw last night. How you operate, I mean.' That lazy, slow smile spread across his face, and for some reason, Nikki felt heat fan her face. She looked away.

'So, number one, we build a picture. Sure, it's about evidence, but remember, an absence of evidence is not evidence of absence. It's there, under your nose. The best pieces of evidence hide in plain sight. We don't bother to look because we believe what the suspects, or non-suspects, tell us. Rule number one, we question everything. OK?'

From the look on their faces, she could tell they were interested, even Monty.

'Number two, we dig deep into our suspects. And our victims. Yes, the victim needs justice, but what has he done to deserve this? We leave no stone unturned. Any detail, however trivial, can make or break a case.'

All three of them nodded. Monty sat back in his chair, a thoughtful expression on his face.

'Number three. We build an iron-clad case for the prosecution. The CPS is there to help us, so let's help them. If it means we have to travel abroad to interview a victim of historic crime, so be it. If it means we have to pressure a lord or minister, we do that. We want the whole story. Not just what we hear. We want the truth.'

She stopped. All three of them were listening intently. Nikki felt a bit self-conscious. She could get carried away with her love for the job. She straightened an imaginary fold on her blouse sleeve. Then she walked up to the whiteboard and picked up the black marker pen. She wrote down Brian Allerton's name on the top.

'After SOC have been today, we will have fingerprints and DNA samples. Anything else?'

She wrote down *fingerprints* and *DNA* as numbers one and two.

'Have we checked with the uniform squads to see if there were any sightings of suspects overnight?'

Monty said, 'No, but that's first on my agenda.'

'OK. We didn't find a murder weapon. It seems to be a knife, and a sharp one at that, given the depth of cuts he suffered. We need to ask Uniform about that, and also organise a search party around the college grounds and outside.'

Monty said, 'Will do. There're also the signs that need to be strung up today.'

Nish cleared his throat. 'And the door to door over a two-mile radius that you wanted, guv.'

'Good.' Nikki pointed the marker pen at the younger man. 'Enlist the help of a uniform team for that. We need to get that done by today as well. I don't have to remind you the first forty-eight hours in a murder investigation are the most important. The killer is most likely still around the local area and prone to making a mistake.'

'We need to find out who wanted him dead.' Kristy spoke for the first time. Monty snorted and was about to talk, but stopped short when Nikki glared at him. She nodded at Kristy.

'Good point. The professor must've had at least one enemy. We know that most victims are murdered by someone they know. So far, we have the wife, who was also first on the scene. Now we need to find his friends and colleagues, and any other family he might have.'

'Students as well, guv. They would know about him,' Nish chipped in.

'Definitely. All the college staff, to be honest, and don't forget the cleaners and maids – they often know things others don't.'

Monty sighed. 'Looks like we got our work cut out. But don't worry. The uniformed units will help with taking statements. I can also ask the MIT from Kidlington North HQ to give us a hand.'

Nikki nodded. 'That would be helpful.'

ELEVEN

There was a knock on the door. A woman with black hair opened it a fraction and leaned inside.

'Not disturbing anything, am I?' Her eyes fell on Nikki and she observed her for a few seconds. 'You must be the new DI for Kidlington South Murder Investigation Team.'

'I am indeed.' Nikki extended a hand. The woman pumped it enthusiastically.

'Hetty Barfield. Henrietta actually, but everyone calls me Hetty. You can too.' She grinned. 'I'm the head of Forensics.' Her rosy cheeks bulged with mirth as she smiled, and her black eyes danced.

'Nikki Gill. Nice to meet you.' She pointed at the white-board. 'You're right on time, Hetty. We were just discussing when SOC was going to attend. Now, right?'

'Yes, I just came to check if you had any instructions before we went in.'

Nikki pursed her lips. 'The crime scene is a room upstairs, which is great for isolation. However, there are footprints outside the window which could be interesting. And there

might be more down the quad. As this is a college, I fear
evidence could get tarnished easily.'

Hetty inclined her head. 'Definitely. All those students
running around. We're going to set up a tent anyway. If you
want to put that crime scene under lockdown, that would be
better.'

Nikki shrugged.

'OK. Let's do that.'

'Thanks. I will pop down there in a couple of hours.'

Hetty waved goodbye. Nikki turned to her team and went
back to the whiteboard.

'What about his phone? Or laptop?'

Nish looked at Monty, who was frowning at the whiteboard. Monty said, 'Did Dr Raman mention anything? She
looked inside his coat pockets.'

'I did too,' Nikki said. 'I didn't find anything in his trouser or
coat pockets. Nothing in the drawers of his desk either. The
desk had some papers, a pen holder, but I didn't see a laptop.'

'Maybe he had the laptop at home,' Kristy suggested.

'Possible. Can we please ring the wife and arrange a time to
see her at the family home?'

'Yes, guv,' Kristy said.

Nikki continued. 'Get the prof's timetable from his secretary. We need to know his daily work schedule. From his wife,
we should get his daily routine. When he woke up, when he
came home, that sort of thing. Let's build a picture of his day-to-
day life.'

Like brush strokes on canvas, she wanted to add, but kept it
to herself. She loved this part of her job, starting with a blank
page and slowly adding colour. Watching the faces, their secrets
and lies emerge.

Nikki stuffed her shoulder bag into the bottom drawer of
her desk and straightened as Nish opened the door for Justina,
the uniformed PC from last night.

'Nothing to report, guv,' Justina said. 'Our skipper is doing a report as we speak. But he asked me to inform you.'

Every force had its own name for their staff, but skipper was a term Nikki had heard before. Unless she was mistaken, skipper was shorthand for sergeant.

'What's your sergeant's name?'

'Damien Pitkin, guv. He will probably meet you on-site, he said.'

'OK. Just to clarify. The team outside on the road didn't see anything either?'

Nikki knew very well the squad car wouldn't have been there the whole night. It was unfair to expect that, without a formal surveillance operation in progress.

Justina shook her head. 'No. But they are there again now. Any instructions?'

'No, thank you. I will catch up with them when I'm on-site.'

Justina left, and Nikki shut the door. 'Monty and Nish, head up to the college and find out more about the professor's timeline yesterday, and get contact details of the staff and students he knew. We need a list to comb through.'

Monty nodded, and Nish wrote something down on a pad.

'Kristy, you and I are headed for the crime scene. See you lads there.'

TWELVE

Kristy glanced at Nikki, who was concentrating on the road. Traffic was getting heavy in the morning rush to work.

'How you settling in, guv?' Kristy asked.

Nikki shrugged. 'Not bad. Usual teething problems, you know.'

They were silent for a while. Nikki was aware the young detective was looking at her, but she focused on the road.

'You met the guv, DI Sen. He's a funny sort.'

'Monty? Yes, he fancies himself, doesn't he?'

Kristy laughed. 'He tries to. He's actually harmless, once you get to know him.'

'How long have you worked with him? He was giving you a hand till I came along, correct?'

'Yes. We didn't have a DI, and instead of being allocated to other teams, DI Sen came over from Kidlington North to be acting DI.'

They drove in silence for a while. Kristy said, 'He's all right. You'll get used to him.'

'He's well used to himself,' Nikki said drily. 'All those fancy suits he wears. Thinks he's on the catwalk.' A thought struck her then, and she glanced at her younger colleague.

'Is he...?'

'No.' Kristy shook her head. 'He's divorced and got a daughter. Loves his little girl. Showed us photos of her. She's fifteen and really tall. That was sweet.'

'How about you?'

'Me?' Kristy glanced at Nikki, and they both smiled. 'I'm too young to have a family, guv. Only twenty-three.'

'Enjoy it,' Nikki said. 'I wish I was twenty-three again.'

'How about you, guv? If you don't mind me asking,' Kristy added hastily.

Nikki put a brave, fake smile on her face.

'I'm single. Got a daughter from a previous marriage. She's sixteen and tells me what to do.'

They both laughed.

It was mid-morning by the time she and Kristy arrived at New College. The college car park reserved a space for her, and she put her permit on the dashboard before she locked up.

The car park was next to the Holywell Street entrance, but the access to the college was through a narrow alley, which opened onto a cobbled street that skirted around the boundary walls. Nikki walked down to the ramparts that lined Longwall Street, pausing to inspect the ground. Here, the ramparts were like a castle's, with steps going up to the top. A sentry could patrol up there, and these ramparts featured in the larger Oxford colleges, a remnant of their medieval past. They were designed to protect the colleges, and the priests who ran them, from hordes of highwaymen and robbers.

Nikki did exactly what a sentry would've done centuries ago; she climbed up the stairs slowly.

'Watch how you go,' she called out to Kristy, who followed behind. 'It's not as strong as it once was.'

'Tell me about it, guv,' Kristy said. 'At least it didn't rain last night.'

Nikki nodded. A lack of rain was also good for preserving evidence.

Although they climbed up slowly, worried about cracks and gaps, the entire structure was lovingly maintained. Nikki got to the top and gazed down the other side. The drop to Longwall Street was at least ten feet. Unless one had a ladder, it wasn't easy scaling these walls, nor climbing down from them, which was harder.

She turned around and examined the buildings within the college lawn. Yes, the killer could've escaped through here. But it was risky. She crouched on the rampart and focused on the ground below. A couple of cars went past. She could see a squad car to her right, with a driver inside. The pavement was narrow, enough space for two people to walk side by side. Opposite, a row of terraced houses took up the street.

'Long way to go down, guv,' Kristy observed. 'If he or she did that, they might have had help on the other side. Like someone to hold a ladder.'

Nikki nodded. 'Good thinking. But let's base it on some evidence. Let's have a look at the wall outside to see if there are any marks.'

They went down the steps, Kristy going first this time. Nikki was glad both of them had rubber-soled flats on. On the street outside, she waved at one of the PCs who was getting into the car. He waved back, then jogged over.

Nikki stood in front of the stone wall. Although it was well maintained, several parts of the wall had chipped off. She walked along, her gaze on the ground. She stopped and looked up at the rampart. From here, it looked even more foreboding.

She spoke to the uniformed PC. 'Please walk to both ends of this road and along the perimeter, to see if you can find anything. It could be a discarded glove, a phone, or anything that fell out of someone's pocket. Not easy, I know, but do your best.'

The PC nodded and set off to speak to his colleague.

Nikki and Kristy sauntered down the lawn. Frost had claimed the grass in early morning, and it was yellowish in colour. The college buildings across the lawn looked majestic. They were built in the eighteenth century and were not as ancient as the main quadrangle. But the limestone façades were still imposing, even more so in the summer when the lawn was lush and flowers bloomed everywhere.

Nikki's phone beeped, and when she saw it was Rita calling, she smiled. She moved out of Kristy's earshot.

'Hi, darling,' Nikki said.

'Hello, Mummy. Are you solving a murder mystery right now?'

Nikki laughed. 'I might be. What're you doing?'

'Oh, I'm like busy, you know. Mel's coming over later. We're going to have a sleepover.'

Melanie was Rita's bestie, and Nikki knew her well. 'Oh nice. Say hello from me. Are you OK?'

'Yes, fine.' Rita's voice was a bit low now, and Nikki picked up on it.

'What's the matter?'

'Nothing.'

Nikki knew Rita wouldn't call if there wasn't an issue. She was lucky if the teenager called in the weekdays, to be honest.

'Talk to me,' Nikki said. 'What is it? Are you in your room?'

'I am.' Rita gave an exaggerated sigh. 'Don't worry. It's all OK. Just wanted to talk.'

'I miss you,' Nikki said, feeling a heaviness in her heart. It was never easy. She counted the days when she would see Rita again. 'Would you like to come over?'

'Too much to do this week. Maybe next week?'

'Sure. How about we do a Facetime this evening? About 8 p.m.?

'That sounds good.' Rita sounded upbeat now, and Nikki felt a twang of sorrow. She wanted to be closer to Rita, see her face. They missed each other.

'Excellent. And if you want, I'll come over this weekend and we can go out somewhere. OK?'

'Shopping? I need to buy new shoes. How about Westfield on Saturday?'

'Now, now.' Nikki grinned. 'You've got shoes.'

'I need new ones. Come on.'

'OK, we'll see. Got to go. Love you, darling.'

'Bye, Mummy. Solve that crime now, OK?'

Rita laughed.

'Do your homework.' Nikki laughed back.

'All done. I'm organised, you see.'

Nikki kissed on the phone, then hung up. As usual, she felt lighter, bubblier after she'd spoken to Rita. She couldn't wait to see her again. Nikki walked back to where Kristy was hovering.

The trees were bare and the hedges gnarly with the absence of leaves. The lawns were huge, and she didn't have time to go traipsing round the whole place. She needed to ask a couple of uniform teams to scour the area. She walked into the main quadrangle. In front of the crime scene, a white forensic tent had been erected, as Hetty had indicated. Nish was standing in front, and he stood to attention when their eyes met.

'Hetty's in there, guv,' Nish said.

'Good,' Nikki said. 'Has she found anything?'

'She said she wanted to speak to you.' Nish shrugged. 'I think she has.'

THIRTEEN

Nikki clapped the young man on the shoulder, then entered the narrow archway, which was further constricted by the forensic tent. She went upstairs to the crime scene. Hetty Barfield was on her knees, inspecting the black blood-mottled Persian rug. Her ample frame was encased in a blue Tyvek suit. She lowered her mask when Nikki entered the room, to check Nikki's shoes, and she smiled when she saw the plastic shoe coverings.

'Good to see.'

Nikki grinned. 'Surely you didn't think I would contaminate a scene?'

Hetty smiled, her cheeks pink. She blew away a strand of hair that fell across her face. 'Doesn't hurt to check.'

'What you got for me?'

'Skin fragments from the floor, along with hair. Blood as well, obviously.'

'Some samples will be from the wife. And the murderer.'

'Yes,' Hetty agreed. 'Please get the wife's DNA swab when you see her next. I suspect he had students come here, right? For tutorials.'

Nikki nodded. 'More than likely. In which case, we might find a variety of DNA. That's depressing.'

Hetty shook her head slowly. 'Not necessarily. I'm concentrating around the body.'

Nikki hooked a thumb behind her. 'No signs of damage to the door. Or the window facing the quad. So his attacker had to be someone he either knew, or was expecting.'

Hetty nodded. 'Yes. Swabs from the door handle and window frame revealed nothing. We dusted for prints, but only found the victim's.' Hetty pointed to the portable digital fingerprint scanner, which was a convenient way to take prints, and it was connected to IDENT-1, the national criminal print database.

Nikki wondered if the door had been open when Arabella arrived. She took out her black notebook and scribbled a reminder to ask her.

Nikki kept her book open. Speaking to Hetty was making her mind open up in new directions.

'Murder weapon?'

'I saw the body,' Hetty confirmed. 'Dr Raman will tell you more, but we're dealing with a long knife. Almost like a mini sword.'

'How long?'

'To stab someone in the neck without getting close isn't easy. Hence I think it was more than a knife.'

Nikki stood and pursed her lips together. 'A sword is a stretch as a murder weapon. It has to be hidden and transported.' She winked at Hetty. 'However, it might make our search for the weapon easier.'

'Because there aren't many swords around?'

Nikki scratched her chin. 'Yes, and also not many who are proficient in using one.'

Hetty raised her eyebrows. 'I doubt this person is proficient. He hacked at the victim. But I could discover something interesting. Metal fragments in the neck skin, at the site of trauma. I won't know until we do our lab testing.'

'Spectrum analysis?' Nikki remembered a case where a murderer was caught by the unusual metals on a ballistic report.

Hetty grinned. 'Not much gets past you. Yes, metals show up at different wavelengths on the spectrum chart. Let's see if we find an interesting pattern.'

'Good,' Nikki said. She looked around the room slowly. Her eyes fell on the paintings again. The sad, haunting face of the young woman with fair hair and a black bandana stared back at her.

It was an arresting image, the woman's soulful, glinting dark eyes capturing her attention. She scribbled a reminder to contact an art expert and find out more about it. Hetty joined her, admiring the painting.

'Brueghel's black-eyed girl,' she said. Nikki frowned and turned to look at her.

'You know about Brueghel?'

Hetty gazed at her for a few seconds. 'I used to work in art restoration at the Ashmolean before I did my forensics course.'

'Did you really?'

'Yes. They have a Dutch collection.' She pointed at the frame. 'I've not seen this Brueghel before, but it's well known. Also worth a fortune, if it's the original.'

Nikki pointed to the lower-right corner of the canvas. 'Look closer.'

Hetty inspected the signature for a while. Then she nodded. 'Looks like the other Brueghel signatures I've seen.'

'Can you do me a favour, please? Have a look at the other paintings. Are they the real deal?'

It took Hetty ten minutes to go through the remaining four paintings. By the end, she was clearly excited.

'There's two by Kalf. He's a master as well, not as well-known as Brueghel, but famous nonetheless.' Her dark eyes shone as she grinned, looking like a kid in a candy store. 'I think they are originals, but we might need to get a Dutch Old Masters expert in here.'

'What about the other two?'

'A Hals, and the other a Ruysch, can't remember her first name. Female Dutch masters are rare to find. The professor has quite the collection.'

Monty appeared at the doorway and said hello to both of them. Nikki left Hetty to her devices and stepped out.

'Have we lined up people from the college?' Nikki asked.

'Yes, guv,' Monty said. 'The bursar has agreed to speak to us. We got a list of all the teaching staff in the history department, and Nish is going around asking for them.'

'Good. What about a list of the professor's students?'

They were outside and walked down the path bordering the lawn. Nikki had always wondered how the quad lawns stayed so green even in the winter. One of the estate gardeners had told her it was fertilisers, carefully pumped into the turf, and high-powered lights that covered the quad like a blanket at night once all the students and visitors had gone. It never ceased to amaze Nikki the lengths an Oxford college would go to keep appearances intact.

'Still getting a list from the university. The college only knows about the students he had tutorials with. Apparently, he didn't have much contact with the undergrads. Mostly graduate and PhD students.'

'I see.' Nikki thought for a while. Professors did teach undergrads, but she also knew some profs chose to focus on research and only teach more senior students.

They walked around the quad, and then through the arches, emerging at the back of the college, where the newer admin buildings were located. Monty stopped in front of a large Greco-Roman-style building. From the side, Nikki could see the sprawling lawns that led to the boundary ramparts in the distance.

The limestone building was four floors tall and imposing. It had floor-to-ceiling windows and Greek-style columns holding up a central pediment on the roof.

'Shall we go in?' Monty asked. Nikki nodded, taking the lead.

They went up the steps to the broad patio, with fluted columns on either side. The huge door was open, and Nikki's feet sank in the soft rug laid out over the mahogany parquet flooring. A woman slid out from behind the glass counter at the rear of the room, checked their warrant cards and asked them to wait.

Nikki and Monty stood, eyeing the oil paintings of deans and dons on the wood-panelled walls, and the tall potted, tropical plants with broad leaves that gave the reception room a warm, cosy atmosphere.

A middle-aged bespectacled man, wearing a grey suit, approached them. He had sparse blond hair and sallow cheeks with a pasty complexion from too many days inside an office. His eyes flicked from Monty to Nikki.

'You must be Inspector Nikki Gill,' the man said, his tone well-modulated and Oxonian.

Nikki introduced Monty and they shook hands, as he added, 'Richard Moffatt, the college bursar. Please, come into my office.'

FOURTEEN

Mr Moffatt's office was covered in dark-panelled wood, and the dark-red leather gilt armchairs looked deep and comfortable. A couple of nice framed landscapes hung on the wall, and Nikki counted at least three statues around the room – each a Greco-Roman study of a woman and child. They looked old but well preserved. Framed photos of the bursar with dignitaries Nikki didn't recognise adorned the wood panelling.

'Would you like a cup of tea, or coffee?' Mr Moffatt asked. Nikki declined and took out her black notebook. Monty did the same.

'A terrible thing, this,' Mr Moffatt said, his eyebrows meeting in the middle. 'Never happened in the history of the college.'

The bursar's lips were pinched together, and he looked troubled.

'May I please start by asking you what you were doing yesterday evening between the hours of 4 p.m. and 8 p.m.?'

A frown rippled across his face as he stared down at his desk, then at an invisible object on the floor. 'I... had a series of meetings yesterday. Meeting some alumni and fundraisers.

Then there was another meeting in the evening with the governing body.'

'What time did the governing body meeting end?'

Mr Moffatt was lost in thought. 'Around 8 p.m., I would say.'

'And when did it start?'

'Oh gosh, I'm not sure I recall.' He took out his phone and flicked through the screens. 'Here it is. Around 6 p.m., I think.'

Nikki wrote down the times and circled the words *governing body*.

'We would like to speak to everyone here who knew Professor Allerton. I take it you did?'

Mr Moffatt was looking at Nikki with wide eyes, visible behind his glasses. 'Well, I knew him as a member of the governing body, yes. Or the GB as we call it.'

Nikki angled her head to the left. 'Professor Allerton was a member of the GB, but he didn't attend the meeting?'

'Not everyone can attend every meeting, Inspector. Sometimes members have teaching commitments, and so on.'

Nikki had investigated a couple of burglaries in Oxford colleges in the past, and she knew about the powerful governing bodies.

'GB meetings are important, aren't they?'

There was a moment's silence. Nikki kept her expression blank, but a hint of suspicion was brewing in her mind. The bursar lost his composure when Nikki asked him for an alibi, and he hadn't recovered. Something was bothering him.

Mr Moffatt coughed into a fist. 'Yes, they are.' He said nothing more. Nikki allowed the silence to lengthen.

'The college makes decisions about hiring new teaching staff, and expenses on the property, during these meetings, don't they?'

Mr Moffatt lifted the tips of his shoulders. 'Sometimes they do, yes. Among a variety of other matters.'

The bursar's reticence to disclose much about these closed-door meetings was in part a reflection of the college's strict privacy policy. Nikki also knew Mr Moffatt was a traditionalist, or he wouldn't have the influential job of the head bursar, essentially the money manager of the college.

'Despite these meetings being important, why didn't the professor attend last night?'

'He had a seminar. It was a university-wide thing, with many attendees. He was presenting his latest research as well, at the seminar. He apologised for the absence.'

Monty shifted on his chair, and Nikki glanced at him. Monty cleared his throat. 'Approximately how many people came for the seminar?'

'I am not sure. About fifty I would say, because they fitted into the auditorium.'

Nikki asked, 'Do you know what the professor was doing before he went to the seminar?'

'I do not know his exact schedule, but I daresay he was around the college as it was a working day. Unless he had external commitments.'

'Such as?

'Fellows and professors are often members of university groups. I mean the University of Oxford.'

Nikki nodded. She knew the colleges were fiercely independent, although they all came under the umbrella of University of Oxford. But in modern times, which meant from the late eighteenth century, Oxford dons actively participated in university life.

'Did the professor have a secretary? We need to know his movements for the sake of the investigation.'

'I believe he did, yes. She didn't belong to the college however, as he had a history departmental role at the university. She was his departmental secretary. I didn't know her, but I'm sure I can find her contact details if you wish.'

Monty asked, 'Is it possible to look for it now?' He glanced at Nikki, who nodded swiftly. 'It's rather important that we establish his commitments yesterday.'

Mr Moffatt smoothed the few strands of hair on his balding pate. 'Of course, no problem.' He lifted the phone and spoke to someone, then hung up.

'I should have the details of his secretary soon.' He glanced at his watch. 'Is there anything else I can help you with?'

Nikki remained impassive, but the kernel of suspicion she had was hardening. 'There is, in fact. Is it fair to assume the professor knew members of the governing body?'

Mr Moffatt licked his lower lip before responding. 'Well, as he was a member he would have had contact with them, yes.'

'In which case, we would like to speak to them. How can we get in touch with them?'

Mr Moffatt inclined his head slowly. 'Certainly. I can get in touch with them for you.'

'No need to bother yourself.' Nikki smiled. She had expected that response. 'Please provide us with the details of each member now and we will contact them ourselves.'

Monty spoke up. 'We also want to speak to the students he recently taught, or had contact with.'

'That will depend on his diary. His secretary will have the details of his tutorials, and I shall see if I can get hold of them for you.'

Nikki said, 'When did you last see the professor?'

Mr Moffatt appeared lost in thought. 'I was wondering about that. To be honest, our paths didn't cross that much. I knew him, of course, but we were busy with our own jobs. I remember the last GB meeting, which was last month.'

'Do you have a date and time?'

Mr Moffatt looked peeved, but fished out his phone and scrolled through a few screens. 'Yes. The tenth of October was the last meeting, at 6 p.m.'

'Exactly four weeks ago,' Nikki said. 'Did the GB meet every month?'

The bursar shrugged. 'It's not set in stone. It can be, depends on what's on the agenda.'

'What was on the agenda at the last meeting?' Nikki asked. Mr Moffatt sat very still. His cheeks were flushed, and a few beads of sweat had appeared on his frontal scalp. His Adam's apple bobbed up and down frequently, and he shifted on his seat. He was showing many signs of anxiety, and Nikki wanted to know why.

'A number of issues. I'm afraid I can't remember all of them.'

Nikki decided to press. 'There must've been one or two important matters.'

Mr Moffatt's head sank on his chest. Nikki and Monty glanced at each other. The bursar raised his head. He adjusted his glasses and stared straight at Nikki.

'Inspector Gill, I am struggling to understand what the GB meetings have to do with this matter.'

'I'm just trying to build a picture of what the professor's duties were. His working life might throw up clues about his death. He must have known many people through his work in the college?'

'Yes, of course.'

Nikki went on, 'And most murder victims are killed by people they know. Hence, an idea of his working day and the people he met would be valuable to this investigation.'

Mr Moffatt cleared his throat and swallowed again. 'I see your point. But you must realise that minutes of the GB meetings are very private. Each college has their own. Under no circumstances can they be released.'

'Even for a situation like this?'

Mr Moffatt unfurled a handkerchief and wiped his brow. 'The governing bodies are chartered by the Privy Council. The

Council sets down rules which all governing bodies obey. I'm afraid I have to ask the Privy Council for their guidance.'

He spread his hands, and his jaw hardened. 'I have not dealt with a situation like this before. The Privy Council, which is part of the main university Council, has to sanction this before I can release confidential material.'

Nikki and Monty exchanged glances again. Nikki continued. 'You'll need to seek that guidance now, Mr Moffatt. In the meanwhile, we'll also need the contact details of the professor's colleagues.'

Monty added, 'In the governing body and outside it. And also, his secretary please.'

Her instincts told her Moffat was holding back. She understood the reasons the colleges were reluctant to hand out confidential details. But there was something more. Mr Moffat was worried, and Nikki wanted to know why.

FIFTEEN

Mr Moffatt's secretary came in with a printout. Monty took it with a murmur of thanks. He looked through the document that bore the most recent names and contact details of New College's governing body members, and the professor's university secretary.

Nikki took the two sheets of paper from Monty. Mr Moffatt was rubbing his hands together, and Nikki caught the movement from the corner of her eye.

'Do you know if any of these members are in the college now?'

The bursar shook his head. 'No, I'm sorry. Some of them might be out. Without knowing their schedule I'm afraid I cannot tell you.'

Monty made a sound in his throat. Nikki knew exactly what it meant. The list was of no use to them at this point in time. Nikki persisted, aware that Mr Moffatt was increasingly impatient to get rid of them.

'There must be other teachers of history in the college. Professor Allerton would have been in touch with them. Is it possible to meet them today?'

Monty jumped in. 'If you don't know we can ask your secretary. She can ring some of the fellows or tutors in history.'

Mr Moffatt's lips were stretched in a thin line. 'Of course. Let me see what I can do.'

He picked up the phone and a few moments later his secretary re-entered the room. Mr Moffatt took his glasses off and rubbed them on a silk cloth.

'Rachel, please contact the history staff and see who is free to speak to the police.'

Nikki smiled at Rachel, who held her eyes for longer than necessary. She was young, in her mid- to late twenties. Nikki turned her attention to the bursar.

'As far as you know, did Professor Allerton have any enemies?'

Mr Moffatt's eyebrows hiked north. 'My goodness, no. I mean, not that I know of.'

'Well, clearly, someone didn't like him that much,' Monty observed drily. Nikki smirked at her deputy, before continuing.

'Did his students complain about him? Was he late for tutorials?'

'Not that I know of. To be honest, such matters are dealt with by the pastoral head of the college. Any student can approach him. If there was a problem however, I would have heard.'

'The professor wasn't in any financial difficulties, was he?'

Mr Moffatt hesitated slightly before replying. 'Not that I know of, no. I am not aware of his personal finances, of course. He was paid on time, and he lived comfortably.'

Monty asked, 'Did you ever visit him at home?'

Mr Moffatt nodded. 'He had a summer party in his garden last year. Many of us were invited, including some of his postgraduate students. He lived in Jericho. He lived well without being extravagant, from what I could see.'

'Thank you,' Nikki said. 'We will visit his wife later today.'

Rachel came back, flashed a smile at Nikki, and handed her a piece of paper. It bore a name and number.

Rachel said, 'Miss Sue Pollard is a senior tutor in history, and she shared several classes with Professor Allerton. She is in the Senior Common Room at the moment. She can meet you in her office.'

Nikki rose to her feet. Rachel arched her neck to look in her face. Nikki smiled. 'Could you please show us the way?'

'Certainly.'

Nikki nodded at Mr Moffatt. 'Thank you for your help. If you could please get us the minutes of those meetings.' It was a statement, and Mr Moffatt's eyes hardened.

'I can try, Inspector,' he said stiffly. 'It is not my decision, as I explained.'

Monty held out a card, and Mr Moffatt took it. 'Please call us if you remember anything about the professor. Any small detail could make a big difference, however irrelevant.'

The bursar cleared his throat. 'I will of course.'

Rachel walked slightly ahead of Nikki and Monty.

Monty lowered his voice. 'Wonder what's eating him?' he said.

'So do I.' Nikki's mind was running in slow loops. This was the beginning, and she had to keep an open mind. The net had to be cast wide. But she couldn't shake the feeling Mr Moffatt knew more about the professor than he was letting on.

They had walked out into the quad. It was cold, but an austere sun was dazzling in an empty blue sky. A broad shaft of sunlight angled in past the main clock tower and lit up the golden yellow limestone building enclosing the lawn. A priest in a black smock came out of the chapel and hurried across the quad.

Rachel walked to the end and turned left, walking close to the many arched, narrow gateways that framed the corridor covering the quad building. She went inside one at the opposite end to the chapel, making sure Nikki and Monty were following her. Bare branches hung with ivy dropped down from the arched opening, and Nikki had to brush them away with a hand before she ducked inside.

They passed through the students' quarters and up some steps. Rachel stopped outside a black-painted door and knocked. A woman opened it and looked at them inquisitively, her glance flicking from Rachel to the two detectives.

SIXTEEN

Sue Pollard was in her sixties, Nikki guessed. She had short hair cut to the neckline, grey-coloured with splashes of white. Behind round glasses she could discern sharp blue eyes. She wore cream trousers and smoothed down her blouse as Rachel introduced them.

Nikki and Monty stepped inside a large but cosy room that looked like a library. There was a fireplace opposite the door, a long and elaborate affair with a thick mantelpiece. It had been kept as originally intended, but was unused now. It was large enough to roast a couple of hogs side by side. An iron grill protected the front. On the brass mantelpiece several photos were arranged.

Bookshelves covered the entire room, from floor to ceiling. They occupied three walls, apart from the bay windows that faced the quadrangle. The walls were of ancient stone and the room seemed like a time capsule. If a fire had been blazing in the hearth, Nikki could easily have imagined this place nine hundred years ago, except for the salient fact that Sue Pollard would certainly have been a man – perhaps in a priest's smock, belt and collar, with a long, bushy beard.

'Please have a seat,' Miss Pollard said, indicating the well-worn brown leather sofa next to the fireplace. There was a coffee table in front of the sofa, with books and magazines neatly piled in one corner. Nikki and Monty sat.

Sue sat on her armchair at the desk facing the bay window and swung around to face them.

Nikki opened proceedings. 'Thank you for seeing us today, Miss Pollard. As you know, this is about the tragic death of Professor Allerton.'

Miss Pollard sat motionless with her hands folded on her lap. Light streamed in from the window behind her, making it difficult to see her face clearly.

'Please, call me Sue. Yes,' she said. 'And very disturbing, the way it happened.'

'When was the last time you saw Professor Allerton?'

'As it happens, it was yesterday afternoon. We were having lunch in the Senior Common Room.'

'Did anything about him strike you as unusual? Was he different in any way?'

'Not that I can recall. We said hello, read our papers, then had lunch.' Sue furrowed her brows. 'Come to think of it, he was a bit quiet. He spent some time staring out the window, even when Bernard had announced lunch.'

'Bernard?' Nikki crinkled her forehead.

'The butler.' A faint smile played along Sue's lips. 'Senior Common Rooms have service staff. For us humble fellows.'

'Ah yes.' Nikki grinned back. 'Anything else wouldn't be civilised now, would it?'

'Quite.' She seemed lost for a while, eyes downcast. 'Don't get me wrong. Scholars like their quiet moments, like anyone else. So Brian having some time to himself isn't unusual.'

'What was he like normally? Life and soul of the party, or the quiet type?'

'I would say a combination. He could be loud and jocular,

but also observant.' She waved a hand. 'We go to the SRC to relax, you see. Sometimes also have a lunchtime tipple. But drinking is more commonplace at night.' She smiled. 'The wine cellars at the college are impressive.'

'I bet they are. Was Professor Allerton drinking at lunchtime yesterday?'

Sue hesitated, then pressed her lips together. 'He was, yes. He had a glass or two of sherry. I wasn't keeping count.'

'No, that's fine, thank you. Was he fond of a drink?'

The hesitation came again, and Nikki knew the answer. It wouldn't be the first time she had heard of boozy academics.

Sue shrugged. 'It was well known, I guess. He enjoyed his wine. You must know, Inspector, drinking habits are well entrenched in our circles.'

Nikki inclined her head, and Monty grinned. Nikki asked, 'Would you say he had a drinking problem? Did he ever turn up to his tutorials or classes drunk?'

Sue shut her eyes briefly before opening them. 'I wouldn't say drunk, but he did drink in the daytime. Sometimes you could smell it on his breath.'

'How long did you work with him?'

Sue looked up at the ceiling, obviously doing some mental calculations. 'I joined New College about ten years ago. He was already here. He was a senior tutor for several years, then he was awarded the Regius Professorship.'

'Did you know him personally?'

Sue shrugged. 'We were colleagues. We met each other's partners at parties and gatherings.'

'But you were not friends?'

Sue's blue eyes contracted a touch. 'It's often not a good idea to mix business with pleasure, as I'm sure you must know, Inspector. Like I said, we knew each other.'

Nikki decided to change tack. There was something here, and Miss Pollard was trying to avoid it.

'You were a member of the governing body, along with the professor.' It was a statement, not a question.

'Yes.'

'Was he an active participant in the meetings?'

She shrugged. 'I guess so, yes.' She opened her mouth to say something, then stopped.

Nikki held her eyes. 'Did you like him, Sue?'

She waited a few seconds before replying, and Nikki had her answer. There wasn't much love lost between them.

She raised her eyebrows. She pointed to Monty. 'As much as you like your colleague here, Inspector. We worked together and hence got on with each other.'

Nikki smiled. 'Could you please answer the question?'

She frowned. 'Yes, of course.' She was more agitated now and shifted in her chair, then crossed her legs. 'We worked together for a long time.'

'You never had any arguments with him? Or conflicts?'

Sue shook her head swiftly. Too swiftly, Nikki thought.

'No, I didn't.'

Nikki glanced at Monty, who took over. Monty cleared his throat. 'Where were you between the hours of 4 p.m. and 8 p.m. yesterday?'

'I had a couple of tutorials, lasting till 5 p.m. Then I went back home to Iffley, where I live with my partner.'

'Was your partner at home?'

Sue shook her head. 'No. He's away on a business trip.'

Monty bent his head, writing on his pad like Nikki was. They both knew what this meant. Miss Pollard didn't have an alibi.

Nikki asked, 'Were you at the seminar hosted by the professor?'

'It was hosted by the college actually, and I organised it.' She lifted her chin. 'Brian read out my research article and answered questions.'

'I see.' Nikki was interested. 'Why were you not there to read out your own article, if you organised the seminar?'

Sue swallowed and then adjusted her glasses. She seemed uncomfortable, and Nikki guessed she had strayed too far. She was beginning to see the academic's true colours, and they were intriguing.

'Well, it was agreed at the GB meeting that it made more sense if a Regius did the seminar. Brian's name had more attraction you see. He was a star in his field, so to speak.'

'It was your field as well, correct? Modern English history?'

The older woman nodded in silence, blinking twice.

Nikki glanced at Monty, who snapped his pad shut and shoved it in his pocket. They rose in unison, and Nikki did a half bow for Miss Pollard, which made the woman smile.

'Thank you,' Nikki said, handing her card to Sue. 'Please call us if you remember anything.'

SEVENTEEN

'She hated him,' Monty said flatly, as they walked down the quad towards the crime scene. It looked out of place, a white tent covering the entrance of the arched walkway.

'She gave it away when she made no effort to hide his boozing,' he continued. 'And she almost came clean at the end. I got the feeling she was tired of playing second fiddle to him.'

Nikki was thoughtful, eyes on the flagstones beneath their feet. 'She didn't want to share the seminar with him. She did all the work...'

'And he took the glory,' Monty finished for her. 'Was that a pattern?'

'She also doesn't have an alibi. Maybe one of the neighbours saw her getting home, we need to check.'

Monty nodded sagely. He pulled out a packet of cigarettes, cursed and shoved them back in his pocket. It was daylight and he couldn't get away with a cheeky one now.

'She probably had motive and doesn't have an alibi,' he mused. 'Suspect?'

'Maybe,' Nikki said. 'Let's not rule anyone out right now.'

They had come upon the forensic tent and Nish ambled over to them.

'Dr Raman called. She's done with the post-mortem. Wants you to give her a call.'

'Thanks, Nish. Scene of crime all done now?'

'Yes, guv. They're taking photos, but will pack up in a couple of hours.'

'Have they finished taking samples from the corridor and out here?'

Nish hesitated. Nikki smiled. 'They will probably cover every inch of the passage down to here. Knowing Hetty, she would do the whole quad if she could. Not that she'll get much with the students trampling everywhere.'

'Shall I check with them upstairs?'

'No. Leave them be. You stay posted here, under no circumstances is anyone allowed in.'

'Roger that, guv.'

Nikki stepped back, almost to the grass verge of the precision-cut lawn. She looked up at the window, which now had its curtain drawn. Monty followed her.

Nikki spoke in a low voice, almost speaking to herself. 'The victim finished the seminar around 6 p.m. Where is the auditorium, by the way?'

Monty pulled out a map. Tourists were handed these when they visited the college during the summer holidays. Nish strode forward. The young constable had an eager, warm voice. He had clearly overheard their conversation.

'The auditorium is through the passage and in the new buildings at the back. Where the bursar has his office.'

Nikki smiled at him. 'Good work. What else did you find out about the place?'

Nish flushed at the praise. 'It's used for stage and theatre work by the students, but it's only used for college activities. I went to have a look, when Kristy was here to guard this place. It was closed, guv.'

'OK, thanks.' Nikki resumed looking at the window. 'Around 6:30, the prof was back in his room. Then he leaves the premises. We don't know where he goes. His wife finds him at ten thirty p.m. in his office, dead. I want to know where he went.'

Nish said, 'CCTV doesn't pick him up leaving. There are multiple CCTV blind spots in the college; I've just been watching them with Winston. The prof could've left via one of the back doors.'

'And then he's brought back here and left in his room.'

'We don't know that yet,' Monty reminded him. 'No one's come forward as yet, but someone could have seen a person enter or emerge the staff quarters.'

Nikki tapped her black shoe on the stone. 'This is Oxford. Not very traditional to come forward and divulge information. Have we put up signs?'

'Outside the college and as soon as you come in.'

'I want some posters up here as well, on tripods so they can be clearly seen.'

Monty blew out his cheeks. 'We tried that. Apparently not allowed, due to health and safety.'

Nikki flexed her jaw. 'Nonsense. Can we please do it? If anyone takes them down ask them to speak to me. It is vital we remind students of the incident. One of them might have seen something.'

She continued, 'In any case, our murderer either knows this place inside out, or he or she got extremely lucky. At 6:30, there would be people around. Some of them would be leaving the seminar. There's a high chance one of them witnessed something.'

She turned to Monty. 'Are there any other entrances to the upstairs apartments?'

Monty shook his head. 'Not that I know of. But wouldn't be surprised if there was.'

Nikki was feeling a little frustrated. Mr Moffatt could have made her job a lot easier. She needed a guide to the college. Then she thought of Winston. She asked Monty to get him, and he rushed off, no doubt eager to have a quick fag by the outside gate. Nikki beckoned Nish over.

'Could you please chase Professor Allerton's secretary at the university? And ask the researchers at HQ to track down the governing body members.' Nikki pulled out her notebook, and Nish took a photo of the relevant pages on his phone.

Monty came rushing back, Winston behind him, struggling to keep up with the DI.

'You won't believe this,' Monty raged, his cheeks mottled. 'There's two reporters out there, with microphones and cameras. They want to know what's happened.'

Nikki swore under her breath. It was a matter of time, of course, given the police presence all around the college. She had hoped against hope the press would stay away. A suspicion nibbled at the back of her mind. When she looked at Monty's face, her worst fears were confirmed.

'No,' she said.

'Yes,' came the response from Monty's dark, thundering face. 'They know someone's died here. Asking if it's a murder investigation.'

Nikki closed her eyes and looked skyward. She shook her head. 'Do they know the victim's name?'

'They didn't mention names.'

Nikki turned to Winston. He lowered his eyebrows. 'Any ideas, Winston?'

Winston shook his head. 'No idea. It was only you and me at the gates last night. And all the students who turned up later.'

'But they wouldn't know any better,' Nikki said. 'I guess word can spread. We are in a college, after all.'

She indicated to Winston. 'Let's go upstairs.'

Monty stayed by the tent, as Nish had gone to make the calls. Nikki stopped at the unmarked wooden door that led to the steps upstairs. The arched ceiling met her eyes, gables and sculptures adorning the cornices. The corridor wrapped around the quad.

'Winston, is there any other entrance to upstairs?'

The older guard thought for a while. 'Don't think so. The scholars aren't allowed to take food into their living space. They have to attend the great dining hall or the SCR.'

'I see. So no entrance for butlers or servants.'

'That's right.'

'What about interconnecting hallways upstairs?'

Winston shook his head. 'The scholars are the most powerful people here. Or the priests who made them a thousand years ago, to be more precise. They put the fear of God into the builders. They wanted total privacy where they lived.'

Nikki frowned. 'No other entrance. Right. So our killer had to enter and exit via this route. And he carried a body back, which couldn't have been easy.' She looked at Winston. 'You've sent us all the CCTV, right?'

'Yes. But as I explained to your man, there are some CCTV black spots around the college ground. However, the main quad and the living quarters are all well covered.'

Nikki said, 'And yet, no sighting of the prof leaving the college and then someone bringing him back. How is that possible?'

'Maybe the prof knew where the black spots are.'

Winston made a face. 'I can't see how he would know, or why, to be honest. But Prof Allerton smoked cigars. I've seen him on the grounds at night. And those areas aren't covered by CCTV.'

'Right.' Nikki pointed a finger, aware of the importance of what Winston just said. 'Was he smoking there last night?'

The porter spread his hands. 'I don't know. I was busy at the gates. What he did after the seminar was over is anyone's guess.'

'We know he came up to his room. That's on CCTV. He crosses the quad and goes up the stairs. At some point, he leaves, but clearly not via the quad, or the back, as there are cameras there.'

Winston had his hands folded behind his back as he leaned against the stone wall. 'He could've waited until it was dark, then walked downstairs, but stayed out of the quad. That way, he could stay out of the cameras, go to another side of the building and get access to the grounds. I'm just guessing.'

Nikki smiled. Winston was proving to be invaluable. 'That's a good guess. It makes sense. But the million-pound question is why he wanted to keep his movements secret. I think he made a deliberate attempt to do so.'

Winston shrugged. 'Can't help you with that. Are you sure he went out of the college grounds by the way?'

'There was grass and mud on his shoes. He had to be outside. He could've been on the college grounds as well, in one of the blind spots. Our people are scouring the place, but they've found nothing so far.' A thought occurred to Nikki. 'Are there any other parks around the college?'

Winston frowned. 'Outside the college it's central Oxford. The other colleges have their own lawns. He could've gone to one of them.'

'What's that big park in the middle, with the pond, and the River Cherwell running through it?'

'University Parks,' Winston said. 'But that's a five- to ten-minute walk from here.'

'And he would be on the main streets for that, I presume.'

Winston nodded. Nikki was grateful to the porter. 'We might be able to get him on CCTV outside the college. Thanks, Winston, you've been a great help.'

EIGHTEEN

Nikki felt her phone buzz as she came down the stairs. It was Dr Raman, calling from the morgue at John Radcliffe Hospital.

'Thought I'd give you a call in case you're busy with the investigation,' she said.

'Thank you,' Nikki replied.

'You're welcome,' she said. 'Nothing like the first stiff of the winter, eh?'

Nikki laughed. 'First and last, we hope.' Humour was one way of alleviating the stress of the job. Both knew the situation was far more serious than most they had encountered.

'Yes, let's hope it is.'

'What have you got for me?' Nikki was outside now, and she walked down the quad, her eyes on the faces of students and staff she passed.

'He lost a lot of blood very quickly, as the carotid artery was severed. Interestingly, he had cuts on his elbows and wrists as well. That's where the basilar and radial arteries are situated.'

'That hastened the blood loss,' Nikki said.

'Yes. It means the killer had some basic knowledge of anatomy.'

Nikki stopped at a corner of the quad and leaned against a stone wall. 'Hetty said a long blade was used, longer than an average kitchen knife. Do you agree?'

'Yes, I do. Lacerations from a kitchen knife leave jagged, uneven marks. Most have serrated edges for ease of cutting. But the lacerations on our victim are different. The weapon used was blunt, and the killer needed to inflict several blows to achieve the effect of a sharp kitchen knife.'

Nikki frowned. 'Are you saying the weapon used wasn't very effective?'

Dr Raman made a noise between a sigh and a smothered laugh. 'Well, it did the job hence it was effective. If you're asking whether a professional knife murderer, if I can use such a term, would use the same weapon, then I doubt it.'

'Because it was blunt where – at the edges, or the tip?'

'I don't know. You need to ask the murderer. However, he or she needed a fair few blows to the neck in order to perforate the important arteries. In the process, the killer made a mess of the neck muscles and tendons. A sharper knife would have sliced through those structures.'

Nikki observed her feet again. Her mind was churning. 'I daresay that a blunt knife is one that has not been used for a long time. It could be an antique piece. Maybe like a dagger?'

Nikki could hear the pathologist smile down the phone. 'Great minds think alike, Inspector Gill.'

'Unless the killer used something like an old machete. Is that possible?'

There was silence for a while. Dr Raman cleared her throat.

'If you come down to the morgue I can show you. A machete would leave bigger marks. It would cleave through the neck muscles. The cuts on the victim are more delicate. Yes, the weapon was used several times, in a frenzy, if you like. But it didn't hack the head off, if you know what I mean.'

'I do,' Nikki breathed. Her pulse was quickening. Having

an idea about the murder weapon was critical, especially if it was unusual. 'It's safe to assume the blade was long and thin, and maybe rusty. Hetty mentioned that as well. If it was an old weapon, then the chemical composition would be different. Correct?'

'Precisely. Most modern knives are made from a combination of aluminium, nickel and steel. Older knives would mostly be steel, I think. I'm not sure though. Hetty might know more. I have sent her tissue samples already.'

'Thank you. Anything else?'

'Skin samples from his nails show a different DNA to his. Once you have DNA swabs from the suspects, we can do a cross check.'

'He fought with his attacker, and scraped his skin?'

'I think so. Our victim has lacerations on his knuckles as well, which would go along with that. He also has tobacco stains on his nails.'

'He smoked cigars,' Nikki said, remembering the box of Cohiba in the drawer, and also what Winston had told her. 'Maybe cigarettes as well.'

She paused, thinking about the rest of the crime scene. 'Anything in the lower body?'

'Blood splatter, but no specific injury. I would say the killer repeatedly stabbed him around the neck and chest region. The large arteries in the chest cavity are better hidden under the ribs and muscles, but he definitely perforated the lungs. That would have hastened death,' Dr Raman continued.

'Are there any signs of where he was killed? I mean, does the grass or mud on his shoes point to anywhere specific?'

The pathologist sighed. 'I thought you might ask me that. I sent the soil sample from his shoes for analysis. They came back with the same clay type we see all over Oxfordshire. Nothing more specific, I'm afraid.'

'We think he left the college and walked to a park nearby.

Hoping to pick him up on the street CCTV if he did. After the college lawns, University Parks is the nearest, right?'

'Hmmm, yes. But after 7 p.m. the Parks main gate is shut. I hear there are other entrances, but only the students will know.'

'Or the academics,' Nikki said. 'Thanks, Sheila, that's helpful. If you find anything else please let me know.'

She hung up and, head bowed against the wind blowing across the quad, walked quickly to the crime scene.

Monty stood there, coat pulled tightly around his body, shifting from one foot to the other. His eyes narrowed when they met Nikki's.

'What'd she say?' he asked. Nikki explained, and Monty nodded slowly, then pointed up.

'We need to find out who else lived in the staff quarters. Professor Allerton wasn't the only one. Winston said he would find out. He needs to ask the staff accommodation officer.'

'So could we,' Nikki said. 'I want to know if all the staff quarters have the same entrance, or if they're different.'

Monty shrugged.

'Stay here,' Nikki said. 'I need to check something upstairs.'

Nikki went up the circular stone stairs. The old wooden door at the top was similar to the one downstairs with one exception – it could not be locked. Not for the first time, that struck her as strange.

Daylight was fading, and there was minimal light coming in from the tall windows. Nikki flipped on the light switches on the landing. After the small landing, there was a hallway, which led to the study, and a double bedroom and bathroom opposite it. Nikki wondered how much time the professor spent here. He had his own home in Jericho. His wife would know more.

Nikki walked to the end of the hallway and met a stone wall. It was limestone-coloured, fading yellow with tinges of brown, and solid. She knocked on it, hoping to find a hollow sound. She found nothing and turned on her heels. The bedroom door was open. Hetty and her officers had done their job, but Nikki hadn't examined the bedroom.

The double bedroom had low stone arches overhead. It was large enough for a king-size bed and a big desk in one corner by the windows. The bed had been slept on, she noted. With a gloved hand, she raised the duvet. The sheets were wrinkled, on both sides. She wondered if Hetty had taken DNA swabs already. Was the professor sleeping here with his wife?

Arabella, the wife, had said she came from their house. Nikki didn't know if that meant she had stayed the night there, or slept here, then went home to get ready. And if not the wife, who could the professor be sleeping with?

Nikki looked at the desk. A stack of journals on history were stacked neatly to one side, and a couple lay on the bedside table. Clearly, the professor read them before he went to sleep. Both the bedside table and the desk were made of dark mahogany wood. The corners and legs had delicate floral patterns. They looked old, period pieces. Well maintained, but the marks of age were obvious. The corners had flattened, the top was covered in ridges and marks. Probably hundreds of years old.

Nikki opened the drawers. More journals, and some ring binders with what looked like dissertations or theses inside. She shut the drawers and turned to the windows. The wooden frames were polished and the panes criss-crossed with a pattern. She saw movement outside in the garden. A woman walked out from behind the corner of the next building. She stood still, watching the window.

Nikki retreated, keen not to be seen. The woman had black hair and was of medium height. She wore a grey coat and a turtleneck jumper. From what Nikki could see, she was pretty. She wasn't a casual observer. Her eyes lingered over the window, then she looked down. Her shoulders slumped.

Nikki stepped forward, keeping to the shadows. She got to the curtains, then peered out. The woman took one last look at the window, then shook her head slightly. An expression of sorrow convulsed her face. She wiped her eyes then headed down the garden. Nikki sprinted for the staircase, eager to catch up with her.

NINETEEN

Nikki came out into the garden to find the woman walking ahead, head bent low. She stepped on the stones laid out as a garden path. This was the scholars' garden, and it was large, sloping down to a bank of trees at the back. Apart from the woman, the garden was empty.

Nikki lost her between two large topiaries, and she increased her pace. She brushed across the sculpted hedges as tall as her shoulder and stopped short. A row of circular topiaries lay ahead of her, more than two metres high. She couldn't see the woman. She ran forward and saw the flash of a grey coat move rapidly to the left.

She called out before she lost her again. 'Excuse me?'

The woman stopped and turned around. High, naturally sculpted cheekbones, large, expressive, grey-blue eyes, the shadows underneath hinting at lack of sleep. No make-up, a natural beauty. Jet-black hair lying in wisps around her shoulders, stirring in the gentle, but cold wind.

Nikki raised her warrant card, holding it close to her face so she could read.

'May I please know your name?' Nikki asked.

The woman blinked. She was silent for a few seconds, then appeared to make her mind up. 'Tracy. Tracy Ishihara.'

'Thank you, Miss Ishihara. There has been a death in the staff quarters of New College which was reported to the police last night. I saw you walking on the premises just now, and I was wondering if you saw or heard anything yesterday evening.'

She didn't tell her that she had seen her already. She wondered if the woman knew that she had been spotted.

'Who died?' Tracy frowned, and Nikki couldn't tell if she was lying. Tracy said, 'I saw the police cars outside and realised something had happened. I thought it was theft or burglary. I didn't realise...' Her voice trailed off.

'Professor Allerton,' Nikki said.

Tracy stared at Nikki for a while longer, blotches of colour spreading up her neck, into her cheeks. 'I can't believe it,' she whispered. 'Brian's dead?'

Nikki nodded soberly. 'I'm afraid so. Did you know the professor?'

She nodded. 'We worked in the same department. My specialism is medieval history of Scandinavia, but there is some overlap with English history, particularly in northern England.'

'When did you last see him?'

Tracy's chin lowered to her chest. 'Not this week. Maybe last. Yes, last week.' She put a finger to her cheek and looked into the distance. 'I can't remember where. It might have been in the library, or in the department.'

'Do you have lunch and dinner in the staff common room? Like the Senior Common Room, for instance.'

'Not always, no. However, I have met Brian in the Senior Common Room at dinner sometimes, along with my other colleagues.'

'Did you know him well?'

'Yes, I guess so.' Tracy shrugged again. 'We had worked on a project together in the past. We had friends in common in the department.'

'If you don't mind me asking, do you live in the staff quarters?'

She shook her head. 'No. But I live close by, in Cowley. It's at the other end, near town.'

'Close to the High Street, you mean?'

Tracy nodded.

Nikki said, 'What brings you here today?'

'I come to the department on a daily basis. I do some student tutorials and contribute to the research in the department.'

'So you came to work today?'

'Yes,' Tracy said. She looked down the path. Topiary hedges surrounded them. In the middle there was a clearing with a fountain.

'When did this happen?'

'I cannot go into details of the case right now,' Nikki said. 'But may I please ask where you were between the hours of four and eight yesterday evening?'

'I was at the library, working on one of my papers.' The tips of her shoulders lifted. 'I work as a non-stipendiary post-doctoral fellow in New College.'

'I see,' Nikki said.

Tracy waved a hand in the direction of the staff quarters. 'I was aware that something was happening. But not the death of Professor Allerton.' She stepped closer to Nikki. 'Can you please tell me what happened? How did he die?'

Nikki considered her questions. She had been looking up at the window and it was more than likely she knew the professor. But how well?

'Apart from the fact that his death is now a police investiga-tion, I can't tell you any more. However, if you can remember anything at all about yesterday, then that would be very helpful.'

'I've got to get going, Inspector Gill. This is very disturbing news. I'm rather shocked.' She crossed her arms over her chest.

'Of course,' Nikki said. 'Would you mind if I gave you a call sometime, or asked you to come down to the station to give a statement?'

Tracy's forehead wrinkled. 'A statement about what?'

'You knew Professor Allerton. We need to build a picture about the kind of man he was. Anything you can tell us would be very helpful, I'm sure.'

Nikki gave her a card. Tracy took it, glanced at it briefly, then put it into her jacket pocket. She nodded at Nikki, then walked off towards the fountain. Nikki watched her go, thoughts churning in her mind.

Tracy knew more about Brian Allerton than she was letting on. That much was clear from her attitude. Exactly how much, and what sort of relationship Tracy had with Brian, Nikki needed to find out ASAP. Tracy's shock could be an act. In which case, she couldn't be discounted as a suspect.

TWENTY

Monty was speaking to Nish in front of the main entrance. They turned as Nikki strode out to join them.

'I just met the mysterious Miss Ishihara,' Nikki said. Monty raised his eyebrows and Nish looked confused.

'She's a colleague of Professor Allerton. But much younger, I'd say she's in her late twenties or early thirties. Given the prof was in his sixties, I think the age gap was considerable.'

Monty frowned. 'What's so mysterious about her?'

Nikki puffed out her cheeks, then exhaled. 'I saw her looking up at his bedroom window with sad eyes. She knows more than she's letting on, I think. She said she's only met the victim casually, but I think there's more to it.'

'What did she tell you?' Monty asked.

Nikki shrugged. 'Not a great deal really. She's much junior to him. Not sure where in the pecking order a fellow is, but I suspect it's lower than a lecturer.'

'Sounds about right,' Monty agreed. 'Lecturers become assistant professors, and after five or seven years, full professors, right?'

Nikki shrugged. 'Anyway. She said she's non-stipendiary,

which means she doesn't get a salary. But she's a post-doc, which means she's finished her PhD.'

'Worth following up?' Monty asked.

Nikki nodded. 'She was in the library between four and eight yesterday.' She clicked her tongue against the roof of her mouth in exasperation. 'I forgot to ask her which library. She might've meant the New College library.' Often, Oxonians said library when referring to the Bodleian. But there was a host of other libraries at the university, and each college had a substantial collection of books.

Nikki said, 'I think we need to ask everyone in the history department about our victim. See what you find. Did you give his wife a ring?'

'I did,' Monty said. 'She will meet us at 3 p.m. at her house.'

Nish said, 'I managed to track down some people on the governing body list. A man called Daniel Blatherwick, who is a professor of chemistry. And a woman called Peggy Moran. She is a lecturer in archaeology, and she knew the victim well, as they had worked together in the past.'

'Good work,' Nikki said. 'Set up interviews with them. I think we have time for a quick lunch, then let's go and meet the wife.'

Professor Allerton's house turned out to be a charming period semi-detached property on the outskirts of Jericho. The wooden eaves were painted white. The front garden was well maintained, with a little pond that had running water. Jericho was full of lovely Victorian properties such as these. Very few new buildings. Monty led the way. They went up the flagstone staircase, and Monty rang the bell. The sound of barking came from inside. The door opened soon, to reveal Arabella, wearing a blouse and jeans, and holding an excited golden retriever by the collar.

'Daisy gets a bit excited,' she apologised. 'Please come in.'

They stepped inside the wooden hallway, which had a high ceiling. Light-brown oak panelling covered the walls. A door to the kitchen on the left was open, and Nikki thought she saw some movement inside, but couldn't be sure. Daisy was straining at the collar, keen to sniff the two strangers who had arrived. Nikki crouched and petted the dog. Daisy got up on her hind paws, a tongue hanging out as she evidently enjoyed Nikki stroking her head.

'There you go,' Arabella said, 'she likes you already.'

'Nice dog,' Nikki said, trying to stop an enthusiastic Daisy from licking her face.

'Hard work, sometimes,' Arabella said with a smile. She became serious. 'Mind you, she's been a godsend since yesterday. Keeps me busy.'

She put Daisy into one of the rooms on the right and shut the door. They heard her nails scratching on the door as she whined loudly.

'This way please,' Arabella said, leading the way into their kitchen. The open-plan kitchen was modern and nicely done. A white granite countertop wrapped round the length of the kitchen. There was an island in the middle with a sink. A woman was sitting at the dining table close to the bi-folding backdoors that opened out into the garden.

The woman looked like she'd been crying. Her brown hair was straggly and needed a wash. She didn't have any make-up on, and she wore a thick brown woollen jumper that had seen better days. She was in her late twenties, Nikki guessed. Her blue-grey eyes swivelled from Arabella to the strangers. Slowly she closed the book she was reading.

'Julia, this is the police,' Arabella said.

Nikki and Monty introduced themselves. Arabella said, 'Julia is my daughter.'

They both said hello. The younger woman mumbled something incoherent and got up from the table. She was walking out the kitchen door when Nikki stopped her.

'We would like to speak to you as well, if that's OK.'

The woman stopped in her tracks. There was open hostility in her eyes as she looked at Nikki. 'Shouldn't you be out there catching the person who killed my father?'

'Julia,' Arabella said, her cheeks colouring. 'Please don't speak to the detectives like that.'

Julia glared at her mother. 'What's the point of them being here? It's not like we killed Dad, is it?'

'Julia, please. Calm down.'

Julia shook her head and swallowed. Unshed tears brimmed in her eyes. 'Daddy's dead, and all the police can do is ask *us* questions.' She turned to Nikki, her gaze sliding to Monty. 'Do you think that's fair?'

Nikki was used to this, though it was the part of the job that never got easier. There was no good way to break bad news. She just had to show Julia that she was on her side.

'I'm very sorry for your loss, Julia. We need to ask questions to everyone who was involved in your father's life. You might not believe it now, but a little detail can make all the difference. That's why we need to speak to you.'

Nikki's words seem to have an effect on Julia. Tears rolled down her cheeks, and she wiped them, sniffing. She shrugged. 'OK. I'll be in my room.' She left and crossed the landing, then went up the stairs slowly, looking back once.

TWENTY-ONE

Arabella shook her head sadly. 'She was close to her dad. She's taken it badly, not that I can blame her.' She sighed. 'I must say, the manner of his death has shaken me as well. I feel awful.'

Monty said, 'Shall I make you a cup of tea? Why don't you sit down?'

'No, that's fine. The kettle's boiled already. Please have a seat, and I'll be with you. Would you like tea or coffee?'

Monty and Nikki refused with a murmur of thanks. They waited while Arabella made some tea and sat down at the table.

Nikki opened her black notebook and flicked to an empty page. 'Please tell us exactly what happened yesterday.'

'We were meant to attend drinks with the college warden. This was a post-dinner invite for 8:30 p.m. I was rushing, as I was late. I had to take a cab down to the college, because neither Brian nor I wanted to drive back after the drinks.'

'What time did you leave home?' Nikki asked.

'I left around ten to eight. I got there about 8:15.'

Nikki nodded. That fitted in with the records Winston had provided. Arabella had checked in at the Holywell Street entrance at 8:17.

'Please tell us what happened after that.'

'I went in through the front gardens and into the main quad. I walked down the quad, and into the archways that led to his office upstairs. I went in, and saw—' Arabella stopped, her face draining of colour. Her eyes were fixed on the table.

'Was the door open, or did you have to open it?'

'The door was shut,' Arabella replied after a few seconds. 'I'm pretty sure. Yes, I did turn the handle.'

'And when you were walking down the quad, did you happen to look up to see if the window was open?'

Arabella pressed her lips together, then closed her eyes. 'I can't remember if the window was open. But the light was definitely on. I do remember seeing that.'

'Thank you,' Nikki said, making a note. 'Please carry on.'

Arabella shrugged. 'What else is there to say? I saw him lying there, and I didn't know what to do. It was clear that he was dead. I still went inside, to get a closer look.' She stopped speaking again, looking downcast.

Nikki asked, 'Had you noticed anything different about your husband's behaviour over the last few days or weeks?'

Arabella seemed confused. 'How do you mean?'

'Was he doing anything out of the ordinary? For example, did he seem very quiet, or was he angry? Was he coming home very late, or always talking on the phone to someone? That sort of thing.'

Arabella thought for a while. Then she shook her head. 'Work was his life, and he was busy with it. But we had a social life as well. Most of it within academic circles, as you can imagine.'

'Did you often go out for dinners and the like?'

Arabella waved a hand in the air. 'Tea with the undergrads, or dinner with the lecturers organised by the colleges, sometimes external companies or foundations held events as well.'

'All in the college?'

'Mostly, yes. You will find in Oxford the colleges have the best premises.'

Nikki smiled. 'Oh yes. Nothing like the grandeur of the old days.' Her expression became serious. 'Had you been to any events recently? With your husband, I mean.'

Arabella thought for a while. She rolled the tip of her thumb against a finger. Nikki watched her.

Arabella was the perfect picture of the grieving wife. Nothing excessive. She was bearing it with dignity, but her sorrow was palpable.

'At the start of term, in October, there are always some events, you know. Like the ones I mentioned. When term starts in earnest, the studies take over I guess. In answer to your question, we did go to a couple of events in October, but not since.'

'Thank you. Did your husband stay mostly at his quarters in the college during term time?'

Arabella took her time in answering. 'No. This was his home, and it's not exactly far away.'

She looked away, the frown still creasing her face. Nikki decided to gently pursue. 'So, he came home every night?'

'Yes, he did, unless there was a late meeting.'

'What sort of late meeting?'

'I'm not sure. It could be before exam time, when the examiners met to discuss the passing grades and such.'

'Did anything like that happen recently?'

'I'm not sure, to be honest. I don't stay up late every night. And I see my friends sometimes as well.'

'So, he could've come home late one night when you were out?'

'Depends what you mean by late. When I visit my friends for dinner, I am back home by 11 p.m. And Brian is back by then, definitely.'

'And can you remember the last time he came home late?'

Arabella frowned and stared at the wall for a few seconds.

'It was occasional. He called to tell me he would be back late. I think it happened twice in the last few weeks. So not very often.'

'I see.'

Nikki consulted her notebook. 'Do you work as well?'

'Yes, I am a librarian.'

'Which library? The Bodleian?'

'No. All Souls College.'

Arabella looked tired.

'I see.' Nikki scribbled on her notebook.

Through the glass-panelled back door, Nikki could see the lawn. The garden was well kept, and she could see nicely trimmed hedges and flower beds on the corners. The sky was a leaden grey and a whispering rain had started.

She pressed her lips together and glanced at Arabella. 'Did your husband have a study in the house? Or his own room?'

Arabella nodded. 'Yes, he did. It's upstairs. Shall I show you?'

Nikki and Monty followed Arabella outside into the reception area. They went up the wide staircase, to the first floor. The landing was wide, and it led to a hallway with several rooms branching off it. Another flight of stairs went up to the second floor. Arabella walked to the first door on her left after the staircase. She opened it and went inside, and Nikki followed.

The room was oak-panelled, similar to the reception lobby downstairs. It was tastefully decorated with a chocolate-brown gilt armchair and a dark-wooden desk. The dark-wooden panelling came up to a couple of metres and ran the length and breadth of the room. A bay window opposite the desk looked out over the garden. Bookshelves lined the walls, groaning with the weight of heavy tomes.

Nikki read some of the titles, most of them were historical, and there were several magazines and periodicals belonging to the History Society along the shelves. The desktop had a printer and also a monitor screen, but no computer or laptop. Nikki put her gloves on, and so did Monty.

'Did your husband have a computer in this room?'

'We have a desktop that both of us use, downstairs. But it was mostly me, it was like the family computer. He has his own laptop, which I haven't seen here.'

Nikki pointed to the set of drawers on either side of the desk. 'Could it be in there?'

The older woman shrugged. 'By all means, take a look. I haven't checked.'

Monty strode forward and knelt on the carpet. His gloved hand opened and closed all the drawers. He rifled through sheaves of paper and folders. Then he stood and shook his head.

'Nothing here, guv.'

Nikki looked around the room. There was a locked filing cabinet to one side.

'Do you have the keys, Arabella?'

'I'm not sure where he kept them. You could try one of the drawers.'

Monty had a root around in one of the drawers and found a key which opened the cabinet.

'Do you mind if we have a look around here?'

Arabella hesitated. She twisted her hands and looked around the room. Then she locked eyes with Nikki. 'To be honest, I never come up here. This is his place, and the door was locked when he wasn't around.'

'He locked the door and took the key with him?'

Arabella nodded. 'I found the key in the package that Winston gave me. I think you found it in his pocket last night, right?'

Nikki nodded. 'Yes.' She observed Arabella carefully. Was she lying? Did she know where the laptop was?

Why was Professor Allerton so secretive about his study? Nikki thought to herself.

'Please have a look and let me know if I can help you with anything,' Arabella said before leaving the room.

'Thank you.' Nikki waited until Arabella had gone, then she shut the door.

Monty was staring at her.

'Well, that was odd, wasn't it?'

'Not only did he lock the room, he also locked his filing cabinet.'

Nikki nodded. 'Right, let's take a look. You handle the drawers, and I'll look through the filing cabinet.'

Nikki went through the cabinet systematically, taking out all the papers inside each file and spreading them on the floor. It was mostly bank statements, receipts and invoices. After several minutes of searching, she found something interesting.

It was a payment to a company called New Frontiers Publishing. It was a receipt, signed by someone called Simon Douglas, Treasurer. The amount made Nikki whistle. A cool £250,000. Why would the professor make such a large payment to a publishing company? If anything, as an academic who wrote books, he should be getting money from them. Nikki took photos, then put the receipt in an evidence bag. 'I found something,' Monty said spreading out the contents of all the drawers. 'Invoices from builders. Looks like the prof was investing in a block of flats.'

Nikki examined an architect's plan of a row of houses to be demolished and made into blocks of flats. She pointed at the development address. 'That's Longwall Street, close to New College.'

'Yes, and it looks like those terraced houses would be converted into student halls of residence. And the professor was investing in that?'

Nikki ran a finger down the document. 'Yes, it would seem so. But it's the college that's responsible for it. I wonder why the prof got involved? Either way, the bursar should know about this.'

Monty said, 'The colleges are very rich, you know. Why did they need their professor's money?'

'More to the point,' Nikki said thoughtfully, 'I wonder where the professor was getting the money from. Certainly not from his academic's salary.'

TWENTY-TWO

The man had parked four houses away from Brian Allerton's. Through the trees in the front garden of Brian's house, he watched as the detectives went inside. He knew this street well. He had followed Brian back here many a time. Building up Brian's routine. Getting to know his prey. The thrill of the hunt had consumed him. The killing had been even better. When he sent Brian that text, he knew he'd come. He had to. He could destroy Brian with what he knew.

And that's exactly what he did. As he thrust the knife repeatedly into Brian, all he did was transmit the years of rage and agony he had accumulated. Brian now knew his hurt, his pain. And soon, so would the others.

The man waited patiently, watching the house. He had to be careful, this street had CCTV cameras. He didn't want to get out and show his face. He did have a disguise; a peaked hat, the uniform of a parking attendant, and dark glasses. Last week, when he did his final surveillance on Brian, he had pretended to check the cars for permits, while he actually monitored Brian going into his house. That could work again, but the stakes were higher. The thrill ignited in his bloodstream, catching his breath. This is what he'd been waiting for. Now the police were involved, and he had to be more careful, while also subtly showing his handiwork.

Bringing Brian's body back into the college had been a nice touch, he thought to himself. It was pleasing. He wanted to leave the body where it would cause the biggest shock. Arabella's screams had made it all worthwhile.

That DI Nikki Gill had been on site, which was a pain. She fancied herself, that one. Where was she when he needed help? When they all needed help? Well, he'd show her a thing or two. She'd remember this case for the rest of her life.

The man drank some coffee from a Thermos and checked his mirrors. He didn't see anything suspicious. He took out the binoculars and looked through them briefly. The front door was still shut.

He wanted to see more of Nikki Gill, and get a feel for her. She would be a difficult opponent, the first signs suggested. And that lanky detective who went around with her, he could also be trouble.

The other reason was he wanted to keep an eye on Brian's family. His wife and daughter. It was only fitting that they suffer as well. At the very least, they must know the truth. He suspected that they did. Arabella in any case. Maybe he would get the chance to ask them one day.

He detected movement from the corner of his eyes. The front door opened and the two detectives stepped out. They stood on the porch, chatting for a while to someone inside. Once they drove off, he gave them a few seconds head start. Then he started the engine, and set off slowly. As he went past Brian's house, he slowed down.

A young woman was coming down the steps of the front door. It was Julia, Brian's daughter. The man parked up, and watched her. Julia was a pretty girl. Her shoulder-length brown hair was done up nicely, and she looked good. When he was sure she wouldn't see him, he got out of the car, and followed behind her.

Julia walked on to the main road, and then to the bus stop. The man stopped there too, pretending to wait for the bus. As he waited, he watched Julia. She had put her sunglasses on. As his eyes moved over her body, he felt a tingle of desire. He'd not had a young woman like her in a while. But that's not what he wanted Julia for. That might come later, but first, he had a burning itch to get to know her a little, and ask her about Brian. How she felt, knowing her father was hacked to death. He liked those details, learning how others suffered and felt hurt. Because he had suffered all his life, and watched his loved ones die around him. It made him the person he was today.

The bus for the town centre arrived, and Julia got on it. The man followed. He wanted to find out Julia's daily routine, just like he'd done with her father.

TWENTY-THREE

'Back to the nick, guv?' Monty said as Nikki got into the car.

'No,' Nikki replied, as her phone pinged with a text from Dr Raman. 'Let's go to the morgue. Sheila has managed to do the post-mortem.'

John Radcliffe was a teaching hospital, and the mortuary also had a dissecting room for surgical trainees. Right now, it was empty, and their footsteps echoed in the wide, white-washed concrete hallway.

Monty pressed on the buzzer, and a black woman opened the door for them. She was dressed in surgical blues, and her black hair was done up in braids. She smiled when she saw their warrant cards.

'I am Shola, Dr Raman's assistant. This way, please.'

They followed Shola to the changing room. Through the window, Nikki could see the rows of gurneys. Most of them were empty, but some of them had body bags, all zipped up. She got changed and slipped her feet into a pair of crocs. They were surprisingly comfortable.

Shola and Monty were waiting outside by the time Nikki finished. They walked over to a row of desks, at the margins of the huge room. Sheila Raman was perched on a high chair, reading her laptop screen. She saw them and hopped off. Sheila wasn't tall, she only came up to Nikki's chest. Her large, dark eyes were sharp and glittering, but friendly. Her lips split into a smile.

'We meet again, Inspector Gill,' she said.

'We do indeed. Please call me Nikki.'

'OK, Nikki. How are you settling in?' Sheila asked.

'Not bad, thank you. It's a change of scene from London, but so far it's been OK.'

Sheila nodded. 'I used to work in Surrey, a place called Chertsey. Have you heard of it?'

'Yes. It's not far from south London. It's straight down the A3, isn't it?

'Yes, not far at all. We were quite happy there, but then I had to move—' She stopped short, and a smile on her face faltered.

Nikki didn't say anything. Sheila recovered, and the smile returned, but it was forlorn. The glitter had gone from her eyes. 'My husband passed away. I needed a change of scenery and applied for this job five years ago. Since then, I've been here.'

'I'm sorry to hear that,' Nikki said. 'That makes both of us outsiders, right?'

'Yes, it does.' Sheila raised a finger. 'Mind you, in many ways Oxford isn't that different from anywhere else. Peel back the layers, and you'll see all sorts of nefarious things are going on.'

'What do you mean?' Nikki asked, intrigued.

Sheila pointed at the gurneys around her. 'I have a recent death from poisoning. A couple of suicides. A missing person who just turned up in the river with his abdomen slashed open. Make no mistake, Nikki. Crime thrives everywhere. Shall we?'

Sheila smiled and extended a hand like she was inviting them inside her house.

Arla, Nikki's mentor at the Met, had always maintained a good pathologist was a great teacher in the art of murder. Arla had learned a lot about the biology of dead bodies from her mentor and friend, Dr Banerjee. Nikki hoped she could develop a similar relationship with Dr Raman.

She followed Dr Raman to one of the gurneys. Monty had been listening with interest, and he stood just behind Nikki as Dr Raman flung the cover off Brian Allerton's dead body.

'We know how he died. Severe blood loss due to the knife wounds. It was a frenzied attack, as you can see by the deep gashes on the head, neck and chest.' Sheila pointed at the wounds.

Nikki looked closely. The wounds were dry now, but the knife had cut through to the muscles.

The eyes were taped shut. There was a suture line across the cranium, where the skull saw had made its cut.

'Nothing to report inside the cranium,' Sheila said. She moved down to the chest. 'More laceration marks from the knife, as you can see. I would say the victim was facing to his right when the attack happened from the side.'

Sheila stepped back from the gurney and lifted her right hand up as if she was holding a weapon. 'The killer had to be right-handed to land the blows he did. A left-handed attacker would have been more full-on straight. But the marks are on the victim's right-hand side, and they were made by a right-handed murderer.'

'Do you think it was a man? He certainly had to be strong,' Nikki said.

Sheila shrugged. 'Not necessarily. A strong woman could have done this, if the knife was long and sharp. I have sent samples off to look for the metal residues. I'll let you know if I find something. By the way, fingerprints on IDENT-1 didn't show anything.'

'Thank you. Yes, Hetty mentioned that as well,' Nikki said.

'Blood samples were sent for toxicology and are now back, courtesy of being labelled as urgent. The results show something interesting, but not that surprising, to be honest.'

Nikki's eyebrows lowered. 'Recreational drugs?'

Sheila smiled. 'Correct. Any guess as to what type?'

'Cocaine? That's the commonest.'

'Yes, correct,' Sheila said. 'You would be surprised at how rife use of cocaine is in Oxford. And it's not just the students I'm talking about.'

Nikki raised her eyebrows. 'Academics as well?'

Monty spoke from her left. 'We've caught a couple of professors with possession. There're big cocaine-dealing gangs in and around Oxford. The academics love it, actually.'

Nikki grinned. 'Reading all those books must get boring, right?'

'Exactly,' Sheila answered. 'Cocaine is a neuro stimulant, and in the nineteen hundreds it used to be sold in shops as a painkiller. In fact, a certain type of cough syrup still contains a lot of codeine, which is nothing but an analogue of cocaine.'

'I should get myself some of that, instead of the white wine I drink,' Nikki joked. They laughed.

Sheila returned to the body. 'His hands have some lacerations as well. He obviously raised his hands to protect himself, and the knife stabbed him in several places.' She showed Nikki the regions.

Nikki asked her, 'Any DNA underneath the fingernails?'

'Yes. I have sent samples off to the lab. I will let you know as soon as I have a result, and if there is a crossmatch.'

Sheila continued. 'His internal organs are unremarkable. The stomach contents show digested food from lunch I think, hence there isn't much. I think that's about it. I have sent off the stomach contents to look for poison as well. Again, if we find anything, I shall let you know.'

TWENTY-FOUR

Thirty years ago

Tommy hated going back to the care home after school. The bus was full of boisterous kids, joking and laughing, but he sat at the back, staring out the window. Another boy sat in the seat in front. Riley, his name was, and he was Tommy's age. Tommy had seen Riley come out of Robert's room one night, holding his hand, staring at the floor, ashamed.

He knew exactly what Riley had been through. And it made him sick when he thought of what might happen tonight. Paul had gone to the pub to meet this man, whoever he was. Tommy missed Paul when he wasn't here. He wished he could've gone to the pub as well, but Paul said no. He would be back soon.

The bus got to its stop, and the boys piled out. A group of the older boys who lived in the care home walked ahead. They were in years ten and eleven, and they didn't care what happened to Tommy. No one did, apart from Paul, who had been through the same hell as him. Tommy felt a desperate sadness as he watched the taller, older boys. He wished he could be like them, but he couldn't imagine having to go through all the days, months and years to get bigger. His days and nights were filled with terror, and he just wanted it to end.

He wanted to grow wings and fly away. He had dreamed that last night. He was sinking in a black, foaming sea, calling out for help. An angel came down, and she had the face of the girl he had seen with his mother, his so-called sister. The girl had feathery wings, dark as the sea that rippled around him. But she enclosed him in those black wings, their feel so soft around his face and body, it cooled his bones, lulled him to sleep. He went high, higher up with his sister, and she never let him go. That was the only good dream Tommy had in ages, and he didn't forget it.

No, Tommy couldn't face this anymore. He stopped as the boys went inside the care home. The wrought-iron gates were huge and heavy, they loomed like the doors of a prison. The actual old manor house had belonged to some wealthy landowner. Now, under state maintenance, despite all its periodic charms, it seemed hideous to Tommy. Riley, the younger boy, walked with his head bent, eyes fixed on the floor. Tommy wanted to grab him and run. But he had nowhere to go.

Tommy headed for the side entrance which opened out from the kitchen and pantry into the side gardens. That door was often open, and Paul used it to slip out when the kitchen wasn't busy. Perhaps he could use that to go into the main hall and then go upstairs to his room.

The kitchen was busy. He could see the chefs, in their white shirts, moving around inside. But the pantry was quiet. The door was ajar, and Tommy slunk inside. He darted past the cupboards and peeked through the door that led into the kitchen. All the chefs had their backs to him. Tommy ran the short distance that led to the dining hall, which was empty. He sighed in relief as he came out into the passage that led to the main landing and lobby.

He skidded to a halt as Robert came out from one of the rooms. His eyes narrowed when he saw Tommy.

'Where have you been?'

'I... I just got back from school,' Tommy stammered, trying to sidestep his way to the staircase. Robert blocked his way.

'I didn't see you come back with the others. Were you trying to sneak in through the back?'

Tommy gulped, fear shaking his spine like a twig in a storm. 'No... I just took the longer route back home.'

'No you didn't. You lying bastard.' Robert got hold of his collar and dragged him towards the room.

'No, no!' Tommy protested, digging his heels into the wooden floor, but it wasn't any use. Robert flung him inside the room and shut the door. Bert was standing there, with Riley in front of him. Riley was looking at the floor, and Tommy knew he was scared out of his wits. He looked up briefly, and his eyes met Tommy's. Then he looked down again.

Robert dragged Tommy up to the pair and forced the schoolbag off his shoulders.

'I found this one trying to sneak in through the back.'

'Well, well,' Bert said, coming closer. His eyes were big, cheeks sunken and scarred with lines. His breath stank of cigarette smoke. His hands ruffled Tommy's hair, then pulled him nearer. Tommy shrank away, but it was no use.

'Who's been a bad boy now then, eh?' Bert whispered. His hands roamed all over Tommy's body now, and he closed his eyes. Breath was stuck in his chest, the air trapped inside like an iron balloon.

'I'll tell you who's been naughtier, though,' Bert said, standing. 'Riley here won't do as I tell him. Tommy, you know what happens to the boys who don't listen, don't you? The boys who are naughty?'

Tommy kept his eyes closed. Fingers gripped his cheek and squeezed, hard. He felt Bert's foetid, revolting breath on him again. He opened his eyes to find Bert's face inches from his. Robert stood behind him, a hand on Riley's shoulder.

Tommy gulped. 'I need the loo. Can I go, please?' He looked at Robert. 'Please?'

A wolfish smile appeared on Robert's lips. 'Piss on him.' He pointed at Riley.

Tommy's mouth opened in shock. He shook his head. Bert also had an evil grin on his face, like a psychotic joker.

'You heard him. Go on, do it. Otherwise you know what happens.'

Tommy shook his head again and stepped backwards, but Bert grabbed his collar, restraining. He slapped Tommy across the face, a stinging blow that made him cry out. Tommy felt Bert's hands all over him again, and he closed his eyes, trying to forget he existed.

There was a knock on the door. Bert huffed angrily at the interruption. Robert opened the door and stood in front, blocking any view inside.

'What are you doing here?' Robert barked.

'Stuart sent me. He needs to see you.'

Tommy turned at the voice, because it belonged to Paul. There was a scuffle at the door, then Robert dragged Paul inside. Paul put up more of a fight, and Robert was red in the face. Paul stopped struggling when he saw Tommy, his eyes widening.

'Piss on Riley,' Robert ordered Paul, then cuffed him around the head. 'I said do it.' Robert shoved Paul forward.

'You heard what he said,' Bert said softly. He was more menacing, Tommy thought. With his quiet voice and weird, widely spaced eyes.

'No,' Paul shouted. 'Let them go. I'll tell the teachers.'

'You can tell the Queen of England if you like,' Robert sneered. 'No one cares. It's us putting a roof over your head.

Food on your plate. You're so worthless no one wants you. Do you want to end up on the streets?'

'Better than here,' Paul said, for which he earned another slap on his head.

'Do it,' Bert said, his face inches from Paul. Then he stood and lit up a cigarette. He puffed in silence, regarding the boys. A dangerous light started to glint in his eyes.

'Will you do it, or not? You know what happens to bad boys here, Paul. This is your last chance.'

'We can't have disobedient boys,' Robert echoed. 'What will the Ofsted inspectors say? They gave us a good rating last year.' He exchanged a quick smile with Bert.

Paul's hands were fists and an angry snarl curled around his lips.

'Last chance,' Bert said, taking a deep pull on his cigarette and blowing the smoke into Paul's face. Paul said nothing. Without warning, Bert took his cigarette and pushed it into Paul's shoulder. The skin sizzled as it burned.

Paul screamed and jumped backwards, then fell on the floor. The men laughed, and Tommy put his hands over his ears. The laughter echoed, getting louder, then fading, a relentless wave of evil noise that battered his ears.

Nine-year-old Nikki raised her voice. 'Mummy! Mummy!'

There was no response. Her father was also out, at the pub, or wherever he went in the evenings. Nikki couldn't think of the last time she'd seen her father at home. She heard sounds late at night, shouts and screams, that woke her up. She clutched her teddy tight and prayed the fighting would stop. Nights like those, she cried herself to sleep. And tonight, she was glad it was just her mother and herself. It was quieter that way.

Nikki had finished her dinner, and then her homework. But the house was dark, and it scared her. She flicked on the light of the hallway, and the yellow glare showed the empty space, the exposed floorboards, the cracked mirror next to the doorway. The ground was freezing beneath her feet. She went upstairs, and turned the light on in the narrow landing. It was a typical two-bed council house, and it had seen better days. The heating was paltry, and she shivered in the cold. Clarissa lay on the bed, face down. The glow from the bedside lamp light fell on her hair. An arm hung down to the floor. Nikki saw the two bottles next to the bedside table, both empty. Clarissa had drunk herself into a stupor and then passed out. Nikki was getting tired of seeing her mother like this.

She was even drunk when she picked Nikki up from school, although she vehemently denied it when asked. But Nikki knew. She always knew when her mother lied to her.

She crept forward, and put a hand on Clarissa's shoulder. She shook it gently, but Clarissa didn't stir. A harder shake had the same effect. Clarissa's once pretty face was getting bloated and puffy. Her eyes looked swollen. Nikki glanced at the table-top. Two photo albums were stacked there, and the top one was open. Nikki had never seen these albums. She took them, and sat cross-legged on the floor. The photos showed a younger and smiling Clarissa with a baby. It was a boy, she could tell that much. He had a blue vest with the word *Tommy* written across it. Her father, Peter, also held the baby. Her parents looked so different. So much happier.

She flicked through the photos, and picked one up for a closer look. Tommy had started to walk, and her mother held his small, chubby fists as he took his first steps, an excited look on his face. Nikki could see the similarity between the baby and the boy she had seen in the care home. Her brother, whom she saw once every six months. It was stranger than the story books she read. She felt sad for Tommy. She wished she had known him better, before he died.

She glanced at her mother, who was fast asleep. Her nostrils puffed, and her chest rose and fell with each breath. But apart from that, Clarissa was dead to the world, and Nikki wondered if her mother wanted that. She got up, and went to her room, then shut the door firmly.

TWENTY-FIVE

Nish and Kristy had left their cars in the St Aldate's police station car park and walked up towards Christ Church College.

From the town centre, Christ Church's imposing clock tower was visible, dominating the landscape. Both detective constables had worked in the area for a few years now, and they were used to the stunning architecture in Oxford. But it wasn't every day that they stepped inside one of its most famous colleges.

They showed their warrant cards at the Porter's Lodge. The security guard lifted the phone and, a few moments later, a man hurried across the main compound. He walked down the paths that skirted the perfectly manicured lawn. He was dressed in a suit, and came to a halt opposite the two DCs. Nish and Kristy flashed their warrant cards again. The man nodded.

'I am Simon Probyn, I work for the bursar's office at Christ Church. I understand you wish to see Professor Daniel Blatherwick.'

'Yes. We rang the college, and were told that he's here today.'

'Professor Blatherwick is currently busy with tutorials, and I think he is just finishing up the last one. Would you mind having a seat in the admin building, and when he is ready, I can take you down to his office.'

The detectives followed Mr Probyn through the main compound, the buildings encircling them. Christ Church really was palatial, Nish mused. He had never been inside. It was a tourist attraction as well, and in the summer one could buy tickets just to walk around the main quad. But the chapel could be visited on selected evenings and was free for all.

Luckily, most tourists didn't know this. Christ Church chapel was unique in that it was also a cathedral. When the Church of England split from Roman Catholicism, Christ Church had become the headquarters of the Anglican Church. The new Bible, and the manifesto for the Church of England, had been written inside Christ Church chapel. Hence, this particular chapel was a powerful institution.

They were directed to a group of low-rise but ancient stone-walled buildings at the back of the college compound. They had to walk through several archways in order to get there.

Mr Probyn pressed his ID against a digital keypad, and the incongruous-looking glass doors slid silently apart. They stepped inside a building where, apart from the carpets, everything seemed to be a thousand years old. The stone walls were deliberately unpainted, and the stained-glass windows, rising from floor to ceiling level, gave the place the look and feel of a cathedral. People worked at desks, and a few faces looked up as they walked down. At the rear of the office there was a partitioned seating area with bookshelves and a flower vase. Mr Probyn directed them to a sofa.

'Would you like anything to drink? Tea or coffee, perhaps?'

Nish and Kristy declined with a murmur of thanks. It was very quiet here, the thick stone walls, and the deep carpet absorbing all sound. Only the faint hum of breathing and the even softer hum of distant servers and computers pervaded the atmosphere. Nish felt he had to whisper in order not to disturb the peace.

'Funny place this, isn't it?'

He pointed to the ceiling, where thick wooden beams criss-crossed. They had been varnished, but left to their original colour. 'I hope the roof doesn't fall on our heads.'

Kristy also lowered her voice. 'After dark, maybe they light candles and sacrifice animals over here.' She giggled, and Nish stifled a laugh.

Nish asked, 'Did you call everyone on the list?'

'I didn't get around to all of them,' Kristy whispered. She took the piece of folded paper from her pocket, and also opened up her phone. 'There's two lecturers and another professor I need to call. One of them is abroad. These academics always travel, don't they?'

Nish nodded. 'My sister teaches at Manchester University. She's a lecturer in the Department of English.'

Kristy raised her eyebrows. 'Is she really? I didn't know that. What about your parents?'

'Dad was a chemist. Mum was a housewife. I'm the first person in our extended family to become a policeman.' There was a tinge of pride in his voice. He winked, and Kristy smiled.

'Didn't you want to become a chemist, or a doctor?'

Nish shook his head. 'Too much studying. I'd be bored to death.'

'You must be very different from your sister. She must love books to become an academic.'

'She does. But she was always the boring type. Miss Goody Two Shoes.'

Kristy made a face. 'Nothing wrong with that. What were you, life and soul of the party?'

Nish narrowed his eyes at her. 'Haven't you seen me dance at the office parties?'

He smiled as Kristy's cheeks coloured a little. At the

Summer Ball for Thames Valley Police, they had danced together a lot and had come close to a cheeky kiss. It didn't happen, and neither of them had been brave enough to mention it since, but he wondered if one day it might.

Their attention was distracted by Mr Probyn walking into the seating area. 'I rang the professor to check, and he is free to see you now.'

The detectives rose and followed Mr Probyn and they went out into the main compound, where there was an elevated walkway that wrapped around the central lawn and fountain. An austere November sun fell across the clock tower, and lit up the opposite side of the building. They walked past the chapel, where a service was in progress, then into another arched passageway, and came out into a corridor which led to student accommodation in the floors above.

Nish and Kristy found themselves in a cosy, comfortable room with a gas fire burning in the fireplace under the mantelpiece. The structure of the room was similar to the one in the admin building. The wooden beams in the ceiling were painted black, and the stone walls were whitewashed.

A number of paintings hung from the walls. Virtually all of them were landscapes, showing blue seas and boats.

Professor Blatherwick was a sprightly, average-height man with a balding head. Most of his hair grew in wisps at the back and on the sides. He didn't wear glasses, and Nish wondered if he had contacts in. His blue eyes examined both of them, and lingered on Kristy till she looked away and cleared her throat.

'Please come and have a seat,' Professor Blatherwick said. Four chairs faced his large desk. They were clearly for students who had just left a tutorial. The elderly man moved papers from his desk, trying to make the space neater. There was a laptop, and a separate monitor on the desk. Bookshelves lined the walls around the desk. There was also a whiteboard on the right wall, with chemistry equations and formulas written on it. There was a photo of a woman and two grown-up children on the desk. Nish assumed it was the professor's family.

'Dreadful news this, about Brian.' The professor clutched the arms of his chair, and stared at them.

Both Nish and Kristy took out their notebooks. 'Yes,' Nish said. 'It is a very sad event. Did you know Professor Allerton well?'

'I did. I used to be at New College, and we were in the governing body together. I saw him on a regular basis then, but we were friends from before as well.'

Professor Blatherwick settled back in his chair, and steepled fingers in front of his face.

'We were quite close in Cambridge. Both of us used to row. We made it to the first team, which as you know is quite prestigious.'

Nish and Kristy both nodded. Everyone knew about the famous Oxford and Cambridge boat race. Nish had never understood what the big fuss was about, it was just a race after all.

'But after our undergrad years, we lost touch. I saw him every now and then at conferences in the USA and in Europe. Both of us got married, and led separate lives. We caught up again once we were in Oxford.' There was a smile on his face, but it faltered.

Nish asked, 'When do you remember last seeing him?'

The professor thought for a while. 'I would say a couple of weeks ago, at a university Council meeting.'

'University Council?' Nish asked, curious.

'The Council is the central decision-making body of the university. They elect the chancellor and vice-Chancellor.'

'Were you and Professor Allerton members?'

'Of the Council? Good heavens, no. But like all academics, we know the twelve Council members. We have to elect them, after all. They're all academics, who now do administration duties.'

'What was the Council meeting about?'

Professor Blatherwick looked uncomfortable. 'I can't see what that has to do with the case.'

Nish and Kristy looked at each other. Kristy shrugged, and Nish continued. 'There might be a relevance. If it was one of the last meetings that he attended, we need to know what it was about.'

The professor sighed. 'It was about the university funding.'

He stopped and Kristy prodded him. 'Can you please elaborate?'

The professor cleared his throat. 'As you know, the individual colleges of Oxford have their own money. Most of it is historic endowments, a lot in the form of land. The university is rather short of cash. It wants the richer colleges to help it out.'

'I see,' Nish said slowly. 'What was discussed at the meeting?'

Professor Blatherwick squirmed in his seat. 'That is confidential.'

'Like my colleague said,' Kristy spoke patiently, 'what we discuss here is also fully confidential.'

There was silence for a while, then the professor sighed wearily. 'Very well. If you must know, it's always a tussle. The colleges and the university have this fractious relationship. In this case, it was a development of student accommodation on Longwall Street, near New College.'

Nish and Kristy looked at each other, frowning. Both of them had heard, from Nikki, about the planning documents from Professor Allerton's study. They also knew not to talk about it.

'Please carry on,' Nish said.

'Well, it's going to cost millions, demolishing a whole street of houses and building new quarters. Student accommodation in Oxford is rather good, considering it's only for students. The university wanted a stake in the development, and New College was refusing.'

'And the two of you went as representatives of the college?'

'Yes.'

'Was anyone else from the college there? Such as Mr Moffatt, the bursar?'

Professor Blatherwick's gaze was quiet, but Nish could sense something behind it. The older man nodded. 'Yes, he was.'

Nish asked, 'Did anyone on the university Council dislike Professor Allerton?'

'Not that I knew. Like I said, these money matters are always a source of friction. The Council wants a piece of the pie the colleges own, and the colleges keep it to themselves.'

Nish asked, 'The last time you met the professor did he seem out of sorts in any way? Sad, or angry perhaps?'

'Not that I saw. He seemed like his usual self. He liked to have a drink, and he was always quite a charismatic man.'

'Did you ever meet his wife?' Nish asked.

Professor Blatherwick nodded. 'Yes, quite a few times. At college dinners and university social events.' A smile touched the corners of his lips again, then faded.

Kristy picked up on it. 'Did you know his wife and family well?'

He shrugged. 'Yes. Oxford is a tightly knit academic community, and people become friends easily.'

'Have you spoken to her recently?'

'No. But I must give her a call. See how she is.'

Kristy said, 'Do you know if the professor had any enemies?'

The question startled the professor. His eyes widened, and his jaw went slack. 'Enemies? I'm not quite sure what you mean.'

'Professor Allerton was killed in a violent manner. We're

just trying to find out who could have done that to him. Did you ever hear any rumours about him? I understand that many years ago he used to teach in Christ Church College.'

Professor Blatherwick had been frowning, but the skin on his forehead cleared. So did the crinkles around his eyes. His spine was straighter, and his expression serious. His eyes flicked between the two detectives.

'Brian was a charming and engaging man. He liked women. I heard whispers that he had affairs with his PhD students. Or maybe just one student. I'm not sure.'

'When did you hear these rumours?' Nish asked.

'They swirled around academic circles for a few years.' Professor Blatherwick didn't elaborate any further. There was a guarded look on his face.

Kristy asked, 'Did you see any evidence of his extramarital affairs? Maybe you, or someone you know, spotted him?'

Professor Blatherwick sighed. 'I think one of my PhD students saw him at a nightclub in Cowley once. He was dancing with a girl half his age. He was wasted, and she barely recognised him. But it was him, she told me.'

'Can we speak to your PhD student?'

The professor hesitated, then nodded. 'Her name is Emily Blanchard. I can give you her contact details, if you wish.'

'Yes please,' Kristy said. She took down the details in her notebook.

'Can you think of anyone else we can speak to, regarding these rumours about Professor Allerton?' Nish asked.

Professor Blatherwick shook his head. He looked at his watch. 'Now if you'll excuse me, detectives, I have another tutorial in ten minutes' time.'

TWENTY-SIX

The man whistled as he walked down the side alley that led to Christ Church College. He'd had a productive day. He'd followed Julia Allerton to the Bodleian, and he even got close enough to see what books she was reading. He realised she was going to be there for a while. He had more important things to do so he left the library, planning to return soon.

First, he needed to put the second stage into action. Now that Inspector Nikki Gill was involved, there was a high possibility she would realise who his next targets were. He couldn't let her put guards around them. He needed to strike now.

As he got closer to the gates, he slowed down. The porters were present, and so were a couple of tourists. During Mass time, it could get crowded. He saw something else that concerned him. A man and woman, dressed in suits. They didn't look like students, or academics. Neither were they building surveyors, or tradesmen.

The man frowned as he watched them come out of the main gates, and then walk down, deep in conversation. He noticed the bulge in the man's breast pocket. Was that a radio? Were they detectives?

If that was the case, he didn't have any more time. He didn't go in through the porter's lodge, for obvious reasons. They kept a log of all visitors. He went around, to the trade entrance, and to his annoyance, found it shut. He had to walk all the way around the ramparts, till he came to another gate. He slipped inside, his hat turned down low over his face, dark glasses on. He knew where the cameras were. He was dressed in overalls, and he looked like a decorator. That disguise had worked in the past. It also allowed him to keep his weapon hidden inside the long overall pockets. His gloved hand now encircled the knife handle. Adrenaline surged in his arteries, and his mouth opened as he breathed faster.

He walked down the main quad, then into the arched corridor that encircled the quad and the fountain in the middle. As he got to the office he wanted, he felt the calmness, and a moment of clarity descended upon him. He knew this was the right course of action. It would define his life. He had felt the same way before meeting Brian in University Parks the night before.

He knocked on the door. A voice bade him enter. The professor raised his white- haired head as he came in and shut the door behind him. Daniel Blatherwick looked confused, and then narrowed his eyes as the man got closer.

'Who are you?' he asked, rising from his seat.

The man took off his hat, and sunglasses.

Professor Blatherwick frowned, then his eyes widened.

'You? What are you doing here?'

'To settle a longstanding score,' the man said, getting closer.

TWENTY-SEVEN

Back at the office, Nikki sank into her armchair, and put her feet up on another chair she'd pulled up.

'Long day, guv?' Kristy asked.

'You could say that. I think I'm getting past the running around phase. Leave it to young people like you.'

'You're still young, guv. Don't let anyone tell you different.'

Nikki opened her eyes and saw Kristy smiling at her. It was a genuine smile, and she wasn't being cheeky.

'I'll take that as a compliment.' She barked a laugh. 'Have to, at my age.'

'You're still in shape. You look good.'

'It's because I can't be bothered to cook. The less I eat, the less I put on.'

'Intermittent starving, guv. Best frigging diet I know. I tried every diet, nothing worked till I started that. And cutting out carbs.'

Nikki frowned at her. 'There's hardly anything of you. No point in being dress size zero, is there?'

'I feel better as well. Honestly. Less carbs, more veg and protein. I have more energy.'

'I get my energy from coffee. Used to be cigarettes as well, but thank God I kicked that habit.'

'Shall I get you a coffee now?'

'That would be great, thank you.'

Kristy left for the canteen, while Nikki looked at the papers on her desk.

There was something strange about Julia's relationship with her mother. Julia seemed angry and defensive. She clearly admired her father and was devastated by his loss. More so than Arabella, who seemed to be a devoted wife, and appeared to have had a good relationship with her husband. Or did she? Nikki knew wives could keep secrets that lasted a lifetime. However, Arabella's grief was genuine. Nikki believed her, but that didn't mean she would stop digging around.

She flipped out her phone and did a search for New Frontiers. It was a publishing company that specialised in books about sociology and politics. Most books on the website were academic. There was a thump on the door, which was Kristy tapping with her foot. Nikki opened it, and Kristy came in with a tray bearing three cups of tea and biscuits.

'Monty will be back soon,' Kirsty said, indicating the third cup. She took a sip of scalding coffee and sighed, that felt good.

'I hope you don't mind, guv, but I looked through the rest of those papers,' Kristy said. 'The skipper said I could.'

Nikki grinned at her. 'So he doesn't have to do it. Glad you did, anyway. Find anything?'

'As a matter of fact, I did. Brian Allerton's been an academic in Oxford for almost three decades. Shortly after he started, he was a warden at St Jude's Hall. And so was Daniel Blatherwick, the professor who's a member of the college's governing body.'

'I see. What is St Jude's Hall? Doesn't sound like a college.'

'The Halls are like smaller colleges; they were originally set up by Jesuit monasteries ages ago, for their monks from all over to study in Oxford. A hundred years ago they became full member colleges. St Jude's Hall ran a children's care home in Evesham. Both professors worked there part time, too. They were post-doctoral fellows then, junior academics. Not sure why they worked in a care home. But they did, and maybe that's where they became friends.'

Nikki frowned. 'Where was this care home?'

'In Evesham, not far from here, in the Cotswolds. It was called Dunston Hill Care Home.'

A distant memory boomed in Nikki's mind, like surf pounding against a rocky cliff. She felt a whiplash in her spine, and breath left her lungs in a gasp. It could be a coincidence. Could there be another children's care home with the same name in Evesham...?

Nikki turned to Kristy. Her throat was dry, and she had to clear it twice before she could speak.

'What was the name of this children's home again?'

'Dunston Hill, in Evesham. But it's shut down now.'

Dunston Hill.

The words hit Nikki like two bullets between her eyes. She examined her nails, and sat back in her chair, trying to act casual. Her hands trembled, and she gripped them together in her lap, under the table.

'St Jude's Hall used to run the care home?' she asked.

Kristy Kirsty gave her a funny look, and went to say something, then thought better of it.

'Yes, they did, with the county council. The council rented the building from them.'

Nikki's heart knocked loudly against her ribs, in slow motion. She was aware Kristy was watching her, and she leaned back in her chair, trying her best to act normal.

'Guv, you all right?' There was a tinge of concern in Kirsty's voice.

'Yes, I'm fine,' Nikki said quickly. 'Just puzzled why they

both worked in this place at the same time. Did you say the care home is now shut down?'

'Yes, it closed in 2003. I found some newspaper articles about it. Looks bad, guv. Apparently there were allegations of abuse to the children there.'

Another sonic boom thrashed against Nikki's eardrums, the sound of her raw heartbeat, arousing demons from the past.

It couldn't be, but it had to be.

She got up, and went to Kristy's desk. 'Show me the paperwork.'

Kristy had it on her tablet screen. She scrolled to the right page and held the tablet out for Nikki. It was a photocopy of a printout from the Oxford Council webpage, twenty years ago. Dunston Hill Care Home was officially closed down, and on the next page, Kristy had pulled up newspaper articles. Nikki's head spun as she read the headlines. Allegations of physical and sexual abuse had surfaced at the care home.

Many years ago, when she was at university, Nikki had looked this up. She had found national newspaper articles when she did a search for the care home. She had never forgotten the name – Dunston Care Home. The articles were short, and she recalled them now. There was a scandal, but no one was found guilty. The care home was shut down, and that was that.

Kristy was speaking, and her voice seemed to come from far way, through a long tunnel. Nikki jerked her mind out of the past, and focused on Kristy.

Kristy said, 'The two profs were there when the abuse happened. But as far as I can see, they were not implicated in it. No names were mentioned.'

Nikki leaned against the wall, reading the newspaper report. The allegations were raised by the older children who had left the care home. Nothing was proven, but there was a police investigation. The article bore a statement. The police had spoken to St Jude's Hall, and the county council. The investigation ended without any conclusion.

'Dig out the investigation if you can,' Nikki said. 'Records were digitised from 2005 as far as I know. Ask the researchers to look in the paper archives.'

She felt dizzy as she handed the tablet back to Kristy. There was a knock on the door and Nish came in. Nikki made an excuse and went outside.

She crossed the open-plan office, smiling absentmindedly at the few people who greeted her. Then she was in the staircase, which was always empty. She went up a couple of floors, and sat down on one of the steps.

She needed time to think. She pulled out her phone and typed the care home's name in the search engine. Sure enough, the old news article popped up. The same one she had just seen. There was another; about the closure of the home and how the abuse allegations had dogged the place. The newspapers were small, local presses like the *Cotswolds Tribunal*. Nikki checked for their offices and found nothing. Perhaps they'd folded.

There was a photo in the article. An old building, large and quadruple-fronted, with black wrought-iron double gates. The front lawns were overgrown with grass. It was a black and white image. As Nikki stared at it, that old pain returned, knifing through her heart.

This was the place where Tommy had stayed and never returned from. He'd fallen off a cliff in Evesham and died, his death ruled a tragic accident. But was it?

Nikki's head sank in her hands. A heavy hand lay on her heart, making it hard for her to breathe. The past was catching up with her, and she didn't know what to do about it.

TWENTY-EIGHT

Nikki forced herself to think. Was Brian Allerton working at the care home a mere coincidence? It had to be. She didn't know what he did there, or how involved he was. In fact, Nikki knew nothing about the care home. Over the years she had tried, but there was never much online, and there was no one to speak to. She had tried calling the reporters who wrote the article, but she never got through to them.

The care home was still there, as far as she knew. She hadn't looked into it recently. Now she knew she had to.

However... nothing would bring Tommy back.

She got up and rubbed her forehead once. She needed to get back on the case. Her mind was abuzz with possibilities. Although it could be coincidence that the two professors worked at Dunston Hill, she wondered if there was another angle to this.

She went back into the office. Monty was at his desk, and he looked up as Nikki entered.

'So, what did you make of the Allerton family?' Nikki asked.

Monty sipped his tea before replying. 'The wife was genuine. I don't think she was lying. She let us look around everywhere.'

Nikki nodded slowly.

'Do you want me to get statements from the Handelsbanken account?'

'Definitely, and all his other bank accounts as well, including his wife's. We have a financial crimes unit, right?'

'Yes, downstairs. I'll give them a call.'

Nikki tapped the desk with a black-painted fingernail. 'Did Scene of Crime mention anything at his quarters in New College?'

'Nope.'

Nikki checked emails to make sure she hadn't received any reports from Hetty. There was a knock on the door and Justina poked her head in, then came inside.

'Uniforms found the broken cover of a phone. It was red with blue stripes. It had the victim's name on the inside.'

A jolt of excitement sparked Nikki's spine. This was good news indeed. 'Any sign of the phone?' she asked hopefully.

Justina downturned her lips. 'Sorry, guv.'

'Where on the road did they find it?'

'Near the junction between Crosby and Longwall Street.'

Nikki took out her laptop and opened a map of Oxford. She checked the area and then used Google Maps to zoom into the location.

'That's exactly where they found it, near that lamppost.'

Nikki peered closely at the screen. 'Aren't there any manholes, or sewers around there?'

'I was there when they found it. Actually, I think there is a sewer not far from that lamppost.'

'We need to look inside the sewer for the discarded phone. Do you have the IMEI number?'

Justina nodded. 'The last signal from the phone was at
10 p.m. last night. We triangulated it to Magdalen College.'

Nikki frowned and looked at the screen. 'But Magdalen
College is right next to where they found the phone cover.'

She drummed her fingers on the desk. Flashes of inspiration
were bouncing in her brain.

Monty asked, 'What do you want to do?'

'We need to send a camera down the sewer to see if they
find something.'

She checked the map on the screen again. There was a
bridge over the River Cherwell next to Magdalen College. She
pointed at the bridge. 'That's the other place the phone might
have been dumped. But, if the phone was chucked into the
sewer, that opens out into the river anyway, right?'

'Yes,' Monty said.

Nikki stood. 'I need to speak to the boss to get a diving unit
to search the river.'

She strode out and knocked on DS Patmore's door. A gruff
voice asked her to enter. Patmore was typing on his keyboard,
and he glanced at her briefly before returning his attention to
the screen.

'We've got a good lead on the case, sir. I believe the phone is
either in a sewer, or in the Cherwell.' She explained her
reasoning to Patmore. He took his eyes off the screen and settled
back into his armchair. He stared at Nikki in silence.

'Diving units aren't that easy to come by. This isn't the Met
you know.'

'I know that, sir. That's why I'm asking you. Surely the
force has a diving unit?'

Patmore sighed, then nodded.

'I'll see what I can do.'

'I can speak to them, sir, if I have your authority. Time is of
the essence, as you know.'

Patmore looked stressed, and Nikki looked at the screen, but couldn't read from that distance.

'Ring switchboard and ask for the number of the diving unit. Tell them I gave you permission.'

Nikki grinned. 'Thank you, sir.'

TWENTY-NINE

Nikki had laid out the various documents she had retrieved from Professor Allerton's home study.

She had put the Handelsbanken private bank account statements in the top-left corner followed by the research grants he had received from New Frontiers, the publishing company.

In the middle of the desk, she had placed the architectural plans and drawings of the buildings on the street opposite New College.

The drawings were detailed and each terraced house was shown to be demolished, with new student accommodation being built in its place. The architect's address was in Oxford. Druitt and Poole Architects. She got the phone number and gave them a ring. A secretary put her through to one of the partners at the firm.

'My name is Detective Inspector Nikki Gill. Who am I speaking to, please?'

There was a hesitation on the other end. Then a male voice cleared its throat. *'Mr Poole. How can I help?'*

'I'm calling with regards to the student accommodation development project opposite New College.'

Again, there was a pause. Mr Poole eventually spoke. *'Yes?'*

'Could you please tell me more about the project? Where is the funding coming from? And who are the decision-makers involved in this project?'

There was a longer silence, punctuated only by the hiss of static. Mr Poole said, 'May I please know what this is about?'

'It's about a police matter, and it concerns the murder of Professor Brian Allerton.'

'What?'

'This would be a lot easier if I came to see you, Mr Poole. Is it possible to make an appointment today?'

'Well, my secretary has to check my diary and—'

Nikki cut him off. 'I'm afraid this cannot wait. You're not far from us, and I can be at your office in the next half an hour.'

A few seconds ticked by. 'All right then,' Mr Poole said, a note of wariness in his voice. 'I shall see you at my office in half an hour.'

As Nikki put the phone down the door opened and Kristy stepped in, followed by Nish.

'How did it go?' she asked them before they had a chance to sit down.

'We spoke to Professor Blatherwick, but Peggy Moran wasn't in. We can see her tomorrow, her secretary said. Prof Blatherwick knew the victim from way back when they were at Cambridge together.' Kristy relayed the important parts of Professor Blatherwick's statement and Nikki listened attentively.

'Dancing at a nightclub in Cowley with a woman half his age? Not quite the dutiful husband Arabella seems to think he was.'

Nish said, 'And that's not all, guv. I got the distinct feeling Professor B was good friends with the victim, as he stopped saying more. It wouldn't surprise me if Allerton had a string of affairs.'

'Who was the colleague who witnessed this?' Nikki asked.

Nish looked at his notes. 'Emily Blanchard. She's a PhD student at Christ Church.'

'Get hold of her, ASAP. Her statement is important, and we also need to find the woman she saw the victim with.'

Kristy said, 'Prof B told us about the friction between the university and New College over this student accommodation project.'

Nikki raised her eyebrows. 'Oh yes? The one whose details are here?' She tapped the architect's plans on her desk.

'Yes, that one. The university wanted to get into the project, but New College was refusing. There were some heated exchanges, but Prof B denied that Professor Allerton had any enemies at the university.'

'Interesting. Seems there was a lot of interest in the development project. Big money normally brings big problems.'

Nikki looked at her watch. 'Right, I need to meet up with Monty at the college. See you later.'

THIRTY

Nikki caught up with Monty inside the security gate lodge of New College, talking to Winston and looking at the visitors' entrance ledger.

'Found anyone interesting?' Nikki said.

'Winston says governing body members are not classed as visitors, and as they have passes, they can come and go as they wish. But I did find one person who came the day before the murder. Mr Poole, the architect at Druitt and Poole.' Monty rested a forefinger on the white paper, and Nikki leaned in to have a look. 'Mr Poole's signature was on the paper and Winston has written down his name in full next to it.'

Nikki looked at the senior security man approvingly.

'Well done, Winston. If you hadn't entered the name we wouldn't know that he had been here.' She raised her eyebrows at Monty. 'He conveniently forgot to mention this, didn't he?'

Monty shrugged. 'I wasn't there, guv.'

'I know. I wonder why he lied to us? Anyone else of interest?'

Monty shook his head. Nikki turned to Winston. 'You said

all governing body members have cards, right? Do they come in through this entrance?'

Winston shook his head. 'This entrance is mainly for students. We also take deliveries of small objects. But governing body members can use this entrance, also the Longwall Street gates. Their cards also function as fob keys.'

'In which case, there might not be any record of them going in and out of the college, is that right?'

Winston nodded. Nikki and Monty thanked him, and walked out onto the cobblestones of the college grounds. They crossed the front lawn and porter's lodge area, and came out into the main quad. To the right, the white forensic tent was still present. Notices were attached on the quad walls, asking for witnesses. Nikki said, 'Any sign of Emily Blanchard?'

'She's at Christ Church College, guv. She's there now, I rang to ask Professor Blatherwick's secretary. Apparently, they're doing a tutorial together. Miss Ishihara is meant to be here, but not for another hour.'

'In which case,' Nikki suggested, 'let's go and see Emily Blanchard at Christ Church first.'

The walk through the back roads of the colleges to Christ Church was always a nice one. A group of students hurried past, dressed in sub fusc, the black gown that all Oxford students had to wear when sitting exams.

Nikki got a text.

When are you coming over?

It was from someone she couldn't avoid, but who had left her with conflicted, bad memories. Her mother. Nikki sighed. Who was she kidding? A big reason why she'd moved to Oxford was to make amends with her mother. Maybe one day they could have a normal relationship again. Maybe it was a hopeless dream. But she had to get back in touch with her. She sent a quick text back.

Maybe tonight. I will let you know.

Professor Blatherwick's office door was locked, but the adjacent room was occupied. They could hear voices. Monty knocked on the door, and the talking stopped. A petite brunette woman opened the door. Not yet in her thirties, Nikki guessed. The woman stared at them with questioning eyes. Colour drained from her face as Nikki showed her warrant card. She glanced back towards the room, holding the door.

'Are you Emily Blanchard?' Nikki asked.

'Yes.'

'We need to speak to you about Professor Allerton.'

Emily's eyes opened wider. 'I didn't really know him.'

'Regardless, we need to speak to you.'

'I'm still doing a tutorial for a couple of undergraduate students,' she said in a low voice. 'Can you please come back later?'

'No, is the short answer,' Nikki said. 'We are sorry to bother you, but this is a police investigation, and we need to speak to you urgently.'

Emily blinked a few times, then she nodded. She spoke to the students, and then came outside, shutting the door. She pointed to the end of the hallway, where there was an exit to the back garden. Nikki and Monty followed her. The cobblestoned courtyard, with a small garden in the middle, was empty. Nikki looked around her. She couldn't spot any eavesdroppers. She glanced at Monty, who got the drift. He walked around the courtyard once, then came back.

'All clear, guv,' he said.

Emily looked uncomfortable, Nikki thought. She twirled a strand of hair in her hand, and shifted from one foot to the other.

'You're doing a PhD with Professor Daniel Blatherwick?' Nikki asked.

'Yes, that's right.'

'He knew Professor Allerton, who has died recently. Have you heard about his death?'

'Yes. Professor Blatherwick mentioned it.' Emily pressed her lips together, and looked away from Nikki.

'Apparently, you saw Professor Allerton dancing in a night-club with a woman. Is that true?'

Emily blinked again, and looked even more uneasy. Her face was white as a sheet. 'Look, I don't want to get into any trouble. I didn't know Professor Allerton.'

Nikki raised a hand, and lowered her voice. She didn't want to scare her. 'Don't worry. We just want to know if you saw him in that nightclub, or not.'

Emily nodded slowly.

Nikki asked, 'When was this?'

'A couple of weeks ago. I was there with some of the under-graduates, after a tutorial. Some of my PhD colleagues also turned up. We stayed till late. I saw him on the dancefloor.'

'Who was the woman?'

'I've seen her around,' Emily said. 'She works in the history department, and as a scholar at New College.'

'What did she look like?'

'I would say mixed race,' Emily said. 'Maybe Japanese, or Chinese. She definitely had some Asian and British features, if you know what I mean.'

Nikki and Monty exchanged a glance. Nikki asked, 'What was she wearing?'

Something flashed in Emily's eyes. 'I remember that she was quite tall. Almost his height. She was wearing a cream dress with a low cleavage. Sorry, maybe I'm saying too much.'

'No, not at all,' Nikki assured her. 'We need as much detail as possible.'

'OK. The dress had a low back. There was a slit in either side, showing off her legs. They were dancing close together, and kissing.'

'Did you see them leave?' Monty asked.

'As a matter of fact, I did. The club shut at two in the morning. I saw them outside, getting into a cab.'

'Before this,' Nikki asked, 'when did you see Professor Allerton?'

Emily frowned, and looked at the ground. She shook her head slowly. 'A while back. Professor Allerton was also a member at Christ Church, Professor Blatherwick said. I met him at a Senior Common Room dinner once. Maybe a few months ago.'

'Did you hear any rumours about him?'

Emily had a guarded look on her face. 'What do you mean?'

'Did he have a reputation as a womaniser?'

Emily swallowed, and pressed her lips together.

Nikki said, 'His death, and this investigation, has nothing to do with you. We just need more information about him, that's all. And everything you tell us is fully confidential.'

Emily folded her arms across her chest. She shivered slightly, and Nikki didn't blame her. She had her coat on, but Emily had a thin cardigan over her blouse.

'I've heard that he tried it on with some of the younger lecturers, and PhD students.' Emily stopped, and looked at Nikki, before averting her eyes. Nikki picked up on the hesitation.

'Go on,' she urged. 'What else?'

Emily scratched the back of her neck, then seemed to make her mind up. 'Apparently, he was also seen kissing a man. Men also stayed the night at his staff quarters. But look, I can't verify this. These are only rumours I've heard.' Emily raised both hands.

'Don't worry,' Nikki repeated. 'What else did you hear?'

'Some of my PhD colleagues are attached to New College. They mentioned it. Young men were seen leaving his staff quarters in the morning. I also heard he squeezed a male undergraduate's thigh at a freshers event.'

There was silence, as the Nikki grappled with the revelations.

Monty asked, 'Could we please have the names of your PhD colleagues? We would like to speak to them. In confidence, of course, and we will not mention your name.'

Emily closed her eyes, and sighed. She put a hand over her forehead. 'Look, this is why I didn't want to speak to you guys. But Daniel, the professor, said it might help you. I don't want my friends being harassed.'

'They won't be harassed,' Nikki said, in her most reassuring voice. 'We'll just ask a few questions, then leave them alone. And as Monty said, your name will not be mentioned.'

Emily folded her arms tightly against her chest, and her shoulders shook as a stiff wind blew across the courtyard.

Nikki said, 'Let's go back inside. You can give us your phone number, and we can just call you about the contact details of your friends.'

Emily reluctantly agreed, and they walked back to the office. They bade Emily goodbye, and walked out of Christ Church.

'Well, well,' Monty said. They were walking back through the winding, narrow streets, heading for the dome of the Radcliffe Camera. It seems Prof Allerton batted for both sides.'

'Yes,' Nikki murmured, frowning. 'We need to speak to Arabella again. I wonder if she knew any of this?'

'And if she did, why she didn't tell us anything?'

'Embarrassed, and I can't blame her. But wives have a habit of getting to know things. Oxford is a small community. Secrets can spread easily.' Nikki was lost in her own world, almost speaking to herself.

She was aware of Monty's eyes on her. She shook her head, coming out of her reverie.

Monty said, 'For someone who's just moved here, you know a lot about Oxford, guv.'

Nikki laughed, but it sounded hollow and false, even to her own ears. 'I guess all small towns are the same.'

'But you're from London, aren't you? Nothing small about that place.'

Nikki looked at him askance. 'I was generalising, Monty.'

Monty gave her a look, and then shut up. Nikki was grateful. They walked back to New College in silence.

THIRTY-ONE

Monty had dropped Nikki off at the nick, and she'd collected Nish to go and see the architects of the New College student accommodation project on Longwall Street.

Druitt and Poole Architects had a large, four-storey building next to the covered market near St Aldate's. It was prime Oxford real estate – buildings here now fetched multiples of ten million pounds – early Victorian, its columns and flutes were beautifully maintained.

Mr Poole was a tall man. He had a red, swarthy face, probably the result of eating too much meat and consuming excessive red wine. He wore a waistcoat and on his left wrist there was a Rolex Submariner watch. His brown hair was receding at the temples, and Nikki guessed he was in his mid- to late fifties. They shook hands after Nikki had shown him her warrant card.

'Please take a seat,' Mr Poole said. 'Tea or coffee?'

They politely declined. They sat and Nikki got straight to the point.

'Could you please tell us a bit more about the project on Longwall Street, opposite New College?'

Mr Poole looked uncomfortable. He spread his hands. 'To

be honest, this is confidential information. The plans have not been submitted to the council as yet. I do not foresee any problem with planning permission, but I'd be intrigued to know how you got the information.'

Nikki reached inside her coat pocket and pulled out the roll of white paper. She gave it to Mr Poole who spread it out on his desk. His eyebrows hiked north as he gaped at the plans, then back at Nikki.

'How on earth did you get hold of this?'

'I will ask the questions if you don't mind, Mr Poole,' Nikki said with a smile. 'This is a criminal investigation, as I'm sure you are aware. Professor Allerton was murdered, and I believe he was involved with this plan?'

Beads of sweat had sprouted on Mr Poole's large face. He had a bulbous red nose, the kind many drinkers had. The tip of his nostril twitched. He took out a handkerchief and wiped his forehead. 'How did Mr Allerton die?'

'I'm afraid I cannot discuss an active investigation. Could you please answer my question?'

Mr Poole licked his lips and swallowed. Nikki found his reaction interesting. The man was shaken and all she was doing was asking a question. A nugget of suspicion was hardening in her mind. There was more in these architectural drawings than met the eye.

'He... He, I mean Brian Allerton, and several others from New College, current and past staff, had a say in where the student accommodation would be, and also what type of accommodation they wanted.'

'Is it normally the governing body of the college who decides that?'

'The college holds the funds, and yes, the governing body agrees how to use the funds. But the university's approval is also needed, although the final say belongs to the college. We liaise with our contacts at the college.'

'And in this case Brian Allerton was one of your contacts?'

'Ah, yes.' Mr Poole folded his hands on his lap and looked away from Nikki.

'Who else?' Nikki asked.

'Oh, a couple of other people.' Mr Poole was deliberately trying to be vague, and Nikki's patience was wearing thin. She leaned forward and put her elbows on the table.

'Mr Poole, you are reminded again this is a criminal investigation. Any information you withhold from us, if found out later, can lead to your arrest and potential prosecution. Do you understand?'

Mr Poole's Adam's apple bobbed up and down. He wiped his forehead again. 'Now, let me see. Mr Moffatt, the bursar, was also a person I spoke to. And there was another, a female lecturer from New College.'

Nish pulled out a piece of paper from the inside pocket of his coat. 'I have a list of the governing body members, if that helps. Shall I read them out to you?'

Mr Poole shook his head. 'I've just remembered the name. Sue Pollard.'

Nikki nodded slowly. 'Yes, I've met her already. So, Mr Moffatt, the victim and Sue Pollard were your contacts at New College?'

'Yes, that's right.'

'How much was the college investing into the project?'

Mr Poole opened his mouth, then closed it. He licked his lips again. 'I'm afraid I'm not at liberty to disclose that information.'

Nikki stared at him, letting the silence deepen. Mr Poole looked increasingly uncomfortable. He dug a finger into his collar and pulled at it.

Nikki said, 'Anything you tell us is strictly in confidence, Mr Poole.'

'OK,' Mr Poole said, shaking his head slightly. 'The project is a substantial one, as you can see. A number of different builders and structural engineers are involved. Each one of these terraced houses is large and has a current valuation of £1.2 million. They have to be demolished, and there's thirty of them on the street. People have to be rehoused. And then new, state-of-the-art accommodation built. The entire project will cost sixty to seventy million. But with any building project, costs can go up. Hence, the college has agreed to a ceiling of £100 million.'

Nikki absorbed the information, wondering how many hundreds of millions the college actually held in its coffers. She knew the Oxford colleges had huge amounts of money that they received in endowments over the centuries. Oxford University was unique in that way. The individual colleges were far wealthier than the actual university, which was just a stakeholder organisation. 'Who in the college was responsible for handling the money?' Nikki asked.

'That would be the bursar, Mr Moffatt. But as I understood it, Professor Allerton and Miss Pollard had invested in the project as well.'

'Do you know how much they had invested?'

Mr Poole shook his head. 'Inspector, I have told you everything I know. Probably more than I should have. Please keep it completely confidential.'

'You have my guarantee on that,' Nikki said. 'Thank you for helping us.'

Nish asked, 'Did you ever meet Professor Allerton?'

'Yes, I did. He came to this office a couple of times with Miss Pollard and Mr Moffatt.'

'Can you remember when that was?' Nish asked.

'It was a while ago, at the beginning of this year I would say. January or February, maybe when we had finalised the plans. I had met him at the bursar's office in New College as well, but that was last year.'

'Apart from this, did you know Mr Allerton? Personally, I mean.'

'No, I did not.'

Nish asked, 'Is there a specific builder taking the lead role in this project? Architects often work closely with builders, don't they?'

Mr Poole wiped his forehead again. The heating was on, but it wasn't that hot inside. He took his time in answering.

'For a big project like this, lasting several years, a committee decides who the builder will be.'

'Was such a committee formed? And if so, who do you think they would be most likely to appoint?'

The perspiring architect wrung his hands under the table.

Nikki observed him with interest. He was being frank, she thought, but it was clearly bothering him. Maybe he was just the nervous type. Or had he expected Professor Allerton to die?

'Well, there is one name that springs to mind. Terence Conran.' He stopped and glanced at them.

Nish said, 'Do you have his address? We would like to speak to him.'

THIRTY-TWO

When Nikki and Nish came out of the architect's building, she noticed Nish had fallen behind. He came up quickly.

'My nine o o'clock,' Nish whispered.

Both Nikki and Nish were in plain-clothes; Nikki had her usual black work trousers and black blazer over a white blouse. Nish wore a dark-blue suit. There was no reason for anyone to suspect they were detectives.

Nikki took her phone out and pretended to make a call. She spotted the man almost immediately. He was average height, wearing a hooded top and dark glasses that were unnecessary in the tepid November sun. He had on black tracksuit bottoms and black trainers. When he met Nikki's eyes, he turned away, heading for the shops opposite. He went inside the large Boots store and disappeared from view.

'Have you seen him before today?' Nikki asked.

'Yes,' Nish said. 'I didn't think it was important at first. Outside the Hollywell Street entrance to New College. I saw him the first night, and I remember as he came up to the skipper to ask him why we were there. He was wearing the same clothes as now.'

'What did Monty tell him?'

'Usual stuff. It's a police matter so clear off. He joined the rest of the crowd outside Hollywell Street.'

'And after that?'

'When we went to Christ Church College, he was hanging around outside. When I saw him, he walked away.'

'Are you sure it's the same guy?'

'Yes, positive. I mentioned it to Kristy. She didn't remember seeing him before. But I definitely did.'

Nikki thought about following the man into Boots. She checked her watch. It was past four and light would be fading fast. She had important leads to follow up now, the first being another meeting with the bursar, Mr Moffatt.

'Keep an eye out for him. Let's head back to the nick now. We've got work to do.'

While Nash drove the black Ford Everest 3.2L Titanium CID car, Nikki got on the phone to Monty.

'Have the divers started working now?' she asked.

'Yes, guv. They actually went down half an hour ago. Do you have any instructions?'

'We are in the car, so will head down there. Why don't you and Kristy see if you can track down any more of the governing body members?'

'OK, guv.'

Traffic was building up as it was school breakup time. The High Street leading down to Magdalen College was jammed with cars. Nish turned into an alley and put the car on the kerb.

'It's about a ten-minute walk from here, guv, but driving there might take a lot longer.'

'Good thinking,' Nikki said getting out of the car.

The sun was out, but a stiff breeze blew hair over her face. She thrust her hands into her coat pockets and followed Nish. They walked past the main entrance of Magdalen College and went down the slope of a gravelled path that led to the river.

There was a boatyard, with a few tourists looking on inquisitively. A squad car was parked on the left and there were no
other parking spaces. A uniformed sergeant and Justina were
standing by the river, and the sergeant was arguing with a man
who was clearly unhappy. Justina waved at them as they
approached.

Nikki nodded at her, then looked at the man arguing with
the sergeant. He was complaining about the lack of business
because no one could take a boat out for rowing. He was clearly
the boatyard owner.

'What sort of a police matter?' the man yelled. 'You can't
just get my customers out of the boats and act like you own the
place.'

Nikki stepped forward. 'Sir, I am Detective Inspector Nikki
Gill. There has been a significant incident, and by allowing the
police to search this section of the river, you are helping us in an
important criminal investigation.'

The man stared at Nikki for a while, then lifted a hand
towards the river. 'Who's going to compensate me for the day's
earnings?'

'We will be gone soon, I promise. No more than an hour.'

The man seemed mollified and the sergeant thanked her.
His name was Darren Stevens. Nikki walked down to the edge
of the water.

The cobblestones disappeared beneath the muddy waters of
the Cherwell. The bridge was to her right, and the river flowed
beneath the arches.

The longer punting boats, and also smaller rowing boats,
were tethered by hooks to the nearest arch. There was a black
rigid inflatable boat bobbing up and down in the water. A
sergeant from the specialist diving unit was manning the boat.
He had a cap on and a blue uniform. Scuba-diving gear was visible, but both divers seemed to still be underwater. Justina
pointed to a section of the water just under one of the arches.

'Bubbles there, guv. It must be one of the divers.'

Nikki craned her neck and saw the bubbles. As she watched, one of the divers surfaced. He trod water, then the rigid inflatable boat chugged towards him. The sergeant helped the diver into the boat. The diver took off his gear, then looked towards the bank. He waved towards them, clearly excited as he lifted a plastic specimen bag. The sergeant turned the boat and it puttered across the water to the boatyard.

'Found this.' The diver held the specimen bag aloft. There was a phone inside. He turned the bag and pointed to the left rear corner of the phone. The remnants of a red cover with blue stripes were still visible.

'That has to be it,' Nikki said, excited. 'The cover is a match.'

'Not just that,' the diver said. 'The initials BC are engraved on the back. Those are the victim's initials, right?'

'Yes,' Darren, the uniformed sergeant, said. He leaned across the boat and grabbed the bag from the diver.

'Great work, guys.' Nikki almost clapped her hands in joy. This was a real breakthrough.

Someone grabbed her arm and yanked her back. It was Nish. His hand was pointing up towards the bridge. She followed his line of vision. A man in a black-hooded jacket was leaning over the bridge. There wasn't anyone else around. With his phone, he was taking photos of the scene below. It was the same man who was following them around.

'Get him,' Nikki said.

The man saw them and turned away.

Nikki raced up the slope, Nish charging ahead of her.

'Stop, police!' Nish shouted.

THIRTY-THREE

Nish almost barged into a couple as the pedestrians scattered at the top of the towpath. Nikki was right behind him. Nish took off to the left, across the bridge. He was much faster than Nikki, and he had clearly seen where the suspect was, so Nikki simply followed him. The only problem was she wasn't as quick as she used to be. Her lungs were burning as she struggled to keep up with Nish.

'Move, police,' she screamed as she weaved in and out of groups of students and tourists. A busload of Japanese tourists had arrived, and they were milling around, happily snapping photos of the bridge and river. Several of them lifted their cameras and took photos of Nikki as she raced past. She thought of giving them a wave, but then decided against it.

The suspect was headed straight across the roundabout and then towards the road that went into Cowley. Nish was doing his best to alert people in advance, by raising his voice, but there wasn't much he could do when the man suddenly crossed the road ahead.

Cars honked and screeched to a halt. The black-hooded figure jumped on the bonnet of a car and slid across. There was a bus stop, and he pushed into the crowd and disappeared from view. Nikki was lucky to find a zebra crossing, and she ran across, before Nish could. She was first at the bus stop. The bus wasn't moving yet, passengers still boarding. Nikki heaved in a breath as she looked around. She couldn't see the man with the black-hooded top. What if he was already on the bus?

She had to move in front of people, drawing irritated looks and complaining words. She showed the surprised bus driver her warrant card.

'You need to stop the bus now. There could be a dangerous individual on board, and we are searching for him.'

Nish had boarded the bus already and was looking at the back. She started at the front, scanning the faces on the seats.

The man could easily have taken off his hooded top and discarded his glasses. He was Caucasian, she knew that much from his hands. That didn't exactly narrow the field. Nikki grew frustrated as she checked the faces. Nish met her in the middle. Sweat was pouring off his face, dampening his collar. He shook his head.

'Let's keep looking. He couldn't have got far.'

They jumped out, looking around on the crowded pavement. A Caribbean woman came up to them. 'You looking for the man who just push me to the ground?' She looked angry, and she was holding her left hip. Her hair was in dreadlocks, and she had a range of colourful beads on her neck. Her bright floral skirt hung down to her ankles.

'What did he look like?' Nish asked.

'He was wearing a black top, hood over his head, with dark glasses. He pushed me so hard, I fell to the ground then he just ran off, without even saying sorry.'

'Where did you see him?' Nish asked quickly.

The woman pointed with her hand. 'He just went to the right over there.'

Nish ran, and Nikki followed. The road on the right was an

alley, and it was less crowded. They were just in time to see a black-hooded figure duck into a terraced house on the left.

A woman opened the door, with a baby on her hip. Before she could open her mouth, there was a loud crash at the back, followed by a child's cry. Nish rushed past the woman heading for the rear of the house.

The back door that led to the small garden was open, and the man with the black top was scrambling over the back fence. Nikki grabbed a chair from the kitchen and used it to climb the fence. At the other side there was a narrow path that separated two rows of houses. Nikki whipped her head to the left and saw Nish disappearing into an open street on the left. She jumped over the fence and followed.

A fresh breeze struck her in the face, and she came upon a river. There was a bridge across it, and she saw Nish running after their target.

The suspect disappeared over the bridge, and Nikki saw him jump onto a passing boat. It was a small boat that had seen better days, but its motors were clearly powerful. The boat revved its engines and took off down the river.

Nish stopped, both hands on his waist. He kicked at the ground in frustration. Nikki was on her radio.

'Suspect headed down Cherwell River. Alert all units.'

As the boat dwindled from view, she knew it was futile. The man had escaped.

THIRTY-FOUR

Thirty years ago

Grey clouds scudded over the sky, a harsh rebuke to the morning sun. The light was paltry and the wind whined outside. Paul climbed down the bunk bed and stood on the cold stone floor, body shivering, teeth chattering. The heating never came on till later in the day, when they were at school. He put his coat on, then sat next to Tommy, who faced the wall, sleeping.

'Wake up.' Paul shook his shoulder, and Tommy stirred. He curled up into a tight ball again, pulling the duvet over his head. Paul knew the men had taken Tommy again last night. He had lain awake till Tommy got back. He heard the boy crying himself to sleep. He hadn't slept well himself, tormented by strange dreams. For some reason, he felt responsible for Tommy. He couldn't explain why. In his bleak, dreary life, looking after Tommy was the solitary warm glow. One day, the two of them would escape this horrible place and never come back.

Gently, he turned Tommy around. He was shocked when

he saw the bruises on his shoulders. The boys cheeks were streaked with dry tears.

'What did they do...' The words died on Paul's lips. He knew what they'd done. It made him want to vomit. He held Tommy's hand, but it was limp and cold. A rage flamed to life in Paul's guts. One day... someday, he would take his revenge.

'Let's go to school. It's easier there. Come on. It's time we told our headteacher. I'll come with you to his office. Don't worry.'

After a lot of persuading, Tommy finally sat up in bed. They got ready and left for school, later than usual.

They took the detour past the industrial estate as they normally did.

The land opened up into the wide open spaces by the Cherwell River. They climbed up a small hill. Paul could feel the scar from the cigarette burn, it rubbed against his clothes. He found a resting spot, and sat down with his back against a flat rock. Tommy joined him.

Paul had a big packet of crisps in his bag, and he took it out. It was barbecue beef, their favourite flavour. Tommy took a swig of water from his bottle.

'What do you want to be when you get out of here? When you grow up, I mean.'

Paul grinned. He stuck out his fists and pretended to hit someone. 'I want to be a boxer. I'm going to join a gym soon. There's one on the High Street.'

Tommy looked at him with big eyes. 'Wow.'

'What do you want to be?'

Tommy lowered his head, and frowned. 'An astronaut.'

Paul shot him a quizzical look. 'Eh? Is that like people in space or something?'

Tommy grinned. 'Yes, silly. An astronaut has to be trained a lot to go inside a rocket and then into space. Imagine them going so far away.' The smile fell away from his face. 'So far away from here.' He pointed to the sky. His hand shook, and he lowered it slowly.

They finished their packet of crisps, then drank some more water and stood up. They started going up the slope.

The hill was steep and one side of it had a sheer hang that looked down into rocks and bushes far below. The boys avoided that side and kept to the right slope that undulated down into the green fields below.

Paul sensed Tommy wasn't behind him as he descended. He stopped and looked up and frowned when he couldn't see him. He climbed back up to the flat top and found Tommy standing near the cliff edge, staring down. Paul's blood ran cold. He ran for Tommy, then grabbed his shirt and pulled him back from the edge.

'What the hell are you playing at, you silly bugger?' Paul asked angrily. 'Can't be standing there.'

Tommy looked up at him, his blue eyes shining in the meagre, cold sunlight that had peeked through the clouds.

'I had a dream last night. I was flying, and free, like the clouds.' He had a wistful look on his face, and the shadow of a sad smile played on his lips.

'That was last night,' Paul said, pulling him along, away from the edge. 'Now we have to get to school.'

Paul didn't pull him too hard, because he had seen the bruises on Tommy's shoulder. The smaller boy shrugged off Paul's arm.

'Free. Do you know what that means? It means I don't have to worry about anything any more. It's like what it says in the Bible. There's freedom in heaven.'

Paul frowned, a worry tightening inside him. 'What are you talking about?'

'We need to make ourselves free. Otherwise, we'll never be. I saw that in my dream last night. That girl with black wings, she came down and took me away. It was so nice. She was so warm.

'What girl?' Paul shook his head. 'You're talking rubbish.'

'My sister. The one who comes with my mother. When I'm free, I can live with her. She'll come down with the wings, and we can fly away.'

Paul felt a dagger of sorrow twist his insides. This boy really didn't have a clue. He hugged Tommy and spoke softly in his ears.

'Listen to me you, you idiot. Your mother can't have you back. I've seen this with another boy. She can't cope with two children in the house.'

'It's not my mother,' Tommy said, pushing him away. His cheeks were getting tinged with red, and he was angry. 'It's my sister. She's going to help me.'

'She's just a little girl. Now come on, let's get to school.' Paul turned his back to Tommy and made for the slope to the fields. He heard running steps and turned to give Tommy a smile. His smile vanished when he realised the steps were running away from him, the sound fading. He looked up just in time to see Tommy's head disappear over the crest of the slope.

'Tommy! No!' Paul screamed. He ran up the cliff his lungs burning. He arrived at the flat peak and saw Tommy back where he was, at the edge. It seemed to happen in slow motion. Tommy didn't look back. He bent his knees, then jumped as high as he could, spreading his arms wide. He seemed to hang in the air for a few seconds, a momentary prisoner of the blue air, the cruel sunshine. Then he was gone, and Paul was screaming his name hoarse and rushing to the edge.

He stopped just before he toppled over himself, small rocks and dust scattering in the wind, then plunging far down into the bush and rocks. With horror-stricken eyes, he saw Tommy's little body dropping like a stone, the bag flapping in the wind, his arms flailing like he was trying to catch something. Downward the boy plunged, and his body became smaller, till it hit the rocks with a small puff of dust and a faintly audible crack. as the tears.

Paul averted his eyes, covered his face with his hands and crumpled to the ground as the tears burst from him.

THIRTY-FIVE

Thirty years ago

Nikki stood on her tiptoes, watching the shiny white and blue car park outside. She knew it was the police, she had seen their cars before. Her breath made fog on the glass. She wiped it and watched the car. In their narrow street of terraced council houses, most of the cars were either old, or dirt cheap. The big police car made the other cars look even worse. Right opposite their house, an abandoned car stood on bricks, its wheels taken by thieves, windows smashed in. Nikki heard her mother complain to the council, but they took ages to respond.

Across the street, she saw the net curtains twitch. Mrs Hardy, the nosy parker of the neighbourhood. She might be elderly, but she did like to gossip. In the five years that Nikki had lived here with her parents, Mrs Hardy had stopped her on the streets and asked her about her family more times than Nikki could count.

A policewoman in uniform and a man and a woman in suits, got out of the car. They approached their house, and Nikki ran from the window. She went to the landing and called upstairs.

'Mummy! The police are here.'

The bedroom door opened, and Clarissa's bedraggled face appeared over the railings. She coughed, furiously combing her hair with the brush in her hand.

'What? Are you sure?'

Nikki might be eight, but she already had a wise head on her shoulders. 'Positive. They're outside.'

Right on cue, the doorbell went. Clarissa descended the stairs rapidly, still clutching the hairbrush. She put it on the mantelpiece and checked herself once in the mirror before opening the door. Nikki stood behind her mother. She heard a female voice introduce herself as the inspector something, and then she spoke further in a lower voice. Nikki couldn't catch the words, but she saw her mother's body go rigid, like she'd received an electric shock.

'What about him? What happened?' Clarissa asked. The policewoman spoke again, and Nikki retreated to the staircase and sat down on a step. She watched as the man and woman in suits came inside. Nikki gaped at them, unsure of what to do. She felt very shy. The couple followed Clarissa into the living room and the door shut. Nikki heard their footsteps creak on the bare floorboards. The room didn't have any carpets, like the rest of the ground floor. She heard them sit down on the sofa, and she crept to the door. She put her ear to it and heard the muffled voices.

It was hard to make out the exact words. But one sound suddenly rose above all others. It was a high-pitched wail, and it came from her mother. It was followed by the sound of sobbing. Nikki's heart beat faster. She felt scared and didn't know what to do. Their father was at work and there wasn't anyone else in the house. She heard her mother babbling, her words strung out between gasping sobs.

'Where? How? Tell me!'

The female police officer was speaking, and her voice was

soft, so Nikki couldn't hear. She pressed her ear harder on the door. Only certain words were audible.

'...bottom of the cliff... accident, we don't know. Another boy... Paul was there. He reported... school alerted.'

The woman stopped and the man spoke. His voice was louder. 'Did Thomas mention anything the last time you saw him?'

Her mother kept sobbing, unable to speak. Her voice was wobbly and hard to understand. '...four months ago... so thin, not happy in that place. I could tell... he didn't say anything.'

'Will you be OK to come with us to identify the body? Perhaps with your husband.'

From across the door, despite being invisible, Nikki could feel her mother slowly coming apart, dissolving in sorrow. She didn't understand what was happening, but it was bad. Really, really bad.

Then her mother said something, and there was silence for a while. The policewoman spoke, and Nikki could hear her now.

'Are you sure you can come now?'

'Yes,' her mother said. 'I need to see him.' The floorboards creaked as they stood.

Nikki retreated to the stairs, and this time, went further up so they couldn't see her. But before she did, her mother screamed again, and she halted on the steps.

'It's your fault,' Clarissa shouted. 'You kept him from me. You did this!' There was movement and sounds of a struggle from the room. Then Nikki heard her mother's wailing again, an awful, plangent sound that she would remember for the rest of her life.

The door opened eventually, and the policewoman emerged first. Her lips were pinched, face pale and drawn. Then Clarissa emerged, supported by the policeman. Clarissa's eyes were barely open, and her face was twisted, full of hurt and pain, like someone had just punched her in the gut.

'Would you like to get changed?' the policewoman asked. Then she caught sight of Nikki, sitting on the upstairs landing. Their eyes met, and the woman looked down at the ground.

'I'll go like this,' Clarissa whispered.

Nikki stood and came down the stairs.

'Go where, Mummy?'

All four adults turned to look at her. Clarissa stood straighter. Her lips parted, then she seemed to rethink her words. Nikki had never seen her mother look so helpless.

'I just need to go with them to the police station. I'll be back soon.'

Nikki got scared. Were they going to take her mother away? She clutched the banister tightly. 'Why? What's happening?'

The woman and her mother started to speak at the same time. The woman's voice was clearer, with more authority.

'We just need to speak to your mum once, then she's going to be back. However,' the policewoman looked at Clarissa. 'I'm not sure we can leave your daughter home on her own. How old is she?'

'I'm eight,' Nikki said promptly, and the woman glanced at her and smiled.

'She needs to come with us. It's OK, we have a family liaison officer who can look after her.'

The woman turned to her again and smiled. 'What's your name?'

'Nicola, but you can call me Nikki.'

'Come here,' Clarissa said.

Nikki ran down the stairs, and Clarissa enclosed her in a deep hug. She sank to the floor and her shoulders shook as she held Nikki.

'What is it, Mummy?'

Clarissa dried her eyes. 'I'll tell you later.'

Outside, a couple of the neighbours were walking past and stopped when they saw them. Clarissa kept her eyes averted, but Nikki watched them. Mrs Hardy was standing outside her door. The woman next door to her, Mrs Donald, stood beside her. They kept watching the car as it drove off.

It was the first time Nikki had seen the interior of a police station. She had seen it from the school bus before, but it seemed very different now. It was all grey floors and white walls. They parked at the back, and she clutched her mother's hand tightly as they went through the sliding double doors. There was a big reception area, and a man in a white uniform stood behind the counter. He nodded and pressed a button when he saw them, and another door at the end of the reception area slid open without a sound.

Once inside, they were shown into a room with sofas, a small table with flowers on it. This room seemed more homely than the corridors outside. A woman in a blue uniform came in and introduced herself as Katie, the family liaison officer. She had a kind face, and she smiled at Nikki.

'You stay here with me, and your mummy will be back in a minute.'

Nikki looked at Clarissa, whose nose tip was quivering, eyes sunken. She forced a reassuring smile on her face, but it didn't convince Nikki.

'What's happening, Mummy?' she asked.

'Nothing. Just stay here and talk to Katie, OK? I'll be back soon.'

The policeman who had come to see them held the door open. The policewoman went out and Clarissa followed. The door shut softly behind them.

'So,' Katie asked, 'which school do you go to?'

Nikki talked to her, but she could see this was just a distraction. Katie was nice enough, but the adults were hiding something. At the house, Nikki had heard the words *Thomas*, and *boy*, and she knew this was about her brother at the care home. The brother that she had never really known. Thomas, or Tommy, had never been to their house. She had asked Clarissa why he didn't live with them, and her mother never answered.

It was hard to think of Tommy as her brother. Clarissa barely spoke about him. She didn't see any photos of Tommy at home. And yet, something had happened to Tommy. Nikki felt it in her bones, and she wished the adults would just tell her.

Katie took out a Monopoly board game and gave Nikki some sweets. Nikki pretended to enjoy them, but her mind lay with Clarissa.

Eventually, the door opened and Clarissa appeared. Her eyes were swollen red with a haunted look to them, like she'd seen a ghost. Nikki went to her, and Clarissa gripped her so tight it hurt.

She let go and collapsed on the sofa and wept.

Nikki had seen enough.

'What's happened to Tommy? Is he in trouble?'

Clarissa shook her head and then banged it against the wall. Katie had to restrain her, helped by the policewoman.

Nikki watched, scared out of her wits, then she started to cry. She knew her mother's life had changed for ever.

THIRTY-SIX

Mr Moffatt relaxed in the soft leather seats of the Bentley Continental. The six-litre, sixteen-valve turbo-powered engine purred softly as the car drove through the lush green Cotswolds countryside.

He stared at the scenery, the gently undulating hills always a treat to the eye. His mind, however, was far away. He was caught in a trap and couldn't see a way out. But there had to be a way. Squirming out of tight spots was exactly what Mr Moffatt had done all his life.

First as an investment banker, rising all the way up to director level in the mighty Yank bank, where he had spent twenty-three years of his life. Oxford University had presented fresh challenges, ones he had relished.

The university's vast financial reserves were well known in the City of London. A number of investment managers in the City handled the university's portfolio. But that dwarfed the financial staff who actually worked at the university in Oxford.

Mr Moffatt had put his old contacts to good use. He had allowed a lot of his college's money to be handled by investment firms in the City. They had given back a good return, which had bolstered his standing not just in the eyes of New College, but at the university in general.

Christ Church and St John's, two of the largest and wealthiest colleges in Oxford, had asked him to join their financial board. Things were looking up for him, until Professor Allerton's untimely death.

As the powerful car whisked down a slope and then made easy work of climbing a steep hill, he thought of the roller coaster of recent events. Brian Allerton had been a fool. He would not listen, and he had courted his own death. And now... He would have to pick up the pieces.

It struck him as unfair that poor financiers had to deal with the affairs of a person who left debts behind. The bankers got a good return for it, all that asset-stripping. Not to mention a sizeable bonus on top. But still, it wasn't as juicy as taking bets in the derivatives market. Hey ho, Mr Moffatt sighed as he rubbed his hands together.

It wasn't that Brian had left financial debts. His burden was entirely of a different kind.

The car slowed, humming like an aeroplane coming to the end of its stroll after landing. The driver stopped, got out and entered a code at the wooden gates. They swung open, and the big car drove down a tarmac road.

Dense forest covered the road on either side. In front, the huge spiked iron gates of the Darlington country estate were visible. Mr Moffatt had been here before. It was a beautiful twelve acres of land, nestled within the hills and lakes of Burford, in the heart of the Cotswolds countryside. The massive portcullis slid open silently, and they sped through, coming to a halt on the gravel drive that led up to the steps of the mansion.

Mr Moffatt was shown in by a man who was dressed in plain clothes, but was a butler in every other sense of the word.

The red and green carpet, decorated with the Darlington family crest at regular intervals, was soft under his feet. He rose and walked over to the huge original fireplace, with a real wood fire crackling. The oil paintings of Darlington's ancestors and other landscapes were nice to look at. He turned when he heard someone clear their throat. Tarquin Darlington was dressed in a dark-blue light jacket and freshly ironed blue, matching trousers. He wore a white shirt and had loafers on his feet. He was tall and slim, with sloped shoulders. His cheeks were sunken, and his face had that unusually long, thin look that some tall men have.

He had old-fashioned, round-rimmed glasses that rested on the bridge of his nose. He was in his forties, but dressed like a much-older man. Rich people liked doing that, in Mr Moffatt's opinion. Or, they wore crumpled and old clothes that made them look like beggars. Sometimes, they also smelled of those old clothes. Who cared, when they had tens of millions in their personal accounts? The smell of money was always stronger than their aftershave.

Mr Darlington had floppy salt-and-pepper hair. He had a habit of flicking it off his forehead as he spoke

'Richard,' Mr Tarquin purred. 'How nice of you to come.'

His handshake was warm, but his fingers soft and delicate, like a woman's. His blue eyes had flecks of gold in them as they bore into Mr Moffatt unnervingly.

'Shall we?'

'Oh yes, of course, please do sit,' Mr Darlington said, as if he had forgotten the sofas existed. 'Would you like something to drink? Tea or coffee, perhaps?'

Mr Moffatt needed to fortify himself for the meeting. 'A cup of coffee would be nice.'

They sat down, and Mr Darlington reached out a long, thin arm and plucked up the receiver of a phone on the table next to the sofa. He spoke briefly to the butler, then hung up.

He lifted his glasses up slightly and smiled at Mr Moffatt again. His smile never touched his eyes. They always remained flat and cold. Like the eyes of a fish. Mr Moffatt smiled nervously, then rubbed his hands together.

'Are you cold, Richard? I can always put some logs into the fire.' Mr Moffatt raised both hands. It was cold, actually, but he wasn't about to admit that. Mr Darlington sensed his discomfort. He lit the fire, then used a poker to stir the logs. 'No, I'm fine, thank you.'

'How are things at the college?' Mr Darlington's smile never left his face.

'Difficult, as you must know. Brian's death was unexpected. Well, I say that but...' Mr Moffatt looked at Mr Darlington, whose smile had slipped a fraction, frozen in place. He gulped and changed track.

'Anyway, we are doing the best we can. The police are involved, and they have questioned me.'

'Are you helping the police?'

'Yes, of course, I have to.'

Mr Darlington inclined his head. 'Yes, you must. But there is a limit to what you can do. It is their job, after all, to find who did this.'

They stared at each other for a while, and Mr Moffatt was the first to look away. That smile was still in Mr Darlington's face like it had been painted on. It was unnerving, to say the least. He was glad when the butler came in.

'Thank you, John,' Mr Darlington said.

John placed the tray on the table, poured out two cups of coffee and a dash of milk, then left without a word.

'Have you been in touch with Arabella?' Mr Darlington asked.

'Yes, I have. She's beside herself with grief, obviously. The police have been to see her as well.'

The cup stilled in mid-air, inches from Mr Darlington's face. 'The police have been to Brian's house?'

'Yes.'

'Did they search the house as well? As far as I remember, Brian had a study in his house.'

Mr Moffatt briefly considered saying that no they hadn't, but the truth was he didn't know. He was good at concealing the truth, but he had learned with experience that Mr Darlington had a way of finding things out. He decided to come clean.

'I'm sorry, I didn't ask Arabella that.'

Mr Darlington smiled and took a sip of his coffee. He put the blue china cup back on its blue saucer. 'This might be worth asking. After all, we don't know how much material Brian stored in his home office. From what you know, do the police have any indication of Brian's role in the Longwall Street development?'

'I certainly haven't said anything. The police do seem interested in the governing body, however.'

Mr Darlington narrowed his eyes.

'Why are they interested in the governing body?'

'I had to disclose that Brian was a member and that he came to meetings. That's where we last met, in fact.'

'I see. What about Sue Pollard? Have the police interviewed her?'

'Yes. There's also the others, but not all of them know about the arrangement, obviously.'

Mr Darlington drained his cup, then stood. He clasped both hands behind his back and walked to the roaring fire. Mr Moffatt wanted to join him and stretch his hands out to the inviting warmth. But he stayed put.

Mr Darlington spoke in a soft voice, the tone of regret unmistakable. 'I was willing to help Brian as much as I could. But he wouldn't listen, would he?'

Mr Moffatt didn't say anything. It was better to listen when Mr Darlington spoke.

'We need this to go away, Richard. Can you do that?'

Mr Moffatt was afraid it would come to this. He spread his

hands, his throat turning dry, despite the coffee. 'I'm not sure what I can do.'

Mr Darlington turned his head, while the rest of his body faced the fire. The smile had slipped. His eyes were cold as ice, and they were fixed on Mr Moffatt.

'You need to think of something, Richard. There's a lot at stake, and we have to protect it. I'm counting on you.'

Mr Moffatt wasn't aware he was holding his breath. He exhaled softly, then nodded. 'I'll do my best, certainly.'

'Make sure your best is good enough.' He turned. 'That book from New Frontiers won't get published, will it?'

Mr Moffat shook his head. 'Brian gave New Frontiers the money: two hundred and fifty thousand. They didn't ask for more, and, far as I know, the book's not coming out this year.'

'At least Brian got something right. Make sure you keep track of that book. I don't want it being released by any other publisher.'

'No problem,' Mr Moffat said sincerely, and he meant it. He knew what that book contained. It would never see the light of day.

THIRTY-SEVEN

Twenty years ago

Nikki was walking back home from school. Her A levels were looming, and she was working hard to get good grades. But the situation at home was getting worse. Her parents quarrelled all the time. A lot of it had to do with her father's drinking, and the fact that he didn't want to stop. He had been for therapy, but nothing had worked. Worse, the bruises on Clarissa's face were now appearing with alarming regularity.

'Look!' Clarissa had shouted last night in the kitchen, when their father was out at the pub. Clarissa stabbed a finger at the bruise on her left eye. "See what your father did to me?'

She didn't bother hiding it any more. Nikki's heart froze, fear and shame sinking in her guts. She felt paralysed and cold. At the same time, she acknowledged the rage on her mother's face. Clarissa had a right to be furious. She flicked her eyes to the kitchen door.

Clarissa sank onto a chair. She opened the kitchen cabinet, and pulled out a bottle of gin, pouring herself a drink, then sipped from it. 'I'll drink as well now.' Her voice shook as she clamped down on her jaw. Her eyes became red-rimmed. 'I'll kill the bastard if he does that again,' she hissed in a low voice. Nikki wasn't meant to hear that, she realised. But she did. She turned from the kitchen cabinet and walked to the dining table, where Clarissa was sat, holding her head in her hands.

'Mum, you've got to tell someone. You can't live like this. We can't go on like this.'

Clarissa's head hung down, and her shoulders shook with sobs. Nikki hugged her mother.

'Don't you think I've tried? I've done everything. But he's changed. He's become a brute.'

Nikki grabbed her mother's hand. Her voice was calm and detached. 'Then maybe...' She gulped before she had the courage to speak. 'Maybe we should leave.'

Clarissa looked at her daughter. 'Leave and do what? You want to live in a horrible area the council gives us?'

Nikki stood and poured herself a glass of water. 'Then what do you want to do?'

'I don't know.'

Clarissa finished the rest of her drink. 'Just leave me alone.' She went into the living room and slammed the door shut. The TV came on. Nikki didn't bother to go in. Instead, she went upstairs. She closed the door of her room and sank on the bed. She turned the table lamp on and picked up the latest true crime book she was reading. But her mind wandered.

She thought of the little brother she never got to know, but who always remained at the back of her mind. Their little Tommy, whom they would never see again. Clarissa never spoke of him, but she could see the sadness in her eyes. Clarissa was slowly destroying herself with drink, but what could Nikki do? Speak to social services? She remembered what Clarissa had said. She didn't want to end up in a council house in the wrong part of town. Neither did they have rich grandparents, or aunts to fall back on. This was all the family she had.

Her choices were not just limited. They were non-existent.

Nikki heard a sound downstairs and came out to investigate. Someone was scratching at the door, or trying to fit a key into the lock.

'Who is it?' Nikki called out. Her eyes went to the living room; the door was ajar and the light still on.

Suddenly the door opened. Her father, Peter Gill, lumbered in, stinking of booze and cigarette smoke. Nikki stiffened and flattened herself against the wall. Peter slammed the door shut, then stood in front of her, swaying. He wiped a trail of mucus from his chin. Then he brushed past Nikki, and she closed her eyes. Dad had never touched her. The one thing she was grateful for. He seemed to take his frustrations out on her mother.

He kicked the living room door open, and went in. The door stayed open, and Nikki could hear the TV was on low volume. Her mother was in there.

'Still up, eh?' Peter's slurred voice came through. 'Not been out to see one of your bitch mates? Talk behind my back?'

'Shut up, Peter!' Clarissa screeched. She swore loudly at him. From her voice, Nikki could tell her mother was drunk, too.

'Why do you come back anyway, you layabout?'

'It's my house, in case you forgot!' Peter shouted back. He hurled abuse at her. Nikki's heart ran cold. She knew what would happen now. It was time she made herself scarce. But something made her stop. She'd been running away from this her whole life.

She heard her mother stand, and then another sound, like two bodies bumping into one another.

'Get off me,' Clarissa shouted.

Nikki heard the sounds of a struggle, and her heart rate went nuclear, a cold fear turning her heart numb.

'You stupid bitch! You couldn't even look after your own

son! Lucky I picked you up from the gutter you...' His words were lost as Clarissa screamed, and Nikki heard a crashing sound as something fell to the floor.

She turned, and went inside the room. Peter had his back to the wall, and Clarissa was trying to claw his face. Peter was a big man, and he held her off easily, and raised a hand to slap her.

'Dad, no!' Nikki shouted. Her voice broke, became a wail. 'Stop it, both of you.'

In slow motion it seemed, Peter lowered his hand. His eyes locked on Nikki. They were red-rimmed, and unfocused, but he clearly saw her. Clarissa was also frozen, her fingers slipping down from Peter's face.

Peter grunted, then shoved Clarissa away from him. She crumpled on the sofa, covering her face with her hands.

Peter swore at her again. Without looking at Nikki, he barged past her, and they heard the front door slam again.

THIRTY-EIGHT

Nikki and Nish had stopped at a café on the way back. Nish was hungry after all his running round earlier, and once the adrenaline settled, his tummy was clearly rumbling. Nikki looked on as the young man ordered an egg and bacon baguette with crisps and a bottle of Coke. She shuddered. She got the chicken Caesar salad and a fruit juice. That would be more than enough till evening. She drove on the way back, letting Nish eat.

'What did you think of Professor Blatherwick?'

'He knows more than he's letting on,' Nish said, swallowing. 'About Brian Allerton, I mean.'

'Do you think we should bring him in?'

Nish thought for a while as he drank some water. 'He's going to lawyer up, guv. Then we might get even less out of him.'

'Well, if we think he's hiding facts, then that jolt might be just what he needs. I'll read his statement again. The two men were close. I need to find out more about their early years in Oxford.'

Nikki changed tack, focusing on the matter at hand.

'What was the address on the man's stuff again?'

When Nish had grabbed the man, a wallet had fallen out. It contained an ID card and an address, with a couple of bank cards.

Nish put down his packet of crisps and reached for the evidence bag by his feet. He put on a pair of gloves and took the pamphlet out. 'It's 29 Culverwell Street, OX1 2BH. And the student ID card in his wallet says *Trevor Anthony*. Not Oxford Uni though; he's from Oxford Brookes Uni.'

Nikki nodded. The difference between the two universities was like day and night, Oxford Brookes a polytechnic that achieved university status in 1992 compared to the centuries' old history of Oxford University.

Nikki entered the postcode on the satnav. The map blinked to life, with a red dot pulsating at the location. Their car was a green dot, moving slowly. 'We're only a couple of miles away. Let's check it out.'

Nikki parked outside an alley just off the main street. The dreaming spires of the colleges were to her left, and the road ahead led to Iffley. The buildings here were all terraced houses, most of them converted into office blocks. The door at number 29 was brown, bland, and weather-beaten.

Nish rapped on the door. After a short wait, a younger man opened it. He was a skinhead, with a small brass earring in his left earlobe. He wore a tight-fitting black shirt and black trousers. His neck and shoulders were thick with muscle. He glared at Nish.

'What do you want?'

'DC Nish Bhatt.' He held up his warrant card and held it close to the skinhead's face. 'Does Trevor Anthony live here?'

'Why do you want to know?'

'So he does then,' Nish said, putting his warrant card away. 'Can I come in?'

The skinhead barred the door, folding his thick arms across his chest. 'I didn't say he lived here. Now piss off.'

Nikki stepped forward. 'Detective Inspector Nikki Gill. Mr Anthony was behaving suspiciously at a crime scene, and he was also interfering with a criminal investigation. He resisted arrest and escaped. We need to find him without delay.' She raised her eyebrows. 'Unless you'd rather come down to the station and give a statement.'

The skinhead scowled at them. 'Wait here.' He slammed the door shut.

Nish raised his eyebrows. 'What now, guv?'

'We give them five minutes, then press the bell again. If they don't answer, we return with a search warrant.'

'That will take a couple of days to be approved by the court.'

Nikki shook her head. 'We just need to scare them. Although I am surprised that his friends are like this.'

'Yes, I thought so too. But God knows what he's mixed up in.'

Nikki had barely finished speaking when the door opened again. A middle-aged man in a brown corduroy suit stood there, the skinhead behind him. 'Can I help you?' the man asked.

'We are here to look for Trevor Anthony. He ran away, resisting arrest.'

The man looked at Nish with barely disguised contempt. He smiled condescendingly. 'Not much of a police officer then, are you?'

Nish clamped down on his jaws, and Nikki decided enough was enough. 'What's your name?'

'Simon Douglas. Owner and treasurer of this company.'

The name rang a bell, and Nikki frowned. 'What company is that?'

'New Frontiers Publishing.' The man's attitude softened a little. 'Look, we don't want any trouble with the police. But our premises was searched once because we published material about a politician, who sued us and made life difficult. Hence, we don't like your lot. Nothing personal.' He glanced behind him. 'Jim here is in charge of security. Apologies if he came across a bit rough.'

Nikki's mind was darting around like a ball inside a pinball machine. This was the company that Prof Allerton had paid all the money to?

'Can we come in? We just need to speak to you about Trevor Anthony. Does he work here?'

'Yes, he does.' A shadow of concern dropped over Mr Douglas's features. 'Is he all right?'

Nikki and Nish climbed up the stairs, and Jim the skinhead shut the door behind them. They followed Mr Douglas into his office, which was at the end of a larger space with four desks. Three of the desks were occupied and two women and a woman looked at them inquisitively. Mr Douglas shut the door behind them and they took a seat opposite his desk. Nikki said, 'Mr Anthony was taking photos of an ongoing investigation and following us around. Is he a journalist?'

'Not really,' Mr Douglas dragged the word out slowly. 'We publish books, we are not a newspaper.'

'He's been present at a crime scene that we are investigating, and he also met with the victim, we think, before the victim died. So you can imagine, we need to speak to him.'

Nish said, 'And he ran away when we tried to speak to him, which doesn't look good, does it?'

Mr Douglas was looking more and more confused. 'What crime scene?'

Nikki said, 'Before I answer that, can you please tell me if Mr Trevor was covering the local crime beat?'

'Not as far as I know. As I already mentioned, we are book publishers, not a newspaper.'

Nikki considered his response. 'So it seems Mr Anthony

was acting independently, if he was hanging around a crime scene and following us.'

Impatience was written clearly across Mr Douglas's face. 'What crime scene?'

'A professor has been murdered in a college nearby.'

Mr Douglas paled. 'Professor? What college?'

'I cannot disclose details, but I do understand the victim had some dealings with you.'

The light that appeared in Mr Douglas's eyes became a fire that seemed to singe his eyebrows.

'Dealings with me?'

'Professor Brian Allerton. He paid this company £250,000, and you signed the receipt.'

Mr Douglas was turning green. Nikki felt like reaching forward and supporting his jaw as it dropped to the floor.

'Brian Allerton? Murdered?'

'Yes. I cannot tell you more. You can see where this is heading. He pays you a lot of money, then a reporter who works for you starts to not just appear at the crime scene, but take photos and follow us.'

Mr Douglas wiped his forehead with his shirt sleeve. 'Oh my god. This is unbelievable.'

Nikki gave him some time. 'Why did Prof Allerton pay you that money?'

Mr Douglas breathed heavily, then stared at Nikki. 'It was to settle a dispute.'

'What sort of dispute?'

He swallowed heavily, as if a fishbone was stuck in his throat. 'It was an out of court settlement for material he had used without consent from one of our published books. Like a piece of research.'

Nikki stared at him till Mr Douglas cleared his throat and looked away. She didn't believe him.

'Do you have proof of this plagiarism?'

'I can supply you with the relevant work, yes.'

'And what book did Prof Allerton publish that contained this plagiarised work?'

Mr Douglas breathed like a fish out of water. He wiped his forehead again.

'That, ah, I cannot remember. He didn't publish the book, we found the material before publication. Give me some time and I'll get back to you.'

'Are you sure this was the reason?'

'Yes.' Mr Douglas frowned.

'It seems like a lot of money to pay for plagiarism.'

'Not really.' Mr Douglas made a wheezing sound, then coughed into a fist. 'A professor being accused of plagiarism is a big deal. If word spreads, he'll lose a lot of face. Academics and authors are very particular about plagiarism.'

'Were lawyers involved?'

The older man's Adam's apple bobbed in his fleshy neck. 'We concluded matters before it got that far. Hence it was an out of court settlement.'

Nikki observed him for a while. Mr Douglas was clearly uncomfortable.

'Did you agree the amount he had to pay? Or was it mutual?'

'Well, it was based on the advance he could've earned if the book was published. We contacted his publisher, who are a big firm in the academic world. They had sent out marketing copies to us. That's when we saw it.'

'When you say we, who do you mean, exactly? You? One of them in the office?' Nikki hooked a thumb behind her back.

Mr Douglas tugged at the damp collar of his shirt. 'It was Trevor, actually. He noticed it. This was a large piece of research by one of our authors. Almost a third of the book. Brian claimed the research was originally his, hence it was free for him to use it. But that wasn't true.'

Nish was taking notes, and he went to say something. Nikki nodded her assent.

'Did Trevor contact Professor Allerton about this?'

'I don't know. He came to me, and I got in touch with our legal team. But the lawyers were never officially involved.'

'Do you know where Trevor Anthony is, now?'

'I can give you his home address. I have nothing to do with what he's been doing around the crime scene. It's most peculiar.'

Nikki nodded thoughtfully, not removing her eyes from a clearly squirming Mr Douglas. 'Very peculiar. I agree.'

She gave him a thin, icy smile. 'If we have more questions, we will be back.'

THIRTY-NINE

Nikki and Nish got back to the office to find Kristy at her desk.

'I found something interesting. Looks like the prof and the people we interviewed were involved in some financial dealings,' Kristy said. She came forward, a folder in her hand. She put it on Nikki's desk. The folder contained annual statement filings from Companies House. Professor Allerton had been in a company called New Street Holdings, with Richard Moffatt and Sue Pollard. Daniel Blatherwick's name was the other one she recognised.

'Look at page twenty-seven, guv. It breaks down the company ownership.'

Nikki turned to the page and whistled. 'Wow. They each owned twenty-five per cent, but if one died, or left the company, then their share would be equally divided between the other three?'

'Which means if Professor Allerton's share was up for grabs, the other four directors get it. That's more than eight per cent to each of them. How much did you say each share was worth?'

'I don't know,' Nikki said truthfully. 'But given the cost of the total investment is almost a hundred million, I would say a large amount.'

'Blimey.'

'Indeed.' Nikki settled back on her chair, reading the page. 'This gives all of them a good motive to bump off our victim.'

Her mind was churning. What were Mr Moffatt and his mates up to? She flicked through the pages of the folder again.

'Where's the DI?' she asked.

'He went to look for that woman, Miss Ishihara,' Kristy said. 'Said he wanted to go on his own.'

Nikki was reading through the Companies House filing, but she heard. Her eyes met Kristy's. 'He said that? Why?'

Kristy shrugged. 'Don't know, guv. He had some errands to run, and he would track her down while he was at it.'

It sounded weird to Nikki. She shrugged it off and returned to the papers.

'Four directors are named and we know all of them, right? You two met Daniel Blatherwick.'

'Yes, guv.' Kristy sat on her chair.

Nikki leaned her head back. 'Now we know all of them had motive. One thing about Professor Blatherwick bugs me. If he knew the victim, why did he rat on him?'

Kristy looked confused and so did Nish. Nikki said, 'He said Professor Allerton was dancing with this PhD student, right? And that he had a roving eye. He didn't have to mention that, did he?'

'But he wanted to cast the prof in a bad light,' Nish said, light dawning. 'To give someone else a motive to kill him.'

'Exactly.' Nikki smiled. 'A jealous partner, or an angry wife.' She continued, 'This Miss Ishihara will be an important person in this case. I wonder if she was the woman Prof A was dancing with in the nightclub?'

'She's not a PhD student, guv. She's a non-stipendiary post-doctoral research fellow,' Kristy reminded her.

'Which means she's finished her PhD but doesn't have a job,' Nish said. 'There must be a lot like her in Oxford.'

Kristy turned to Nish. 'Maybe that depends on what subject she studied. Possibly, for English history. Do you mean she was dependent on Professor A for a job? That's why she was sleeping with him?'

Nikki raised a hand. 'We don't know she was sleeping with him. It might've been in the cards, we don't know for sure.'

Kristy rolled her eyes. 'Come on, guv. You saw her looking up to his bedroom with sad, lovelorn eyes, right?'

'Lovelorn?' Nikki grinned. 'But I take your point. She knew him, as they worked in the same department. And it was strange the way she was lurking around in his back garden. Like she'd done it before.'

She shook her head. 'But we need to keep an open mind. Let's see what Monty comes back with.'

She looked at the papers on her desk. She picked up the bank statements again. Her eyes were drawn like a magnet to the large cash deposits in the Handelsbanken private account.

'Who on earth would give a professor handouts like these?'

The two constables stared at her in silence. Nish was the first to break it. 'Rent money? Maybe he owns lots of student digs in Oxford, and he has an agent who goes round collecting cash from them.'

'Good thinking. We assume he was an old school academic, but like any old dog, he could get up to God knows what.'

Kristy said, 'Expanding on that, guv. Dr Raman said she found cocaine in his blood sample. He had a snorting habit. What if...?'

Nikki cocked her head to the left. 'What if he was dealing as well? That's a stretch. He's got too much to lose if he's discovered to be a supplier of Class A drugs. Using it occasionally is a different thing.' She pointed a finger at Nish. 'What you said makes sense. It might not be cheap rental digs for students.

Could be another source of income.' She frowned as she stared down at her feet. The bottom of her trousers had flecks of mud on them.

'There could be a number of reasons why he was getting cash. But let's not keep guessing. We need evidence. That might come from talking to others.'

'Sue Pollard,' Kristy said. 'Now that she's named in this company, time to speak to her again?'

'Definitely. And the main man, Richard Moffatt.'

She picked up her phone and rang Monty. He answered the first time. *'Yes, guv.'*

'Where are you?'

'At the college, guv. I'm trying to track down Miss Ishihara, that woman you saw.'

'I'll see you soon, Monty,' Nikki said. 'Look for Emily Blanchard.' She hung up.

She pointed at the folders on her desk. 'Take this down to Financial Crime. And chase up the phone records from the lab. They might have something for us later today.'

FORTY

Tracy Ishihara's office was not only tiny, but she also shared it with two other post-doctoral fellows. A slim young man with a beard opened the door when Monty knocked. He introduced himself, and Nikki showed her warrant card. The room was lined with bookshelves and there were three desks. The other two people in the room looked up, and Nikki spotted Tracy at the back. She approached her table and smiled down at her.

'We meet again, Tracy,' Nikki said.

Tracy was looking at Nikki as if she had two heads. Then she frowned. 'You're the inspector I met the other day, right?'

'Yes. Is there somewhere we can talk privately?'

Nikki and Monty followed Tracy after she put on her coat and walked outside. They came out into the main quad and Tracy headed for the college grounds at the back, by the rampart walls. There was a sheltered area next to one of the buildings, with trees around them to block the cold winds. Tracy sat down on a bench, and Nikki sat next to her. Monty stood behind them. Nikki got straight to the point.

'The last time we spoke, you didn't say that you were in a relationship with Brian Allerton.'

Tracy went white as a sheet. Her lips moved, but she couldn't speak. She swallowed and looked down at her lap. Her fingers were pressing into her palms.

'You acted surprised when I said he had died, but you knew already, didn't you? That's why you came to the garden behind his quarters.'

Tracy's nostrils flared. She looked past Nikki, towards the lawn.

Nikki kept her voice soft. 'Why don't you tell me everything, Tracy? If you've done nothing wrong, there's nothing to worry about, right?'

Nikki held Tracy's eyes. Slowly, the younger woman nodded. 'That's right. I haven't done anything wrong.'

She was silent for a while, clearly gathering her thoughts. Her eyes were focused on the mid-distance. 'Yes, Brian and I were seeing each other. A lot of people knew, it wasn't exactly a secret. It had been going on for more than a year. But...' She closed her eyes and sighed. Nikki gave her some time.

'Brian was under pressure. The funding for his chair was being withdrawn.'

Nikki frowned. 'So he was about to lose his job?'

Tracy nodded. 'I'm not sure of the details. But the college had recently diverted funds from the history department to the humanities. Apparently, the college wanted to attract better-quality undergraduates into subjects like Classics. All the colleges in Oxford compete with each other for the best talent, and the governing body felt New College was losing to the others. They felt the history department was too big.'

'How long had this been going on for?' Nikki asked. Her notebook was open, and she was scribbling.

'I started in the college two years ago. Definitely from then. The restructuring was already underway. Brian had been told he would lose the chair.'

'What were his options?'

Tracy shrugged. 'He could apply for a different role in Oxford University, and he might well get it. Or he had to move to another university. I know other colleges in Oxford were interested, but he would have to have accepted an associate professorship. And work his way up again. Brian was angry. He felt the college had betrayed him.'

'Do you know how long Professor Allerton had worked at New College for?'

'Decades,' Tracy said. 'Almost twenty years, I think.'

'And what about your job? If Brian lost his, then surely your position was also untenable.'

'That's right,' Tracy said. 'My fellowship was tied to his research.'

'You published some books together, didn't you? They were published by New Frontiers Publishing.'

Tracy's shapely eyebrows met in the middle of her forehead. A curious look flitted across her features, and Nikki couldn't read it.

'How did you know about that?'

'We have our means,' Nikki said. 'Please tell me a bit more about his research.'

Tracy pressed her lips together and settled back on the bench. 'Brian's field was modern European history, specialising in England. We were looking at ways Oxford University had been funded from its inception in the twelfth century. The books we submitted for publication were based on that.'

'And what were your findings?'

Tracy folded her lower lip beneath the top one. She looked down at the ground. 'We found ancient documents in the Bodleian. The Bodleian has a large underground section. We found some records that showed a lot of traders and merchants had donated money to the monks when the colleges were being built.'

It was Nikki's turn to frown. Tracy had stopped and either was unable to carry on, or didn't want to.

'Tracy?' Nikki asked.

Tracy sighed. 'A number of these traders and merchants made their fortunes in the slave trade. It was common practice in those days. We discovered there are libraries and chapels in Oxford that were built with slave traders' money.'

Nikki rubbed her chin, thinking. 'That's nothing new though, is it? It's old history. Slave traders were rich, and they built lots of palaces and houses. Some of them even have statues, like that guy in Bristol. I can't remember the name, but the statue was taken down.'

'Yes,' Tracy said. 'The Colston statue. And although many people know of Oxford's links with the slave trade, it's never been published by a professor.'

Tracy went quiet. Monty leaned forward. Nikki looked up at him. Monty said, 'Do you think Professor Allerton was losing his job because of this research?'

Tracy shook her head. 'It certainly raised eyebrows and caused some friction, but Brian knew he was losing his job before he started the research into university finances. So no, I don't think the funding for his chair was linked to this.'

Nikki said, 'But the far-right political group found out, didn't they? The National Socialist Movement.'

Tracy rolled her eyes. 'Oh, those idiots. Yes, unfortunately they have a couple of students at the university. They're trying to set up a far-right student club, and the university's student union are resisting it.'

'We came across one of their members. His name is Trevor Anthony. Does the name ring any bells?'

Tracy frowned, deep in thought. Then she shook her head. Nikki said, 'He is about five feet ten, average build, and he wore a black-hooded top. Dark jeans and white trainers.'

The confusion cleared from Tracy's face. 'Ah yes, I

remember a man like that. He came to a couple of the seminars where Brian and I talked about his research. I didn't know his name, as anyone can attend these seminars. But I remember a man who matches that description.'

'Did this man ever follow you and Brian, or act threateningly?'

Tracy shuddered. 'Yes, I remember him staring at me. He followed me as well, and I was on the verge of contacting the police. And Brian said he had seen him outside his house and also outside the Holywell Street gates.'

'How many times did he follow you?'

'Two or three times. It was always after I finished work and walked back home. Sometimes, I stayed here with Brian.'

'Did you ever see this guy inside the college?'

'Only at the chapel a couple of times, where it's free entry. And at the seminar.'

'The day Brian died, was he giving a seminar on this research?'

Tracy nodded. Her eyes widened, and she stared at Nikki. Both women knew the thought that was circling in their minds. 'He was there,' Tracy whispered. 'I remember him clearly.'

Monty said, 'Can you remember what time you saw him?'

'The seminar ran till 5:30 p.m. It started at 4 p.m. I was next to Brian, and I saw him. He was in the second row, and he kept looking at me and smiling like a perv. He scowled. It was disgusting. Once Brian delivered his speech, it was question time. He became really agitated. He wanted to know why we were undermining British history by publishing such research.'

'Did he swear or shout?'

'He didn't swear, but he was definitely shouting. Other people in the audience would definitely remember him.'

Monty said, 'Did you watch him leave the seminar?'

Tracy shook her head. 'No. I stayed with Brian.'

Nikki narrowed her eyes. 'Please carry on.'

'I had to go and do some shopping and then was heading back to my flat. Brian's wife was coming, and they had a wine and cheese party after dinner at the Senior Common Room.' Tracy smiled, a ghostlike, ironic emotion that floated across her lips and then vanished. 'I have been to the Senior Common Room with Brian before. But not when his wife was coming, obviously.'

'So you left the college after the seminar to do shopping and then went home. Do you live with anyone who can vouch for that?'

'No,' Tracy said. Her eyes hardened, and her jaws clamped down. 'I live alone. I'm telling you the truth. I've got nothing to hide.'

Nikki kept her voice low and non-judgemental. 'You knew he was married, and his wife visited often. How did that make you feel?'

'How do you think it made me feel?' Tracy asked, her face expressionless. 'Not great. Brian didn't want to leave his wife. He said he couldn't afford a messy divorce. Even his pension would be divided, as his wife's earnings were a lot less than his.' Tracy bent her head and inspected her hands. She moved her palms slowly across her thighs, then clasped her hands together. 'But we were happy. I thought we had a future together. One day, Brian would leave his wife, despite the expensive divorce.'

'Did you know everything about Brian?' Nikki asked gently.

Tracy locked eyes with her, and Nikki saw understanding in her gaze. She inclined her head. 'Yes, I knew he was bisexual. That didn't stop us from having an honest and committed relationship. Brian didn't sleep with a man while he was with me.'

'Are you sure about that?'

Tracy's jaw hardened, and her nostrils flared. 'Yes. I love Brian. And I know he loved me, too.'

Nikki wrote something down in her notebook. She lifted up the cover, so Tracy couldn't see. She was trying to organise her thoughts. Tracy didn't have an alibi, and she could easily have gone into Brian's room after the seminar and killed him. However, so could Trevor Anthony. There would be witnesses from the seminar, Nikki realised. This was a real breakthrough. But it didn't mean Tracy was off the hook.

She took out a card and so did Monty. They gave them to Tracy, who accepted them without a word. 'Please give us a call,' Nikki said. 'Anything you remember could be very useful for us.'

Sadness flashed across Tracy's face. 'Yes, I will. To be honest, I'll help in any way I can to find the bastard who did this to Brian.'

FORTY-ONE

Monty was driving towards a Iffley, taking the scenic back route. The sun was out, shining on the river as it snaked beside the road. The tide was up, and Nikki watched a couple of rowers bending their backs against the current.

Sue Pollard lived in a detached house that wasn't far from the river. The road sloped upwards, leaving Iffley Lock down below. The lock was critical to the functioning of the canals. It was from Iffley Lock that the Oxford regatta used to start, back in the 1800s. The tree-lined road had a church at the end, its steeple rising high in the air. Houses on the hill close to the river were not cheap, Nikki knew.

'Nice place,' Monty commented as he shut off the engine.

'She can't afford this on her department lecturer's salary,' Nikki said. 'Maybe it's her partner's money.'

Monty locked the car, and they walked up the drive and knocked on the door. Footsteps approached, and there was a wait as someone looked through the peephole. The door cautiously opened, and Sue Pollard peeked through.

'Yes?'

'We met yesterday,' Nikki said, holding up her warrant card. 'This is my colleague, Detective Inspector Monty Sen.'

Sue opened the door further and looked at them inquisitively. Her hair had more flecks of white, and Nikki wondered if she dyed it. Her round-rimmed glasses were missing, and Nikki thought maybe she was wearing contacts.

'What can I help you with, inspector?' Sue asked.

'Can we please come in? It's about the matter we spoke of to you. Professor Allerton's death.'

'I believe I told you everything I know.'

'There are things that have recently come to light, and we need to ask you about them. May I?' Nikki stepped forward. The reluctance on Sue's face was clear, but she stepped aside.

They walked into the wide reception area, the hardwood floor creaking under their feet. The place was rustic, done up in a farmhouse style. The wooden beams on the ceiling were not painted. Horseshoes hung from the walls, with a few framed portraits of horses.

'This way please,' Sue said, leading the way to an open-plan kitchen and diner. A large set of doors at the back opened out into a long garden. Sue was cooking, and there was a nice smell in the kitchen. A pot bubbled on the hob, and there was a humming sound from the oven.

'Sorry to bother you,' Nikki said, 'but this couldn't wait any longer.' Sue's blue eyes focused on Nikki's face, searching. She kept her expression blank.

'Shall we sit down?' Nikki asked.

They sat down near the door, on one of the large wrap-around sofas. Nikki took out a notebook. 'When we last met, you knew that Brian was going to lose his chair, didn't you?'

Sue swallowed, then briefly licked her lower lip. Her hesitation was the answer Nikki was looking for. Sue nodded. 'Yes, I did. It wasn't anything new, after all, it had been discussed for the last couple of years. We were giving Brian time to find an alternative, and suitable, job.'

'Why didn't you tell us?'

'Because it didn't come up in our conversation. You asked me if I knew him well, and the answer was not really.'

'While the seminar was going on, you were at the college?'

'This again, I've told you this already. Yes I was, but then I returned home.'

'What time did you leave the college, and when did you get back home?'

'I left the college about 6 p.m., and I can't remember checking the time when I got back home. Normally with traffic it takes about half an hour.' Sue fixed Nikki with a stare, then shifted her attention to Monty, before glancing back at Nikki. 'Is this what you wanted to talk about? We've been through this already.'

'I just want to check,' Nikki said. 'And you said your partner wasn't home that evening.'

'No, he was away on a business trip. He still is, by the way.'

Nikki nodded. She tapped her pen on the open page of the notebook. 'Professor Allerton was a director in a company called New Street Holdings. Have you heard of it?'

Sue went very still. Her face lost colour as she stared at Nikki. Nikki hooked one eyebrow north. 'Have you?' she repeated.

Sue appeared to be fumbling for an answer. She opened and shut her mouth a couple of times, then cleared her throat. 'It was a company that was set up to manage our investment in a student accommodation venture. I believe Brian was one of the directors, yes.' She spread her hands. 'What does this have to do with his death?'

'It's the fact that if one director left the company, his shares would be equally divided between the other directors. One of those directors was you. Is that correct?'

Sue's face was rapidly turning white as a sheet. 'I'm not sure I know about this. I need to ask my accountant.'

'Well, we have looked at the company particulars. I can assure you that this is correct. Are you saying you didn't know about this rule?'

'I'm afraid I cannot deny nor confirm it,' Sue said.

Nikki smiled. Sue was clever. She just gave a no comment answer, but dressed in a different language.

'You stood to benefit handsomely from Brian's death, didn't you? The building project would come to almost a hundred million, and its value would be more than that. Perhaps a lot more. Is that not correct?'

Sue's mouth hung open. 'Are you—'

Nikki raised a hand. 'No. I'm not accusing you of anything. True, you don't have an alibi for when Professor Allerton was murdered. However, we checked the CCTV at the college's car park. You drive a cream-coloured Volkswagen, don't you?'

'Yes,' Sue said.

'CCTV showed the car leaving the college at 6:10 p.m. So, we have proof that you did leave the college at that time.'

Sue looked visibly relieved.

'Do you know why New Street Holdings was formed? As we understand it, it is unusual for academics to have such a large investment in a college project.'

'I'm afraid I cannot discuss that,' Sue said.

'Any reason why?' Nikki asked.

'It is a confidential matter. I am not sure where you got this information from, in any case.'

'We have our sources.' A thin smile played on Nikki's lips. 'I know you can ask for a court order to verify the evidence, but I can assure you, we have the correct documents.'

Sue clamped down on her jaws. 'I have told you where I was the day Brian was murdered. I came home, and you have proof of that on CCTV.'

Yes, Nikki thought to herself. But we don't know if you went back, leaving your car here.

There was a stony look on Sue's face, her blue eyes focused and sharp. 'I won't say anything more to you without a lawyer present, Inspector Gill.'

FORTY-TWO

'Back to the nick, guv?' Monty asked as they got into the car.

Nikki was preoccupied with Sue Pollard's statement. She narrowed her eyes, thinking about what she'd just heard.

'Guv?' Monty asked again.

Nikki startled. 'Sorry, I was miles away.'

'Back to base, or somewhere else?'

Nikki's phone chirped. It was her personal phone. She had a missed call from Rita and another number that she knew very well. It was in Oxford, and she didn't want to call it back. She held the phone, the usual dark memories emerging from the chasm in her soul. She was also aware Monty was waiting on an answer. She shook her head, hoping that movement would pull her out of the funk. She had too much on her mind.

'No,' she said quietly. The corner of her thumb rubbed against her lower lip. 'Let's see if Daniel Blatherwick is at the college, or at home. I want to see him.'

'Shall I track him down now?'

'Yes. Nish and Kristy are at the nick, right?'

'Yes, guv.'

Nikki got out of the car and called Rita. She answered on

the first ring. Nikki's heart lifted with sunshine when she heard her daughter's voice.

'Hello, Mummy.'

'Hi, darling. Back from school?'

'Yes. Just sitting down to homework. How are you?'

'Fine, just busy with work. Have you eaten?'

'Yes. Mum? Can I come this weekend?'

Nikki considered. She was duty SIO this weekend, which meant she could get called out. That didn't mean Rita couldn't come. However, she wouldn't be able to give her her full attention, and she would be tired. Also, in an ideal world, she wanted to sort out the cottage. Give it a lick of paint, sort out the damp patches in her bedroom.

'This is your weekend with Daddy, love. I'll tell you what. Why don't you come down the week after, on a weekday. I can drive you back if you like.'

'Kind of difficult that, with school work and everything.'

'OK. Then do Friday after school? Then we can have a long weekend together.'

'Hmm. OK, that works.'

There was silence for a while, and she knew what Rita was thinking. Nikki spoke before her daughter could.

'See you next Friday then, darling. And if you really want to come this weekend, just come down. I might be busy, that's the only problem.'

'OK, Mummy.'

Nikki hung up, then clutched the phone tightly in her hand, like she was afraid to let it go. Monty came out of the car.

'Guv?'

Nikki sighed and turned to him.

'Professor Blatherwick's secretary says he's at the college now and in between tutorials. I can't get hold of him on the phone though. Shall we head down? It's on our way back anyway.'

Nikki agreed. The evening rush was building on the roads. Iffley was quiet, but the main roads were packed.

Nikki rang the professor twice, but both times it went to voicemail. She rang base and spoke to Kristy.

'Financial crime haven't sent a report yet, guv. I will chase them again,' Kristy said.

'Did you speak to the accountant of New Street Holdings?'

'They're not picking up. The financial guys will try as well. But I did get through to New Frontiers Publishing. Arranged a meeting with their boss for tomorrow.'

'Well done. Anything from the tech lab about the phone?'

'Not as yet. I rang them an hour ago, and they're still trying to turn it on. It's been at the bottom of the Cherwell for the last two days.'

'Yes. I hope they can make it work. Any sight of Trevor Anthony?'

'Nish is with Traffic, they're looking at CCTV footage along the river where he jumped on the boat.'

'OK. I want to speak to Professor Blatherwick, then we'll meet you at the nick by 7 p.m.'

Nikki hung up. Traffic had built up steadily, and Monty put the siren on to get past the gridlock. They managed to get to Christ Church before six in the evening.

'Back again?' The portly security guard at the porter's lodge smiled at Nikki.

'We like to keep busy.' Nikki waved at him as she and Monty walked past. They hurried through the majestic quad, heading to the right, where Nish and Kristy had seen Professor Blatherwick before. They went up the steps and crossed the landing to the covered archway that led inside the building. As Nikki was about to enter, a woman came running from the other side, crashing into her. Nikki fell backward, losing her balance. She slammed into Monty, who was only saved by the wall.

Nikki's chest hurt and breath exploded from her lungs. The woman looked at her with huge, wild eyes, her mouth open in shock. It was Emily Blanchard. Nikki straightened herself and caught Emily by the shoulders. Emily was in shock, her lips quivering, unable to speak.

'Emily! What's happened?'

Nikki had to repeat herself twice before Emily blinked and focused on her. She gasped, then pointed behind her. Doors stretched at regular intervals, office rooms for the teaching staff at the college.

'I saw... I just saw... blood...' Emily panted, and her whole body shook.

'Emily!' Nikki raised her voice. 'Look at me. Here!'

The terrified woman turned her saucer eyes to Nikki. 'Dead. I think he's dead.'

'Who?'

'Daniel. Professor Blatherwick.'

Monty had run ahead of her and opened the door to the professor's office. Nikki, close on his heels, caught her breath at the sight.

Daniel Blatherwick was sprawled on the floor, face down. Blood seeped out from his body, darkening the carpet. Monty put gloves on and knelt by his body. He felt in the neck, then shook his head.

'No pulse.'

FORTY-THREE

Emily was sitting on the edge of the raised landing that wrapped around the massive quad. Uniformed police guarded every entry into the college, including the chapel to their right. A red blanket was wrapped around Emily's shoulders. An ambulance stood in the quad, a curious and ugly anomaly in the stately surroundings. A gurney was lowered from the ambulance, and the paramedics discussed between themselves how to bring the body down.

Nikki brought a steaming cup of coffee that she'd just purchased from one of the cafés opposite the college. The huge doors of the main entrance were firmly shut now, and although the chapel service was on, no one but the college staff and students were allowed in.

'Drink,' Nikki said.

Emily took the coffee cup without saying a word, then stared at the ground. Nikki reached out and guided the cup towards Emily's face.

'Drink. It will make you feel better.'

The young woman looked at Nikki with vacant eyes that drifted to the cup. She took a sip, then grimaced.

Nikki sat down next to her. Evening shadows were lengthening across the quad like long, dark needles. The towers and turrets of Christ Church were darkening, a chill settling from the sky. Nikki noted with approval that Emily was drinking.

'I know you don't want to talk. But it's best if you do it now, while it's still fresh in your mind. Not easy, but actually, better than having to do it later. We can take you back home, or to the police station if you wish.'

Emily shook her head. 'No. I'd rather stay here. Or maybe outside.'

'Outside is the station or your home.'

Emily flicked her eyes at Nikki. 'I don't want you there.'

Nikki shrugged. 'Fine.'

Emily screwed her eyes shut. 'Sorry. That came out the wrong way.'

'No problem.' Nikki knew people reacted to shock in irrational ways. 'Take your time.'

'To be honest, I'm not sure where I want to be right now.'

'That's understandable. As you knew Professor Blatherwick, we will keep a squad car outside your home tonight.'

'Thank you.' Emily's eyes were bright liquid pools of light. She was grateful.

'You'll be fine.' Nikki gave her an encouraging smile. 'What did you do after I saw you this morning?'

'I was busy with my own work, and then getting ready for the tutorials.'

'Did you see Professor Blatherwick in between?'

'Yes, I did. He was at the Senior Common Room for lunch.'

'Did he seem all right then? Not worried, or scared?'

'No. He wasn't there for long. Said he had to meet someone after lunch.'

'Who?'

'He didn't say. But I could tell it was important. He had lunch quickly and left.'

'What time was this?'

'About 1:30 p.m., I'd say. Half an hour later I went to the library, and I remember seeing the time there. I worked there for a while, then came to the tutorial.'

'Did you see the professor again?'

Emily shook her head. 'No. He was meant to be in his office, but when I came back, it was locked.'

'Hmm.' Nikki narrowed her eyes. 'So he met someone and then left? Maybe he went to meet someone outside the college?'

'Maybe. Or the meeting was over quickly. I didn't see him, in any case.'

Nikki wrote down the times in her notebook. 'What happened after your tutorials?'

'I took a break. I didn't go to his office. I got a coffee and came back. When I opened the door to his office, I saw...' Her gaze drifted down to the ground. She put her cup down.

'What time was that?'

Emily shook her head.

Nikki asked, 'What time did you finish your tutorials?'

'Not long. It was almost 6 p.m. by the time I was all done.'

'You did tutorials from 2 p.m. till 6 p.m.?'

Emily glanced at Nikki. 'No. I didn't start the tutorials till about 4 p.m. I had two booked, and they lasted longer than I thought they would.'

'From 1:30 p.m. till 6 p.m., you didn't know where the professor was?'

'Yes.'

Nikki pressed the tip of her pen against the open page of her notebook. The students could provide an alibi for Emily. She was first on the scene, and despite her shock, which seemed genuine, she was also the obvious suspect.

'How well did you know Professor Blatherwick?'

Emily stiffened her shoulders for a second, then relaxed. She sighed. 'He was my PhD supervisor, obviously. So, I knew him reasonably well. He wasn't married, but had a partner. No children.'

'I'm just wondering why you told him that you saw Professor Allerton dancing at the club with Tracy Ishihara. I mean the woman you saw him with.'

'What do you mean?'

'He said you saw them. Which means you told him. Why? It's not the kind of thing that a student raises with her teacher, if you know what I mean.'

Flecks of colour touched Emily's neck, then moved up to her cheeks. Nikki had suspected as much.

'Were you more than friends?'

Emily kept her eyes on her hands, clutched tightly together on her lap. She didn't reply. The tip of her nose turned bright red.

'Your reaction to the murder suggests you knew the victim very well. And the fact that you confided intimate secrets to him. The two professors were friends when younger, but recently their relations were not that good, right?'

Emily nodded. Then she looked up at Nikki. Tears rolled down her cheeks, and she brushed them away with her sleeve.

'Yes, we were more than friends. And you are right about his friendship with Brian. I didn't know Brian well, but he talked about him sometimes.'

'What did he say?'

'Nothing specific. I met him at a seminar, and Daniel introduced me. He said later they used to be friends, but he had gone off the rails recently. He was in trouble with his college.'

'New College, I take it. What sort of trouble?'

'Daniel didn't explain. I saw Brian with that girl shortly after that. I had heard the rumours about him earlier anyway. They did the rounds.'

'Hmm. Hope you don't mind me asking this. Any rumours about Daniel?'

Emily looked up sharply. She frowned. 'No. He had a part-ner, a woman with whom I think it was almost over. He wasn't like Brian, if that's what you mean.'

'Do you know his partner's name?'

'Emma Dunstan.'

Nikki wrote the name down. 'Does she live in Oxford?'

'No. Not sure where she lives. Daniel lived in Kingham, not far from here.'

'Have you been to his house?'

Emily sighed. 'A couple of times. It was in between when Emma was there, which I didn't like. Daniel had an apartment in St Giles. That's where he often stayed during the week, and where we met up.'

There was a commotion behind them. The paramedics were wheeling the gurney down the archway to the stone landing that wrapped around the quad. Emily and Nikki rose to make way for them. They watched as the paramedics took the gurney down the steps, Monty helping them. The zipped-up black bodybag was held in place by rubber straps.

'Come on,' Nikki said, pulling lightly on Emily's arm. 'Let's get you back home.'

FORTY-FOUR

Nikki was about to leave, when she saw the petite and prim figure of Dr Sheila Raman stride into the quad, clutching her briefcase. At least, it looked like her. She was walking in from the direction of the porter's lodge, and the huge expanse of the quad, with the darkening skies, meant Nikki had to strain her eyes.

'You're becoming rather busy these days,' Dr Raman remarked as she came face to face with Nikki. Her eyes slid to the paramedics, who were locking up the back door. One of them waved at her, and she waved back.

'I'd rather be at home with my feet up.' Nikki grinned. 'Emily here found the body.' She indicated Emily Blanchard, who was standing next to her.

Nikki beckoned Monty over. 'Please arrange for Emily to get back home and have a squad car parked outside her house. The car should stay there till tomorrow morning, at least.'

'Thank you,' Emily said.

Nikki gave her shoulder a squeeze, and she walked away with Monty.

Dr Raman and Nikki went up the flagstone steps onto the

broad landing, and crossed it to enter the arched balcony. A white tent was being erected outside Professor Blatherwick's office. Hetty Barfield hadn't arrived as yet, and one of the crime scene technicians Nikki had never seen before nodded at her, and she returned his greeting. They put on shoe coverings and gloves, then entered the crime scene. Professor Blatherwick wasn't a tall man. Less than six feet, Nikki guessed. He was lying face down, in a pool of blood. It seeped out from under him, creating a macabre crimson halo around his head and neck. The cream-coloured carpet was already turning black.

Dr Raman tiptoed across the body to the other side. She knelt and took his pulse, then inspected the body. Nikki stood behind the pathologist. She could see the deep gashes around the neck, and she suspected more lay in the chest region. The professor was wearing a navy-blue suit, and the jacket was darkened with blood. She helped Dr Raman turn the body over. The wounds looked similar to the first victim's. They were jagged, rough marks. Dr Raman pointed to the upper angle of the neck.

'Seems our killer is getting better. The lower part of the neck is protected by the strong sternocleidomastoid muscle. But the upper triangle of the neck is more vulnerable. The carotid vein and artery pass through here. Both of them have been perforated.'

She pointed to the rips in the jacket and shirt. 'More stab wounds, and these were made with considerable force. The blows have gone clean through the ribs. There must be damage to the supraclavicular arteries, and the top of the lungs. I won't know more detail until I take him down to the morgue.'

'Same MO,' Nikki said quietly.

'Yes,' Dr Raman agreed. She stood and crossed the body to the other side. She raised a hand and brought it down in an arc.

'The killer swung from behind and got him in the neck region first. The trajectory of the blows suggests the prof was sitting down at the time. The knife was pointing down, and that's why the lungs were also damaged. Then he must have turned, and the killer stabbed up like this.' Dr Raman pushed a fist up in the air, like a boxer doing an uppercut.

'Sitting down?' Nikki frowned. She looked at the large desk, and the armchair behind it. There were three chairs opposite the desk, and a wooden glass cabinet to the right. The body lay near the cabinet, on the floor.

Dr Raman followed Nikki's line of vision. 'Yes. I think he was stabbed from the back, then staggered over here and collapsed.'

Nikki went round the desk, noting the blood marks on the floor. She hoped the blood splatter expert would be coming soon, but then realised in Oxford, she would have to do with Hetty Barfield.

Behind the chair, the curtains were drawn. Drops of blood had fallen on the armchair handles. They glistened as dark marks on the black leather. Nikki had to peer closely to notice them. The papers on the desk were strewn around. Quite clearly, the professor had staggered to his feet, and he'd made a mess of the table. An open laptop was pushed to one side, and a pair of glasses lay on the floor. They had been trampled on. Nikki left everything as it was and knelt down. Drops of blood were present on the carpet, smudged by the victim's feet. She straightened and examined the curtains. They were made of heavy, embroidered drapery, and hung from ceiling to the floor. She parted the curtains with one finger and peeked through. The window was closed. There was no lock on the sash window, and she noted it could be opened from outside. The garden outside was the place where she had interviewed Emily Blanchard in the morning. To the left, in the middle, she could see the circular green area with potted plants. It was a secluded place, and it was empty. Nikki noticed the high walls at the rear of the garden, and the windows of the buildings on either side inside the compound that looked into the garden. To her right, lay the warden's building, and to the left the dean's accommodation. She frowned. Clearly, the killer had come in through this window. Before he left he shut the window and then drew the curtains.

Had anyone seen the killer coming through the back garden?

Dr Raman said, 'I'm almost done here.'

'What's the time of death, doc?'

The pathologist pursed her lips together. Her short black hair shone in the yellow light from above, and her dark eyes glinted.

'Hardly any rigor mortis in the body. Temperature is close to ambient. And you can see a lot of the blood is fresh. Death happened a few hours ago. Between two to four hours, I'd say. I need to do more measurements in the morgue to be precise.'

'It's now 6:30 p.m.' Nikki glanced at her watch. 'So he died between 2:30 p.m. and 4:30 p.m.?'

'About right, I'd say.'

Nikki left Dr Raman to her work and went outside. The chapel service was ongoing, and it was faintly ridiculous, with the sound of the choir singing filtering out, while a white forensic tent was being constructed just a few yards away. Nikki went down the stone steps and crossed the quad, to the porter's lodge. A uniformed sergeant was chatting to one of the burly porters. He tipped his hat to Nikki.

'Guv. Everything OK?'

'Yes, thank you.' Nikki turned her attention to the porter. 'Does anyone live in the accommodation that faces the back garden of the professor's office?'

'You mean the dean's quarters, and the warden's chambers?'

'Yes.'

The porter scratched his head. 'The dean lives there, but he is away giving a talk in Yorkshire. His family have gone with him. I don't know if anyone would have been inside the warden's chambers.'

'Who is the Warden?'

'Jeremy Pollard,' the porter said.

Nikki frowned. 'Is he related to Sue Pollard?'

The porter looked surprised. 'Yes, they are married.'

Nikki hid her astonishment the best she could. While she hadn't asked Sue Pollard specifically about her husband, she would have expected Sue to give her that information voluntarily.

'Do you have a list of people who came and went today?'

'Yes, unless they have one of the back door passes at St Giles.'

'Christ Church has a back door at St Giles?'

The porter managed a wry smile. 'Yes, one that we know of. Five years ago we found the basement underneath the chapel led to a tunnel that opened out near the River Cherwell. Honestly,' he added, looking at the surprised expression on Nikki's face.

'OK,' Nikki said. 'I need a list of everyone who came in and out from Christ Church today. If you have any visitors to the victim, can I please see them?'

She went inside the porter's lodge and looked at the signatures on the page.

The porter shook his head. 'Sorry, ma'am. No one came to see the professor today.'

Nikki tapped a finger against her lips. 'That's not true. I know for a fact he left the Senior Common Room at 1:30 to see someone.'

'He might have,' the porter said. 'But that visitor didn't come through here.'

FORTY-FIVE

Nikki put the window down as she drove back home to Kidlington. The night air was frigid, and it didn't have the invigorating effect she had hoped it might. Her hands shook as she put the windows up and put the heating on full blast. Traffic was less now, thankfully. To be honest, even at peak times the traffic in Oxford was nothing compared to what she was used to in south London. She was stopped at a traffic light when she heard her personal phone beep. She glanced at it, and her heart froze. She didn't recognise the number, and she stared at the message

I know what happened to Tommy

A car honked behind her. The lights had gone green. Nikki touched the accelerator and crossed the four-way intersection. She pulled over as soon as she could. The screen stared back at her, the meaning of the letters reaching deep into her heart, clawing and scratching. She put the phone down and looked ahead. Then to her sides and all around her. Her fingers hovered over the keyboard, then pressed.

Who are you?

She waited a beat, and the reply came. *A friend.*

How do you know Tommy?

I can only tell you when I see you.

Nikki wasn't about to meet a stranger who sent weird messages. She replied:

How did you get my number?

As she expected, there was no response this time. But the question gnawed at the corners of her mind. This was her personal number. One she didn't hand out easily. She could count on her fingers the people who had this number. However, she did give it to switchboard. In over twenty years in the police force, switchboard had never leaked her number. An operator who did that would be easily discovered, the call traced and they would lose their jobs. No, this leak didn't come from switchboard.

From where?

The stranger didn't respond further. Nikki started to drive, the drumbeat of her heart raking up disturbing memories.

Now she also knew she had to go and see her mother. She had put it off for long enough, which was funny, because her mother was one of the reasons for her return to Oxford. She picked up her phone, and sent her a text to say she would be coming tonight.

FORTY-SIX

Twenty years ago

It was a hot day, and the sun's rays were stinging. It hadn't rained for more than a week, and England was basking in glorious weather. Nikki had spent the day by the river in Iffley, where the River Cherwell was broad. Unlike many, she stayed in the shade, thereby avoiding sunstroke. It was past dinnertime when she waved goodbye to her friends and packed her bags. She was slightly woozy from the Pimm's she had drunk.

Shadows were lengthening as she walked back home, but the sun still glared at her with an evil eye. She had been drinking because she wanted to forget the dire situation at home.

It was a Friday, and next Monday, Nikki was finally leaving home. She was off to study Forensics at Bristol University. She was looking forward to it, eager to leave the mess of her family life. She would miss her parents, even if they had failed to give her and Tommy a safe, secure home.

It left her with an incomplete, frustrated feeling that gnawed at the corners of her soul. She felt angry, and yet desperately sad. She wanted her mother to be happy, and her father to get help. She knew neither would happen. Nikki kept to the shade, stumbling as she walked back home. She wanted to crash on her bed and not think about dinner. Clarissa might be out with friends, or drunk at home. She hadn't seen her dad for a couple of days either. No one knew where he was, and frankly, no one cared.

Nikki remembered the days when she was little, and her dad had been different. She didn't know what happened, what had caused his transformation into a drunken bully who gambled and lost all his money. She didn't want to think about it. She wanted to leave this toxic life and make a new one for herself.

As she turned the corner and into the street, she stopped short. The flashing blue lights of a police car were visible, and an ambulance was parked in front of her house. Nikki increased the pace, her throat suddenly dry. The front door of her house was open, and a policeman was standing outside. He came forward and spoke to her gently.

'I'm afraid there's been an incident in your house. Your mother called 911.'

Her mother? She thought Clarissa had been out with friends. Obviously not. 'What's happened?' Nikki asked breathlessly.

She started to move towards the door, and Sergeant Thacker followed her.

'Your father fell down the stairs and, unfortunately, he has passed away. He sustained severe trauma to his head and neck. By the time the ambulance crew arrived, he had stopped breathing. He was pronounced dead at the scene.'

Nikki was inside the house, but she whirled round to stare Sergeant Thacker in the face. Her jaw was on the floor, and her pulse surged in her ears. The policeman came forward and gently guided her inside the living room and onto the sofa.

Nikki's brain was a blur, and she didn't know what she was thinking, or feeling. Through hazy eyes, she saw her mother in the armchair. For once, Clarissa was sober. She was sitting straight in the armchair, her spine rigid. Her eyes were red-rimmed from crying. Her neck moved a fraction, and she registered Nikki. Mother and daughter stared at each other for a few seconds, then Clarissa's face crumpled. She bowed her head and tears rolled down her cheeks. A black weight was lodged in Nikki's throat, not letting her breathe. She shuffled close to her mother and cradled Clarissa's body against hers.

'What happened, Mum?'

Clarissa spoke through her tears. 'I came home. I opened the door and found him slumped on the landing. He wasn't moving. I tried to rouse him, but he wouldn't budge. That's when I called the police.'

A man and woman, both wearing suits, came into the living room. The man introduced himself as Inspector Cromwell, and Nikki's suspicions were confirmed. They sat down opposite Nikki and Clarissa.

'When did you come into the house?' Inspector Cromwell asked Clarissa.

'About one hour ago,' Clarissa said, sniffing loudly.

Nikki gave her a tissue, and Clarissa dabbed at her nose.

Inspector Cromwell asked, 'Was your husband at the house when you left?'

Clarissa shook her head. 'No. No one was in the house when I left.'

'So, you didn't know where your husband was?'

Inspector Cromwell and his assistant exchanged a glance as the pause deepened. Nikki felt obliged to answer on her mother's behalf.

'My dad was at work.'

Inspector Cromwell turned his attention to her. He gave her a brief smile. 'Your father is unemployed. The social service records show that. He had a history of drunken and disorderly behaviour and also of domestic abuse.'

Breath caught in Nikki's chest as she felt Clarissa stiffen as well.

Inspector Cromwell said, 'Mrs Gill, will you please come to the station to give a statement?'

'Why can't you take a statement here?' Nikki asked. 'She's been through enough, can't you see that?'

Inspector Cromwell softened, and he nodded. 'OK. Please answer as clearly as you can. When was the last time you saw your husband alive?'

Clarissa was gripping Nikki's hand. She said, 'Yesterday. At dinner time. After dinner, he went out.'

'Do you know where he went?'

Clarissa shook her head. 'No.'

'Did he come back?'

Clarissa's grip on Nikki's hand was getting tighter. Nikki rubbed her mother's hand, trying to reassure her. Clarissa said, 'I don't think so.'

'You didn't see him this morning?' Inspector Cromwell asked.

'No, I didn't. Like I said, I left to do some shopping and then I came back.'

Inspector Cromwell looked at Nikki. 'Where were you?'

'I was out with my friends. By the river. I didn't see my father today either, by the way.'

Inspector Cromwell stared at Nikki thoughtfully, then at Clarissa. Then he stood. 'If we need to ask any questions, we can either come back, or ask you to come to the station.'

'Does anyone else live in the house?'

'No.'

Inspector Cromwell stared at both of them for a while, then smiled. 'Thank you.'

. . .

Matters got worse over the next couple of weeks. Clarissa wasn't arrested, but she had to attend the station several times to explain where she had been and about the state of her marriage. Nikki had to delay going to university. She went with her mother to the police station, and demanded to be present at every interview. They had a solicitor, as well.

Although the police didn't say it, Nikki knew Clarissa was suspected of her father's death.

Nikki watched policemen knocking on their neighbours' doors and asking questions. She knew they were trying to verify Clarissa's alibi and her whereabouts. In the end, there was nothing to indicate it had been any more than an accident. Mr Gill had slipped at the top of the stairs, then fallen down in a drunken state and broken his neck. His blood tests showed high levels of alcohol, and also diazepam.

FORTY-SEVEN

Jericho was the nicest place to live in Oxford. It was also dull and quiet, particularly when Nikki was growing up. Now, she noticed with approval, there was a cinema hall showing the kind of highbrow, arty films the dons would love, and a smattering of chic food halls and cafés. A far cry from the two dreary pubs and supermarket when she was younger.

She had parked her car at Christ Church College and then walked, because nothing in Oxford was very far from the nexus of colleges in the main square. It was pleasant to walk, despite the cold. She needed to clear her mind, in order to deal with what lay before her.

She turned into the street of old two-storey, Victorian terraced houses. There was only one house with weeds overgrowing the front lawn, flies buzzing from rotten food left out of the waste bin. She stopped in front of it, crinkling her nose at the smell. The timber frame of the windows had damp, and one window had a panel missing, replaced by a wooden panel. Bricks were crumbling everywhere, and patches of damp were spreading below the windows.

Nikki steeled herself, but the battle continued inside.

Visions like jagged shards of glass perforated her composure. She made her hands into fists, fighting the hollow ache gripping her heart.

Maybe this had been a mistake. But she had to do it. This visit was long overdue, and now that she was here, she might as well finish it.

She opened the rickety, rusty gate. It screeched noisily. Nikki averted her eyes from the overgrown front lawn – it was small, but still a total mess. The green door had remained the same, but paint peeled from it now, and the wood frame was rotting. She took a deep breath, then knocked. She had to knock louder, three times, before she heard a human voice. It was high-pitched and female.

'Who is it?'

Footsteps shuffled closer then stopped. The voice called again, louder and gruffer. 'Who is it?'

'Nikki. Mum, it's me.' She raised her voice, making sure her mother heard.

There was silence the other side. Then a chain rattled, and after a while, the door opened.

A silver-haired woman with a small, wizened face stood there. Her hair was thin at the top, but fell in waves to her shoulders. Her eyes were glassy and unfocused. She wore a long dress that had food stains, and a baggy jumper with cigarette burns. She stepped closer, peering at Nikki, and the stench of alcohol wafted over.

Nikki fought the impulse to step back. Sorrow fought against rage and frustration in her soul, leaving barren, scorched earth. It had been like that for a while now.

The woman smiled, revealing yellow teeth. 'Nikki, it is you. Come in.'

Nikki clamped her jaw tight and stepped inside, shutting the door behind her. The small hallway opened into a lounge that looked like a cyclone had ripped through it. Books were piled on the floor, along with magazines, CDs and DVDs. Clarissa had become a hoarder, and endless amounts of bowls, lanterns, small statues and paintings were arranged haphazardly. It was hard to walk without hitting something. A silent TV stood opposite the sofa, which housed a Monty cat with green eyes. Empty bottles of rum lay strewn on the floor, and white packets of Marlboro Lights. Cigarette smoke hung in the air like a cloud.

Nikki remained standing as Clarissa sat down, simply because there was nowhere to sit. The two armchairs had a ton of crap on them.

'You need to open the windows, Mum.' She put her handbag down and threaded her way to the sash window that faced the front lawn.

'No, leave it,' Clarissa screeched. Her voice was now coarse with cigarette smoke and age.

It was freezing cold inside, in any case. Nikki walked to the far wall and checked the thermostat. She turned the heating on. Down the hallway into the kitchen was a similar mess. The cat had followed her and jumped on the kitchen counter. It began to sniff an open packet of ham. Nikki liked cats, and she thought this one was cute, but it had clearly developed bad habits. She shooed her off the counter, and she jumped off reluctantly. She mewled and rubbed herself against Nikki's leg.

Nikki opened the cabinet doors and found a bowl. She opened the fridge and opened a milk bottle that didn't smell like it had gone off. She gave the cat the bowl and it started to slurp noisily, indicating it was hungry. Nikki felt a pang of guilt. She rummaged around in the cabinets till she found a carton of cat food. She gave it to her, and the cat blinked its green eyes at her, then purred loudly.

Nikki walked to the garden door and peered out. If it was a mess inside, this was a jungle. She shook her head and checked the lock. It was open. She locked it, then walked past the cat who was happily eating.

She stood in front of the sorry wreck Clarissa had become. 'How are you, Mum?'

Clarissa peered at her like she was seeing her daughter for the first time. She shrugged. 'You got a job in Oxford now, right?'

'Yes, I have.'

'Hmm. Your father would've been pleased.'

His ghost still clung to the grime-stained walls of this near-derelict home. His baleful eyes still watched her mother, sliding into an abyss of no return.

Nikki blinked away the awful memories. Nights spent listening to her parents fighting. The alcohol-fuelled rages her father went into, capable of destroying—

Her mother's voice broke into her waking nightmare.

'Why did you come here?'

Nikki scrutinised her mother. 'Have you not been texting me non-stop this afternoon?'

'Was I?' Clarissa upturned her lips. 'Can't remember much these days, sorry.'

It was BS, and Nikki knew it. For years, her mother had blamed alcohol, and now dementia. She didn't have dementia, and Nikki suspected she could easily cut out the booze if she wanted to. But she wouldn't. Even while her father was alive, she had started drinking. It was an attempt to numb the pain of Tommy's loss, but it never worked.

'No time for your poor mother.'

Nikki took out her phone and read from the screen.

'I'll be dead soon and you'll be sorry.'

Nikki looked at Clarissa, who avoided her eyes. 'You don't remember?'

Nikki moved some books from one armchair and perched

on the edge. 'Why don't you get some help, Mum? I mean, this is crazy. Why do you have to live like this?'

After a few seconds, Clarissa turned to Nikki. Her vision sharpened, and for a moment, a new light shone in her eyes. She blinked and the mask returned. Her chin sank down to her chest.

Nikki felt the despair again. For years, she had tried to rescue Clarissa from this hell. She suspected her mother had suffered at her father's hand more than she could ever imagine.

'Mum, did you hear what I said?'

Clarissa reached behind her and a small flask appeared in her hands. She unscrewed the top and took a long swig. Nikki got to her feet. She leaned forward, grabbed the flask and pulled. Clarissa resisted, but Nikki was stronger. Her face was flushed red, and Clarissa was coughing and spluttering by the time she had wrenched the flask out of Clarissa's hand.

Nikki stood, her lips trembling, a black weight pressing at the back of her throat.

'Stop it now,' she said, hating it when her voice broke. 'No more.'

Clarissa glared at her, wiping her lips with a dirty sleeve. 'And what would you know, eh? Miss High and Mighty Detective Inspector. You left as soon as you could and...'

Nikki stood there, her chest heaving. She blinked back tears. 'And what? Carry on.'

Clarissa shook her head. 'You're just like him. You act just like he did.'

Nikki frowned, a lethal cocktail of hurt and anger swirling in her veins. She wasn't aware she was shouting, but she was.

'I'm nothing like him! You know that!'

'No, I don't!' Clarissa shouted back, then succumbed to a fit of coughing. She bent double at the waist. Nikki sank to her knees and rubbed her back, but Clarissa flung her arms away.

She straightened, and the older woman's lined cheeks were wet with tears.

'Leave me alone. Why did you come back?'

Nikki trembled, her heart in pieces. She wiped her cheeks, but more futile saline drops budded in the corner of her eyes.

'I'm nothing like him, Mum. As for why I came back...'

She ran out of words. Clarissa knew anyway. Nikki had come back for her. For the new job, yes, but more so for some closure. For a sense of guilt that ate away at her insides, shrivelling her soul.

Clarissa wasn't allowed to keep both of her children due to her alcohol and drug addiction, even after treatment. She had relapsed in the past, and Tommy was considered too vulnerable. Clarissa had never fully opened up, but Nikki had read her social services file. When Tommy was a baby, a neighbour saw how thin he'd become and alerted the services. They found Clarissa passed out in the bedroom, and Tommy scavenging in the rubbish bins for food. No one knew who Tommy's father was. He had vanished leaving Clarissa a single mother, and a drug addict, when the social services got involved with Tommy.

Clarissa got Tommy back a year later, but she relapsed again, and Tommy was neglected. This time, social services kept Tommy away from her.

Shortly thereafter, Clarissa cleaned herself up in rehab. She met Nikki's father and seemed to turn over a new leaf. After Nikki was born, the family moved out of the area. But Tommy was still deemed too vulnerable for Clarissa to look after and Nikki was already on the social services watch list. Clarissa knew if she could remain sober, hold down a job and pay rent, and look after her little girl, sh'd get Tommy back. But that day never came. Clarissa hardly played any role in Tommy's short and tragic life.

· · ·

Memories of Tommy filled the room, seeping between the peeling wallpaper, pouring out from the discarded bottles of gin. His presence would never fade, and neither would the rot that had claimed Clarissa's life.

Clarissa knew, and hence she wouldn't look Nikki in the eye. Sadly, Clarissa shook her head. Her voice was a desultory whisper.

'Just go, Nikki.' She raised a hand without glancing at her daughter. 'I'll be all right.' She leaned back on the sofa. 'You can't change anything.' She appeared to be speaking to herself.

'It's not about that,' Nikki said, her eyes downcast. 'You must let it go.'

Clarissa looked at her then; a long, haunting stare that hollowed out her eyes, darkened her soul with grief.

'I wish you'd talk to me,' Nikki said, a heaviness engulfing her heart. She sat back down on the armchair. The cat walked over. It sat down at Nikki's feet and nudged its head on her slacks. Nikki stroked her absent-mindedly. 'I miss Tommy as well,' she whispered, almost to herself. She knew Clarissa was looking at her. 'I was young, but I remember.'

Clarissa's eyes flickered away, then she nodded. Nikki sat in silence for a while.

Perhaps it was a mistake to come back. Her mother was right, the past was immutable. It was too late to change anything.

FORTY-EIGHT

Nikki woke up feeling groggy. She stumbled down the stairs to put the kettle on, then back up to the bathroom. Her eyes were puffy and she had fallen into a dreamless, dark sleep that had lasted till now. It was six thirty in the morning and freezing cold. She turned the heating on as she brushed her teeth. In an hour's time, she was driving down to the station. Her commute was super-short, less than ten minutes, even with traffic. She was grateful for the little things that went her way.

Nish and Kristy were already at their desks when she pushed the office door open. She greeted them and eyed Monty's empty desk.

'Where is he?' she asked.

Both the detective constables shrugged. 'No idea, guv,' Nish said.

'Anybody want coffee?'

'I'll get it for you, guv,' Kristy said, standing. 'Nish has something to show you.'

'Thank you,' Nikki smiled, walking over to Nish's desk. Nish opened a folder and pulled out a stack of papers.

'Call list, guv, from Professor Allerton's phone. The lab sent them over this morning.'

'Excellent. Have you been through them?'

'Kristy and I were doing just that. The text messages have also arrived. Think you might find these interesting.' Nish gave her another set of papers, several parts of which were underlined.

Nikki sat down and read through the text messages that Kristy and Nish had highlighted.

'These are quite threatening, aren't they?' she said, glancing up.

You will die a horrible death. Traitor to the cause.

'Do we know whose phone number it is?'

'Yes,' Nish said, stretching his arms out. 'Trevor Anthony.'

'Interesting,' Nikki said. 'Any sight of him yet?'

'He wasn't at his student accommodation in Oxford Brookes yesterday. Two uniformed constables went out there. University staff are now aware to give us a call as soon as they see him.'

'Good. He's a suspect now. Not only was he threatening him, but he was also at the seminar, being abusive, just before his death.'

The door opened and Monty came in. He looked flustered. 'Sorry to be late, guv,' he said. 'Got caught in a parent–teacher interview.'

'No problem,' Nikki said. She pointed at the papers. 'We started without you.'

There was a knock on the door, and Justina leaned in. 'Traffic just asked me to contact you, guv,' she told Nikki. 'They've got the CCTV footage around Christ Church, if you want to have a look.'

'Excellent,' Nikki said. 'Can you please ask them to email it to me? I'll have a look right now.'

Justina nodded and left. Kristy came back with four cups

perched precariously on a tray with two plates of biscuits. Nikki opened the door for her and helped set the tray on the table.

'Chocolate bourbons, my favourite.' She winked at Kristy. 'Unfortunately, I can only have one. The rest are for you lot.'

'You can have more than one,' Kristy said.

Nikki shook her head ruefully. 'When you get to my age, things are different.' She sipped her coffee and opened up her laptop. The emails from Traffic had arrived. She opened one, clicked on the largest video file and hit Play. The porter's lodge faced the main street, which was busy. Nikki watched people going in and out of the college for a while. They were mostly tourists with their cameras and backpacks. The staff car park was at the rear and it opened up into Christ Church Meadow, the huge expanse of land where deer and cattle roamed. Nikki looked at the time stamp and focused her attention on the cars that came in after 1:30 p.m. She saw a chauffeur-driven black Bentley with the number plate DAR1 slide into the car park at 1:45.

The man who got out was tall, slim and clean-shaven. He had grey hair that flopped over his forehead, and he wore round-rimmed glasses that looked old-fashioned. But he was no more than early fifties, she guessed. She copied the car's registration number and posted it on the DVLA website. It was registered to an estate in the Cotswolds and belonged to a Mr Darlington.

A quick search on the internet told her exactly how rich and powerful Mr Darlington was. The family estate went back for generations, and Mr Darlington's father had been the owner and chief editor of a national newspaper. His son looked after the media and real estate business and was an up-and-coming councillor for greater Oxfordshire. He was also one of the patrons of both New College and Christ Church. He had graduated from New College, and had a master's in Law from Christ Church before he had left to train as a solicitor in London.

Nikki went back to the email attachments and found the file that showed the CCTV footage inside the quad. At 2 p.m., she saw the tall figure of Mr Darlington walking down the quad. He stopped near Professor Blatherwick's office, went inside the arched walkway, and was lost from sight. She speeded up the tape. At 3 p.m., Mr Darlington was visible again, walking down the quad, in the reverse direction. At 3:08 p.m., he got back into the Bentley, and it drove away.

Nikki sat back in her chair, thinking. The visitor Emily Blanchard had mentioned had to be Mr Darlington.

Was he also the killer?

FORTY-NINE

The conference inside Oxford County Hall was in full swing. Nikki and Kristy jogged up the steps. In the reception area there was a big sign that said:

KEEP OXFORD GREEN – SAY NO TO PROPOSED NEW BUILDS.
CHAIRED BY TARQUIN SMYTH DARLINGTON COUNCILLOR, CONSERVATIVE

There was a crowd milling around, but most people had already gone inside. The sound of clapping and loud cheering came as the speaker said something the crowd liked. Nikki pushed her way in through the double doors and then pulled open a door that led into the auditorium. The tall, sprightly figure dressed in a light-grey suit at the podium looked similar to the man she had seen on CCTV. He addressed the audience gathered around him, who were listening with avid interest.

'Our rivers are getting polluted by new developments. Marine life is getting caught in plastic waste and dying. Fifty years ago the River Cherwell had crystal-clear waters, now it is as muddy and opaque as the Thames in London. How can we reverse that?' Mr Darlington held up a hand and pinched his thumb and forefinger together. 'Just a drop, that's all it takes. One drop of mercury from a factory can kill an entire shoal of fish. Our ecosystems are being destroyed by new developments, and we cannot sit by and watch it happen.'

There was thunderous applause.

'So, I ask you,' Mr Darlington said, raising his voice, 'if the developers won't listen to us, if the factory owners and industry leaders can lobby the government, and if the government turns a blind eye and deaf ears, then who will take the message to them?'

After a significant pause, he answered his own question. He pointed to the public, and swept his hand up and down and sideways. 'You will. That's why we live in a democracy. You, I, we, us. We will rise to this challenge, which is a generational problem that we need to resolve now, and not let our children's future be affected by degrading the environment they will hand over to their children.'

There was a standing ovation. Nikki had to give it to the man. He knew how to play the crowd and exactly what to say. She found it ironic that the Darlington family had such extensive real estate businesses themselves. She had looked online; a couple of their companies bought land for new developments and sold it to the highest bidder. She wondered if the wildly applauding public knew about that.

A woman in a charcoal business suit got up on the podium. Mr Darlington stood to one side. The woman worked for the council as well, and her name badge said JANE ASHTON, ADMINSTRATOR.

'Thank you, Mr Darlington, for helping us protect our environment. If you have any questions for Mr Darlington, please form an orderly queue to the right side of the podium.' Miss Ashton pointed. 'The rest of you are welcome to leave, and please email us your questions and we will be happy to answer them.'

Nikki nudged Kristy, and they made their way through the crowd towards the podium. Mr Darlington had come down from his lectern and was sitting at a table on the floor. There was a queue of people waiting to speak to him. Nikki strode up to them. Miss Ashton saw them first and turned an inquisitive eye at the warrant card that Nikki displayed. Her face fell.

'Could you please ask Mr Darlington to come to one side? We have some important questions to ask him about a recent homicide.'

Jane Ashton blinked, then started a reply. 'As you can see, he's busy. Can this wait?'

'No, it cannot.'

The woman cleared her throat. 'Well, it's just that—'

Nikki didn't have time to waste. She smiled at Miss Ashton, then stepped towards Mr Darlington, who was speaking to a man.

He turned and looked down at Nikki.

'Mr Darlington?' Nikki flashed her warrant card. 'Can I please speak to you about Professors Blatherwick and Allerton?'

The mild and easy smile that rested on Mr Darlington's thin lips faltered slightly, then recovered. His features remained congenial. He spoke to the man in front of him. 'Would you please excuse me for five minutes?'

He turned to Nikki and extended an arm, bowing slightly. 'This way please, inspector.'

They walked past Miss Ashton, who looked mortified. Mr Darlington raised a hand to reassure her and hooked a thumb towards the waiting crowd. Miss Ashton got the drift and scurried forward to speak to the people waiting in the queue.

They went round the podium to the back, which faced a set of stairs descending to the backstage area. Mr Darlington stared at Nikki, the easy smile wider now.

'Yes, of course I know Professor Allerton and Professor Blatherwick. May I know what this is about?'

'I'm afraid they're both dead. Professor Allerton died two days ago, and Professor Blatherwick died last night.'

Mr Darlington's Botox-smooth forehead crinkled, and his jaw went lax. 'My goodness me. I didn't know that.'

Nikki didn't believe him for a second. It was a good act, and to the untrained eye, it might look genuine.

Mr Darlington continued to shake his head. 'I really cannot believe this. Are you sure this actually happened?'

'I've seen their bodies with my own eyes, Mr Darlington.'

His face had become pale, and he looked agitated. He coughed into a fist. 'Do you mind if we sit down?'

Nikki nodded, and they pulled up a couple of chairs.

'When did you last see Professor Blatherwick?' Nikki asked, after she flipped open the black notebook. She watched Mr Darlington's face closely. It remained blank, but he blinked a couple of times, taking his time to answer.

'That's what I'm so shocked about,' Mr Darlington said. 'I saw him yesterday. I can't believe this.' His eyes drifted down to the floor.

'At what time did you see him?'

'Sometime in the afternoon. Maybe after 2 p.m.?'

Nikki nodded. 'What did you talk about?'

'Oh, I wanted to start a scholarship for PhD students who studied Organic Chemistry. My mother was a chemist, and she studied at Oxford. She wanted to leave something for the students in her will. I knew Professor Blatherwick, or Daniel, as I called him, from his days at New College, when he was on the governing body.' Mr Darlington frowned and seemed to lose his train of thought. 'Anyway, that's what I came to see him about.'

Nikki asked, 'What were you doing in New College when he was a governing body member there?'

'I graduated from New College. I remained a member of

the alumni board, and I am sometimes called to interview new students.'

'You got to know the professor while you were a student, or later?'

'Later, when I returned as a member of the alumni board.'

'Did you know Professor Allerton as well?'

The skin around Mr Darlington's eyes contracted. 'Is that relevant to this discussion?'

'Yes it is, as both of them died within two days, and knew each other quite well. Could you please answer the question?'

Mr Darlington gave Nikki a patronising smile she didn't like and spoke slowly, like he was explaining to a child. 'My question about relevance centred on the fact that I know a lot of academics in Oxford. Why is it important whether I knew Professor Allerton?'

Nikki stared him down and, eventually, he answered. 'Yes I did. After all, I studied History and Classics for my undergrad degree, hence I was taught by him.'

'Where were you on Wednesday, the fifteenth of November between 4 p.m. and 7 p.m.?'

His jaw relaxed, and his eyebrows rose a touch. 'Why?'

'Again, please answer the question.'

Mr Darlington ground his jaws together. 'Miss Gill, I must say I am rather perplexed by your questioning. Is there a reason for this?'

'It's Detective Inspector Gill, actually.' Nikki smiled. 'And the reason is simple. Professor Allerton died during those hours. Hence we need to know your whereabouts at that time.'

'Am I a suspect?'

'Not yet, no. Answering the question would help to eliminate you as one, however.'

They held eyes for a few seconds. Mr Darlington didn't look away. 'I was at the home office, as it happens. My wife and staff at home can confirm that.'

'Thank you. Did you know Professor Allerton well?'

'Not particularly. He was my teacher when I was younger, but I didn't have much contact with him recently.'

'When was the last time you spoke to him?'

Mr Darlington pressed his lips together and looked down at the floor, thinking. He shook his head slowly. 'To be honest, I can't recall. A few months ago, when I was at New College for an alumni board meeting.'

'I see.' Nikki cleared her throat. 'Regarding your meeting with Professor Blatherwick, when did you leave? And where did you meet, by the way?'

'We met in his office. I left just after 3 p.m., I believe. I had to be at the station to catch a train down to London. I just came back this morning.'

'Did he seem scared, or worried about anything?'

Mr Darlington paused for a few seconds, his eyes moving from Nikki to Kristy, who was standing behind. He shook his head slowly. 'No, he was his normal self. Could you please tell me what happened?'

'I'm afraid I cannot comment on an ongoing investigation. Is there anyone who can vouch for your movements after you left Professor Blatherwick's office?'

Mr Darlington's eyebrows lowered. 'What do you mean?'

'I mean an alibi, Mr Darlington.'

The corners of his eyes crinkled. 'I'm not sure what you're trying to get at, Inspector Gill. Do I need a lawyer?'

Nikki shrugged. 'You always have the right to a solicitor. Is that what you'd like to do?'

Mr Darlington stared at her, his spine stiff, his jaw set rigid. 'I have nothing to hide, Inspector Gill. After I left Professor Blatherwick, my driver took me to the station, and I boarded the 3:35 to Paddington, London.'

He looked up and behind Nikki. Kristy shifted, and Jane

Ashton arrived. She glared at Nikki, then blinked at Mr Darlington, who rose to his feet.

'I am afraid we are out of time, Inspector Gill. If you wish to speak to me again, please make an appointment with my secretary.'

FIFTY

The uniformed constable standing guard outside Professor Blatherwick's apartment in St Giles nodded at Nikki and Monty and held out a clipboard. They signed their names and went inside. The Victorian block faced St John's College.

The ground floor housed a school of English language, and a dentist's chambers. The buildings were large, and, in the eighteenth century, had accommodated entire families. The tradition had continued, but the living quarters were now smaller, designed to be two-bedroom apartments for professors and administrators of the university.

On the second floor, they went through a series of doorways, till they came to a corridor with apartments at regular intervals. They had to sign their names once again before they entered Professor Blatherwick's apartment. A white Tyvek-coated figure was kneeling on the floor in the hallway. The forensic officer looked up at them and smiled. Nikki greeted him and walked carefully across, stepping on the planks that had already been laid.

Hetty Barfield, wearing oversized forensic goggles and her sterile outfit, turned as Nikki entered the room. She held a couple of books in her gloved hands and carefully put them back on the shelf. The living room was large, with tall Georgian windows looking out at St Giles. The road outside was busy with traffic and pedestrians. The painting of an unknown, but well-dressed man was on the wall above the ornate fireplace. Bookcases lined the walls, and opposite the set of sofas there was a widescreen TV. 'Not bad for an academic, eh?' Hetty said, lowering her mask.

'Not bad at all,' Nikki agreed. 'What have you found?'

'It's still early days,' Hetty said. 'We started off in the hallway and living room. Not done the two bedrooms as yet. There is a master bedroom and a smaller guest one. Feel free to have a look, as long as you don't touch anything.'

Hetty grinned, and Nikki smiled back. 'If I do touch anything, I'll put it in a specimen bag, don't worry.'

The kitchen lay next to the living room. It was good-sized, but the presence of a large dining table made it look smaller. There were plates in the sink and the kitchen had been used recently. She opened the drawers and had a look. Apart from the usual pantry items, and cups and plates, she found nothing. The master bedroom was opposite the bathroom, and she went into the bathroom first, followed by Monty. She found two toothbrushes, a woman's make-up bag, and shaving kit. They were inside the mirrored cabinet above the sink. She looked at the bath tub and at the corners of the sink. She knew Hetty would take DNA swabs from everywhere.

Monty had already stepped inside the bedroom, and she followed him. Like every other room in the apartment, it had high ceilings, with ornate mouldings in the corners. The place had been well maintained, at the university's expense. She wondered if the professors had to pay for this, or got it courtesy of their jobs.

She asked Monty, who shook his head. 'Last year we investigated a burglary at one of these apartments. It wasn't here, it was at St Aldate's. It was an associate professor's apartment. She rented from the university at a reduced rate, which came off her salary. She wasn't allowed to buy it though.'

Nikki nodded. That made sense, if it was the university's property. 'This must belong to Christ Church College, right?'

Monty nodded. 'The colleges own most of the properties in Oxford, guv. Not to mention the land.'

Nikki knew that already. Money from the properties, and from renting out the land to developers, was a good source of income for Oxford University. The king-size bed had been recently slept in. With a gloved hand, she lifted the duvet. The bed sheets were rumpled. There was a study table next to the bed, with a table lamp. There was a laptop on it, and papers arranged neatly to one side. There was a dresser, and Nikki opened both doors.

It was mostly men's clothing, a few suits, shirts and trousers. Three pairs of black shoes and a couple of running trainers lay at the bottom. She parted the clothes and found two women's dresses. They were a size eight, which fitted Emily Blanchard's size. She took photos of the dresses, intending to check with Emily to make sure they belonged to her. If they didn't, it meant the professor was seeing someone else.

'No phone here, guv. Only the laptop,' Monty said. He had opened the drawers of the study desk and had also looked under the bed. 'There's a suitcase in there,' he said. He pulled it out and raised a small cloud of dust when he opened it. There were a couple of photo albums and some old books inside the suit-case. The chemistry textbooks were expected, but the old photos looked interesting.

Nikki looked at a faded photo where a young Daniel Blath-erwick held hands with a woman, and another couple stood next to them. They were in a city, by the river. Nikki leaned closer, finding the other couple's features familiar. Especially the woman. Then she realised. It was Arabella Allerton and her

husband, the recently deceased Brian. She flicked through the
other photos. Brian and Daniel were drinking at a bar, and
someone had taken the photo. The Allertons and Blatherwicks
seemed to have gone on holidays together.

'Take the laptop and everything in that suitcase,' Nikki said.
She went out into the hallway and entered the smaller guest
bedroom. This had a double bed that didn't look slept in. There
was a mirrored wardrobe, and a table lamp on a bedside table.
The room looked unused. Nikki crouched under the bed and
had a look, but didn't see anything.

She came out and went to the living room, where Hetty was
kneeling on the floor, using a hand-held brush on the carpet.
Nikki told her what she had found.

'I'm going to take the photo albums and laptop back with
me. Hope that's OK.'

'No problem,' Hetty said. 'If I find anything here, I'll let you
know.'

The wind had picked up outside and it blew a gust of gnarled
leaves across the pavement. Nikki tightened the coat around her
waist.

Monty said, 'Where to now, guv?'

'Let's check out his place in Kingham. You've got the
address, right?'

Monty nodded, and they walked the short distance to the
black BMW. The drive to Kingham took almost forty-five
minutes. Nikki used the time to call Dr Raman.

'Any news, doc?'

Sheila Raman sounded upbeat.

'I do actually. We found metal fragments in his neck. It's all
iron, and some of it is rusty. The chemical composition is iden-
tical to what we found on Professor Allerton's body. We put it

through our mass spectrometer machine. This type of iron was used in old knives. Some of them are still around as antiques, and I daresay many Oxford colleges still keep them.'

'So we are sticking to the theory that an old knife was used?'

'Not only that,' Dr Raman said, 'I wouldn't be surprised if the same weapon was used in both murders.'

FIFTY-ONE

Kingham was a charming Cotswolds village. The main street had cobblestoned pavements and lots of small boutique shops. Modern chains like Boots and Starbucks had also landed, somewhat spoiling the village's originality, but once Nikki looked away from them, it was all local businesses. Narrow alleys led into courtyards and roads ran down the hill to green fields that undulated to the horizon. White sheep dotted the green hills, grazing in flocks. Most of the Cotswolds was built on these hills, and since ancient times, sheep farming and wool had built the region's fortunes.

Monty drove along the main street, going up and down the slopes, till he came to a wider street with a row of semi-detached residential houses. He stopped outside a thatched house, which looked like it was plucked out of a fairy tale. The roofs were low and the windows had blue shutters on them. There was a front garden with sunflowers and daisies that had run wild, and the grass was overgrown. It still looked very pretty. Nikki went up and knocked on the door.

The woman who opened it was tall and well past middle age. She had numerous crow's feet around the eyes, and the skin folds of her neck had sagged. Her brown eyes were without mascara, and they were red-rimmed. She had a tired expression on her face.

'You must be the police,' she said. She opened the door wider, without asking for their ID. 'Please come in.'

They sat down in the kitchen that opened out to the garden at the back. The garden rolled down towards the hills, and from the kitchen they had a spectacular view of the countryside.

'Please sit.'

'You must be Emma Dunstan,' Nikki said. She showed her warrant card, and so did Monty.

The woman nodded, and they took their seats.

'I'm very sorry about your loss. Were you here yesterday?'

'Yes,' the woman nodded. 'I work at Oxford University Press, in Jericho. But half the time I work from home.'

'So you were here the whole of yesterday?'

Emma nodded. Her brown hair had silvery streaks in it. She tucked a couple of loose strands behind her left ear. 'I went out shopping, to buy some groceries. I'm sure people will remember me in town.'

'Thank you. How well did you know the neighbours?'

'Quite well. A couple of them are families, and some are retired folk. In fact, Jacqueline, who lives opposite, can vouch for me as well. I spoke to her in the morning, and she came round for a cup of tea in the evening.' Emma looked down at her hands. 'I didn't feel like being alone last night.'

'Of course not. I can understand.' Nikki gave her a minute.

The tip of Emma's nose reddened, and she pulled out a piece of tissue and wiped the corners of her eyes.

Monty cleared his throat. 'How long have you lived here for?'

'On and off, for about five years. Our relationship wasn't going well. We had decided to bring it to an end, and I was going to move out. My mother lives in Cowley, and I was going to move in with her for a few months till I found a place of my own. It would make the commute for my job much easier.'

'Did you and Professor Blatherwick have any arguments recently?'

She shook her head. 'I knew about Daniel's life. He was sleeping with that woman, half his age.' Her jaw hardened a fraction, and her lips quivered for a few seconds, but she didn't speak.

Nikki asked, 'Which woman do you mean?'

Emma's eyes locked with Nikki's. The ghost of a smile flicked at the edges of her lips. 'Was there more than one? I only know about Emily.'

'How did you find out about her?'

'I saw them in a café in Oxford one day. I had seen her at Christ Church College a couple of times, hovering around his office. I knew something was up, but watching them hold hands on a table was kind of a giveaway.' She swallowed, then exhaled slowly. 'Daniel wasn't even trying to hide it.'

'Did you decide to break up with him after you found out about his affair with Emily?'

'No. We had lost the spark, you know? We tried to get it back, but it wouldn't work. He was always busy with work, anyway. He was hardly here.'

'Did you know much about his work?'

'In the college, you mean? Yes, I went there occasionally as his partner for the dinners and seminars. He also used to be on the governing body at New College, and I visited him there, too.'

'Do you remember anyone from New College?' Nikki asked, interested.

'Yes, he was friends with Brian Allerton, I remember him. He's died as well recently, hasn't he?'

Her eyes flicked from Nikki to Monty. A look of alarm

creased her face, and she frowned. 'Do you think the deaths are related?'

'We don't know,' Nikki said. 'But we are looking into it. I'm afraid I cannot say any more than that.'

'I understand.' Emma nodded.

Nikki prompted her. 'You were saying about his friends at New College?'

'Oh yes.' Emma wiped the tip of her nose, then put the tissue in her pocket. 'Brian he knew quite well. He also knew Richard Moffatt, the bursar, and that other woman.'

Emma frowned as she tried to remember. Nikki helped her. 'Sue Pollard?'

A funny gleam came into Emma's eyes. 'Yes. That's her name.'

'What about her?' Nikki asked, leaning forward.

'I didn't like her. She was quite arrogant. She was a senior member of the governing body, and seemed to know everyone's business. She seemed to have this hold on both Brian and Daniel. They listened to her, but I could tell neither of them liked her.'

'Did Professor Blatherwick ever say he didn't like Sue Pollard?'

Emma nodded. 'All the time, in fact. He called her a bitch, because she interfered with everything. She had contacts at the university Council, which means she had powerful friends. Her husband was also the warden of Christ Church College.'

'Jeremy Pollard?' Nikki ventured. She had heard the name from the guard at the porter's lodge.

'Yes. He spends a lot of time away, but he will see him every now and then. Husband and wife are cut from the same cloth. Speak the Queen's English, you know?' She raised her eyebrows.

Nikki smiled. 'Surely there's a lot like that in Oxford?'

'Oh yes.' Emma swiped a hand in the air. 'A lot of Oxonians

are a bit up themselves, I'm afraid. But Sue Pollard had power. Not sure where she got it from. Her and Richard Moffatt were always whispering about something. I've heard they make a lot of money from the college.'

'How so?'

Emma shrugged. 'I'm not sure. You'll have to ask them.'

'Who told you they make a lot of money?'

'Daniel did. He mentioned it a couple of times. Called them greedy pigs.'

There was silence for a while. Monty shifted in his seat and looked at Nikki, as if he was ready to draw the interview to a conclusion.

Nikki reached inside her pocket and took out her phone. She had taken pictures of the old photos she found in Professor Blatherwick's suitcase. She showed them to Emma, who looked at the screen with a confused expression. As she examined them, the knot of tension on her forehead cleared.

'That's Daniel, isn't it?'

'Yes. Do you recognise the others?'

Emma looked at the screen for a while, then her eyes widened. 'Yes. That's Brian, to his left.'

FIFTY-TWO

They were back at the office in Kidlington station, and Nikki slumped into her chair with a sigh. She put her feet up on the stool next to her chair.

Nish walked over to her and placed a folder on the desk. Nikki opened her eyes. 'What's that?'

'The rest of Trevor Anthony's phone texts. Many of them are to Professor Allerton. Worth looking at.'

Nikki put her feet down and reached for the folder. Nish had underlined the messages of interest.

You're a traitor.

Immigrants are our enemies. But the worst enemies are those who betray our own people. That's what you are.

Nikki looked through the rest of the hateful messages. Then she looked up at Nish. 'What's this all about again? That research Professor Allerton was about to publish about slave traders' money funding some of the libraries and chapels at the university?'

Nish nodded. 'It made him a target.'

Nikki thought for a while, her mind wandering back to her conversation with Tracy Ishihara. 'Did Trevor Anthony follow the prof back to his quarters after the seminar? Did we find any witnesses?'

Kristy spoke from her desk. 'We asked around in New College, guv. No one has come forward as yet.'

'And what about Tracy herself? She went back to her apartment after the seminar finished. She doesn't have an alibi, right?'

Kristy's face brightened. 'Actually, no, she does.' She opened up her laptop, and her fingers flew over the keyboard. She pulled up a CCTV image and turned the laptop around so Nikki could watch. Kristy pressed Play, and the film showed people moving in and out of New College's main gate.

Kristy said, 'There she is.'

She pointed at the screen, and Tracy was visible, walking out the gates. Kristy paused the film, and the timestamp read 5:35 p.m.

Nikki asked, 'Could she have come back after she left? Did anyone see her go shopping and then go back home?'

Kristy and Nish looked at each other, then shook their heads. 'No idea,' Kristy said. 'However, the professor's phone does have some texts. They came from Tracy's phone, and were sent late on the night of the murder.'

Nikki went back to the folder Nish had just placed on her desk. She flicked through the pages till she found the texts. Tracy had asked the professor to call her, at 10:30 p.m. She had also wished him good night at 11:15.

Nikki tapped the table with a finger. 'I can't see why she would send these texts if she knew he was dead. Unless, of course, she was trying to mislead us.'

Nish said, 'She seemed quite scared when we met her, guv.

Do you think she's capable of murdering someone and then covering her tracks?'

'No.' Nikki frowned. 'She doesn't seem the type. But then again, who does?' She folded her arms behind her head and leaned back into the armchair. 'What interests me are the publications she did with the professor. Surely she became a target for the right-wing loonies as well, right?'

'Probably,' Nish said. 'We're still waiting to hear back from New Frontiers Publishing. We have also put in a freedom of information request to get all the research Tracy did with the professor.'

'Good idea.' Nikki smiled. She lapsed into her thoughts again. 'This whole thing about Prof Allerton getting kicked out of New College. The decision was taken before he published the slave trader studies, right?'

'Yes,' Kristy said. 'Do you think he did the research on the slave traders, knowing it would be controversial and put the college and university in a bad light?'

Nikki blinked at Kristy, surprised. 'Now, I never thought of that. If he did so, would that give someone in the college a motive to kill him?' Her question hung in the air. Nikki spoke slowly. 'I doubt it. Unless...' She narrowed her eyes. Her thoughts were taking shape, but it was still a vague outline.

'Unless what, guv?' Nish asked.

'What moves the world around? What oils all wheels?' Nikki asked.

Nish grinned. He lifted up his right hand and rubbed his thumb against two fingers. 'Money.'

'Exactly. I wonder if the university could be asked to make financial reparations as a result of slave traders' money funding parts of the college? That might be worth thinking about.'

'But who in the college would murder him for that? They're a bunch of academics,' Kristy said.

'They might be,' Nikki said, her head bent, eyes fixed on the threadbare carpet. 'But they are also cunning. Look at how much money the governing body members in New College stand to make from the property development.' She looked up at the constables, her eyes shining. 'We already know Sue Pollard and Richard Moffatt were due a windfall if Prof Allerton died.'

'And Daniel Blatherwick as well,' Kristy reminded her. 'But now he's dead.'

Nikki nodded. 'Therefore, his share will now also go to Sue Pollard and Richard Moffatt. If you ask me, those two will make a mint from the murder of the two professors.'

Nish said, 'Were they angry with Prof Allerton for his research into the slave traders? That gives them more of a motive.'

'What do we know of Richard Moffatt's whereabouts the day of the murders? And Sue Pollard's, for that matter.'

Nish opened up his notebook, and so did Kristy. Both DCs flicked through the pages. Kristy was the first to speak.

'Monty and you interviewed Sue Pollard the day after the murder. She had organised the seminar, remember? But she wasn't there. She was at a tutorial, and we confirmed it with the student. He's called Brad Williams, a master's history student at the university.'

'Well, that puts her out of the picture,' Nikki mused. 'What about Richard Moffatt?'

'He was at the office,' Nish said. 'He did see the professor before the seminar. That's from his statement. Around 2 p.m., they met at his office. We verified that with Mr Moffatt's secretary.'

Nikki narrowed her eyes again. 'That's funny. I'm pretty sure when I interviewed him he said he hadn't seen the professor for a month. They last met at a governing body meeting, he told me. I didn't know they met a few hours before his murder.'

The door suddenly flew open, and Monty rushed inside.

His chest was heaving, and his face was red. 'Tracy Ishihara just called 999. There's a group of hooligans outside her house and they're trying to break in.'

FIFTY-THREE

Tracy lived in a narrow street close to Cowley. It was over the bridge from Magdalen College and just outside the main university quarter. The street was run-down, with small terraced houses packed together. A police car had parked on the kerb at the entrance of the street, and the road was packed. Cars honked as they tried to get in and out of the street, causing traffic to build up. A group of men waved placards about. They read:

TRAITORS TO THE CAUSE. IMMIGRANTS OUT.

Nikki and Monty walked up to the uniform sergeants managing the crowd.

'How long have they been here for?' Nikki shouted above the chanting.

'We don't know,' the sergeant shouted back. 'The woman called us an hour ago. Her house is number thirty-four.'

Monty had already moved ahead, and Nikki followed. As she walked through the crowd, she kept her eyes open for Trevor Anthony. There was another gaggle of protesters outside

number 34. Several of the neighbours had come out and were
talking to the police who formed a ring around the rabble-
rousing group. More placards waved in the air.

Monty held up his warrant card to a tall uniformed
sergeant who seemed to be in charge. He spoke to his men, and
they squeezed in through the gates. They knocked on the door,
and after a while, a frightened-looking Tracy opened it. Nikki
and Monty slipped inside, and Tracy slammed the door shut.
She was dressed in her pyjamas, and she was shivering. Her
face was drawn and pale, and her arms were crossed over her
chest.

'Sorry this is happening,' Nikki said, pointing outside.
'When did you notice them?'

'Maybe a couple of hours ago. I just had a shower and
stepped out. I was drying my hair and looked out the window. It
was shocking, really. There was a group of them, with their
placards. Within minutes the group seemed to grow, and the
whole street was blocked.'

Nikki asked, 'Did they try to hurt you? Like throwing bricks
at the window?'

Tracy shook her head. 'No, it's just been the chanting.' She
put a hand to her forehead. 'I can't believe it. Is this about the
research Brian and I did?'

'Possibly, yes,' Nikki said. 'Can you think of any other
reason?'

Tracy shook her head. She slumped against the wall, and
her hands dropped to her sides. Then she sank down on the
staircase. 'Can you please get them out of here?'

Nikki looked at Monty, who shrugged.

'We will try,' Nikki said. 'But we don't want to make the
situation worse, either. Please stay indoors. You're well
protected by the police outside.'

Tracy looked up. 'And what happens when they leave?
What happens tonight, when I'm going to work tomorrow? I

told you that guy follows me around. This time, he brought his friends.'

'Trevor Anthony?' Nikki asked quickly. 'Have you seen him out there?'

Tracy nodded. 'I'm surprised you didn't see him.'

Nikki yanked open the door and stepped outside. The crowd increased their chanting when they saw her. She scanned the crowd. If Trevor had turned up, he might have fled before the police arrived. She looked around and caught movement at the corner of her eye. The other end of the street opened up into a park. She saw a man wearing a long black leather jacket, slipping through the park's entrance. The figure was familiar. She grabbed Monty's sleeve and pointed. He nodded, and they walked down to the pavement, and the police again pushed the crowd back to let them through. Nikki broke into a run, almost barging into a neighbour who suddenly appeared in her way.

'Get these yobs out from our street,' the old man bellowed. 'What's the world coming to?'

Nikki had swerved to avoid the old man and almost tripped and fell. Monty spoke on her behalf. 'We're doing our best. Please stay indoors so that the situation doesn't get worse.'

The old man wasn't going anywhere. He stood in Monty's way. 'Get worse? How can it get worse than this? I've not seen this in all the fifty years I've lived here!'

Nikki pulled Monty away. 'Come on, we don't have time to waste.'

They ran towards the park. The man in the black leather coat was nowhere to be seen. They stood, breath heaving in their chests, scanning the area. Then Monty shouted, pointing to his right. There was a children's play area and after that a crop of trees. The man in the leather coat was running now, disappearing under the trees.

Monty sprinted after him, and Nikki followed. So much for a quiet life in Oxford, she cursed to herself. Not even a week in the new job, and she was running round more than she had done in south London. The man in the black coat heard them coming. He turned round, and Nikki recognised his face. It was Trevor Anthony.

'Stop,' she screamed.

Trevor turned and ran. The undergrowth was dense and the park covered a large area. The ground was wet beneath their feet. Trevor dodged his way between tree trunks, but slipped and fell. Monty caught up with him just as Trevor was getting up. He flung himself at Trevor, grabbing his waist in a rugby tackle. He brought the younger man down, and Trevor fought back. Nikki ran harder to catch up with them. Trevor raised a hand to swing his fist at Monty, while he was trying to take a pair of handcuffs out from his pocket. Nikki grabbed Trevor's hand and pinned it to the ground. Trevor snarled and spat at Nikki's face. She managed to avert her face at the last moment. She pressed Trevor's fist on the squelchy ground with both hands. Monty handcuffed one hand, then grabbed the other and twisted it behind Trevor's back. They turned him over, and Monty put a knee on Trevor's back, handcuffing both hands. 'Trevor Anthony, you're under arrest.' Monty read him his rights, then jerked Trevor to his feet. All three of them had mud on their clothes, and Nikki was shivering cold.

She set off towards the street, and Monty pulled Trevor along with them.

FIFTY-FOUR

'Wait here,' Nikki said when they came out of the park. The crowd of skinheads were visible ahead, still chanting the slogans. Some of the group had dispersed, and even as Nikki watched, a few of them walked away. The situation seemed to be improving.

'Let's not drag him through the street,' Nikki told Monty. 'I'll ask one of the constables to get a squad car here. You go back with him to the station.'

Trevor shook himself, trying to get free from Monty's grasp. Monty swore and tightened his grip on the man's collar. Nikki took out her radio and turned up the black dial. She issued an order, and within a few seconds, two of the uniformed constables came running.

Nikki left them and walked back to Tracy's house. The crowd was thinning and so was the number of police. Two uniformed sergeants still stood guard outside Tracy's house. Nikki knocked on the door, and Tracy's frightened face appeared again. She relaxed when she saw Nikki.

Nikki stepped inside, and Tracy shut and bolted the door.

'It's getting better outside,' Nikki said. 'We also caught Trevor Anthony, the man who followed you around.'

Tracy frowned. 'The guy who shouted at Brian at the seminar?'

'Yes.' Nikki nodded.

Relief flooded Tracy's face. 'Thank you.'

'Shall we sit down? I need to ask you a couple of things.'

Tracy looked at Nick inquisitively. 'About what? I've told you everything I know.'

Nikki said, 'It won't take long.'

Tracy exhaled, resignation on her face. 'Would you like a cup of tea?'

Nikki nodded. She waited in the living room while Tracy made two cups of tea and brought them in.

Tracy blew on her cup and watched as Nikki took a sip.

Nikki said, 'We know that you left New College just as the seminar came to an end. Can you tell us if you went back to the college that evening?'

Tracy put her cup down slowly. 'We have already been through this, inspector. Yes, I did leave and went shopping. Then I went back home. No, I did not go back to the college.'

'Are you sure?'

Tracy's eyebrows lowered. 'Why are you asking me this? I've just told you I spent the evening at home. Here, as it happens.'

'We need to eliminate you from our investigation, Tracy. I just want to make sure you didn't go back to the college on the evening of Professor Allerton's murder.'

'No, I didn't.' There was a firm, set expression on Tracy's face. Her jaw hardened.

'Do you know what sort of relationship Sue Pollard had with Professor Allerton?'

The question seemed to take Tracy by surprise. She recovered quickly. 'They were colleagues, as you must know. Apart from that, I don't know anything else.'

Nikki locked eyes with Tracy. 'Brian never told you anything?' She used the victim's first name for the first time.

Tracy shook her head slowly and then looked down at her cup. Nikki leaned forward. 'Sue Pollard is a very powerful woman, isn't she? She might be a senior tutor, but she is in the governing body, along with Richard Moffatt.'

Tracy shrugged, a blank expression on her face.

Nikki said, 'It's my understanding that it's not easy to become a member of the governing body. How did Sue get there?'

Tracy raised her eyebrows. 'I'm sorry, inspector. I cannot answer these questions. You need to ask Sue herself. I'm not sure how you expect me to know these things. Is this what you wanted to talk about?'

'Maybe we can talk about something else.' Nikki took a sip of tea, then settled back on the sofa. 'Do you have a list of all the research you published with the professor?'

Tracy narrowed her eyes. 'I guess so. But again, you're already aware of this.'

'The professor paid a publishing company called New Frontiers a lot of money recently. Did he talk to you about that?'

There was a guarded expression on Tracy's face all of a sudden. She inclined her head forward, averting her face from Nikki's. Tracy's fingers moved on her lap. She swallowed, and her mouth opened as she breathed a little faster. Nikki observed her closely.

'Tracy?'

'No, he didn't, and I don't know anything about this.'

Nikki knew Tracy was holding back. She decided to press gently. 'Did you know Trevor Anthony worked for New Frontiers Publishing?'

Tracy's lips parted as her eyes widened.

She breathed faster, the shock evident on her face.

Nikki said, 'If you know anything about this, now is the time to tell us, Tracy. Doesn't look good if we find out later.'

Tracy's face was turning white as a sheet. 'I don't, sorry,' she whispered. 'I know he had some dealings with New Frontier, because Simon Douglas, the treasurer, came to his office one day. I think they had an argument, as I heard raised voices. Later, Brian told me it was about a royalty dispute for one of his books. That's all I know. Honest.'

Nikki stared at her for a while, then nodded. 'Call me if you remember anything else.'

Tracy gulped. 'Look, will this Anthony guy come back? I don't feel very safe here any more.'

'He's going to be in custody now. I'll let you know what happens with him.'

FIFTY-FIVE

Nikki and Monty sat facing Trevor and his solicitor, Mr Chambers. Monty had filled Nikki in about Mr Chambers already. He was a right old pain in the rear, and he loved to poke holes in police cases. He was notorious for freeing an armed robber for lack of evidence, and the man then robbed a bank exactly a week later. He looked like a stuffed parrot, in his pinstripe suit and necktie, Nikki thought. He smiled condescendingly at Nikki, and she ignored him. Monty spoke on the recording machine and they started.

Nikki said, 'Trevor Anthony, could you please confirm that you work at New Frontiers Publishing.'

'Yes, I do.' The young man had a sneer on his face as he looked at Nikki.

Nikki settled back in the chair, going for the relaxed, friendly vibe. She wanted to drag Trevor into a sense of security. She had his measure. He wasn't a career criminal. But he was clearly angry with the police for something. Finding out the reason might go a long way towards answering his actions. 'You were present at Professor Brian Allerton's seminar at New

College the day before yesterday. You're visible on CCTV, entering the compound at 17:15.'

Trevor said nothing.

Nikki continued, 'Then you're seen leaving the college, at 17:45. You were late for the seminar, but that didn't stop you from shouting abuse at Brian Allerton. This is also recorded on the CCTV inside the seminar hall. Can you please confirm?'

'If you know it already, why are you wasting time?' Trevor snarled.

Nikki was glad she was getting under his skin. 'Just procedure. Can you tell us why you were so upset with Professor Allerton?'

There was a sullen look on Trevor's face as he glared at Nikki, then glanced away.

Mr Chambers had a hushed word with him.

'No comment,' Trevor said.

'You abused him verbally. Perhaps you were angry about his plagiarism. Or maybe there was another reason. Then you left the college, but you met up with him later, right? Was it at University Parks? Or in another college?'

Nikki's tone was more strident now, and her earlier smile was replaced by a stone-faced stare. Trevor glared back at her.

'That's where you had another argument with him, then you murdered him in cold blood. You stabbed him several times.' Nikki pointed a finger at Trevor, who was now breathing heavily, a shade of crimson creeping up his neck. 'Then you did the same thing to Daniel Blatherwick.'

'No!' Trevor shouted, baring his teeth. 'I did nothing of the sort.'

'Then why did you run every time you saw us? Why did you follow us around?'

Trevor clutched the ends of the table and looked around him like a trapped animal.

Mr Chambers was the picture of calmness. He pulled on

Trevor's sleeve, but the young man brushed him off, which pleased Nikki. She looked at Mr Chambers sweetly as he slumped back in his chair.

Monty cleared his throat. 'Only the guilty run, Trevor. Tell us what you did. We can help you. Once you're in court, this will only get harder. If you think we're bad, wait till you face a criminal barrister.'

'Inspector Sen,' Mr Chambers said. 'Please don't bully or harass my client. That goes for you as well, DI Gill.'

'Just stating the truth.' Monty shrugged.

'You heard him,' Nikki addressed Trevor, whose eyes were sliding all over the place. She dropped her voice, made it less accusatory. 'What did Brian do to you, Trevor? Tell me.'

Her words had an effect on the young man. He stopped fidgeting and fixed her with a gaze, then narrowed his eyes. Nikki waited. Trevor said nothing. A torment flickered over his face, then his jaws shook. He closed his eyes like he'd just seen something awful and wished to forget it.

'No comment,' he whispered.

A silence dropped in the room.

After a while, Nikki's voice broke it. 'Why did you hate him, Trevor?'

He didn't answer, and Nikki felt the moment had passed. Trevor was hiding something, that was obvious. But she couldn't force it out of him. She changed track and looked at Monty, who nodded and cleared his throat.

'Where were you between 13:30 and 16:00 yesterday?'

Trevor glanced at Monty. 'At the Bodleian. Then I went home and had lunch. Later, I went to the gym.'

'Did you go to Christ Church college yesterday?'

Trevor shook his head. Nikki knew Trevor hadn't shown up on CCTV in Christ Church. Monty asked about his gym address, and he noted it. They could check the cameras there, too, Nikki thought. 'The evening of Professor Allerton's seminar, where did you go after you left the college?'

'I went to the Bookbinders pub. My friends can vouch for me. I left the pub around 10 p.m. and went home.'

Nikki knew the pub, it was a Jericho landmark. She had no doubt it would have CCTV as well. The longer she interviewed Trevor, the stronger her conviction grew. This lad hadn't committed the murders. But he had run from the police for a reason.

She raised a hand as a signal to Monty. 'If you have nothing to hide,' Nikki told Trevor. 'Then tell us why you evaded us for so long.'

'Because you lot exist to make our lives a misery,' Trevor spat out, grimacing. 'Fat lot of good you are when needed. You let us down, then make life difficult.'

'Is that why you were filming us? To record our work?'

'Why not?' Trevor raised his voice. 'I need proof to see—' He stopped suddenly, aware he was talking too much.

'Go on,' Nikki urged.

'No comment.'

The back and forth continued, but it was clear Trevor wasn't going to talk. And yet, she wasn't convinced he was entirely innocent. He might not have committed the murders, but he had dirt on him. 'You will remain under custody tonight. Tomorrow we will question you again.'

'Either you charge him, or let him go,' Mr Chambers said.

'You know we can keep him here for twenty-four hours,' Nikki shot back. 'And we will charge him tomorrow.'

She glared at Trevor, who couldn't hold her gaze.

FIFTY-SIX

Back in the office, Nikki called Simon Douglas and informed him about Trevor. 'Do you know if Trevor had any personal contact with Brian Allerton or Daniel Blatherwick?'

Mr Douglas took a few seconds to answer. 'You asked me this before. The answer is the same. I just don't know.'

'And yet, Trevor was hurling abuse at Prof Allerton in the seminar. Trevor uncovered the plagiarism, according to you. We still haven't received evidence of that, by the way. Due to Trevor's work, Prof Allerton pays you a quarter of a million pounds. Can you see where this is leading to, Mr Douglas?'

Silence greeted her. Nikki filled the void. 'We're getting closer to arresting you and demanding sight of all the documents relating to Prof Allerton's claim.'

'What? Arrest me for what? I haven't done anything.'

'You're withholding the truth from us. You know that. That can be seen as being an accessory to murder.'

The gasp was audible, followed by strenuous breathing down the line. 'Very well.' Mr Douglas's voice was resigned. 'But what I'm about to tell you must remain confidential, and never be reported to the media. I signed a contract, and I can get sued.'

'What sort of contract?'

'A non-disclosure agreement, when we agreed the out of court settlement. There are no void clauses. I'm not allowed to tell you this, but you're not leaving me any choice.'

Mr Douglas sighed, and Nikki waited.

'I can't tell you everything. But Brian paid us that money to stop us publishing a book. Trevor was writing that book. We were going to get sued if that book got published anyway, so we were on thin ice. We knew it was dangerous. When Brian offered us that money, I agreed to accept. Trevor was furious, and wanted to go ahead. But he worked for me, and the final decision was mine.'

'What was the book about?'

'That I can't tell you. You might as well arrest me for that, because if I disclose the book's title, then I get arrested under my NDA anyway.'

Nikki wondered about the book's contents. She also wondered how a professor had £250,000 lying around. It was either half his pension cashed out, or he had a rich benefactor. Nikki remembered her chat with Mr Darlington. He knew Professor Allerton well. A knot etched deeper in the back of her mind, opening up a new space.

'Do you know if Mr Darlington was involved in stopping this book from getting published?'

Only heavy breathing answered her. 'Mr Douglas?'

'Oh my god,' the publisher moaned. 'Miss Gill, please—'

'Whatever you say remains confidential. I assure you.'

Mr Douglas swore inaudibly. Then he appeared to make his mind up. 'Very well. Yes, he was. It was Darlington's lawyers who drew up the NDA. It was also them who acted on Brian's behalf. Informally, of course.'

'And did Mr Darlington provide the money?'

'That I cannot say for certain. You need to ask Mr Darlington.'

Nikki thought for a moment. She understood why Mr Douglas had been quiet about this. He could be sued for a lot of money if he breached the terms of the NDA.

'Thank you. I'll be in touch.'

Nikki's phone chirped, and she frowned at the unknown number. However, the message was clear enough.

Come alone tonight. This is about Tommy. I'll be waiting.

Nikki stared at the screen for a few seconds, then made her mind up.

Why do you want to meet me?

The reply came instantly.

It's about Tommy.

Tell me now.

No, only when I see you. There's an old industrial estate past the BMW factory in Headington. If you don't come alone, you'll never learn what happened to Tommy.

Who are you?

For a few seconds, there was no response. Then a new message arrived.

8 P.M. Don't be late. Come alone.

Nikki put her phone away and walked to the window. She

stared out at the trees undulating in a stiff breeze. The door behind her opened and Kristy and Nish walked in.

Nikki glanced at her watch. 'Did Hetty Barfield get back with a forensics report of Professor Blatherwick's apartment?'

'Not as yet, guv,' Kristy said. 'I'll let you know.'

'Did any of you contact Arabella Allerton? I would like to see her again.'

Nish nodded. 'She is at home, guv. But I must say, she wasn't very welcoming. She said there was nothing else she had to tell us.'

'Oh, I think she does. Give a call and let her know we are on our way.'

<hr>

Nikki and Monty drove down in the black Ford Titanium. The car had all the mod cons, and even had bullet-proof glass. It felt ridiculous driving in a bullet-proof car in Oxford, Nikki thought with a smile. In the mean streets of south London, it made perfect sense. But she couldn't imagine one of the residents doing a drive-by shooting in the genteel environs of Jericho.

Her heels clicked as she went up the steps to the broad portico of Arabella's house. She rang the bell and waited. A tall woman with auburn hair and blue eyes, and a stern expression on her face, opened the door. Nikki raised her warrant card. The woman reached out a hand and asked if she could hold it. Nikki refused.

'I'm sure you can see it perfectly well from here,' she said. 'I'm sorry, but I cannot hand my warrant card over. It's our official ID. May I ask who you are?'

'Fenella Robinson. I am Arabella's sister. And also a criminal law solicitor.'

Now that made perfect sense, Nikki thought with resignation. The expression on her face didn't change, and she maintained a smile. 'Nice to meet you, Ms Robinson. Is Mrs Allerton inside?'

'I believe she has told you everything that she knows,' Fenella said, her eyes boring into Nikki's.

'New evidence has come to light and we wish to ask Arabella a few questions for that reason.'

Fenella reluctantly stepped to one side. Nikki and Monty walked in and immediately heard loud barking from the cute golden retriever. A side door opened, and the dog was visible, Arabella restraining it. She shut the door and wiped her hands on her trousers.

Her face was pale and strained, and her eyes had dark shadows under them. She extended a hand towards the kitchen. 'Would you like to come in here, please?'

Nikki and Monty sat down at the table. Fenella circled round, urging her sister to do the same. They sat down opposite Nikki.

Nikki cleared her throat. 'How have you been?' She addressed the question to Arabella, ignoring Fenella.

Arabella opened her mouth to speak, but Fenella put a hand over her sister's. 'Inspector Gill, I'm sure you are not here to make small talk. Could you please get to the point?'

'Very well,' Nikki said. She glared at Fenella for a few seconds, then switched to Arabella. 'Did you know your husband was having an affair?'

Arabella appeared to be in shock. Her mouth fell open, and she blinked several times. Then she snapped her mouth shut and stared down at the table.

Nikki gave her some time.

Arabella shook her head slowly. 'No, I didn't,' she whispered.

'Did you know Professor Daniel Blatherwick at Christ Church College?'

Arabella's eyes widened, then she frowned. Fenella leaned in towards her and whispered something.

Arabella shrugged. 'I've got nothing to hide.'

Fenella spoke firmly. 'Remember you don't have to say anything. You can give an official statement with a lawyer present.'

Arabella shrugged. 'No, it's OK.'

She flicked her eyes back to Nikki. 'Yes, I knew Daniel. He was good friends with Brian. He used to be married, but got divorced a long time back now. I can't remember when.'

'Did you go on holidays together? As families, I mean.'

Arabella nodded. 'Yes, a long time ago. Goodness, that takes me years back. I can't even remember when.'

Nikki pulled out her phone and showed Arabella the photos she had taken in Professor Blatherwick's apartment. The sisters scrutinised the photos.

Arabella said, 'That was in Germany. Berlin, I think. There was a conference, at Berlin University. I can't tell you the date.' She pushed the phone back to Nikki, who murmured her thanks and put the phone back in her pocket.

'Did you know that Daniel Blatherwick died yesterday?'

Arabella's shoulders slumped and a horrified expression appeared on her face. Her hand went to her mouth. Nikki observed her reaction with interest. She decided to prod gently.

'Did you know Professor Blatherwick well?'

'You don't have to say anything,' Fenella said to her sister.

She cast a venomous stare at Nikki. 'Inspector Gill, what's the point of these questions? Can you not see my sister is already distressed?'

'She can answer if she wants to,' Nikki said, spreading her hands.

'I can't believe it,' Arabella blurted. 'How did this happen?'

'In the same way your husband was killed, I'm afraid,' Nikki said. 'Multiple stab wounds. Do you know if they had a common enemy?'

Arabella's chest heaved as she dragged in quick breaths. She had trouble speaking, and shook her head vigorously. 'No. Not that I know of, anyway.'

'How well did you know Daniel?'

'I can't remember the last time I saw him. Maybe a few months ago, at one of the college dinners. But there was a time when, as families, we mixed often.'

'What was his ex-wife's name? And did he have any children?' Nikki asked.

'She was called Ruth. I haven't seen her for decades. No, they didn't have any children.'

'You don't know Ruth's maiden name by any chance?'

Arabella shook her head. The tip of her nose turned red, and tears brimmed in her eyes.

Fenella put an arm around her shoulder. She turned on Nikki. 'I think that's quite enough now, Inspector Gill.'

'One last question, if you don't mind. Did you ever suspect your husband of being interested in men?'

Arabella's head jerked up as if she had been slapped. Fenella's jaw went slack. Nikki waited. When Arabella didn't answer, she said, 'We've heard reports that men were seen leaving your husband's apartment in the college.'

Arabella gripped the sides of her forehead and closed her eyes. Her voice seemed to come from a great distance. 'Once, I saw photos on his phone. It was a very young man, almost a teenage boy. He was in his underwear and posing.'

'When was this?' Nikki leaned forward.

'A while ago. Maybe three to four years. I asked him about it. He said it was the son of a colleague who was in gymnastics. The proud father had sent him a photo.'

'Did you believe it?'

Arabella closed her eyes again and sighed. 'In my heart of hearts, no. But I didn't know what to do...'

'You said photos. How many did you see?'

Arabella lowered her head into her hands and remained like that for a while. Fenella held her shoulders, and even she now looked troubled.

Nikki exchanged a glance with Monty. His eyes were hard as flints, jaws flexing. She knew what he was thinking. Perhaps Brian Allerton had a secret life neither of them knew about.

Slowly, Arabella raised her head. She wiped her eyes, and moved the strands of hair from her face.

'Many years ago, when we got married, and before Julia arrived... I found this magazine in the boot of his car. It had photos of naked children. It was disgusting. Brian told me he had bought the car from a friend, and that was true. The magazine came with the car, and didn't belong to him. As the car was new to us, I believed him at the time. He sold the car, and told me he'd reported his friend to the police. Before you ask, I didn't know this friend.'

Nikki felt a chill spread down her spine. 'Anything else?'

Tears returned to Arabella's eyes. She sobbed, and Fenella hugged her sister. Arabella said, 'I didn't tell anyone all these years. I was wrong. I was scared. I didn't know what to do.'

'Now is the time to tell us,' Nikki said softly. 'It's alright.'

'He liked hugging boys.' Arabella sobbed. 'One of the school parents complained, many years ago. Brian used to run a private tuition business for children. He only had boys, no girls. These boys came to our house. I once found him with a boy on his knees. Brian had his arm around the boy's waist.' Arabella broke down, holding her head.

Fenella looked at Nikki, her face pale and drawn. She wasn't the hard-nosed barrister any more, she was a distraught sister. Nikki breathed in, pulling air into her constricted lungs. It didn't relieve the pressure on her chest.

She gave Arabella some time, then asked, 'Did you discuss this with anyone?'

'No. No one. I didn't want to believe any of it. His private tuition business shut down, and the boys never came again. Our life returned to normal.'

Arabella fell silent. She was quiet, only the sound of her breathing puncturing the moment, as if she was afraid to speak, afraid what secrets her words might evoke.

Nikki asked, 'Is there anything else you noticed?'

Arabella shook her head. 'Now that I think of it, maybe he was more careful later on. I did look into his phone again, but I didn't see anything. He could have just deleted photos, I don't know. But it reassured me, and I kind of carried on, thinking, hoping for the best.'

'Will you come and speak to us at the station?' Nikki said, looking at Fenella. The barrister nodded. Nikki looked at Monty, who nodded once, and took over.

His voice was grave, like he was dragging it up from his boots. 'Thank you, Arabella. If you don't mind telling us, where were you yesterday between 1:30 p.m. and 4:30 p.m.?'

Fenella stiffened, and she frowned. 'Why do you need to know that?'

'That's when Daniel Blatherwick was killed.'

'It's OK,' Arabella said, touching her sister's arm. 'I was at the library, inspector. You can ask anyone there.'

Nikki's phone beeped. She thought it might be Rita. She excused herself and went outside, into the lobby. When she saw the text, her blood ran cold.

Don't be late tonight. Come alone.

FIFTY-SEVEN

Nikki drove down the deserted road, the headlights of the car scything through the darkness.

Piece by small piece, like a macabre jigsaw, a horrible picture was emerging in her mind.

Brian Allerton liked young boys, as despicable as that sounded.

He also worked at the Dunston Hill Care Home, many years ago, along with Daniel Blatherwick. Now, both those men were dead.

She didn't want to face the awful thought, but like a serpent, it raised its ugly fangs. Could Brian have known her brother? Could he have... done anything to little Tommy?

The thought made her shudder, and also feel sick to the stomach. If Brian had been a paedophile, then was his death some sort of revenge?

Daniel also worked with him, and now he too was dead. Apart from their financial dealings, the thread that connected them was Dunston Hill Care Home.

Had Daniel been the same as Brian? Is that why they were murdered?

Nikki stopped at the red lights. The glow from her car got swallowed up in the blackness outside, like her thoughts disappearing down a tunnel of conflict. She had lived under the shadow of her brother's potential abuse all her life. Now it was coming back full circle... The loops ran around in her head till she couldn't think any more.

She had reached the derelict industrial warehouse just outside Headington. There used to be a steel mill here, and she had seen it as a child. Now the business was long gone, having given way to cheaper competition from overseas. All that remained was a rusting hulk, whose vague shape she could see in the dense, cold night air. She switched the headlights off, as the text had asked her to. Sudden blackness enveloped her. She pressed on the brakes, slowing the car. The tarmac road had grass growing down the middle, but it was still operational. Slowly, her eyes got used to the dark. Outside the main warehouse, she ground to a halt. She turned in her seat and looked all around. She didn't like it here. The road ended in a disused quarry, which was now filled with water. To her right lay dense shrubbery and undergrowth. Her only way out was to reverse the car, to get back to the main road. She decided to be ready. She turned the car round, keeping the headlights off. The back wheels hit a hole in the road, and they spun, unable to get traction. Nikki cursed and pressed on the gas. Thankfully, the car lurched forward, and she straightened the wheel.

She turned the engine off. She had kept the heating on, but the tips of her fingers were cold. Her breath made fumes in the air as she unwound the window. Frigid coldness seeped inside the car. She stared at the warehouse, trying to discern movement. She didn't see anything, but just as she turned away, she caught something in the corner of her eye. It was at the rear of her car. She spun round. A dark shape appeared by the passenger window. The man was of medium height, but broad around the shoulders and bulky. She couldn't make out any of his features. His hands were stuffed inside his pockets, and a hoodie covered his face. Nikki kept her eyes on him, while her hand scrambled in her pocket for the extendable baton. The feel of the hard handle gave her some comfort. She had used it several times to crack glass and human skulls. She took a deep breath and turned the knob of her radio to silent. If she was attacked, she could relay an SOS on the radio. Nikki got out of the car and cleared her throat.

'I'm armed, and I can call for help, which will be here within seconds. Do you understand?'

'I know,' the man said. His voice was muffled, and she realised he was wearing a mask. It was also too deep, and she knew he was doing it to disguise the real tone of his voice. She didn't blame him. He must know she was recording the conversation on the phone. And she knew he was too, which bothered her. He could use it against her later. But the compulsion to know what he did about Tommy roared inside her like sea waves.

The man spoke again. 'I didn't expect you to come.'

Nikki's breath made fumes in the air. A cold futility was seeping into her bones, battling with the surging pulse rate in her ears.

'Who are you?' she asked.

The man didn't answer.

Nikki shuddered, her breath rapid and jerky. Her fingers tightened around the baton in her right coat pocket. 'You sent me the text about my brother. Thomas Gill.'

The man inclined his head in assent.

'Talk,' Nikki said.

A few seconds passed and the man just observed Nikki. She was starting to find it unnerving. It was also an old trick, to make people anxious. She wasn't going to play this game.

'Either you talk, or I arrest you. Shall I call reinforcements?' She raised a hand to her breast pocket, where the radio resided.

Her fingers rested on the round black knob. She only had to rotate it to get a signal. 'Do you know what happened to Tommy? How did he die?' Nikki asked.

'He wanted to go,' the man said. 'He ran off the hill and fell to his death. But he was hurt. He didn't want to live any more.'

'Hurt? Where and how?' Nikki's throat constricted, and her mouth went dry. A pressure hammered against her forehead, joining the nuclear drumbeat of her heart.

The man was silent for a while. 'They did that to him. In that place.'

Nikki knew then. She had suspected it all along. 'Are you talking about the care home? Dunston Hill?'

The man was still as a statue, even his chest barely moved as he breathed. Nikki spoke. 'Why are you telling me this? Who are you?'

'Tommy loved you,' the man said. 'You were the sister he never got to know. The day he died, he talked about you.'

Nikki's brain searched for words and found a barren desert of thought. Her mind was numb like the cold night air shrouding her. The man spoke again in the strangely deep, but muffled voice. 'He wanted you to know that. He's gone. But the others have to pay.'

Nikki frowned, confused. 'What do you mean?'

She went to speak, but the man turned and melted into the bush behind him.

Nikki ran forward.

'Stop!'

She fumbled for the torchlight. She swept the beam around the trees and undergrowth. Leaves and twigs moved where the man had gone through. But there was nothing to see. She debated whether to chase him. In the distance, she heard a car engine start. She didn't see any lights, but the car zoomed away, leaving her in the frigid silence.

FIFTY-EIGHT

Nikki drove back home, feeling lost. She parked outside her cottage and sat there for a while. *You were the sister he never got to know. The day he died, he talked about you.* A weight appeared in her throat, and it grew heavier, wider, till it clogged her windpipe, and she had to open her mouth to breathe. Moisture prickled her eyes. Her hands shook a little, and she gripped them together. She watched the dark windows of her cottage for a while, before she got out. She went inside and switched the lights on. She took off her shoes, shook out the ponytail and went to the kitchen. Like a beacon, the fridge seemed to be calling her. She opened it in a trance, her movements automatic, unthinking, like a machine. Her hand reached for the bottle of white wine. Then she stopped. Her mother's face flashed before her eyes. Her vision blurred and the bottle, the white light inside, the fridge, started to dim and shake. Her eyes squeezed shut, and she wiped them dry. Then she stood and shut the fridge door.

No.

She wouldn't get the bottle out.

There was another way. There always was another way, she

just had to look for it. Her mother had given up and lost her life. Clarissa was scarred and those wounds would never heal. She would never forgive herself.

A dagger of despair plunged into Nikki's soul, and the pain was almost physical, driving her to her knees. She held on to a chair, then lowered herself to seating.

She didn't know how her mother lived. That was the truth. It was easy for Nikki to tell Clarissa to sort her life out. She stood and wiped her face with a tissue. She boiled the kettle and made a cup of tea.

Then she sat down with a pen and paper. The fog in her mind made it hard to see the shapes. But forms were becoming visible, and she forced herself to think as she sipped the tea. Then she started to write.

The others must pay. She circled the word others, then put a question mark next to it.

Could it be the two professors? If it was, then she had just met the killer, and let him slip through her grasp. The thought made her shudder, and hair stood up on the back of her neck.

She looked at what she'd just written. *The others.* Was there someone left to pay?

Nikki couldn't assume this man had killed the professors. Would he be so stupid as to show himself, if he had? She needed evidence.

However, she now knew for certain he had known Tommy. He had been there when Tommy died, if she could believe what he said. Was he a friend from school? Or had he been in that horrible care home?

Nikki gripped the pen tighter as she stared down at the notebook. Unanswered questions filled her mind. Why had this guy got in touch with her now? And what was the reason for all the cloak and dagger crap? He could simply get in touch with her.

He had obviously tracked down Tommy's family, and she

wondered if he'd been in touch with her mother. Nikki hesitated, checking the time. It was almost 10 p.m., but Clarissa would be awake. She rang her. It went to voicemail. She rang again, and this time her mother answered.

Nikki listened to the hush of static for a while. 'It's me.'

'What do you want?'

Nikki sighed. 'Nice to speak to you as well, Mum. Can you turn the TV volume down? I need to talk.'

'About what?' Clarissa hiccupped, and her words were slurred. Sometimes Nikki wondered why she bothered. She tried to suppress the irritation, and failed. It had been a long day, and her nerves were getting frazzled.

'You know what, Mum? Just leave it. Sorry I called.' As soon as the words left her mouth, she felt regret. Also anger, and they collided in a wave of frustration. But she didn't hang up, and neither did Clarissa. Nikki heard the TV sound go down till it was almost silent. She heard her mother breathing down the line. Maybe this wasn't such a good idea, she thought. Maybe she should see her mother in person to have this chat. But she couldn't be bothered to go all the way to Jericho, now. 'I need to ask you something about Tommy.'

She heard her mother's breath catch, then get faster. Nikki wanted to get this over and done with quickly. Before the demons returned.

'Did Tommy have a friend in the care home? Or at school? A friend you remember, anyway.'

Only Clarissa's breathing was audible. 'Why?' she finally asked.

'Can you just tell me.'

'Not that I recall, no. If he did, then I...' Clarissa's voice trailed off, and Nikki didn't press any further. Nikki knew her mother wouldn't know about Tommy's friends. 'Has anyone got in touch with you recently about Tommy?'

'Like who?'

It was a long time ago. Nikki could feel a cold hand on her shoulder, her body chilling. Digging up the past came with a price.

'I don't know. A man sent me messages on the phone. Said he knew Tommy when he was a child. I met him. He didn't say his name, or identify himself. But he did know about Tommy and me.'

Clarissa said nothing, her silence dripping into a never-ending void of regret.

'Mum?'

'Yes.'

Nikki's voice was small and a battle raged inside her. She had read the coroner's report on her brother's death. It was a suicide. Or an accident.

'Who reported Tommy's accident? Do you remember?'

'A boy from the school. Can't remember his name now. He was walking to school with Tommy when it happened. Hang on.'

Clarissa had finally caught on to Nikki's chain of thought. 'You don't think it's the same boy, well he's a man now, getting in touch with you?'

'That's exactly what I think. Can you find his name? I can't remember it being in the file. All the boys' names were anonymised for safety.'

Clarissa was quiet for a while. 'I would've remembered someone like that. They didn't give me the boy's name either.'

Nikki knew then she would have to dig up the old files from the council. She could do it tomorrow from work.

'Thanks, Mum. Can you please let me know if anyone contacts you about Tommy?'

'Yes, I will.' Clarissa hung up before Nikki could say goodbye.

Nikki listened to the buzz on the line for a while, as if she hoped her mother's voice would suddenly reappear. Then, slowly, she put the phone down.

FIFTY-NINE

Nikki sat in the canteen, a steaming cup of coffee on the table in front of her. It was five minutes to eight, and she had started early. On the online portal of the council website, she had managed to pay and download the last filed copies of Dunston Hill Care Home. It was shut down in 2003, due to lack of funding. The old building was still there, but it had been converted into flats. Nikki had her iPad, and she flicked through photos of Dunston Hill. The front façade of the building remained the same. Wisps of strange memories curled around the periphery of Nikki's heart. It still looked grand, but cold and impersonal. Even the large wrought-iron main gates were the same. But the long drive had now become a car park. She found photos of the inside of the flats, they were nicely done and sold for a hefty price tag. Nikki shook her head. If the buyers knew what happened here...

She felt movement and looked up to see Monty and Kristy approaching. They sat down opposite with their coffee and breakfast trays. 'Dunston Hill Care Home,' Nikki said. 'I'm going to visit it today. Given Prof Allerton's involvement with

St Jude's Hall, I think we need to see it. Maybe someone there remembers him.'

'The college still owns the land, but the building is now leased to a development company. Will you find anyone there from years ago?' Kristy said, taking a sip of her coffee.

'That company has made the place into lots of small flats. So they don't own it? It's still owned by the college?' Nikki asked.

'The college owns the freehold. They are the landlords. The building is leased to the development company with the right to alter. It's a long lease, like two hundred something years. The college makes money from the lease rent, which is many thousands per year. I need to look for the figure.'

'Thanks,' Nikki said. 'I got the files for the care home, but they don't say much apart from when it shut down. I'm hoping we can track down the officer in charge at the time. His name's mentioned here.' Nikki read from the screen. 'Jack Taylor.'

Kristy raised her eyebrows. 'I spoke to him when I rang the college. He did say he's been there all his life, so it might be the same person. He still works there in some capacity. Under the lease, the college owns a small portion of the building, where their members can live.'

'Let's go see him.' Nikki glanced briefly at Monty, who had not offered any comment so far. He held her eyes, and she could feel his mind churning.

Monty said, 'I met Simon Douglas, the treasurer of New Frontier Publishing, and he mentioned more about the book that Prof Allerton didn't want them to publish. It's about Dunston Hill Care Home and it's failings. Mr Douglas wouldn't tell me the name of the book.'

'That's why he gave them £250K, basically a bribe to stop them from publishing it.'

'Allerton is connected to that, right? The book about the care home and it's failings.'

'That's why he fell out with New Frontier, his own publisher. They were printing the book,' Kristy said.

'Does the care home have any connection to Blatherwick?' Monty asked. The two women shook their heads.

'But we haven't checked, have we?' Monty continued. 'That will be one thing to clear up when you visit the care home.'

'Can you drive me there?' Nikki asked. 'Kristy and Nish have to stay here to chase up other stuff.'

Monty nodded his assent. 'Best go now. Get it out of the way.' He followed her out of the canteen. They bumped into Detective Superintendent Patmore as he was coming in. The barrel-chested older man stopped in his tracks and glared at both of them. His eyes softened as they fell on Nikki.

'DI Sen is giving you good reports. I'm glad everything is OK.'

'Thanks, guv,' Nikki said.

She gave Monty a quick smile, and his lips twitched back in return.

'How is the case with the murdered professors?'

'Going well,' Nikki said. 'We have a suspect in custody, but he might not be the right person. I'm going to see another later this evening. We should have another arrest by the end of the week.'

'Good, keep me informed.' DS Patmore suddenly stopped and put a finger to his lips, as a thought had just occurred to him. 'By the way, did you see Mr Darlington, the town councillor?'

Nikki's eyes were guarded. 'Yes, I did. He is one of the suspects, actually. He saw Professor Blatherwick just before he died.'

'I see.' DS Patmore seemed deep in thought. 'Can I ask you a favour? Before you go to see him again, please clear it with me.'

'Yes, sir. But is there a reason?'

DS Patmore sighed. 'He's good friends with the Commissioner. They had a chat about him being harassed by a female copper at the town hall. I take it that was you.'

Nikki shrugged. 'If you call asking questions harassment, then so be it.'

DS Patmore grunted. 'I don't like these posh toffs any more than you do. But just be careful whose toes you tread on. OK?' He gave Nikki a smile.

'OK, sir.'

Monty drove the black Ford Titanium, and traffic was light. The rolling green, yellow and brown hills dipped in and out of pretty valleys, villages nestled in their depths. It didn't take them long to get to Evesham. As Monty took the road to the care home, Nikki began to recognise the landscape as vaguely familiar. When he pulled up outside the big gates, she went rigid. Memories assaulted her mind, all of them fleeting, but each one painful.

Clarissa weeping as she was escorted outside.

Nikki with her eyes fixed on Tommy's scared face as she was dragged away.

'You OK?' Monty asked.

Nikki couldn't look him in the eyes. She nodded.

He got out and rang the buzzer, then spoke on the machine. He came back to the car, and the gates opened slowly without a sound. That was new, Nikki realised. Previously, these large gates used to be ajar, and they had to slip through them. The gates used to look old, gnarly, with flaking paint. Now they were glistening black and polished.

Her eyes took in the broad frontage of the house, the row of rooms flanking the large main door. It was all nicely done up, re-plastered and painted. The builders had done a good job, and the place was clearly popular, given the number of residents' cars parked.

But Nikki couldn't stop the sense of dread crawling up her skin. Monty parked, and they got out. Despite the sunshine, she shivered, drawing her coat tighter.

'Sure you're OK?' Monty asked from behind. He had a concerned look in his eyes, and she smiled briefly. She felt his eyes on her as they walked towards the security lodge in front of the main doors.

A man in a grey uniform came out and took their names, then took photocopies of their warrant cards.

There was a courtyard with a small garden in the middle, and the rectangle was enclosed by the building. The balconies with arches and Romanesque pillars were probably not more than a couple of hundred years old. The place looked very different to the cold, dreary, grey place that Nikki recalled. She sauntered slowly through, and Monty strode ahead. He spoke to a receptionist at the counter, and she asked them to take a seat. They stood by the floor-to-ceiling Georgian windows and looked out at the well-maintained courtyard.

Nikki stopped in front of a long wooden board on the wall, where several names were inscribed and dated. The oldest was at the top. It looked like an honours board, and at the top it said, 'Warden's List'.

It was a chronological list of the wardens of the children's home. At the top, she saw a familiar last name: Reginald Darlington. She wondered if he was any relation to the current Mr Darlington.

Monty came and stood next to her, looking at the board. He pointed to another Darlington, about halfway down. Thomas Darlington was the warden from 1937 to 1942.

Monty nudged her in the elbow. 'Look at that.' He pointed at the middle of the board, where two familiar names were carved in the wood.

Nikki's breath caught in her chest as she read the names:

Brian Robert Allerton. Warden from 1995–1998
Daniel Bertrand Blatherwick. Warden from 1998–2001

The next name on the list was Jack Andrew Taylor. Warden from 2001–2002. After 2002, the home had shut down. Nikki and Monty looked at each other. Nikki could see what was whirling in Monty's mind – getting hold of Jack Taylor was now critical.

'Inspector Nikki Gill?' a male voice said from behind.

SIXTY

A thin man stood there; he had round-frame glasses and a bald scalp. He was dressed in an old-fashioned tweed suit, complete with leather patches on the elbows. Everything about him was genteel countryman, but his dark eyes were sharp and alive behind the glasses.

'Greg Rigby,' the man said. 'I'm the site caretaker here. How can I help?'

Nikki said, 'We want to see Mr Jack Taylor, the man who used to be the warden of St Jude's Hall, before all of this.' She waved a hand around. 'We heard the warden might still have kept his old residence here.'

Mr Rigby shook his head. 'Sorry, none of the old wardens live here anymore. That practice stopped a while ago. As for Mr Taylor, I have no idea where he is, sorry.'

'Do you know if the warden's old quarters are still present?'

Mr Rigby hesitated. 'They are, but they're now admin offices for the company that own the site.'

Monty said, 'Were they flats before the conversion?'

'Yes. They were two and three-bedroom flats, converted from a Victorian house.'

'I know they've been converted into offices, but can we please have a look? We need to speak to Mr Taylor, urgently.'

Mr Rigby looked confused, and Nikki didn't blame him. She said, 'If we could just see the old wardens' quarters, then we'll be on our way.'

'OK.' Mr Rigby shrugged. 'I mean, there's people working there now, but you can have a look.' They crossed a well-maintained garden with a small fountain and then came upon a row of three houses. Mr Rigby led them into the first house, which had clearly been renovated recently. Inside, the ground floor was an office, and Mr Rigby showed them around. The upstairs was also a bland office space, and Nikki shook her head in frustration. They went back outside, and Monty was on his phone.

'University archives,' he said, putting a hand over the receiver to mask his voice. 'They often have records of the last-known whereabouts of the staff.'

'You have your uses, Monty.' Nikki nudged him with her elbow.

'That's me,' he said. 'Mr Useful.' He put a finger to his lips, then said hello into the receiver. He listened for a while, then a frown creased his face.

'UKPPS? Are you sure?' He listened again, the frown remaining. 'Is the letter signed off by anyone, and dated?'

Monty hung up, then looked quizzically at Nikki. 'Mr Taylor was taken to a safe house by the UKPPS in November 2001.'

'The Protected Person's Service?'

'Yes. Not sure why. No reason given, apart from the fact that his forwarding address became the UKPPS HQ in Scotland Yard. The letter's signed by a Graham Bartlett from the UKPPS.'

Monty's frown was mirrored in Nikki's expression. 'And no PCN? No arrests?'

'Nothing that the team saw when they looked him up. We

need to speak to Mr Bartlett. He was working twenty years ago, maybe he's still there.'

Nikki nodded, and they walked back to the car. Monty rang switchboard and asked to be put through to Scotland Yard.

Nikki's mind was whirling around in loops. The UKPPS would only get involved if a witness needed protection from a serious threat. An Oxford academic seemed like a far cry. Unless Mr Taylor knew or did something that could damage someone... dangerous. 'Hello? Is that Mr Graham Bartlett?' Monty said on the phone. 'This is DI Monty Sen from the TVP speaking. We are investigating a double homicide in Oxford, and we need to speak to you about Mr Jack Taylor, a former warden of St Jude's Hall.' The phone was connected to the speaker and Mr Bartlett's voice came through. 'Gosh, that takes me a long way back.' He was quiet for a while. 'What is Mr Taylor's connection to the murders?'

'Both of the victims were wardens at Dunston Hill Care Home, run by St Jude Hall. Mr Taylor was also a warden there.'

They could hear the clicking of a keyboard. Mr Bartlett was probably pulling up the old files as they spoke.

Monty said, 'The home shut down in 2002.'

After a brief silence Mr Bartlett came back on the line. 'Yes I've located the folder. Mr Taylor came forward with allegation of CSA, or child sexual abuse, at the care home. He had spoken to the council as well. Back then, there was no specialised police units for CSA. The case was handled by the Oxfordshire Constabulary. Mr Taylor was the only witness who was willing to come forward with the allegations. The case was closed down within three months. Mr Taylor started to get unconfirmed threats on his life, and the police referred the case to us.'

'And what did you do for Mr Taylor?' Monty asked.

'He was in a safe house for three months. The death threats against him were serious. He was roughed up once and went to hospital. He resigned from all college and university positions, we're not sure why. He alleged bullying in the workplace, but nothing was ever substantiated.'

Monty looked at Nikki, and she held his eyes for a while. Then she asked, 'Were any arrests ever made over the CSA allegations?'

'No. There were more allegations, from the children themselves. An inquiry was launched and some of the children who had left the care home, and placed with foster parents, came forward with allegations of historic abuse.'

'Were any names mentioned?'

Mr Bartlett was silent for a while, and they heard sounds from the keyboard. 'It's surprising, but most of Mr Taylor's evidence was redacted. Blacked-out on the paper, I mean. But other children mentioned the names of Robert, Bertie and Stuart. Three carers who committed the abuse, according to them. Their real identities were never uncovered.'

Monty frowned. 'The evidence was redacted? By the Oxford police?'

'No. The case was taken over by Special Branch at Scotland Yard. They conducted the investigation. No one was prosecuted, and there was no trial.'

All three of them were silent for a while. Eventually, Nikki asked, 'What happened to Mr Taylor after that?'

'He still got threatening letters at his home address. Eventually, we gave him a new identity, and he retired to Bognor Regis.'

'Where is he now?'

'Still there, as far as we know. We closed down the case. This is obviously twenty years ago now. I can give you his new name and address, if that helps.' Monty took down the name. Joseph Abingdon. They thanked Mr Bartlett and hung up. Monty rang the team, and Kristy answered. He gave her the name and address and asked her to track him down.

They were on their way back to the nick when Kristy called back.

'Got a Mr Abingdon who matches the age. He's now in an old people's home, also in Bognor Regis. Shall I arrange a visit?'

Nikki said, 'Yes, tell them we are going there this afternoon.'

———

Bognor Regis was further then Nikki had anticipated, and it took them almost three hours before they arrived at the care home. Joseph Abingdon was a resident there, and he was in his early seventies and paralysed after a stroke, so he wasn't going anywhere fast. Sunrise Care Home was a three-storey newbuild in a seedy end of Bognor. It was dark when Monty pulled up in the car park. At the reception, they showed their warrant cards and were taken up to the second floor. Nikki's watch said 7 p.m., and it seemed the nurses were doing their medicine rounds. Monty asked one of the nurses, who led them to the matron in charge of the floor. The matron was expecting them, and she took them to Joseph Abingdon's room. She knocked on the door and they entered.

Nikki saw an old, wizened man, his skin covered in wrinkles, curled up in bed, lying on his back with hands folded on his chest. The matron shook his shoulders gently, and his eyes flickered open. She whispered in his ear, and his body moved under the sheets. A skeletal arm bent at the elbow and rose to his face. The matron moved away and gestured to Nikki and Monty to come forward. Then she went out and shut the door.

The elderly man was peering at them, his chest rising with slow, deep breaths. The lines of his forehead were etched deep, and the skin was paper-thin. His neck muscles were almost gone, the windpipe like reeds shaking in the wind. Nikki wondered if he was fit for questioning. 'Are you Mr Jack Taylor?' she asked. 'You worked at St Jude's Hall in Oxford in the late nineties.' She expected the old man to be surprised, or irritated. But instead, he simply nodded. His face was pale, in his lacklustre, fading eyes rested an acceptance of what was to come.

'Can you talk, Mr Taylor?'

'I'm not dead yet,' the man said, his voice stronger than Nikki had expected. He coughed once and hacked up some phlegm. He indicated at them to help him, and Monty crossed over to the other side and helped the man sit up a little against the headboard.

Nikki handed him a glass, and the man spat into it. He wiped a thin, almost barebone arm across it. The hand shook with the effort. Jack Taylor gave the appearance of a man whose life was leaving him rapidly, but somehow he was still clinging on. Monty pulled up two chairs, and Nikki sat down.

She said, 'We want to speak to you about Brian Allerton and Daniel Blatherwick.'

Mr Taylor's lips parted, and his eyes narrowed. 'Why?' he whispered.

'Unfortunately, Prof Allerton was found dead two days ago. He died of extensive knife wounds.'

Mr Taylor's eyes widened, and his nostrils flared. Patches of colour appeared on his cheeks.

'And Prof Blatherwick was also killed, in a similar manner, yesterday. We think the deaths might be connected. They were friends, we gather. Did you know Prof Blatherwick?'

Mr Taylor seemed more taken aback now. His lips parted, and he cleared his throat.

'I, uh, yes, you could say that.'

'You were the last warden at Dunston Hill Care Home, is that correct?'

The sparkle in Mr Taylor's eyes dimmed and he closed them. 'Yes,' he whispered.

'And you were there with Brian Allerton and Daniel Blatherwick?'

'Yes.' Mr Taylor's eyes remained shut. He remained silent for a while.

'Mr Taylor?' Nikki prompted.

The older man stirred, then his eyelids flickered open. He stared at the ceiling.

'I know what you want. But they destroyed me for it.'

Nikki and Monty exchanged a glance. 'Who are you talking about?'

'Them. The establishment. The men who run the place. I was bullied, harassed, then I got death threats for trying to speak the truth.'

'We found the police investigation case files,' Nikki said softly. 'We know you were taken in by the PSS.'

The frail, wasted old man sighed deeply, his breath rasping in the chest.

Nikki said, 'Both Brian and Daniel are now dead. Perhaps you can now tell us the truth.'

After a while, Mr Taylor nodded. 'What I am about to tell you doesn't leave this room.'

SIXTY-ONE

Mr Taylor's voice was slow and deliberate, like he was dragging the words up from a dungeon.

'The whispers started when Thomas Darlington was in charge. He spent a lot of nights in his office and also had a bedroom in the home.'

'Tarquin Darlington's father?' Nikki asked.

'Yes. He was one of the first wardens of Dunston Hill.'

'Carry on,' Nikki said, a knot of apprehension tightening in her chest.

'He took a lot of interest in the boys. One of the teachers said a boy told him he spent nights with Mr Thomas. Of course, nothing could be proven, and this was a long time ago. Similar rumours started circulating when Brian became warden, in the mid-nineties. Brian, as it happens, was good friends with Mr Darlington senior. He introduced Brian to working at the care home in his spare time.'

Nikki digested this in silence. Thoughts were colliding, sparking, setting off crazy loud bangs in her mind. She tried to gather them together.

'Recently, Prof Allerton tried to stop a book about the care home from getting published. Did you know anything about that?'

'No, but a couple of journalists picked up on the historic complaints. They came to see me as well. They wanted an interview, but I said no. Look at me. That crap destroyed my life.'

Nikki and Monty looked at each other.

'What were the complaints about?' Monty asked.

Nikki felt her heart shrivel, and her body seemed to shrink in the chair. Her hands were cold, fingers clawed. A memory whiplashed against her skull. She heard her mother wailing on the phone as Nikki sat on the steps, listening.

Why don't you do something? Can't you see what they did? They should be in prison.

Mr Taylor breathed out slowly. 'Allegations of historic child sexual abuse. I'm sure you know already.'

Monty nodded. 'Yes.'

Nikki felt his eyes on her, but she stared down at her hands. When she looked up at Mr Taylor, the older man had a blank look on his face, but Nikki could tell something had changed. There was now a sparkle of curiosity in his eyes.

'Carry on,' Nikki said.

Mr Taylor coughed once. The rest of his body remained immobile as he asked for a glass of water. Nikki helped him, and he sank back into the white pillows. 'After Brian started, he called in Daniel. They were only known by their middle names. Robert and Bertie.'

He paused again to take a painful breath. '

I was in the same college, and I knew Brian, who seemed a perfectly nice chap. We used to meet in the Senior Common Room for lunch. Daniel as well. It was Brian who invited me to work here. However' – Mr Taylor coughed into a fist and paused – 'they didn't know that I was raised as an orphan and had some experience of living in care as a child, before being placed with a foster family. I was lucky, my foster family were very loving. But I knew of many children who were not as fortunate as myself. I came here because I wanted to help the children.' He stopped, and his eyes flickered down. 'What I found was disturbing. Many of the children – all boys – had psychological problems. They bed-wetted at night, were either withdrawn or violent and argumentative. Their hygiene was poor, and for many of them, behaviour issues were getting worse. I spent some time there and got a couple of the boys to open up to me. It wasn't easy. They were deeply mistrustful of all adults. Men, in particular. In fact, it was only when my wife joined me in looking after the children, that the boys spoke to us.'

'Is your wife present?' Nikki asked. Mr Taylor pressed his lips together, and a pressure seemed to depress his shoulders.

'No. She passed away earlier this year.'

'I'm so sorry,' Nikki said. 'Your wife and yourself made a big difference to their lives, I'm sure.'

'Thank you.'

Monty said, 'What did the boys tell you and your wife? Did they mention names?'

A shadow passed over Mr Taylor's face. 'This is old news, but saying it again isn't any easier. Yes, the boys directly implicated the men who cared for them. It was very hard for them to actually talk about this. We had to ask most of the questions. They merely nodded, but a couple actually said what happened to them.'

'What names did you hear?'

'Robert and Bertie, as the boys called them. Before that it, was Babs, which was short for Babbage, Thomas Darlington's middle name. There was another man called Stuart. He was called Stu by the boys. His last name was Purdy. I believe he came from the council.' Mr Taylor went on to describe some of the heinous, depraved acts carried out against the boys.

When he finished, a stunned silence lay over them like a

cloud. That heavy, dark weight was back in Nikki's throat, and she couldn't breathe. Tears prickled her eyes, and she dabbed them with a tissue.

Monty was the first to recover. 'So, if Robert was Brian's name in the care home, and Bertie was Daniel's name, they were the ones who perpetrated the abuse?'

In silence, Mr Taylor nodded.

Monty continued. 'And what did you do with this information?'

Mr Taylor shook his head. 'I took it to the board of directors who managed the home. But Brian, Daniel and Mr Darlington, they were all members of the board. I was merely a worker here. They ignored me. I confronted Brian, who told me they were all lies, because the boys were unhappy in general with their lot. I didn't believe him. I told him I would go to the council and he said I would lose my job at the college. I didn't care. I told the council, but it turned out that Mr Darlington had extensive connections with the councillors. The Darlington family had donated millions to the council over the years. They were in each other's pockets, all of them.'

'So you complained to the council? Then what happened?'

'They set up an inspection committee. It was a farce. There had been other inspections in the past. Children had complained to their teachers. But I was the first adult to complain, believe it or not. These children had no parents, hence no voice.'

'So, things didn't change after the council inspection you arranged?'

'Well, it was different because Shelly, my wife, and I were here, a lot more. Brian and Daniel took notice. Nothing happened due to the council inspection. And when Shelly or I weren't here, I'm afraid things continued as they were. But Brian, Daniel, and Stuart now knew I wouldn't be kept quiet.

The college wasn't comfortable with these allegations either. But no real change came till that boy died.'

The last sentence was like a hammer blow to Nikki's heart. Her whole body turned to ice. She couldn't move her eyes away from Mr Taylor's face. The old man went quiet.

'A boy in this care home died?' Monty echoed.

SIXTY-TWO

Mr Taylor spoke again, his eyes closed, only the lips moving. 'Yes, but not in the care home. He committed suicide by throwing himself off a cliff. Give me a minute, I'll remember his name.'

After a while, he opened his eyes, and then he frowned, looking up at the ceiling.

He didn't have to say the name, Nikki thought to herself. She knew it.

Thomas Gill.

The two words echoed in Nikki's mind. She saw his small, pale face, his eyes following her as Clarissa dragged her away.

In slow motion, she watched Mr Taylor's eyes lower to hers. She wrenched herself from her morbid reverie and cleared her throat. 'The boy who died. I know it was a long time ago. But did you ever meet him?'

'Yes, I did.' Mr Taylor's eyes were now hooked on Nikki's.

She stared back, hypnotised.

Mr Taylor's voice was dry and cracked, like the gaps slowly opening up under Nikki's feet.

'He had the same last name as you. Any relation?'

Nikki looked down at her hands. The knuckles were bone white, gripped tight. Her jaws flexed, and she couldn't answer. She heard Monty shift in his seat. She couldn't look at him, or at Mr Taylor.

'That's why you came,' Mr Taylor said softly.

The words scratched along the surface of Nikki's mind, barely registering. She looked at him and shook her head. Her voice wobbled when she spoke. 'No. I came for the investigation.'

'Yes.' The old man nodded his scrawny neck. 'But you also came for Tommy. Thomas Gill. I remember him, now.'

'You met Tommy?' Nikki whispered.

'Yes. He was one of the boys who suffered. He could never speak of his troubles, but another boy called Paul, who was his friend, told us. Then Shelly and I spoke to Tommy.'

A pressure gathered in Nikki's face and forced itself into a pinpoint in her eyes. A teardrop trickled out, dimming her vision.

Mr Taylor continued. 'By that time, the council was already alerted, and so was their school. The inspection was organised. A few months after I spoke to Tommy, he died. I'm sorry.'

Nikki tried to swallow the rock lodged against her throat, and failed. She wiped her eyes, sniffed, angry at her useless tears. She needed to focus.

'How do we know his death was an accident?' She looked at Mr Taylor. 'Who reported it?'

'His friend, Paul. Paul Jameson. I remember speaking to him after Tommy died. The poor boy was in pieces. He was older, and more capable. There was a post-mortem, and death by suicide was the verdict. No police investigation took place, as the death wasn't deemed suspicious. Then the home was shut down.'

Focusing on the facts was helping. Nikki asked, 'Yes, I looked at the coroner's report. Paul's name was anonymised, so thank you. Do you know where he is today?' It was a forlorn hope, but she had to ask.

Mr Taylor shook his head. 'I don't know. He tried to stay in touch, but I had to go into hiding. This was a long time ago, and I'm getting older.' The ghost of a smile flickered across his face. 'They can't threaten me anymore. I'm close to the other side.'

Mr Taylor spoke again, which was good, because she was finding it difficult.

'Because of what happened to him, I remember Tommy. It was hard for him to talk about what happened. But slowly, he did, when he spoke to Shelly. We knew his mother came to visit. Your mother, correct?'

Nikki nodded.

Mr Taylor said, 'I met your mother once, after the event. I had taken over as warden of the hall. She was angry and wanted answers. She wanted to see Paul, which we couldn't allow. It was all... very unfortunate.' Mr Taylor shook his head and exhaled. Then he looked up at Nikki.

'But Tommy did talk about his family. He spoke about his mother, and you.' A sadness weighed on the deep lines of Mr Taylor's face. 'He wished he could see both of you, more.'

Nikki felt her eyes dim and blur, the room slowly dissolving under the burden of her memories. Her heart creaked in its bony cage, and the guilt twisted inside, again. She wiped her face with the tissue, aware she now needed to get out of here.

'Thank you.' She sniffed. 'And sorry about this.' She indicated her face and smiled. She took out her card and handed it over. 'Please call if you remember anything.'

She got up and left, not looking back at Monty.

SIXTY-THREE

Nikki needed air. The closed, stuffy smell inside the nursing home was drowning her senses, pulling her underground. She practically ran out through the reception, dodging a nurse walking an older woman on a tripod. She had given up smoking many years ago, but her lungs now suddenly itched for a cigarette. She walked to the end of the front lawn, and then leaned against the brick fence. She took a deep breath, trying to calm down. It didn't work. The night was humid, congealing around like a black dream. It was sticky and close, regrets and secrets thickening the air. She forced herself to walk. As if in a dream, she went out of the nursing home, her feet moving of their own will.

She must've walked almost a block before she realised suddenly she didn't have any idea where she was. She retraced her steps. Slowly. Her mind was still woolly, but the hard facts were now appearing out of the mist.

Tommy's death forced Dunston Hill to close. Not the police investigation and the subsequent threats that made Mr Taylor seek shelter from the PPS. That gave her an idea of the powerful people behind the scenes. It was typical Oxford, the shadowy individuals who controlled the scenes never revealed themselves.

Except, she now had an idea. The Darlington family was firmly in the picture, and with it, Tarquin Darlington, the current heir. His grandfather was now implicated in this scandal. A scandal that was suppressed. Years later, when this book surfaced, Brian Allerton paid the publisher to stop its launch.

Did the £250,000 come from Tarquin Darlington? A sudden thought occurred to Nikki. It was too late now for any of her team to be at the nick. Switchboard answered, and she asked for the duty uniform team and was put through to an Inspector Len Deighton, whom she had met once.

'Hello, Len. I want a patrol car outside the Darlington Estate. I can't explain a great deal now, but there is a chance he might be the next potential victim after the two professors.'

Nikki hung up and as she entered the car park of the nursing home, she saw Monty leaning against the car. She was glad he didn't come looking for her. She needed the space.

'Back to Oxford? It's getting late,' Monty said, concern clear in the chestnut brown of his eyes.

She nodded. 'Sorry about walking out like that.'

Monty shook his head. 'That was a lot to deal with,' his voice was low. 'I can't imagine what you've been through. That boy, Tommy Gill, he was your brother?'

'Yes,' she responded quietly, trying to keep her voice from cracking.

They got in the car and sat in silence for a while. 'I think Tarquin Darlington and Stuart Purdy are next in line.'

'Assuming these murders are to do with what happened at Dunston Hill.'

Nikki looked at him. His silhouette was obscured in the darkness. 'What other motive can there be?' she asked.

Monty shrugged.

She said, 'I got these texts. From someone who said he was at Dunston Hill. Knew my brother, he said.'

She sensed Monty tense. A muscle ticked in his jaw. 'When was this?'

'Two nights ago. He said that place killed Tommy.'

'Did this guy have a name? How did he get your number?'

'He didn't give a name. And no idea how he got my number.'

Monty touched his forehead. 'Oh God. You realise he could've been our killer?'

Nikki nodded slowly. 'Yes, I do. And I'm sorry I didn't tell you before. I felt I had to go, to see what he knew about Tommy.'

Monty remained silent. Nikki sighed and looked out the window at the dark car park, cones of lights appearing below the lights on the wall.

'That man said Tommy wanted to see me again. He saw me, his sister, in his dreams. He missed his family.' That heavy weight was at her throat again, closing her windpipe, suffusing her eyes with futile tears.

'How he suffered,' Nikki whispered, her head lowering to her chest. She couldn't hold it back this time. She thought of her guilt-ridden mother, her body ravaged with alcohol, wasting away in her broken home. The dam broke inside her, and the black waters burst out in a deluge. She clutched her head and bent over her knees, her body shuddering with sobs.

Monty leaned over and pulled her to him, she felt the warmth of his hand, rubbing her shoulders. Nikki dried her eyes and straightened. God, she must be a mess. She couldn't remember the last time she'd let herself go like this – and in front of a male colleague. Monty held out some tissues, and she accepted them gratefully.

'Let's get going,' he said gently, and she nodded, unable to look at him. She pulled the window down and let the humid night air in. The car picked up speed and the wind pulled out strands of hair from her ponytail; she let them blow around her face. 'Paul Jameson, the boy who was Tommy's friend. We need to find him, and we need to track down the other children in the care home. Your brother and Paul couldn't be the only ones who were abused.'

'They weren't,' Nikki said, in a flat, desultory voice. She felt numb and heavy now, but her mind was still working. 'That much was clear from the council report and police investigation. But no charges were brought against any individual.' She knew that was the cruel victory of the abuser; his victims were often shamed and scared into silence. 'The researchers won't be there now. But I can still access the databases. Let's get on the case tonight.'

'No.' Nikki turned to him. 'It's too late tonight. I've already asked Inspector Deighton to patrol around Tarquin Darlington's house. We need to locate Stuart Purdy as well, who might be anywhere. Paul Jameson too, as you mentioned. When I get back home, I'll do some searching on the laptop.' Nikki could use her ID to remotely access the police databases from her home. She knew she wouldn't be getting much sleep tonight. As the car picked up speed on the motorway, and the night-grimed land streaked past, the lights blurred into her mind. If her life was the tip of the iceberg, Tommy's death was the submerged section, invisible to everyone. Only she felt the pull, and her life had been this battle between shadow and light, half chances and fleeting regrets. She now knew she wouldn't let this go, she had to resolve it once and for all. It was almost 10 p.m. by the time Monty dropped her off home.

'Thank you,' she said, and meant it. She looked at his handsome, lean face, staring straight out the windscreen. Then he turned to look at her, and in the darkness, she felt their eyes meet, then he nodded and looked away.

She wanted to say more, a lot more, but didn't know how to

say it. Perhaps it wasn't important. The silent things, the ones she could never utter, those were the bones and flesh that made her the damaged person she was. Monty had had a glimpse of that today.

'Our discussion with Mr Taylor was confidential,' he said. 'There's no need to bring your personal details into it.'

She looked down at her hands and nodded. 'Apart from what's public record. And Tommy's name is.'

'But it's not in the police record, only in the post-mortem, you said. Let's keep it that way for now.'

She looked at him, grateful. Suddenly, she felt on the verge of tears again. It had been a roller coaster night.

'Thank you.' She smiled, then got out of the car. She watched the red lights of Monty's car as he drove away. Silence descended on the street. All the houses were dark, hunched together, like they were watching her. Nikki climbed the steps of her cottage and opened the door. She flicked the lights on, then shut the door behind her. Her phone buzzed, and she saw she had two missed calls, from a number she didn't recognise. She called it back, and a woman answered the phone. 'DI Gill,' Nikki said.

'Hi, uh, I'm sorry to bother you, but you said to call you if... if anything happened.'

'Who is this?' Nikki frowned.

'Arabella Allerton, Brian's wife.'

'Yes of course. What's the matter?' A pang of anxiety released in Nikki's spine. It was late for Arabella to call.

'It's my daughter, Julia. She's not been home all day, and I can't get hold of her on the phone. None of her friends know where she is, either.'

SIXTY-FOUR

Nikki went into the kitchen and opened the fridge door. She held the phone tightly against her ear as she took out a bottle of water.

'When did you last see Julia?'

'This morning. She left to go to the Bodleian. She's not a student here, but she can use her dad's card. She normally studies until mid-afternoon, then comes home to go to the gym. She has some friends here, and sometimes she meets up with them. I've called all of them, no one knows anything. I'm getting worried.'

Nikki could hear the edge in Arabella's voice. First her husband, now her daughter? God forbid.

'Don't worry,' Nikki said quickly. 'I'm coming over. Can you please send me Julia's phone number and a recent, good-quality photo?'

'Oh, thank you.'

Nikki hung up. She splashed water into a glass, then downed it. She changed into a new pair of black, rubber-soled shoes and went out again. Jericho was normally a half-hour drive, but at this time of the night, it took her fifteen minutes.

The lights were on at Arabella's house, and Nikki heard Daisy barking as she rang the bell.

Arabella opened the door, her eyes red-rimmed. She ushered Nikki inside. They went into the huge kitchen and Arabella flicked on the light switches.

'Sit down,' Nikki said. She got two glasses of water from the sink and put them in front of Arabella.

'I want you to think carefully about the last few days,' Nikki said, sitting next to Arabella. 'Was Julia going out at odd times? Did she come home looking flustered? Or was she different in any way?'

'Nope. She's got a boyfriend in Cambridge who visits occasionally. She just relaxes, studies and sees her friends. She's meant to go back to Cambridge next week.'

'When did her boyfriend visit last?'

'About ten days ago. I've spoken to him. He doesn't know where she is. He's called all her friends. No one's heard from her since 8 a.m. this morning.' Arabella's eyes widened and her fingers became claws on the table. 'What if something's happened to her?'

'I'll send an alert out. Don't worry. It'll be all right.' Nikki called Switchboard and asked them to connect her to the radio frequency of Len Deighton. When she got through she gave Inspector Deighton Julia's appearance, and what she was wearing when she left the house.

'You've been busy tonight, guv,' Deighton remarked. 'Hope there's nothing else.'

'Me too. Any news from the Darlington Estate?'

'Nothing. Done two rounds, and it's all quiet. I'll pass this woman's details to all duty units.'

'Thanks, Len.'

Nikki looked up at Arabella. 'I better go. I'll be in touch shortly, and will also send a family liaison officer to be here with you.'

'Thank you,' Arabella said, her knuckles white, eyes wide. 'Should I do something?'

'No. I know it's the hardest thing right now, but please stay at home. The FLO will be here soon to give you company.'

Nikki stood, and so did Arabella. She clutched Nikki's hand. 'Please find my daughter. Please.' Her eyes were hollowed out, panic-stricken.

Nikki gripped her shoulders. 'We'll get her back, OK? Be strong for Julia, and also for yourself.'

Arabella walked Nikki to the front door. Daisy was barking like mad, scratching the door.

'I'll be in touch.' Nikki turned on the porch. 'Don't worry.'

As she walked back to the car, she rang switchboard, and spoke to the FLO on duty. She was a woman called Charlene Williams, and Nikki gave her Arabella's details. Charlene promised to be over immediately.

As Nikki hung up, she received a text message. Her blood froze as she read it.

Julia will pay for her father's sins.

There was no return number. Nikki replied quickly.

Who are you?

You came to see me. I knew Tommy.

Have you got Julia?

Yes.

Nikki hurried back to her car. Panic was turning her fingers ice cold. She shivered as she slid into the driver's seat. Her shaking fingers poised above the phone as she forced herself to think. This was the same person she had met. Possibly the killer. Why did he tell her he had Julia? If he wanted to kill Julia, he would've done it by now, surely. Left her body where she could be discovered. But instead, he was informing Nikki... fear suddenly whiplashed against Nikki's spine. She looked around her and twisted to look at the back seat. Darkness covered everywhere, with only the dull glow of the streetlamps offering meagre relief. She couldn't see much. Was he here? Hiding and watching her? She messaged him back.

What do you want?

Like I said, Julia will pay for her father's sins.

Who are you?

You know who I am, you saw me.

Are you Paul Jameson?

My name is not important. My deeds will carry my name one day.

What do you mean?

Julia... she will tell the world. Her blood will clean the past.

Fear curdled in Nikki's guts as she stared at the blinking dot after the last sentence. Her breath came in gasps.

Let Julia go. She's not done anything wrong.

You should know better.

Nikki stared at the last sentence. This man knew who she was. He had her phone number. He had to be someone she knew and had seen recently. She didn't give her number out to anyone, and Switchboard would never do that either. And if this guy was the killer... how did he kill Professor Allerton in the park and then bring the body back inside the college? How did he go into Christ Church College and kill Prof Blatherwick in his office? He must be someone who went in and out of the colleges easily. Sparks were triggering in Nikki's brain, lighting up her mind like a Christmas tree. A man who could get through security, and porter's lodge... a brilliant flash of lightning illuminated her mind, thunder clashing in her heart. Her spine snapped straight as her eyes bulged.

Now she knew why that man who knew Tommy looked familiar. He stood at a distance, but his posture, his shuffle from left to right foot...Nikki fired up her car and zoomed out into the main road. She knew what she had to do.

She just hoped she wasn't too late to save Julia.

SIXTY-FIVE

The night roads were empty, and Nikki tore through them, hazard lights flashing. She parked outside New College's fort-like entrance and ran inside. The porter on duty was surprised to see her. 'Where's Winston?' Nikki asked, breathless.

'He's not on duty, he must—'

'I need his phone number and home address. And I mean his personal phone number.'

The porter looked shocked, but Nikki stepped closer, her face inches from his. Her teeth gnashed together as she snarled. 'Right now.'

The porter's face blanched as he stumbled back. He pulled out his phone and started to read the number out. Nikki snatched the phone from his hand and looked at the name and number, then sent it to herself. She asked for the address and called the duty uniform team on her phone. Len Deighton answered.

'DI Gill. I need a location triangulation on a phone number. It's urgent. This man is the main suspect in the two murders, and he's kidnapped the first victim's daughter.'

'Bloody hell, guv. All happening tonight. Leave it with me, I'm on the case.'

Nikki turned to the porter, who was standing there with an aghast look on his face.

'Where's Winston's address?'

The man had scribbled it on a piece of paper, and he handed it to Nikki.

'If you see Winston,' Nikki said, 'if you hear from him, let us know ASAP. Call 999. Stay away from him, he's dangerous. OK?'

The man gulped and nodded.

'When did you last see Winston?'

'This morning. He's got the day off. He came to collect his mail, then left.'

'Did he say where he would be today?'

The porter's eyes darted sideways, and he licked his lips. 'Actually, he told me once he's got a barn outside Headington. He got it cheap, and now he's doing it up. He lives in a flat near Port Meadow normally. I asked him if he would be at the barn today, but he wouldn't say.'

Adrenaline pulsed in Nikki's blood. 'Well done,' she said. 'Anything else you can think of, about Winston? Does he have any family, or friends living nearby?'

'No, he never mentioned anyone.'

'Do you know where his barn might be, exactly?'

'I didn't ask, sorry. He said it was outside Headington, that's all I know.'

Nikki thanked the man again and ran back to her car. She had a dilemma now. Would Winston take Julia back to his flat in Oxford? She doubted that. He would have to take her in and out, and it would be hard to escape from a flat. A derelict barn seemed ideal.

Nikki floored the pedal, zooming down Woodstock Road towards Headington. Her phone rang on the hands-free loud-speaker; it was Deighton.

'Last signal from that number was within two hundred metres from a farm road in Headington. Sending you the coor-dinates.'

Nikki's phone beeped soon. She was almost in Headington, but pulled over and punched the number into her satnav. She followed the directions, which led her past Headington's High Street and into a country lane which had nothing but open farmland for miles. The red dot showing her destination was growing closer. Soon, she had to turn right and go down a dirt track.

The car bumped along the uneven ground. A drizzle had started, and her wipers switched on. Then she saw it. A light on her right, across a dark field. There was nothing for miles. She cut her headlights, but knew the sound would carry. She slowed as she came up to the building. There was a car parked in the front. The barn had a triangular roof, and it was big. Some of the roof was in tatters, and the stone walls had suffered many years of wind and rain. She couldn't see the light inside any more. Someone had seen her and turned it off. She could hear a generator, so there must be an electric supply. She looked up and saw the cables on old wooden poles. Her phone still had reception.

She took out the extendible steel baton, gripping it in her right hand. Raindrops splatted against her face, soaking her hair through, but she didn't care. She put a hand on the car's bonnet, it was still warm. The car hadn't been here long. She got to the thick wooden door, pushing her shoulder against it with all her might. She grunted with the effort, but finally the door screeched open a few inches. That was enough for her to slip through. It was pitch black. She took out her flashlight, and it sliced through the darkness. Old stone slabs lay on the ground and water dripped from a hole in the roof. Nikki gripped the baton firmly and went inside.

SIXTY-SIX

Nikki flashed the torch around the barn. The light beam picked up old farming utensils against one wall. Spades, pitchfork blades and prongs. The barn was deserted, but there was an upstairs she hadn't checked, accessible by a ladder that rested against the woodwork. Nikki listened for any sounds. But apart from the tapping of water that dripped on to the flagstones from the ceiling, she heard nothing. 'Winston?' Nikki shouted. 'I know you're here.'

Her voice echoed in the vast space. She advanced deeper into the darkness, her senses on fire. Ahead of her, there was a large black shape, part of the upper floor's woodwork. Behind that, another space opened up, and two windows on either side let in meagre light. The back of the barn was bigger. The arc of her flashlight showed holding pens for animals. It also lit up something else, and she almost dropped the torch. Her erratic, panicked eyes swerved back to the chair and the woman tied to it, with her head drooped forward, and her hands tied behind the chair, her feet strapped to its legs.

'Julia,' Nikki gasped and moved towards her.

As she did so, she sensed movement to her left. She jerked

the flashlight in that direction, but she was too late. A solid object hit her on the left forearm and pain exploded down her arm, loosening her grip. She cried out, and the flashlight fell from her hand. Nikki fell to the floor and rolled over, then quickly got on her feet, flicking the baton down so it was extended to its full length. Her left arm throbbed like it was on fire, and she couldn't feel her hand.

She saw a man's shape kick the flashlight across the floor. It skittered to one corner, but the cone of light remained, throwing strange shadows across the floor. 'Winston,' she said, breathing heavily. The pain was now like a lance embedded into her flesh. Her left arm hung limp and useless at the side. The pain made her eyes water, but she gritted her teeth. 'Why are you doing this?'

The man stepped forward, and she could now see his features dimly, though he was still in the shadows. It was Winston.

'You, of all people, shouldn't be asking me that question.'

'I know about Dunston Hill Care Home, and the two professors. I know what they did. But why Julia?'

'Why Julia?' Winston echoed. 'Look at yourself in the mirror. If you suffered with Tommy's death, then why shouldn't she?'

Winston advanced, his bulk blotting out the faint light. Fear pulsed in Nikki's heart, but so did pure adrenaline. She held her ground.

'You shouldn't have come here,' Winston whispered. 'Now you're as bad as the others. You, of all people. I wanted to be your friend. You're Tommy' sister. I did this for him.'

'Don't you dare pin this on Tommy. You could've told me, and we could have sought justice in the proper way. Instead—'

'Justice?' Winston laughed. 'Justice?' He screamed suddenly. 'What justice? Where was the justice when we were being abused? Where the fuck were you when your own brother was suffering?'

Rage burned in his words, and he lost control. He lunged for Nikki, who swung her baton as hard as she could. Her aim was good, and it hit Winston in the right temple with a dull thud.

Nikki grunted as the force of the blow reverberated up her right arm. Winston stumbled, and dropped to one knee. But he didn't fall down. Nikki advanced, her right arm raised and she brough it crashing down on his head. This time her blow missed as Winston lunged forward, grabbing her around the waist in a rugby tackle.

He propelled her backwards, and slammed her on the floor. Pain mushroomed in a fireball at the back of Nikki's head, and breath left her lungs in a rush. The baton dropped from her hand. She felt Winston's thick fingers grapple for her throat. She tried to move, but he had her pinned down with his weight. Nikki fought back, but he was stronger, and the blow as she fell had weakened her. She reached up with her right hand, and dug her claws into his eye. She pushed into his eyeball with all the force she could muster, and Winston cried out, trying to move his face.

His right hand lifted from her throat, and Nikki bit it hard, sinking her teeth into his flesh. He screamed, and tried to move his hand but she kept her jaws clamped on it, and moved with him. She tasted the metallic tinge of blood, then a crashing blow erupted on the side of her head, making her vision rock. She let go, but she'd also managed to dislodge him from her chest. She kicked out with her legs, and caught his feet. She rolled out from under him. He was still on his knees, holding his eyes and howling curses. Nikki's arms scratched the floor, searching for her baton. She didn't find it, but her hand touched a piece of wood, heavy and thick. Maybe a piece of timber from the roof. She had to lift it with both hands. Winston was screaming at her and staggering to his feet. Nikki ignored the shriek of pain in her left arm and raised the piece of wood.

'You're not doing this for Tommy,' she shouted. 'You're destroying his memories.'

Winston stood there, feet planted wide, swaying. One hand was clasped over his right eye.

'It was destroyed a long time ago. All of us were destroyed. Those men killed us, Nikki. I tried to tell you that.'

'But you didn't have to do what you did. You could have—'

'Don't you think I tried?' Winston screamed like an animal in pain. 'It all fell on deaf ears. They wanted proof. Proof!'

Winston came forward, and Nikki raised the piece of wood.

She didn't move back. She wouldn't run any more, come what may. She gritted her teeth as Winston came closer, and she could see his ghoulish face, blood pouring out between the fingers holding his right eye.

He pointed to his chest. 'I am the proof. Me. Here is the proof, in front of you.'

His voice broke, and became a wail.

Nikki opened her mouth to speak, but her words were frozen. Tears budded in her eyes, blurring her vision.

'So do what you want with the proof, Nikki. But I won't stop till they're all dead. All of them.'

Nikki wanted to ask who else was left, but Winston lunged for her.

She pointed the wood in her hand like a battering ram at Winston's midriff, and with all the strength left in her legs, she charged at him. A desperate scream tore out from her throat as she hit him hard, the sharp end thrusting into him.

She pushed him against the wall, and he fell to his knees. He didn't move.

Then Nikki collapsed, sweat drenching her body, no strength left in her limbs. She breathed for a while, aware that Winston wasn't moving.

She crawled forward cautiously. Winston was breathing, but his eyes were closed.

'Winston?' she whispered.

'Nikki.'

Only his lips moved, and she could tell he was trying to move his hands, but it wasn't working. He was dying. She leaned forward.

'Yes?'

'Don't...don't...'

She knelt in front of him. She felt his wrist pulse – his skin was cold and clammy, pulse fast and thready. He wasn't going to last long. A strange regret swirled in her heart, like bitter bile in her throat. It became a heavy weight, and she couldn't swallow. She brushed tears from her eyes.

'What is it, Winston?'

'Don't... call me... my name's Paul. Tommy called me...'

'Yes?'

'Paul.'

After a while, he spoke again. 'I was... with Tommy when he... died. He didn't want to live any more.'

Pain stabbed in Nikki's heart, worse than a knife wound.

Winston spoke again.

'Shirt pocket. Left side.'

Nikki understood. She reached for his shirt, and her hand became sticky with blood. She gritted her teeth, and reached inside, finding a piece of paper. It had writing on it, but she couldn't see it clearly in the dim light.

'Stuart...'

'Purdy?' Nikki whispered. 'Stuart Purdy was the third man at the care home. Is that right?'

Winston didn't move, but she could sense his confirmation.

'Kill...'

Nikki's blood ran cold. 'Where is Stuart, Paul? What have you done to him?'

'Find... find him,' Winston said. He couldn't speak any more.

'Do you know where he is?' Nikki asked, leaning over him. Then she realised his chest wasn't moving anymore. She felt for the carotid pulse in his neck, and found nothing. She stared at him, regret and sorrow cascading over her like a waterfall. This man was a killer, but he had also cared for Tommy.

'Goodbye, Paul,' she whispered.

She scrambled to her knees and crawled to the chair. She slapped Julia's face and had to call her name a few times before the girl stirred. She pulled at the nylon ropes tying her, but her fingers slipped against the hard knots. It was useless, there was no strength in her fingers.

SIXTY-SEVEN

Light beams arched through the window, flashing blues. Footsteps pounded the ground, then the barn door thrust open. Loud voices rang out and lights flashed around.

'Over here,' Nikki cried in a weak voice, soaked with tears. Torch beams bobbed in the dark, and then she had strong arms around her, helping her to her feet. She could stand, but not for long. Her legs wobbled, and she collapsed against a wooden pillar, sinking to the cold stone floor. Uniformed officers swarmed the barn. She watched them free Julia and put her on a stretcher, then carry her out. A familiar face crouched by her, looking concerned. It was Monty. 'Why didn't you call me?' he asked, checking her legs and arms for wounds. 'Eh? Why not?'

She whispered, 'I had to get here. Is he dead?'

Monty finished checking her scalp and neck, then nodded. 'Yes.'

'He was Tommy's friend. He loved him. And I killed him.' Fresh tears sprouted in her eyes, and she felt her heart disintegrate into a thousand shards of grief. 'I killed the man who loved Tommy. I killed him.'

She clutched Monty's collar and buried her head in his

neck, weeping uncontrollably. She felt Monty's arm come around her back, pulling her closer. He was saying something, but she couldn't hear it. She gripped him like he was her harbour in the storm, tears drowned her soul, and her body shook with sobs.

SIXTY-EIGHT

Nikki, Monty and the rest of the team had gathered in DS Patmore's office. Patmore read the last page of the report, then flung it on the desk. His hooded blue eyes lingered on Nikki.

'Are you all right?'

'Yes, I am, sir, thank you.'

Nikki was seated directly opposite, next to Monty.

'Do we have enough evidence for the prosecution?'

'Winston had the murder weapon in his room, sir. His fingerprints were all over it. Dr Raman has matched the metal fragments from the wound sites to the weapon. It's definitely him.'

Nikki coughed once. 'CCTV also shows him in both crime scenes at the time of death, but of course, as security we couldn't question his whereabouts. It's only later that I realised.'

'And the motive was revenge for the abuse him and the other boys suffered?'

'Yes, sir.' Nikki's face was carved in stone, devoid of expression.

She glanced at Monty, who sat still, his expression as blank as hers. He had not mentioned Tommy's name in his report, but his name had appeared all the same; he was the reason the care home had shut down. Patmore was aware and, soon, everyone else would be as well.

'I'm sorry about your brother, Nikki,' Patmore said. 'I didn't know.'

Nikki sighed. 'That's OK, sir.' Patmore didn't respond for a while and studied Nikki. He steepled fingers across his face.

'There's been talk of a paedophile ring in Oxford for many years. As you know, it's very hard to prove allegations against individuals. And not many of the victims of historic abuse come forward.'

Like my brother, Nikki thought to herself, bitterness spreading across her heart.

'Maybe not, but they made their voices heard back then. They were silenced, and you know as well as I do, sir, the police were probably complicit in that.'

Patmore passed a hand over his face. 'Hard to say, but yes, I will admit that mistakes were made.'

There was silence for a while. Everyone in the room knew the police bosses then had now retired, but one or two of them had a lot to answer for.

Nikki locked eyes with Patmore. 'Stuart Purdy, sir. We know he was involved. Jack Taylor told us that and so did Winston.'

Patmore looked at the report on his desk, and ran a finger through the lines that bore Purdy's details.

Nikki said, 'He's a sick man in a nursing home, but that doesn't mean he should evade justice. I would like to see him prosecuted for historic sexual abuse crimes.'

Stuart Purdy had suffered a stroke two years before and he could barely speak, could only move with a wheelchair. He had to be fed a liquid diet.

Monty spoke for the first time. 'Some poetic justice there. He abused boys in a care home, and now he's fully reliant on care home staff for his survival.'

'His mind is still intact,', Nikki said. 'I'm not saying he should be put into prison, but his name should be mentioned in the case. And he should bear responsibility for the lives he has wasted.'

They were silent for a while, aware of what abused children were left with – shame, guilt, the inability to speak up, and the lack of listening ears when they did. Most of these tragic beings ended up in addiction, or early graves.

Monty looked at Nikki, and nodded his agreement. When she looked at Patmore, the Super took a breath in, and then sighed.

'How far do you want to take this?'

'I want the victims and their families to come forward, sir. We have the list of children who went to Dunston Hill Care Home. That's a good place to start.'

Patmore nodded. 'This will ruffle feathers, but it needs to be done.'

Nikki sighed in relief. 'Thank you, sir.'

Patmore reached for a paper on his desk. He put his glasses on, then cleared his throat, which became a bout of coughing. Nikki grimaced. The old smoker sounded like a horse being strangled. Patmore recovered and wiped his mouth with a tissue. 'Excuse me. New Frontier Publishing has returned the £250,000 to the Darlington Estate. They will go ahead with the book launch, but they want to contact you first.' He glanced at Nikki. 'Following the book's publication, there might be media interest. Can you handle that?'

'Handle it, sir?' Nikki said with a straight face. 'I've been waiting for answers my whole life. I've got them now, and if anyone else wants to know, I'm telling them.'

'Yes, but you know what the papers are like. Don't let them twist this and create pressure on you. They will turn this back on us and the police in general.'

Nikki knew courting the media was like dancing with the devil. Patmore had a point. But the truth had to be told. It was always a delicate balance.

'I know, sir. I'll be careful. I'll ask the media liaison officer to help.'

'Excellent idea.'

Patmore focused on another sheet of paper. Nikki glanced at Monty, who must have felt her eyes on him, because he smirked at her, once. His cheeks had a few days' stubble. Suited him, she thought, returning his smirk with a smile. She looked away swiftly, but the smile remained on her lips.

'New College have taken over the property company where Sue Pollard and Mr Moffat were directors. Mr Moffat had too much control over the company, they thought. He might also lose his job as the college bursar due to his involvement.'

Monty said, 'Our CPS liaison thinks the trial will be straightforward. But all the evidence will be out there, and we have to be prepared for it.' He glanced at Nikki, who nodded.

Monty continued. 'Six to eight months for a trial date, and that's with pressure from us. The CPS don't have enough judges, apparently.' He grinned, and the others nodded.

Patmore said, 'The big fish, Mr Darlington, is maintaining his silence. He has agreed to police protection around his house. He's got his own bodyguard anyway. In the future, when all this is out there, no one knows how he'll react.'

'He's scum,' Nikki seethed. 'Covering up for his worthless family.'

'Worth a lot actually.' Monty raised his eyebrows, and she flashed her eyes at him in warning.

'In any case,' Patmore said, 'that concludes matters. Take a week off, Nikki. Spend time with your daughter. That's an order, by the way.'

Nikki nodded.

SIXTY-NINE

Wind had scrubbed the skies clear of the clouds, and the rain had relented. The green hills rose and dipped into valleys as Monty drove through the Cotswolds. Nikki watched the land undulate, as if in rhythm to a silent symphony. Evesham Cemetery approached, and the car slowed as it drove through the gates. The sun shone on the trees, on quiet gravestones, on silent people with their heads bowed. Monty parked, and they got out. Nikki helped Clarissa out from the back seat. For once, Clarissa had made an effort, it seemed. She wore a long dark-blue dress that came down to her ankles. She had a dark-brown cardigan on. She blinked in the sun, and her hand shook as she smoothed back her hair. Nikki noticed the tremor in her body and breathed the smell of alcohol on her lips.

'Can you walk?' she asked.

'Yes, of course,' Clarissa said.

Nikki shook her head and took her mother's elbow. Monty opened the boot and took out the bouquet of flowers. Together, they walked slowly past the mourners and went to the corner of the grave where Nikki had yearned to visit since she arrived in Oxford but hadn't quite been able to face until now. Grief, regrets and a strange peace jostled for place in her troubled heart. She had finally got justice for Tommy, but it had come at a cost. Tommy's friend, Paul, aka Winston, was gone. Rage had turned Paul Jameson into a monster, but he had been the last person to care for Tommy. Nikki helped Clarissa lay the brightly coloured tulips on Tommy's gravestone. Clarissa said yellow was Tommy's favourite colour, and the tulips were mostly yellow.

Mother and daughter knelt, and Clarissa reached out to move some old flowers out of the way. Her hands rested on the stone. Nikki covered her mother's hand, and they remained like that for a while. The sunlight washed over them. No words would ever suffice, and they were not necessary. Nikki helped Clarissa up, and they walked back to the seat. Monty stood behind the bench, and as they approached he walked away a few steps.

Clarissa sniffed into a tissue. 'He loved you. When you came, he always wanted to play with you. Unusually for a child with a new baby sibling, he was very gentle with you.'

Nikki smiled through her tears.

Clarissa's voice lowered, then faltered. 'But social services said I was incapable of looking after both of you. I had to choose. What could I do?'

Nikki gripped her mother's hand, feeling the delirium tremens shake her limbs.

'I know, Mum. It's OK.'

'I'm sorry.' Clarissa lowered her head, and she wept.

Nikki put her arms around her mother, drawing her close. She and her mother would never have peace, but at least they had closure. Tommy would always be here with them, and she just wished she could tell him once that she finally had looked after him.

I wish you were here, Tommy, Nikki murmured quietly, her voice breaking as she uttered the words.

.   .   .

Rita was coming down tomorrow to spend a week with her. Nikki had rented a cottage in the Cotswolds, and with Clarissa and Rita, they would take a family holiday. The remains of her family, this nucleus of love she couldn't live without.

Nikki wiped the warm tears from her eyes and lifted her face up to the sun.

A LETTER FROM THE AUTHOR

Dear Reader,

I hope you enjoyed *Stolen Souls*, the first in my Detective Nikki Gill series.

If you'd like to join other readers in keeping in touch, here are two options. Stay in the loop with my new releases with the link below. You'll be the first to know about all future books I write. Or sign up to my personal email newsletter on the link at the bottom of this note. You'll get bonus content and get occasional updates and insights from my writing life. I'd be delighted if you choose to sign up to either – or both!

www.stormpublishing.co/ml-rose

If you enjoyed *Stolen Souls* and could spare a few moments to leave a review, that would be hugely appreciated. Even a short review can make all the difference in encouraging a reader to discover my books for the first time. Thank you so much!

Join other readers in hearing about my writing (and life)

experience, and other bonus content. Simply head over to www.BookHip.com/VKKKXJB

Thank you for reading this book. I lived in Oxford for a while, and got to know the town, and colleges. Through an old friend, I had a unique insight into Oxford college's social life for which I feel very lucky.

The countryside around Oxford, going up all the way west to Bristol and Cheltenham, is called the Cotswolds. In old English, 'cot' means sheep enclosure, and 'wold' is a hill. The region is a series of undulating hills and valleys, and wool farming made the Cotswolds famous in the medieval ages. The land hasn't changed much, and when you drive around the beautiful green patchwork of hills, you can still see the sheep farms, and stone wall villages nestled in the deep valleys.

If you haven't been, the area is certainly worth a visit. Cirencester is the capital, but Oxford remains the spiritual heart of the Cotswolds. I hope that in this book and series, you and I can go on a journey and discover more about this place, and about Detective Inspector Nikki Gill.

Thank you for reading,

M.L. Rose

Made in the USA
Las Vegas, NV
21 August 2023

76415188R00204